'Expertly crafted, suspenseful  memorable novel of loss and diamonds. Set against a 1930 it offers urgent lessons for our own ...

RACHEL HORE, author of *The Hidden Years*

'This is a haunting tale, deeply atmospheric and beautifully written.'

ELODIE HARPER, author of *The Wolf Den Trilogy*

'A gripping story of war and its legacies, building to a chilling climax. Day writes beautifully, drawing together a tale of eugenics, shellshock, courage, and prejudice, as characters still haunted by WWI face the inexorable rise of WWII.'

FRANCESCA DE TORES, author of *Saltblood*

'Set against the backdrop of Hitler, National Socialism, and its English sympathisers, in the long shadow of the First World War and the rising interest in eugenics, this is a compelling story of two women, one English, one German, searching for truth amidst the lies and danger that surrounds them. Chilling and haunting by turns, it twists and grips at every moment. It is a brilliant, captivating read from one of the finest crafters of historical suspense.'

MARY CHAMBERLAIN, author of *The Dressmaker of Dachau*

'A moving, shocking and vital story based around a real-life tragedy on the eve of war.'

CLAIRE MCGOWAN, author of *What You Did*

'An astonishing story, beautifully written. A both tense and deeply moving novel, this is a remarkable evocation of a place and time as well as a study of what individuals can and will do under pressure. Immersive and compelling from the first page.'

IMOGEN ROBERTSON, author of *The Paris Winter*

'A compelling, moving and vividly-evoked novel.'

ANNA MAZZOLA, author of *The Clockwork Girl*

'A superb story of courage and love against the backdrop of Europe descending into the Hell of the Second World War.'

JAKE KERRIDGE, writer and critic

'A sensitive and subtle picture of a deeply emotive story.'

GARETH RUBIN, author of *The Turnglass*

NIGHT CLIMBING

IN PURSUIT OF TRUTH, SURVIVAL, AND FAMILY.

SARAH DAY

Legend Press Ltd, 51 Gower Street, London, WC1E 6HJ
info@legendtimesgroup.co.uk | www.legendpress.co.uk

Contents © Sarah Day 2024

The right of the above author to be identified as the author of this work has been asserted in accordance with the Copyright, Designs and Patents Act 1988. British Library Cataloguing in Publication Data available.

Print ISBN 9781915643124
Ebook ISBN 9781915643131
Set in Times.
Cover design by Rose Cooper | www.rosecooper.com

The excerpt on page 11 is used with permission of Taylor & Francis Group LLC – Books, from *Modest_Witness@Second_Millenium.FemaleMan_Meets_OncoMouse : Feminism and Technoscience* by Donna J. Haraway, 1997; permission conveyed through Copyright Clearance Center, Inc.

All characters, other than those clearly in the public domain, and place names, other than those well-established such as towns and cities, are fictitious and any resemblance is purely coincidental.

All rights reserved. No part of this publication may be reproduced, stored in or introduced into a retrieval system, or transmitted, in any form, or by any means electronic, mechanical, photocopying, recording or otherwise, without the prior permission of the publisher. Any person who commits any unauthorised act in relation to this publication may be liable to criminal prosecution and civil claims for damages.

Sarah Day's debut novel, *Mussolini's Island*, received a 2018 Betty Trask Award and was shortlisted for the Polari First Book Prize and the Historical Writers' Association Debut Crown.

With a background in science communication, she has worked as a press officer, magazine editor and freelance writer, and was Writer in Residence at Gladstone's Library in 2019. She lives in London.

Follow Sarah on Twitter
@geowriter

and Instagram
@sarahd1928

and visit
www.sarah-day.com

For my dad

You, sir, are a steely-eyed missile man

In April 1936, twenty-seven London schoolchildren, aged between twelve and seventeen, were led on a hike in the Black Forest by their teacher, Kenneth Keast. Ill prepared for bad weather, the group became stranded on the Schauinsland mountain, not far from the village of Hofsgrund.

This book is inspired by those events, but is entirely a work of fiction.

'The red fluid is too potent, and blood debts are too current. Stories lie in wait even for the most carefully literal-minded.'

– Donna J. Haraway

Part One

Chapter One

He is climbing. Everything else has become meaningless, as though he dreamed up his life before this and remembers it now in quick, snow-streaked snatches. There is nothing but white, trees and the glimpse of grey sky beyond, an impossible reminder of a world beyond this one, a safe place of warmth.

The snow clings and gathers itself around his waist, pulling him back, forming a tempting pillow around him. There is an urge, almost overwhelming, to lie back in it and close his eyes, give himself up to the numbing silence. The temptation grows so strong he has to bite down hard on his tongue, force himself to pull on regardless, unsure what he is even hauling himself towards except that he can hear bells, somewhere high and far ahead of him.

It had been early morning when they set out but somehow it is dark now, nothing but moonlight reflecting on the snow to light their way. He can't understand how it can have got so dark, when they have surely only been walking for a few hours. He strains his eyes to see anything around him, but there is only the blur of snowfall. The path, which had just now been steep but manageable, has somehow become practically sheer; he is clinging to great fistfuls of ice and earth, each step barely more than a pathetic stumble forward, then a slide further down the slope; is he really going back, rather than forwards? He strains for the bells and hears them faintly – further away, or closer? He can't tell. Within the terror, he must admit, is something close to elation. This is valour, he thinks, this is bravery. This is what they give out medals for, when people return from wars.

He tries to blink snow from his eyes and scans the mountainside for the children. Until a few minutes ago he knew where each boy was, had them marked out in an urgent pattern around him, but the group is beginning to scatter now, until the closest of them are merely dark shapes in the corner of his eye. He tries to shout, but when he opens his mouth it fills with snow. Even if he could make a sound, there is no way to make himself heard above the wind. Once they reach the top of the ridge he will pick the two strongest boys and send them on ahead towards the village to sound the alarm. They have only to get to the top and there will be time to plan, to think things out. He'll show them what he's made of.

A twinge of pain shoots across the sole of one foot and he flinches, determined not to show it. He thinks of the doctor, years ago when he was conscripted, instructing him to walk from one end of a cold room to the other, the sound of his bare feet against the tiles, a scratch of pencil on paper, a soft voice, *gait normal*.

The bells toll again, and he wonders if they are being rung deliberately, if someone knows they're out here. The far-off sound of a sleeping village, of warmth and safety – it seems impossible that he will ever reach it. The likelihood of the boys making it with him, even less. They'll manage it somehow, though. He imagines the looks on those villagers' faces, when, against all the odds, he emerges from the storm. How grateful the boys will be, how grateful their parents, that he has got them through it. He hears his brother's voice beside him, *Come on, Keith, buck up, it's just a little cold, a little wet, you'll be out of it in no time.*

He showed the boys his old war medal, not long before they came on the trip. They'd been talking about Germany, about what they might expect out here; *Are they all afraid of us, will they try to fight us in the streets? Will Mr Hitler be there, are we going to go with guns?*

He'd tried to explain, and in the end he'd pulled out his medal instead, hoping that would do it for him. *I got it for sniping.* The stories had spilled from him; at last, something to hold their attention, something better than German grammar and textbooks. He spoke of crouching in a tiny, bombed-out flat, watching his comrades running through the streets below him. Picking out Germans one by one, the satisfying *click click* as he watched them fall. *You won't have any trouble from them, boys, they know who's boss.* He'd seen it in the children's faces, the awe in their eyes. He'd held up the medal and read out the inscription on it. *For bravery in the field.* It had felt brand new, their admiration, mingled with an edge of fear.

He feels a sudden twinge at his knee; a small hand is clinging to his trouser leg. A voice whispers, 'Sir, I don't think…'

'Nonsense,' he hears himself reply. 'It's just a bit of weather. Get yourself together.'

Another hand reaches ineffectually for his own and he grips it hard, clasping the cold fingers around his, feeling the child's body resisting his onward march. He would reach out and pull the boy onto his shoulders, carry both of them together, only then he fears he will fall and tumble down the sticky slopes, and what help would he be to them then? Besides, there are so many more. He cannot lift them all out of the mire together.

He knows how to climb in the dark. Ever since Cambridge, when he'd learned the routes across college roofs and spires at night. He can still feel the freezing stone between his knees, rough walls grazing his fingers as he clung tight in the darkness, delirious with fear. Urging himself on, determined to prove everybody wrong. *You're stronger than they think.*

Had they had time to give themselves a talking to, all those boys in muddy fields, before the bullets and the shrapnel hit?

Come on now, it's just a bit of weather, just the luck of the draw. You'll be out of it in no time.

He looks up and sees one of the taller boys trudging on ahead of him, forging a path through the snow with slow, determined heaves. The child becomes his metronome in the dark. Keith matches every step to his, every breath to the bells which chime again – surely closer now, surely it cannot be far. The boy and the bells. The boy and the bells. Step by step, minute by minute, chime by chime. Another jolt of pain shoots through his leg and he stumbles, collects himself and focuses on the dark shape ahead of him. There is a pang of shame that this boy is stronger, faster than he is, that he should have need of a child to keep himself alive, but still he begins to shift his own path until he is walking in the trench of snow the boy has trodden, pale walls rising on either side of them like the slopes surrounding ancient roads.

There's talk of another war coming. Back home, it seems to be all anyone can think about. So many people tried to stop him bringing the boys to Germany – what if it happens while you're there, what if you're *trapped*? As though, the moment it broke out, they'd all be rounded up like criminals. As though these Germans don't know who's boss. But he has wondered himself, these last few days, whether they might have been right. Whether he ought really to have come. In Freiburg, they'd passed uniformed men in the streets, boys in military outfits, seen the red and black flag hanging from the town hall, dripping into the square as though a great gash had been opened up in the side of the building, its bloody insides running down the walls, into the gutter. Something was stirring, something that felt different to the time before. He'd wondered, all the way to the mountain, whether they ought not to turn back. Earlier, they'd met a man on the road who'd seemed horrified at the sight of them; they hate the English here, no doubt, they fear us, he'd said to the boys afterwards, trying to explain it away. A storm is coming, the man kept saying to him, over and over, it's not safe, you need to turn around. *Nonsense*. He'd turned back to grin at the boys, to encourage them to laugh at this German peasant shouting warnings at the sky. *It's just a bit of weather.*

He reaches into his pocket and grasps the edges of his medal, rubbing his thumb against the indentations in its surface. *For bravery in the field.*

Without his realising, the small hand has slipped from his. He pauses and kneels to grope in the frozen dark. At first there's only snow, then his fingers find something cold and hard, like a boulder, but a boulder dressed in shorts and a stiff woollen jumper. The skin feels hard, like leather. The boy's body is already frozen to the mountain, as though the Schauinsland does not want to give him up, now that it has him. Keith looks up, wondering who else has noticed, half expecting someone to let off an alarm or a flare. Ahead of him the tall boy, his metronome, has stumbled to his knees and begun to crawl.

That's when he knows. Later, he will tell them he had a plan, he was in control, that it was only a dire misfortune, a tragedy of weather, no one could have foreseen it. But as he watches the boy fall, he knows the truth of what he has done. What he will do.

Distantly, the bells peal out the hour. Snow-blind, he climbs on.

Chapter Two

There was a moment, somewhere between getting up from her seat on the upper deck and leaving the bus, when Sylvia thought she'd lost her son. She was halfway down the stairs when it happened; they'd stopped on the Euston Road, the wheeze of the engine replaced with the hum of traffic outside and the whole bus suddenly still and silent, waiting for whoever was about to get off to go ahead and get on with it.

Not long after Cyril was born, a nurse had taken him to be weighed while she was sleeping and she'd felt it then too: a panic so acute she'd wanted to tear at her skin, hold up bloodstained fingers, just to get someone to notice. She'd searched the room for her husband, remembered where he was and screamed so loudly that when the nurse came back with Cyril in her arms, Sylvia had feared he might be taken away from her for good.

She stood at the open door of the bus, one hand gripping the pole, and with her other hand felt the air around her with her fingertips, expecting to touch his hair, to feel his hand reaching up for her, and finding only empty space, the shadow of where he ought to be.

A man behind her hissed through his teeth and the driver shot her a pointed glare.

'On or off?'

He sounded weary. Outside, London was bright with sunshine, the pavements slick with recent rain. She wanted to move. She wanted to shout at the driver but she couldn't speak because Cyril wasn't there. Her fingers flexed. The rest of the passengers were growing restless now, a rising hum of discontent, and she was about to scream that old familiar scream when she remembered, in a rush of relief which made her insides feel hot, that Cyril wasn't supposed to be there. He was on his school trip, miles away in the mountains of the Black Forest, and not her responsibility at all.

Off the bus, she allowed herself to be swept up in the stream of people making their way towards the university. Now that the moment had passed, she felt embarrassed, as though the people around her could read the unwarranted panic on her face. It had been the same that day the nurse had taken her baby to be weighed – when she'd come back Sylvia had expected to be admonished for the racket she was making, all that fuss, but the nurse had only stood in the doorway for a moment, waiting. When Sylvia's sobs had subsided she had crossed the room, placed Cyril on Sylvia's chest and tutted, patted her damp forehead and passed her a glass of water. *You didn't wake him, thank God.* Sylvia had looked down at his tiny, crumpled face, his little fists pawing at her hair, and wanted to laugh. *We've made it*, she'd whispered to him, pressing her face close to his, *how about that?* She'd closed her eyes, trying not to think about the empty house around them, the fact that when she looked down at her baby she could see her husband's face and not her own.

She concentrated on her feet on the pavement, loud in the leather court shoes she had polished especially for today, the swing of her wool coat at her sides; it was too hot for wool, she had known it would be, but it was the smartest she had and she needed to make an impression. Was the laboratory expecting a younger woman? They must be; at her age she ought to be at home, caring for her husband and child. Women with families didn't answer job advertisements, not unless something had gone terribly wrong. She wondered if she ought not to have worn lipstick. She touched a finger to her mouth and then, thinking better of it, moved it away.

She glanced down at the slip of paper in her hands. 'Galton Laboratory, University of London, University College, Gower Street W.C.1. Apply Miss Eileen Foster, Secretary, Department of Eugenics.'

She'd imagined herself working in a laboratory ever since she'd started her nursing training. She'd seen herself sitting at a long bench, peering at slides through a microscope, testing out miracles in tiny glass tubes. People would laugh at her but she'd known it was possible, things were changing for women all the time. And then Cyril had come, and everything had been different. When the advertisement had appeared in her morning paper, it had felt like a sign.

She'd seen articles in the papers about the Galton Laboratory, all written in a tone of optimistic excitement; they were going to unlock the mysteries of inheritance, find ways of proving paternity, even help people to decide whether to have children, all based on what sort of blood they had. She'd been handed a pamphlet recently at a Women's Co-operative Guild meeting: 'Defects in the family? Is it wise to marry?' She'd shuddered, thinking of Arthur, and quickly handed it back, but the question had lingered, and with it, the thought of what might be possible in the future. If you really could learn everything about a person, how they'd turn out to be, just from their blood, what mistakes might be avoided?

Somewhere ahead of her a clock chimed a quarter to the hour and she tensed, a flood of anxiety jumping up to replace the terror she had felt on the bus. How many others were going for the position? She scanned the faces of the crowd, trying to judge whether they were on their way to the same interview, the same address. *Remember, love* – her friend Ruby's voice calm in her ear – *you belong there, you've got experience. You march in there like you've got the job already.*

A man brushed past her a little too close and she flinched back against some railings, reaching a hand out again for

Cyril. She felt weightlessness at the lack of his slight pull on her arm, the absence of a need to slow her steps to match his. She wondered where he had been, right at the moment she had had her panic on the bus. Maybe he had experienced the same jolt of absence, had felt around him for her hand, the soft cowl of her coat. He'd be in Freiburg by now, in the shadow of mountains and snow. Did he feel the same strange sense of loss, of having cast a part of himself off? Of course not, she told herself, that wasn't how children thought, they weren't supposed to mind. *You didn't wake him, thank God.* With any luck, he wouldn't be thinking about her at all.

She extracted herself from the flow of people and turned on to Gower Street, pausing to smooth her skirt and touch at her hair. There were grey hairs mingled with the brown now; Ruby made her own dye and kept trying to get Sylvia to try it, but Sylvia had never felt quite right about it. *It gives the wrong impression*, her mother would have said. Besides, Ruby's dye sometimes brought her out in great red welts across her scalp, or even caused clumps of hair to fall out entirely. Sylvia had read somewhere that the ancient Egyptians used to shave off all their hair and stick to wigs, which didn't seem like such a bad idea when you thought about it. Still, she wished now she had given the hair dye a go, after all. She might pass for younger than forty, if she really worked at it.

Her mother had only visited once after the baby was born. She'd appeared in a cloud of violet perfume and swept through the house, rearranging furniture and collecting up dirty plates, pausing briefly to put a hand to Sylvia's temple and hold Cyril out in front of her, examining him from every angle like an object in an auction house. *Well then. So much for your career.* She hadn't asked about Arthur or seemed to notice his absence. She'd died a few months later, and Sylvia had always wondered whether, in those last few weeks, she'd known more than she'd let on.

She turned into the courtyard of University College,

looking up uncertainly at the gleaming white facade of the main building, its white columns like a Grecian temple, topped with an ornate dome. She'd imagined herself here, or somewhere like it, for so long it almost felt familiar. She wished there had been some way to bring Cyril with her, for him to share in her excitement at this possibility of a new start. In an awful rush, she remembered: the night before the school trip, his face in the kitchen doorway, red-cheeked and furious, a piece of paper in his hand, the drawers of Arthur's old desk open behind him. She'd looked down at her own hands on the kitchen table and imagined, once again, clawing at her own skin, screaming loud enough to wake the street, something proportionate to the calamity they were suddenly facing.

Inside, she expected to be greeted by a desk and a receptionist, but found herself instead in a vast, dim space so filled with furniture and stacks of boxes and files that she didn't quite know where to step. She stood still for a moment, trying to recover her composure, to push the memory of that terrible night from her mind. They had ten days apart from each other – the longest they'd ever been separated. There would be time to make things right.

She stumbled against a box covered in a cloth and let out a shriek as something moved inside it, a shock of white fur bristling through the wooden slats.

'Mrs Clayton?' A woman was hurrying towards her, holding out a hand. 'Eileen Foster. I'm so sorry.' She gave a flustered smile. 'The professor's just had another consignment of rabbits arrive. They will keep delivering here instead of to the animal house!'

Sylvia held out a hand, attempting a smile in return as they shook hands. She'd been expecting someone younger – the 'Miss' at the close of the letter she'd received – but Eileen Foster was close to middle-aged, more like a housekeeper than a secretary. Sylvia felt suddenly less self-conscious about her age; perhaps this was a place that expected women to be mature and reliable. Who wanted some young thing who had barely any experience, after all? Still, she would do better not to mention Cyril if she could help it. Better to detach yourself from your outside life, from all those ties that made people question your ability to be impartial, to be focused.

That was how she had coped in France, when she really had been a young thing with no experience. There had been the training, of course – basic first aid, home nursing, then a few months in the hospital – but that had hardly prepared her for the real thing. She'd been chasing after her sister, already out there, desperate to prove she could do just as well. And all of a sudden there she was, in a field tent facing rows of young men all lined up on stretchers. In the middle of a war, but there had hardly been time to contemplate that, either. There was just work to be done. She'd been detached and indifferent, there to do a job, impossible to think about the future, to worry about what would be left when it was all over. People hadn't understood that when she came back. They had taken it wrongly, in their neat houses and carefully arranged lives, with their well-meaning questions. *What was it like? How did you do it?* She didn't know what to tell them so she made up stories; bravery, camaraderie, tragedy, it didn't really matter. Really, there had just been blood, and whatever they could do to stop it flowing.

'Please, follow me.' Eileen led her through the maze of shelving and boxes. The light was dim, but Sylvia could make out typewriters and larger machines covered in multiple tiny keys lined up on the long wooden benches. 'This half is all statistics,' she said, waving a hand. 'Postgraduates, mostly.'

Ahead of them, a number of blackboards covered in scrawled equations had been used to divide the space in two; as they passed through them Sylvia blinked at the sudden bright light from two unshaded bulbs overhead. The other half of the space was filled with gently humming machinery, and two long, polished benches, covered with microscopes, slides stacked neatly in wooden boxes, and gleaming laboratory equipment.

'Serology,' Eileen said briskly, as Sylvia hurried to keep up with her.

'What are all these?' she replied, taking in the bulky metallic boxes which lined the walls.

'Fridges, mainly. We need them for storing the blood. There's the centrifuge as well. Shouldn't be animals, though! I'm sorry about that. It's been a year since the professor took over and still, chaos everywhere! This all used to be a museum, if you can believe that.'

Sylvia could believe it. She imagined moving the tall cabinets aside, taking away the benches and chairs to leave a high-ceilinged, wood-panelled atrium, the cabinets filled with tiny drawers and the corridors lined with glass cases; curiosities stacked up in jars and pinned to cards.

'A museum of what?'

'Skulls, skeletons and skins.' There was an edge of distaste in Eileen's voice. 'All those old-fashioned ways we used to try to classify people. Brain sizes, body shape, all that anatomical nonsense. All in the past now.' She swept a hand about the space, taking in the refrigerators lining the walls. 'What matters now is *blood*.'

They had reached the double doors at the far end of the room, which opened on to a narrow staircase.

'You're a little older than our usual candidate. What are you, forty?'

'Forty-two,' Sylvia said as they climbed. 'Just last month.'

'And you've nursing experience?'

'Yes, I went out in 1917.'

'Goodness. So young.'

'I was twenty-three. Older than a lot of the men fighting, anyway.'

The image of a young boy flashed into her mind, lying on a stretcher in one of the tents, staring at her so intently she had to look away. His hand was gripping hers tightly, and somewhere behind her, someone was shouting her name. *Now, Clayton. We can't wait any more. You need to—*

'Gosh, you must have seen a lot of awful things,' Eileen said brightly.

'There was a lot of blood. So, you know. I'm used to it.'

Eileen smiled at her, clearly bemused; they weren't in a hospital, after all. They had reached a long corridor, thick with the smell of cigarettes and burned coffee, wooden doors lining each wall.

'First floor, laboratories and offices,' she announced, as though she was a lift attendant. She led Sylvia to the end of the corridor and opened a door on to a large room looking out on to the courtyard, lined with books and even more cabinets. The walls were covered in framed etchings: bones, mathematical charts and a couple of pencil portraits of men gazing into the distance with scholarly faces. More calculating machines sat on the polished wooden benches and, on a desk near the window, five skulls had been placed neatly in a row.

'Are those…'

'Human.' Eileen nodded. 'There's still some attachment to craniometry. Difficult to persuade everyone to move with the times,' she said, sounding as though she felt it was her own task to do so.

On the opposite side of the corridor, they viewed the department's library, so filled with overstuffed shelves that it was difficult to squeeze in past them, then retraced their steps along the corridor, passing doors marked 'Director', 'Assistant', 'Classroom' and Eileen's own office, labelled 'Secretary'.

'Common room,' she said, opening a door at the end of the hall, and Sylvia caught a brief glimpse of cushioned benches along the walls, the overpowering smell of stale smoke and coffee. 'We share it with the statistics department, I'm afraid.'

As they stood in the doorway, Sylvia heard the unmistakable

sound of heels on polished wood, and turned to see a young woman walking briskly past them, a bundle of papers in her arms. She nodded a curt good morning to Eileen and continued on with barely a glance at Sylvia.

'One of the research assistants. They come in at all hours,' Eileen said, shaking her head disapprovingly. Sylvia stared after her, imagining the woman taking a seat at one of the benches downstairs, peering into a microscope or a calculating machine, picturing herself doing the same.

'And this is you,' Eileen said, guiding her towards a door by the staircase.

The windowless space was tucked beneath the stairs, the roof slanted in a spiral. A mop, two brooms and a pile of rags in a metal bucket were arranged neatly along one wall, and an overall hung on a hook beside them. Eileen reached for a large metal contraption beside them.

'Latest technology!' she said, handing it to Sylvia. 'You just run it over the floors. So, it's just the laboratories, common room and offices on this floor and upstairs. Downstairs, steer clear of serology, they won't want you interfering, but there is the lecture theatre. Floors mopped throughout, then it's polishing and light dusting. I've been taking care of things myself up until now, but the professor is keen for me to devote more of my time to his notes and files. They're not terribly strict with job titles here, but it does seem rather inefficient for the secretary to be doing quite so much dusting.'

'Yes, of course.' She was still holding the vacuum cleaner, feeling its solid weight beneath her fingers. She had always wanted one at home. One or two of her families had had one, imported from America, and had acted as though the purchasing of it had been a gift for her, a special favour for which she ought to be grateful and apologetic. Sometimes she'd thought about tucking it under her arm and making a run for it.

Outside in the university courtyard, a group of women broke into laughter, carrying through the open windows. *Take care,* Sylvia thought as she listened to them, *watch where you tread. Things might not turn out how you think.*

After Eileen had shown her the second floor they went back to her office. It overlooked Gower Street, thick with women hurrying with prams, mothers holding hands with their children, rushing between shops and crowding at the bus stop. As she watched them through the window, Sylvia felt a sting of guilt; there was something else, behind the loss she felt at Cyril's being away, beneath how much she missed him. It was relief; the freedom that came with only having yourself to think about. She hadn't realised how much she'd wanted it until now, watching those tired-looking women through the window.

'So, you're married?'

'No,' she said, turning back to the room.

'Chi-square, that's enough,' Eileen said in a sharp voice. A black cat had jumped down from a cabinet and was gingerly walking across the desk; she picked it up, tutting, and shooed it away. 'You'll have to keep an eye out for her,' she said, raising an eyebrow. 'She moults. Sorry – you said you aren't married. I thought—'

Of course, Sylvia thought. *Mrs Clayton*. Impossible to leave any doubt. She hadn't wanted to talk about Arthur, about any of it, and already he was here in the room with them.

'He died,' she said shortly.

'Oh.' Had a flicker of relief crossed Eileen's face? 'I'm so sorry.'

'It was a long time ago. Just before my son...' And she broke off again, because she hadn't been going to mention him either. Too late now. 'He's twelve.'

'How nice. Well,' Eileen said cheerfully, 'it's one less complication. Not being married, I mean. It hardly matters for the non-science staff really, but we prefer to keep things tidy.'

'Cyril is extremely independent,' she said quickly. 'It's not something that would interfere.'

'I'm sure he is.'

Sylvia wasn't sure he was, but she had liked the confidence in her voice as she had said it. 'He's on a school trip just now. It's the first time he's been away from home.'

'You must be missing him.'

'Yes, of course.' She felt strangely defensive, saying that. 'They're in Freiburg,' she added.

'Germany?'

'Yes, I was surprised too. But it's good, isn't it, to keep things normal? I don't see why we can't all get along.'

It would be good for Cyril too, that's what she kept telling herself. What better way to draw him out of himself than a trip abroad, hikes across pine forests, strange new food and a language he had never heard being spoken in its own country before, by its own people? She thought of him flying south on a train to the fairy-tale forests of the Rhineland. She had never been to Germany herself, but that was what it made her think of: forests and fairy tales, goblins and children lost in the woods, houses made of sweets. Something quite different to what she read in newspapers: Herr Hitler shouting and all those men in stiff uniforms issuing orders. Some of the parents had been unsure about a trip to Germany, when things were so unsettled, but what was the point in living in fear? And besides, it was so difficult to know what was true in the papers these days.

Eileen escorted her back downstairs. The woman they'd seen in the corridor was seated at one of the benches in the serology laboratory, pipetting tiny drops of blood onto a white tray filled with little divots like a paint palette. She glanced up as they passed, and Sylvia met her eyes briefly before she looked back, absorbed, at her work.

At the door, they shook hands and Eileen promised to write. Sylvia wondered if she had undone things with all that talk of Cyril, her impulsive speech about Germany and friendliness. She must have sounded like a child herself. Now that she had felt the jolt of excitement at her freedom, she realised how little of it she really had, even with Cyril away. She thought of the long day ahead, scouring the newspapers for work, writing applications, then the Women's Cooperative Guild later, another long speech on the impending war, no doubt, and what they could do to stop it. Writing letters, signing petitions, hoping that some of it would come to something in the end. She thought of the bright, clean air of the mountains where Cyril was, the clear skies. How it would feel, to be so high up, so far away from anything real. She felt in her pocket for the edges of his postcard; she had barely had time to read the opening 'Dear Mum' that morning before she had heard the bus rounding the corner and made a dash for it.

She'd been surprised to receive it. His teacher must have made them write, she thought; he'd never have done it himself. He'd barely looked at her as he'd picked up his suitcase in the hallway and struggled to pull it out to the waiting car, not allowing her to help, or even to give him a parting hug. She should have gone after him, should have tried to talk before he'd left, but there had been something terrifying about the force of his anger. When he came back, she thought as she wove her way through the crowds to her bus stop, things would be better. She'd forget the yearning she'd felt as she watched that woman in the laboratory, the longing for freedom, the guilt that came with it. She'd be a better mother, stop thinking so much about the past, about all the things she'd lost. Cyril would forgive her and they would begin again, she thought, imagining a blanket of snow falling over the past, smoothing it out like a fresh new canvas.

Chapter Three

'Right, I want to hear everything!'

Ruby was waiting for her on the steps to the church hall on Upper Street, dressed in her best grey wool skirt and a bright blue shirt, her hair pinned up carefully in waves. She always made an effort for meetings – 'Just in case we meet someone' was a recurring joke between them. As if their next husband was waiting for them at a meeting of the Women's Cooperative Guild. She had her white poppy pinned carefully to her collar; Sylvia rummaged in her handbag for her own, feeling a familiar guilt at how little she wore it outside of meetings.

'You look lovely.' Ruby kissed her cheek; Sylvia could feel the lipstick smear she had left behind.

'Stop it, I look a state.'

'So? The interview! Come on, I'm dying to hear. Did you see the labs? Were there dogs with cats' heads on?'

'There were skulls.'

Ruby wrinkled her nose. 'What else?'

'Just lots and lots of machines. Fridges. Oh, and a box of rabbits.'

'Rabbits!'

'White ones, with little pink noses.'

'And have you heard from Cyril?'

'Got a postcard this morning. He's alright.'

Ruby put a hand on her arm. 'You must be missing him.'

'Of course I'm missing him.'

'Goodness. What's got you so het up?'

She linked her arm through Sylvia's without waiting for a reply and led her up the steps into the building as Sylvia fiddled with her poppy, managing to attach it just as they went inside.

'It's exciting, isn't it?' Ruby was saying. 'The job, I mean. A chance to be close to something really important.'

'It's just cleaning, Ruby. Might as well be anywhere else.'

They entered a large hall, rows of seats facing a stage at the far end. Most of the women had already arrived, gathered at one end of the room around a steaming tea urn. They were a mix of ages, from young women barely twenty to elderly matrons, all dressed neatly in their best, chattering politely over teacups. Most were married, although there were widows and spinsters too. Many of the older women had been in service before they married, and now lived in comfortable domesticity, whilst the younger ones worked in shops and factories, or found work like hers, cleaning houses and offices. Ruby had four children at home, and a husband Sylvia had never met; the few times she'd tried to ask about him, Ruby had quickly changed the subject.

'What is it today?' she said, folding her coat over her arm.

Ruby looked down at the flyer in her hand, reading it out in a prim radio announcer's voice. '"Population decline and the impacts of warfare: Are we on the brink?"'

'Wonderful. Should have brought my knitting.'

Ruby giggled, then held the flyer closer, reading the description of the meeting and rolling her eyes. 'I hate it, do you?' she said. 'All this talk about defectives, things getting worse. You'd think it was the end of the world coming.'

'It's just talk,' Sylvia said vaguely, but still, she knew what Ruby meant. Abyssinia, the Rhineland – despite all the talk about peaceful solutions, it was hard not to feel gloomy whenever she opened a newspaper.

They sat down as a tall, smartly dressed woman took her place at the podium.

'*Defectives*,' Ruby muttered derisively, tucking the flyer under her skirt. 'Kids are born how they're born, aren't they?'

The woman arranged her notes, peering out at them from behind thick-framed tortoiseshell spectacles. As she began speaking, Sylvia remembered the postcard from Cyril and pulled it from her pocket. It was a photograph of a mountain, the word 'Schauinsland' printed beneath it. Its slopes were green and tree-covered, but at the summit there was a white edge of snow.

In her head, a distant alarm bell rang. Hadn't there been talk of a climb? It looked like a real mountain, not just a slope to be tackled in an easy afternoon. Surely mountains in the snow were only ever attempted by real climbers? Brave, experienced men, not schoolchildren and German masters. Men like George Mallory – and look what had happened to him.

She shook the thought away. A party of schoolboys would hardly be taken on anything like a real climb, after all. Perhaps Cyril had exaggerated things, in his excitement for the trip. She felt a twinge of guilt at the scepticism she felt; why shouldn't Cyril be up to it, the same as all the other boys? It wasn't fair, thinking about him like that, but wasn't that what the newspapers were full of? Flaws in the parent are passed down to the child. Arthur's flaws – if she'd known, if only she'd known, would Cyril even be here at all? It was unthinkable. He was here, and she wouldn't have anything different. But sometimes, with all the talk of a new war coming, of the challenges they might face, she felt so afraid she wanted to snatch Cyril up and take him somewhere else, far away from conscriptions and medical examinations and words like sacrifice and camaraderie.

She thought back to the last peace rally she had attended with the Guild. She and Ruby had met the night before to make their signs; Sylvia had painted 'I could lose my son' in large black letters on a sheet of cardboard, and afterwards stared so hard at the words they had begun to dance and swim in front of her eyes. The march had been the biggest she had ever seen; they had been jostled and nudged by well-meaning protestors, white poppies pinned proudly to their chests, all the way along Pall Mall. At one point she had found herself walking beside a young man holding tightly to a small girl's hand. The child was trotting to keep up with him, staring up at the crowds in wide-eyed wonder. Sylvia had smiled at her, then looked up at the man's sign, held high above his head. 'I could be gassed'.

'This country is facing a crisis,' the woman at the lectern was saying. 'Mothers are refusing to be mothers, and fathers have been slaughtered on the field of battle.'

Sylvia stared up at her. She looked around sixty, with long silvery hair tied up in a loose bun. Sylvia wondered if she had lost anyone on the field of battle. She could feel the image of the boy on the stretcher very close to her, and thought instead of Cyril in the clean, cold air of the mountains, striding out into freshly fallen snow. Then of Arthur, standing on the doorstep in his uniform, finally home for good, staring at her like she was a stranger. *Love, my love. Come in out of the cold.*

'Another war is on the horizon. Our population is dwindling, but more importantly, its quality is dwindling too. The strong and healthy were cut down, whilst those weaker members of our society remained safely at home. The percentage of those sometimes called "defectives" is currently...'

There was a sudden sound at the back of the room, and Sylvia turned to see a man standing in the doorway, anxiously scanning the crowd, a rain-soaked umbrella in his hand.

'The Eugenics Society is encouraging all groups under the umbrella of the National Council of Women to support our campaign for the legalisation of voluntary sterilisation in Britain. We will be issuing you with pledges to sign...'

She stared as Lydia Ward, the group's chair, hurried towards the man at the door, spoke a few whispered words and then looked back over her shoulder. Their eyes met, and Sylvia felt a strange premonition. Slowly, she stood and shuffled her way along the row, whispering apologies to the women as they stood to let her pass. The man hadn't even removed his overcoat, which was slick with rain. The woman at the podium was still speaking, but she couldn't hear the words any more, just a blur of sound against a pounding in her ears. As she reached the end of the row she began to shake uncontrollably, and reached out a hand for something to hold on to. It turned out to be Lydia, who clasped it tightly between both of hers as they approached the door. *I've always hated you,* Sylvia thought vaguely as she leaned her body into Lydia's. *I wonder if you know.* She could smell the perfume which always clung to Lydia's body: primroses and patchouli, stiflingly strong in the still, close air of the meeting room. She looked up at the man; met his eyes and saw tears in them. A sick feeling settled in the bottom of her stomach.

'Mrs Clayton,' the man said slowly. 'I'm so sorry. I've come from the school.'

Chapter Four

Most of the inhabitants of the small mountain village of Hofsgrund had anticipated the storm. Such outbursts of snow were unusual so late in April, when the thaw had already begun and snowdrops had forced their way through the ice. But the signs were unmistakeable. Hilde had felt it herself that morning as she'd opened the shutters, a shiver that took her back to the worst days of the winter, huddling in the *Stube* as storms raged outside, holding her hands out to the heat radiating from the stove at the centre of the house.

The stove was as needy as a child. Hilde wished now she'd spent more time watching how her mother had tended it each morning, piling up just enough kindling and fuel to keep it alight through the day, warming each room equally, then again each evening to keep it smouldering overnight. Several times during the past winter it had gone out, and she and Anna had woken shivering in their mother's bed, clinging to each other and gasping with the shock of it.

By mid-morning the snow was falling in loose flakes, settling on the herb garden at the front of the house, where Anna was kneeling to pick sorrel leaves half hidden in the drifts. The pigs in their pen by the side of the house were growing restless and uneasy, shuffling and shifting as the snow thickened and the wind rose.

'That storm's coming,' Anna said as she stood and stretched herself out, staring up at the sky. Anna had turned fourteen in the winter; a few days afterwards her blood had at last begun to flow. She and Hilde had stood together in the kitchen with a basin of water, scrubbing at stained rags until the water was copper tinged, and Hilde had tried to remember what their mother had said to her, back when it had been her turn. *Now you're a woman, Hilde.* She'd looked at Anna, her face still rounded and childlike, and hadn't been able to say the words.

'We should get the pigs inside,' Hilde said, rubbing her hands together against the cold. *It warms the blood, sharing your house with animals,* their mother used to say. *Feel the wall, here* – and she would press Hilde and Anna's palms against it and it was true, they could feel a radiating heat pulsing through the wood, like a heartbeat under their hands.

'I'll do it.'

Anna liked to be the one to look after the animals: feed them and gather them in at night, stroke them softly as they settled in the straw. Some of them even had names. And yet, when it came time to prepare the yard for slaughter, she didn't flinch. Hilde envied it, this marriage of compassion and cold reality. It was what you needed on the mountain, it helped you survive. When the knife slid across the pigs' throats, Anna never looked away. It was always Hilde who shut her eyes, always Hilde who felt an uneasy stirring in her stomach at the sight of their carcasses swinging in the yard, then, later, the sound of their fat spitting on the fire.

In the *Stube*, Hilde stood at the window and watched as their neighbours drove in the last of their cattle. They hadn't taken their own out that morning, already mindful of the storm, and Hilde was glad of it now as she watched villagers struggling through the wind and snow. Towards the square, the church spire was disappearing into a thick fog, behind which the slopes of the Schauinsland spread dark and insubstantial, as though it were part of the clouds gathering around its peak.

Some of the villagers talked of a king sleeping under the

mountain, who collected lives for his army. He is coming, they would say, soon he will rise up and defend the country against some great, unnamed peril. Those who die on the mountain are taken into the earth, like so many others before them, taken for his battles, which will be fought at the end of the world. Hilde didn't believe in the stories, but she felt, all the same, that some great peril was coming, that it might have already arrived. She felt it in the way people in the village looked at each other, the tension that hung in the air like a storm cloud waiting to break. The night of the elections, three years ago, they had lit a bonfire on the summit which had blazed its bright light all across the valley; visible as far as Todtnauberg, people said afterwards. Fires had been lit to form the shape of a swastika, and the villagers had come out to watch as a parade of Hitler Youth had passed their way through the village, holding their flames aloft. Anna had laughed and clapped at the sight, running alongside the boys for as long as she could, while Hilde and her mother stood in the doorway watching, saying nothing. The parties had continued all night, all across the valley – all through Germany, a new era was beginning. *The king is waking*, villagers had whispered to each other, *it won't be long now.*

Hilde turned back to the stove, glancing enviously at Gretel, curled up in a chair, her contented purring loud enough to be heard over the rising wind. It was hard to sleep on storm nights. So often, someone would come to the door needing help: their animals had broken loose, a window needed boarding up. A woman had gone into labour or a child was trapped beneath a fallen branch, the nearest doctor hours away. Often she slept by the hearth, just in case she was needed in a hurry. *It's too much*, she thought, as she had thought so often through the unrelenting winter. *Keeping all this going, we can't do it on our own.* The house felt flimsy and insubstantial, the wind strong enough to break it into splinters. The panicked lowing of the animals was reaching a crescendo; she imagined them kicking down the walls, cattle stampeding across the flagstones, through the *Stube* and into the kitchen, out into the snow. She breathed out slowly, one hand on her stomach, counting down from ten the way her mother had taught her long ago. *When you reach one, things will not be so bad. But you have to do it slowly,* Liebling.

'They're all in safely.' Anna's voice, carrying from the kitchen, broke into the silence. 'Just in time, by the looks of it. What are you looking for?' she said as she entered the *Stube*.

Hilde was standing by the window, staring out at the snow. She closed the shutters quickly and turned around. 'Nothing. I thought perhaps everyone would be at the inn. I saw Fritz going that way.'

'You want to join them? I don't mind.'

On storm nights, most of the village would gather together by the fireplace at the inn, playing cards and sharing stories of harder winters past, warming themselves with schnapps brewed in Gertrud Braunling's basement or wine brought on carts from Freiburg.

Hilde shook her head. 'I don't think I'm welcome, am I?'

'Psch, they'll have forgotten all about it by now.' Anna wound an arm around Hilde's shoulder. 'It's like the storm, Hilde. It can't last forever.'

But Hilde had seen the way they all looked at her in the street, how heads turned towards her in church, hands concealed whispers that were just loud enough for her to overhear. *I heard he's asked her three times now, she thinks she's too good for him, well, she's lucky anyone will touch her. Why don't they leave, they've an aunt in Freiburg, don't they? There's plenty of others who would take on the running of that farm, others who know what they're doing.*

It had been wrong to turn Reiner Haas down, she knew that. Even though he was two decades older than her, even though they barely knew each other, just the odd glance exchanged in church. With both parents gone, she and Anna needed help with the farm, and Reiner had money, a horse and cart of his own. The rumours were spreading like a spring flood; *Hilde Meyer is hoarding money in the basement, she's neglecting her farm, she thinks she's better than the rest of us.* Why else would she turn down such a chance? And, now that she had, what was she planning to do with herself? With that sister who looked as though she hadn't had a decent meal in months, who spent her days grinding up herbs for potions and mixing tinctures? *What does she think she is, a witch? We'd have burned them both, not so very long ago. I heard their father was a socialist, well, it's no wonder how they've turned out, is it?*

'I don't regret it,' she said out loud, and Anna nodded, holding on to her tighter. 'I mean, can you imagine? Marriage. *Children*. I mean, can you imagine?'

'I know. It's just—'

'What?' She turned to look at her sister.

'There are loans now.'

'You think I should have said yes.'

'No! Not if you don't want to. But – what are we going to do, Hilde?'

'We're going to carry on like we always have.'

'Just the two of us, and the whole farm to run?'

'Well, we might go somewhere else. We might go to Freiburg, even.'

'Freiburg!' Anna sounded shocked.

'Or anywhere – I don't know, Anna. I'll think of something.' She waited, and although Anna was silent, Hilde knew that there was more she wanted to say. 'What?'

Anna frowned, her brow creasing in an expression that always made her look much older. 'If you do want to get married. If you ever do, I mean. You'll still be you. It doesn't change that, does it?'

Hilde sighed a heavy sigh. 'Why are you always the wise one, Anna Meyer? Maybe they're right, maybe you really are a witch.'

By the fire, Gretel blinked at Hilde, stretching herself out on her chair. She'd produced a litter last spring, like magic, tiny bodies squirming and crawling over one another in the basement, mewling and scratching at their closed eyelids. Hilde had given one to Freida Zettler, who'd exclaimed over the kittens as though they were freshly baked bread; the rest, Anna had taken out to the stream and drowned.

When the knocking started, it shook Hilde out of sleep. She was sitting in her chair by the stove, Gretel snoring on her lap, and at first she thought they'd come for her, imagined a crowd outside the door, torches flaming in their hands, fists raised.

The cold air rushed in at her as she half opened the door. Fritz Feldberg was standing on the porch; Hilde hardly recognised him at first. Most of his face was hidden in layers of wool, ice clinging to his hair and eyebrows. Behind him, the sky was dark, snow battering against the walls of the house.

'Fritz – is someone ill, or—'

'There's people on the mountain,' he shouted over the din of the storm. 'Children.'

'Children?'

'English – two of them came to the inn, half dead – they say there are others. God knows what they were doing, they were barely dressed for a midsummer day in Freiburg. Just wandering about as though they had no idea where they were. I came to ask – your father's skis…'

'Of course. Just give me a moment to change my boots.'

Fritz put a hand on her arm. The harsh winter seemed to have aged him; he looked thin and stooped. When he had first come to the village, not long before the elections and the bonfires, he had seemed like a tree trunk of a man, chopping wood outside his farmhouse or lifting Anna onto his shoulders. Now, he looked as though a storm could blow him from the side of the mountain, and she felt cold at the thought of him going out there, searching for lost children in the dark. He'd come to the mountain to paint; he'd lived in Freiburg before that, and she and Anna had begged him for stories of the city, of the glamorous women in furs, the cathedral and the wide streets. *I ran out of views to paint* was all he'd say, and eventually they'd learned not to ask any more. He made a small living now selling scenes of mountain life, snowy landscapes and, in the summer, panoramas of the summit bathed in sunlight. After their father's death, Fritz had taken it upon himself to look after them all; Hilde, Anna, her mother. He was the only one who didn't seem to care about Reiner, about all the rumours, the decline of her farm. He'd looked out for her and Anna, without caring what anyone else had to say about it.

'I didn't mean...' Fritz said awkwardly, the hand still on her arm. 'I just wanted to ask if we could borrow Walter's skis.'

'Nonsense. I'll come myself.' She was already gathering up layers of clothing, checking the locks on the shutters. She went to the bedroom and looked in on Anna, who was fast asleep in the bed they shared, closing the door carefully before coming back to join Fritz.

'Really, Hilde, there's no need—'

'Children, you said?' She glanced back at the stove, where Gretel was stretching herself out contentedly on the warm tiles. 'Fritz, of course I'll come.'

Chapter Five

It was nearly dark as they drove from the meeting house. A scattering of rain was beginning to fall; Sylvia stared out of the car window at the damp pavements, people running to shelter in doorways, laughing and holding coats over their heads. A couple stood huddled together under a shop awning, his coat wrapped around her shoulders, and she thought of Arthur walking her to her bus in the days when they'd first met, how he'd stood carefully between her and the traffic. And the days after Armistice, when they'd walked together to No More War meetings – had she known, even then? Once, a group of protesters had strayed into the road and a car had braked hard and sounded its horn; he'd stopped dead in the street and begun to shake so hard his teeth had rattled.

By the time the car pulled up outside the school, the rain had thickened to a downpour. The man – Sylvia still didn't know his name, anything about him at all – held open the car door for her and opened his umbrella over her head as they walked together to the gates. They hadn't spoken at all in the car. For a moment, when he had told her he had come from the school, she had grasped at the idea that Cyril had perhaps got himself in trouble on the trip for some minor infringement of the rules. He had stolen another child's lunch, perhaps, or avoided a hike to stay behind and read comics. It would have been a relief, in more ways than one. He had never once been in trouble and it had begun to gnaw at her, as though it were some rite of passage he ought to pass through. Arthur had told her endless stories about what he had got up to as a child: stolen sweets, pranks played on schoolmasters, days spent exploring riverbanks instead of sitting behind a desk. They had laughed about it, with the ease that adults did when forgiving themselves for mistakes they would one day chastise their children for. Sylvia had been bracing herself for a summons just such as this for so long; better than a visit from a policeman or an ambulance, further down the line. She hadn't had to ask the man any questions to understand that it was something much worse than this.

He left her at the gates. A few other parents were arriving now, clinging to each other in pairs as they made their way up the steps. Sylvia, accustomed to her invisibility, hung back just far enough that they wouldn't feel compelled to speak to her. She knew what they thought of her. A single mother, raising a son alone – who could say whether something of her failure, her shame, might not spread amongst them?

It felt strange to be at the school at night. Everything about it looked different, from the dark windows to the long shadows that stretched across the yard, cast by a single source of light beyond the door. She thought of the first time she had seen it: standing in front of well-worn steps while a smartly dressed woman with the air of an efficient housekeeper recounted the history of the building, its illustrious graduates and impressive exam results. She couldn't afford it, not really. She had inherited enough from her parents to cover the first few years, but it wouldn't last and cleaning wasn't bringing in as much as Ruby had promised her it would. She had never imagined all these decisions, all this planning, would be left to her alone. She had walked around the building – sunlit, clean classrooms full of expensive-looking equipment and books arranged neatly on shelves – and thought of her own school days: learning to sew and cook, how to walk with her head held high. She had listened to the woman proudly listing achievements. *Fifteen per cent of our boys will go to Oxbridge.*

One of our swimmers came fifth in the Olympic games! She would make it work, she had decided, and somehow she had.

The other parents were walking in the direction of the gymnasium, so Sylvia followed them, making her way past empty classrooms, metal forests of chair legs stacked on desks, chalkboards neatly scrubbed. As she walked she began to feel as though her body were a separate object, that she was moving without intention towards a disaster that she couldn't avoid, a truth that waited for her like a hangman and a noose. She passed the dining hall and a lingering smell of gravy and suet puddings flooded the corridor. She thought, pausing for a moment to lean forwards with her hands on her knees, that she might be sick. There was a ringing in her ears, a warning bell that took her back to the worst moments of a war long since over. *We are facing a crisis,* a voice repeated back to her. Cyril's face on the doorstep as he left for Germany – had he been apprehensive, or was that just how she remembered it now? The strength of his anger – had she forced him to go, had it been her own selfishness in the end, had she made it happen? *Humanity is on the brink.*

'Mrs Clayton.'

She was in the gymnasium. How had she got there? The headmaster, Professor Franklin, was holding her hands in his, and someone was trying to give her tea. 'How are you?' he was saying, pointlessly, inexcusably, and she took the tea and began circling the room like an animal in a trap, her head filled with the musty smell of dried sweat. A pommel horse stood silent vigil at the centre of the room, towels and kitbags and various items of forgotten equipment and clothing scattered across the floor around it. Sylvia wondered if one of the items belonged to Cyril, and felt an urge to search through them and snatch up anything that did.

'I just want to wait... everyone's here... get started.' Franklin's voice was thin and strained. She remembered the day she'd gone to visit him in his office and he'd told her about Cyril's scholarship, that he'd known she wouldn't have been able to afford the fees any longer without it. *We don't want to lose him.* She'd been grateful, of course, but there had been something so condescending in the way he'd looked at her that she'd almost regretted accepting the money. She'd known then that she'd always feel beholden to him, to the school. Ever since, she'd avoided visiting as much as she could.

The history master was beside him, nodding with a sympathetic tilt to his head. Sylvia imagined them both in dark green uniforms, their shaking hands raising a gun to their shoulders. They encouraged such thoughts at the Guild meetings. *Imagine your sons, your brothers, your friends, not faceless soldiers, when you think of war. Imagine them being mown down in a spray of bullets. Imagine reality, not the lies we've been fed.* Franklin patted her on the shoulder and she imagined a landmine erupting beneath his feet. He must be at least fifty, but his grip on her shoulder was strong. Yes, she thought, he might be safe from the first conscription. Perhaps not the last.

'I'm so sorry to have called you all here with no explanation,' he was saying to the room now, and she wished there was a way to make everything freeze, to give herself more time.

Next to Sylvia, Roger Prendergast had begun to shake uncontrollably. His wife was trying to keep him still but it only got worse, the convulsions spreading to his voice, a stuttering chorus of anxious sounds that echoed in the vast gymnasium like the trillings of a trapped bird.

'The fact is, the news will be in the morning papers, we think. So I thought it better if you all heard the same, directly from me. And...' He looked down, flinching a little. 'I would urge you not to read the reports, when they do come.'

Prendergast was whimpering more loudly now, strange gasping sounds like a dog scratching at a closed door. Someone brought him a chair and a glass of water. Sylvia held her stomach, wondering if she would be sick now, in front of them all.

'As you know, the boys were with their German master, Keith Hughes, in Freiburg yesterday, before setting out for a climb as scheduled. I've had word early this morning that there was a terrible storm in the afternoon, which caught them unawares. They were on the mountain at the time, and…'

There it was again, that image of the Schauinsland on Cyril's postcard. Surely they hadn't really been there? The room was blurring now, replaced with images of boys struggling in snowdrifts, howling wind and Cyril calling out for her. And if they had got into trouble, surely Keith Hughes, whose job it was to look out for them, who had once fought a war himself, wouldn't let them down?

'There isn't an easy way to say it.'

She was sitting on the floor, without any memory of having got there.

'I'm afraid there have been casualties.'

A collective cry erupted. It fell silent as the headmaster drew a slip of paper from his jacket. Sylvia reached for the postcard, still in her coat pocket unread, and pressed one corner of it under a fingernail until the pain made her gasp. She looked at the history master, standing stiffly beside Franklin, tears dripping messily down his chin. Roger Prendergast stood up and threw the chair across the room and she watched it fly in a perfect parabola, imagined an explosion as it landed, the entire school erupting in flames and smoke and splintered bodies.

Chapter Six

Hilde focused on the shadow of Fritz's body ahead of her, leaning forward into the wind. It was biting now, screaming in her ears as her skis quickly disappeared into drifts of snow. There was barely any light to see by, just the faint glow of moonlight and the distant pinpoints of lanterns – why hadn't she thought to bring one of her own, what had she been thinking?

To her left and right, she could make out the shapes of other villagers, some on skis, others struggling on foot, the faint sounds of them shouting to each other in voices muffled and dampened by the wind. She wondered if any of them was Reiner; impossible to tell in the dark, with their faces concealed and the air thick with snow. If she'd married him, would she still be out here? She might be back at the farmhouse with Anna, curled up by the fire beside Gretel, waiting for Reiner to come home. And even though she hadn't married him, there were other choices she might have made – she might be in Freiburg with her aunt Else, she might have died with her father in the mines, she might be anywhere but here, on the mountain, in the dark.

The search party reached the edge of the village; those on skis removed them and they began to climb, spreading out across the ridge in a long, snaking line. Someone a few feet from Hilde shouted out; she couldn't hear him over the wind, and someone else stumbled, had to be pulled from the snow and set on his feet again. She tried to scan the landscape ahead of her for children, but her eyes were blurred by the snowfall and the wind; how could anyone be out here, how could anyone have thought children could survive it, how could they not have turned back? She wished, again, for a lantern, and thought of the night of the elections three years back, all those lights and bonfires, the whole mountain lit up in flames.

Fritz had been with them that night, sitting in the *Stube* with Hilde's father, drinking beer, whilst Hilde and her mother had stood outside watching the procession pass. It was one of Hilde's last clear memories of her father: the cold, impassive expression on his face, the cheers and shouts from the crowds. She'd come inside and stood in the doorway, listening as he and Fritz talked politics. *I heard someone threw stones at his car when he visited Freiburg. I heard they'll refuse the Jewish boycott when it comes. It won't come to anything, Fritz, they'll have to give it up eventually.* When they'd seen Hilde standing there, they'd been suddenly quiet. Later, Hilde's father had stood in the doorway of the tiny room by the kitchen where she and Anna slept, a candle flickering in his hand. *Whatever happens*, he'd said, *remember you're no better than anyone else. No worse either.*

She hadn't understood what he'd meant until much later.

They found the first boy not long after leaving the village, curled up in a hollow of snow which had been sculpted out by the wind. A shout went up and the column of people slowly halted; Hilde felt the cold settling in her bones, the warmth that her movement had generated leaking into the air. The boy was huddled against the ice, his knees drawn up to his chest, a bundle of clothing beside him. He looked almost rigid with cold, but as soon as one of the men approached and knelt in front of him he melted into the man's arms. Someone lifted him over their shoulders and started back for the village, and someone else knelt to the bundle of clothing, only to find it was another child, frozen into the mountain, his face blue and his body stiff.

Hilde opened her mouth with shock and felt the cold air stop her throat.

High up on the ridge, in the shadow of the mountain peak, they found a man, two children huddled close to him. Hilde knelt in front of him and tried to shout, 'How many are out here, how many children?' He stared back at her with eyes ringed with frost, his mouth moving soundlessly, his hands groping in the snow, clinging to her jacket as though he were trying to pull her down into the earth with him.

They carried them to the inn, where the landlady was waiting with boiling water and blankets, bottles of spirit and broth on the stove. Men and women were running in and out with fuel, food, any medical supplies they could find, others bringing their own bed sheets, warm coals from their fire wrapped in cloth. In the inn's main room, a fire had been built up to a steady blaze, and someone was carrying a prostrate child towards it; Hilde put out a hand to stop him.

'Don't! It's not safe, we have to get his circulation up first.'

They laid him down on the cold flagstones, away from the fire, and Hilde seized a broom and began beating at his limbs. She remembered watching her mother do the same, on an impossibly cold night two years ago when Anna had disappeared on the mountain. Anna told them later that she thought she could hear a lost calf, bleating in the snow. Hilde had stood in the kitchen doorway, watching in horror as her sister lay motionless, then in dazed astonishment as she began to wriggle and jump in her mother's arms.

The boy, though, lay still. They carried him over to the fire and stretched him out, rubbing at his limbs, but he only seemed to grow colder and heavier in Hilde's arms. More boys were dragged in, subjected to the same treatment, while the man who'd been with them wandered dazedly about the room, kneeling and whispering to them, staring at the bodies of those who were lying still by the fire. Hilde heard herself shouting orders, people replying, and all the time she was still slapping and shouting at the child in front of the fire, until someone took hold of her shoulders and gently pulled her back.

She went over to the man, who was sitting on the floor now, a blanket draped loosely over his shoulders. Ice was melting from his eyelashes, his eyebrows, streaming in tears down his face. She stared into his eyes; now that she could see him properly, he looked younger than she'd thought, perhaps only in his mid-thirties. He was staring at his feet; the shoes had been removed, and a toe was visible through a hole in one of his woollen socks. She cast about her; where were the other adults, how could he be the only one?

'My English is not…' she began, then in her own language, 'You understand German?'

The man nodded.

'There are four dead,' she said, slowly and calmly. 'You understand?'

He nodded again.

How did it happen, what were you doing, what were you thinking?

'We need to know if there's anyone else out there. Children, or… or anyone.'

He looked at her. She wondered if he was taking any of it in, if the storm had stupefied him; she had seen it before in a body left too long in the cold, it could take days for the mind to recover.

'Do you understand me?' she asked, more slowly now. 'We have to know if we should go back.'

'No.' He shook his head slowly, turning his face to the window, where the snow was still falling in spirals, turning the sky grey and pale. 'No, *Fräulein*, enough.'

They carried the four bodies down to the basement, where the air was cool enough to store meat and supplies, even in summer. Beds were made up for the surviving children, and offered to their rescuers too, but none of the villagers took them. They sat up instead by the fire, listening to the wind screaming in the chimney, watching the blur of snowfall until someone stood up and drew the curtains closed.

Horst Braunling, the landlord, who had himself gone out into the storm, brought schnapps and jugs of wine, and they gathered together sharing stories of the night, exclaiming at how a school party, a party of children, could have found themselves on the mountain so ill-prepared, with so little on their backs.

'Shorts, some of them were wearing. Shorts!'

'One of them had shoes with holes in their soles. One of them had no socks. One of them looked younger than my Oscar.'

Hilde sat by herself a little apart; now they were indoors, she could see Reiner amongst the group by the fire, and preferred not to endure the sideways glances, the uncomfortable silence. Only Fritz joined her, stretching out his legs and arching his back the way Gretel did at the tiled stove.

'We'll send word to the hospital in the morning,' he said, accepting a glass from Horst. 'What can the man have been thinking?'

'He wasn't making much sense,' Hilde said, recalling the teacher's eyes, staring blankly back at her as she asked her questions. 'Fritz, do you think – I mean, if we'd gone out earlier, or had more supplies—'

'Nonsense. Nothing any of us could have done. We'll know more when we can speak to him properly, but I'd say the man has a case to answer. There'll be police here, as well as ambulances, when the storm breaks.'

She nodded slowly, sipping at her own wine, saying nothing.

'You did everything you could, Hilde. It was good of you to come out at all.'

There was a rush of cold air then, as the inn doors were thrown open and Hans Huber came in. He was as bundled up in coats and scarves as the rest of them had been, but he'd still taken the trouble to display his Party badge smartly on his lapel, the black spider standing out against red and white enamel. Hans worked in the mines; unlike so many others, he'd continued to go down after the cave-in two years ago. *Fear weakens us,* he'd say when anyone asked him what that day had been like, how he could bring himself to go back. He was tall, middle-aged, but still with a youthful appearance that had somehow survived his decades underground. For others, those years had brought with them a sloping, crouching posture and a perpetual squint, as though they were still down there in the dark, but Hans' pale blue eyes were as keen as ever. He told people his party number was 5,415. There were more than two million of them now, and his number was considered as much a badge of pride as his return to the mines. *It's lower than Goebbels',* he'd say, though no one knew if that was true either.

'What does he want?' Hilde murmured, as Hans approached the landlord and took him aside.

'Ach, he's harmless,' Fritz said, taking a sip of his wine. 'We could have used his help earlier, mind,' he added bitterly, eyeing Hans over his glass. 'That boy of his too.'

Hilde watched as Hans accepted a glass of schnapps and stood with Horst, surveying the room with those sharp eyes before approaching the teacher, kneeling down and offering a hand to shake.

Fritz was probably right, but she couldn't help thinking of her mother, the fever that had begun as a cold last winter. *It's harmless, Hilde, stop fussing, you'll wake your sister.* How it had bloomed and spread, ravaging her body until there was nothing left to inhabit. Harmless, Fritz had said, but wasn't that what everyone said at the start?

When she finally reached home, she found the *Stube* dark and cold, the fire in the kitchen almost out. She raked the cinders and added more fuel, lit a candle and knelt to stroke Gretel, who leapt away from her cold hands. At the bedroom door she paused, laying her palm on the scorched wood, then slowly pushed it open, placing the candle in an alcove in the wall.

'Are you awake?' she whispered.

'What's happening?'

'Nothing to worry about. Just some children needed pulling off the mountain.' She sat down on the bed beside Anna, trying not to think about the four bodies they'd left in the basement, covered in sheets too thin to hide the contours of their faces. Anna sat up, running a hand across her forehead. In the dim light from the candle, Hilde could just make out her expression, blurry and puffy with sleep.

'Was it really children?'

'They're at the inn. I'll tell you all about it in the morning.' She reached out and pulled Anna close. 'Remember when we lost you on the mountain?' she murmured. 'You went out after that calf – we didn't find you for hours.' *We were frightened, so frightened.*

'Fritz found me, didn't he?'

'That's right.'

Hilde's mother, taking Fritz's hands, her pleading eyes. Rows of people, bright flashes of colour against the snow, calling her sister's name. Her mother in the *Stube*, scrubbing at the table so hard her knuckles were white. The radio in the background: *Following the death of President Hindenburg, Chancellor Hitler has been named as the new president, and will now take the title of führer...*

She squeezed Anna tighter. 'Fritz said you refused to come home when he found you. It was the day of the cave-in, the day Pa – well, they thought somehow you knew.'

'Like a witch.'

Hilde smiled. 'Like a witch.'

It was as though their father had known too. He'd looked for Anna before he'd left for the mines, but they'd all assumed she was playing outside, somewhere nearby. Afterwards, when it was all over, Hilde remembered the way he'd called for her, checked in every room. As though he'd known he wouldn't come back to see her again. She'd never told her sister. *If he hadn't gone straight to the mines, if he'd stayed just a little longer, if he'd realised you were missing, he might have gone with Fritz to look for you too. He would never have gone down there, he would never have—*

'What time is it?'

'I don't know. Go to sleep.'

She lay down next to Anna, burying herself in the blankets until she felt the cold beginning, finally, to leach from her bones.

'Don't you ever go out there in a storm,' she whispered. 'You understand me, Anna Meyer? Don't you ever get lost out there again.'

But Anna was already sleeping, her breath soft and deep, and outside the storm was still raging, rattling at the shutters and drowning out Anna's snores. Hilde lay awake in the darkness, the teacher's voice repeating over and over in her mind. *No,* Fräulein, *enough.* And there had been something else, when she'd first found him on the mountain. Something he'd leaned in close and whispered to her, that had so shocked her she hadn't known what to say, how to react. Even now, she wondered if she'd imagined it, if the cold had got into her own mind as well as his. He hadn't been rational, he hadn't been sane. He couldn't... surely he couldn't possibly... She closed her eyes and allowed the memory to be drowned out by the sound of the storm, slowly dying outside.

Chapter Seven

In the darkness, in a room somewhere on a mountain, all he can hear is the wind. It is outside now, separate from his body, feeling its way through the shutters and the eaves, shaking the windows like an enemy siege. One of the shutters sounds as though it might come loose, but he can't bring himself to open his eyes and look, he is hiding from time, from the world beyond his eyelids.

He can hear them downstairs, still awake and chattering; luckily he can't make out words in the fog of noise, but he can imagine what they're saying, *murderer, monster, child killer.* Two floors below him, they are laying out the dead on the cold cellar floor, a temporary burial, but he can't think about that now, can't picture their pale faces, so he pulls himself back to the rattling shutters, to the darkness of the room they have left him in; he wonders, *Have they locked the door?*

He never had the chance to give his final lecture to the boys. He'd had four talks prepared, planned to be spaced out evenly along the walk. He'd covered flora and fauna, geology, language, and the fourth was to be the human history of the mountain itself, as they rested on its slopes, the reason the city, all these villages, were here. Coffers of silver, buried in its flanks, worked out steadily over centuries by the men of these villages, poured down the valleys and the cliffs to enrich the city below. After the silver had come other, less valuable treasure: zinc, lead, stone. He would bend and pick up a piece of stone as a tool, ask them to visualise all the miles of rock below them, the work it would take to scrape it from the earth, the effort the mountain demands. *Below us* – he practises saying it now in his head – *are hundreds of metres of tunnels, you could get lost in them for days. Whatever we cannot grow comes from the rocks.*

Later, as they'd fought their way through the storm, he'd wondered fleetingly whether they might try to find the entrance to one of those tunnels, whether they might have found shelter that way. But that had only brought to mind images of the enemy, cowering in foxholes. Better to face it head on, better to see it through.

There had been a cave-in at the nearby mineworks two years ago. He'd read about it when he was researching the trip; twenty men or so had died, some of them buried so deeply their bodies had never been recovered. Some of those men might have been from this village, he thinks, they might otherwise have come out to save him. Would it be worse, dying in the earth, than in the open air? In the end, he supposes, it doesn't really matter, but as he'd begun to drift on the mountain, he'd felt glad. He'd thought of those men, buried underneath layers of rock, and felt thankful that his own death would be in the open air, under the stars.

Someone below him laughs a heavy, guttural laugh. He imagines them sitting together by the fire, wine and ale and reddened cheeks, swapping their stories of the night, sharing what little information they'd got from him. They'd knelt and gazed at him as though they were staring at him through water, or a pane of bubbled glass. He knew what they were thinking, *how did it happen, what were you thinking, why were you there?* He didn't have any answers for them. It was as though his mind and his voice had been frozen too.

Only the man wearing the Nazi Party badge on his coat had shown him anything other than incredulity. He'd shaken Keith's hand, and told him his boys were a testament to the strength of youth, to the promise of a better future. *It was a privilege to be able to assist you,* he'd said, and someone else had scoffed loudly, and told the man he hadn't even been there, he'd done nothing to help, only showed up when it was all over and done with. Keith had allowed the argument which had broken out to fade into the background, grateful for the opportunity to slide out of their view.

If they were to come to him now, what would he say? He feels too exhausted, too stupefied to know. He'll need to get his story straight, decide what line to take; all that will be for tomorrow, he'll need time to think it out. There will be questions at home too, though home feels like a fiction now. His parents, the boys' parents, the school. There had already been questions – that girl, just now, demanding he give an account of himself. She'd been the one to find him on the mountain, and he has a dim memory of something he'd whispered to her then, still frozen with shock and the horror of it – had he really said it, had he been so stupid as to give himself away?

He closes his eyes, and his ears are filled with the sound of the storm, of children screaming and a voice calling out to him, *Sir, we can see lights ahead, Sir, it's not far, if we just stick together, it's not far to go now—*

Part Two

Chapter Eight

For a few moments, the morning after the storm, the Schauinsland was impossibly white. The footprints which had criss-crossed its surface, the churned panic of struggle, the smooth action of sledges and skis cutting through it, the deep troughs of boys being dragged and hauled across the snow, all of it had been erased. The snow had continued to fall, smoothed and sculpted by a screaming wind, and now the sun was rising on a still, cold world.

Hilde was woken by the sound of sledges, scraping their way along the path towards the inn. In the *Stube*, Anna was standing by the window, watching as they passed. Hilde joined her, reaching an arm around her shoulder and pulling her close.

'They came quickly,' Anna said, watching as a group of children ran alongside the sledges, shouting and jostling to get closer. Men in uniform turned and waved as they passed; their swastika armbands flashing brightly against the snow. 'You didn't tell me everything last night, did you? Those children...'

Hilde felt the words in her mouth, considered saying them. *Four children died. You're a woman now.*

'I'll tell you this evening,' she said, pulling on her coat. 'I have to go up to the inn, see if they need any more help.'

The streets were busy; on an ordinary day, people would be out in their fields, driving their cattle or working the land. Those unlucky enough to have the use of the fields furthest from the village wouldn't be seen until sundown, stooped and exhausted as they brought the animals back in; some would have walked for an hour or more each way. Today, Hilde thought as she walked to the inn, there must be fields lying abandoned, animals left in their stables as people gathered to share news of the night's events.

At the inn doorway she stopped and turned back to look across the valley, which was glowing now in brilliant sunshine. The weather could turn so quickly on the mountain; snowstorms and howling winds had already given way to a still, bright morning. Far in the distance, she could make out a line of tiny dark figures against the snow, stretched out across the fields.

'Did you sleep?'

Fritz was coming out of the inn, still dressed in the clothes he'd gone out in the night before.

'A little,' she replied.

'There's two men from the police in Freiburg inside, they'll want to talk to you.' A frown crossed his face, and he shuffled awkwardly to one side as Reiner appeared in the doorway.

'Hilde.'

She felt relief, more than she'd expected to. She'd been doing her best to avoid him for weeks, and now here they were, face to face. He looked tired; she must do as well, she thought, feeling her cheeks grow hot.

'Have you heard?' Reiner said, turning to Fritz. 'There's still a child missing.'

'What?' She blinked at him.

'One of the English boys, yes.'

Hilde looked again at the line of people in the distance, moving slowly across the snow.

'But I asked him. The teacher, he said…' She thought back to her conversation with the Englishman, his dazed, blank eyes. He'd been confused, blinded by shock and cold. But he'd sounded so sure. *No, Fräulein, enough.* Had she asked the right questions, had she been clear? And what had he actually said? Just a few words, practically whispered. Had she misunderstood him, misheard?

'You're sure, Hilde?' Reiner said, turning to her.

She swallowed hard. 'I'm sure. I asked him, he said all the boys were there. It doesn't make sense, Reiner.'

He and Fritz exchanged a look.

'I'm sure,' she said again, feeling less so each time she said it.

'So that's what they're looking for,' Fritz said, staring across the valley as the search party made their way towards the horizon. 'Doesn't seem likely they'll find him alive now, does it?'

'He'll be under the earth,' Reiner said, his voice taking on a strange, monotonous tone as though he were reciting a prayer. 'Under the earth, ready for the battle to come.'

'Oh, come on, Reiner,' Fritz said, shuffling uncomfortably, 'you don't believe in all that, do you?'

'Of course not.' He broke into a sheepish smile, glancing sideways at Hilde as though reassuring her that he knew it was all nonsense, just something people told their children, perhaps, to keep them in line. Hilde's mother had told her the stories when she was a child for just that reason, a warning to behave, or else you might be next. Except, after the cave-in she'd spoken of it too, and it had seemed like more than a fairy tale then. *He's come for your father, he's taken another for his army, he takes the strongest, leaves no one behind but weaklings like you.*

'What about Hans Huber?' she said, turning away from the valley, looking at Reiner, finally, full in the face. 'What did he want last night?'

'Who knows? Just asked what had happened, who had been there. Thinks too much of himself, Hans does. Just because he's the only Party member out here, just because of that wretched number, it doesn't make him better than the rest of us, does it?'

Inside the inn, the chaos of the previous night had been tidied away. A fire was burning in the grate and a table had been pulled close to it. Two police officers were sitting behind it, their Party badges shining on their lapels. Hans Huber was standing behind them, his chin drawn up high and a strange, self-satisfied smile on his face. Hilde walked in slowly, her eyes meeting those of Gertrud Braunling, the landlord's wife, who was wiping glasses behind the bar. Something in Gertrud's expression made Hilde stop uncertainly in the middle of the room.

'They said you wanted...'

Hans spoke first. 'Hilde.' He turned to the two police officers. 'This is Hilde Meyer, she was one of those who went out last night.'

He beckoned her over to the table and she sat with her back to the fire, feeling it scorching her neck. The two men glanced up at her, but did not stand. They looked like the same man separated by time; one was disarmingly young, with bright, wide blue eyes and pale yellow hair, the other older, his hair a stark white.

'You were involved in the rescue?' the younger man said, sounding disinterested.

'That's right. Fritz Feldberg came to my door. He will already have told you, I'm sure.'

'Tell us what happened.'

She recounted the brief conversation with Fritz, fetching their skis, then the seemingly endless trek through the storm. 'When we found the first boy – I mean the first who had died – we thought he was a pile of clothing. The other had tried to cover him up with his coat, you see.'

'And would you say they were adequately dressed?'

'No, I wouldn't say that. I mean – I wasn't really thinking. But they shouldn't have been out there at all, should they? I'm sure they were warned – someone in Freiburg must have said something. It was already snowing by midday.'

The two men exchanged a look. 'And the boy who remains missing – what do you know about that?'

She hesitated. Someone might already have told them about her conversation with the teacher. She wondered fleetingly if it could get her into trouble – would they believe her? She'd already begun to doubt her own memory, her own ears – had she been careful enough, had she made sure? She should have taken the Englishman all around the room, had him name every child in turn, made sure he was absolutely certain. If she'd done that, if they'd known...

'He told me all the children were accounted for,' she said, firmly and slowly. 'I asked him, and he said he was certain. He must have been confused, I suppose.'

'I see.'

The older man sat up a little straighter in his seat then, fixing Hilde with a cold, steady gaze. 'Tell us a little about yourself, *Fräulein*,' he said. There was nothing unpleasant in the question, but something in the tone of it made Hilde want to refuse, to stand up and leave. 'Have you lived in this village all your life?'

She nodded. 'I live with my sister. We lost our mother last winter. A fever she couldn't see off.'

'How old is your sister?'

'Fourteen.'

'And she still attends school?'

Hilde shook her head. 'It's not possible. The farm...' She trailed off, feeling suddenly ashamed. Anna was the sharp one, the one with a future. She'd promised their mother...

'An education is important, now more than ever,' the younger man was saying. 'We need the youth of our country to understand their responsibilities to the state.'

She didn't know what to say, so she only nodded, and stayed silent.

'And your father?'

Hilde briefly met Hans' eyes. Why was he part of this? No doubt he was hoping for a job at the end of it, something to lift him and his growing family up. Despite his pride, he couldn't want to be in the mines forever. There was talk, too, that there was precious little left to scrape out of them; the silver was long gone, and what remained was dwindling in value with every passing year.

'There was a cave-in,' she said coldly, 'two years ago, at the mines. He went to help with the rescue, and he didn't come back.'

They hadn't even had a body to bury. They'd had a funeral; or rather, his name had been included in the ceremony with all the other men's names. But without a body, without a coffin to bury, the word *dead* felt inadequate. He'd gone into the ground, and he hadn't come back.

'It was the day Adolf Hitler became führer,' she added, feeling suddenly emboldened.

'What's that?'

'The day of the collapse.'

There was a long silence. Her voice had been slow and purposeful, but now she could feel her legs shaking a little as she stood as still as possible in front of them. In her mind, she recited the rhyme the children sang. *Dear God, make me dumb, so I won't to Dachau come.*

'So you are alone, you and your sister?'

'That's right.'

'That must be difficult.'

'We know how to manage a farm.'

'Have you not thought to marry? You look the right age for it.' She felt the man's eyes quickly and coldly assessing her, a swift movement up and down her body. She imagined the calculations that might be running through his head, a baby by next spring, perhaps, another the following winter. And in a few years, Anna would be next, the family blooming and spreading until there were enough pairs of hands for another field, perhaps, an increase in the herd. In the papers, they wrote about a woman's duty to repopulate Germany with citizens of pure blood; a woman like Hilde had a responsibility to do her part. The rearmament strategy was no longer a secret; the country was fitting itself out for the battles to come, and strong, healthy children, children who would grow into soldiers, were the best weapons of all.

'I'm nineteen.'

'There are loans now. And some of the repayments are forgiven, for each child.'

She stared at the younger man, waiting for something in his expression to break, but he returned her gaze with a cool, calm expression. *He's enjoying himself*, she thought.

'Was there anything else?' she said.

The other man looked up, taken aback. Hans shot her a warning glance.

'We may need to speak to you again,' the younger man said. Hilde nodded, offering a brief, acquiescent smile.

'Hans can tell you where to find me.'

'Alright then. Heil Hitler.'

Both men raised an arm. Hilde stared back at them for a few seconds, feeling her heart beating faster. The day after the election, when all Germany was ringing with the news of Hitler's triumph, a soldier had come to their door and issued the greeting along with the news, raising his palm as Hilde's father had stared coldly back at him. For a moment, standing behind her father that day, Hilde had thought he would refuse to return the gesture. Was that enough to be sent to the camps, she wondered now, was that all it could take to disappear?

She raised her palm, repeating the words. Only when she was outside, breathing hard in the cold sunshine, did it occur to her that she hadn't felt fear, standing in front of those men, raising her hand to answer them. She had felt anger, blooming in her chest like a flag unfurling in the dark.

Chapter Nine

'Have they found him? Have they found anything?'

The man sitting opposite Sylvia coughed nervously and pressed his hands between his knees. The other – a policeman, slightly older, with a kindly, grandfatherly expression – offered her a smile which, she supposed, was intended to be reassuring. Ruby, sitting beside her, gave her hand a quick squeeze.

She'd brought extra chairs through from the kitchen and laid out tea, and all the time her head was filled with an insistent ringing; alarm bells which refused to still. *Missing*. They kept saying the word, and it stubbornly failed to make sense, the more they repeated it. Missing, as though Cyril was a lost glove, a stray cat. In the brief moments of sleep she'd managed, she'd seen the nurse who'd come on the day he was born, walking into the room with the baby in her arms, and she'd woken up clawing the sheets, her mouth open in a soundless scream.

'There's no news, I'm afraid.'

'Has he been arrested?' Ruby asked.

The policeman, sipping noisily at his tea, looked up at her. 'Who?'

'The teacher, of course.'

'The German police are making their own inquiries.'

'But they're British children. He's a British citizen.'

'Well, I'm sure – that is... ah—'

'At the moment,' the younger man said, leaning forward in his chair, his voice patronisingly level and calm, 'we're more concerned with the search for Cyril.'

This one was from the embassy. He was dressed in a smart, well-tailored suit, his shoes carefully polished. The policeman looked shabbier, less put together somehow. *Low-ranking*, Sylvia thought in her mother's voice. Her fingers brushed against a loose thread in the hem of her wool skirt and she pulled at it, feeling the stitches begin to unravel.

'Then what are you doing here?' Ruby snapped.

The silence which descended on the room was broken by the buzzing of the doorbell. It had been ringing intermittently all afternoon; Ruby stood up and marched briskly to answer it. They listened as she uttered a short, sharp 'She isn't interested. Thank you' and slammed the door heavily.

'Vultures,' she muttered as she came back to sit beside Sylvia. 'Don't you give them an inch.'

'Perhaps,' the man from the embassy said nervously, turning to Sylvia, 'we should wait until your husband is home.'

'What?'

'Your husband, Mrs Clayton. Where is he?'

Funny, the way laughter sometimes came at the very worst moments. Some of the boys she'd treated in the field tents had laughed in strange, wild barks as she'd sat with them and explained what had happened to them, what part of them was maimed or broken or missing.

Everyone was staring fixedly into their tea. Their faces blurred into indistinct shapes as exhaustion swept over her in waves.

'There's only me,' she said.

The two men exchanged a glance.

'Me and Cyril.'

'What have you actually done?' Ruby asked coldly.

'A search is being conducted on the mountain,' the man from the embassy said. 'Which is encouraging,' he added, looking appealingly at the policeman, who was still staring into his teacup.

'No reason to give up hope,' the policeman offered brightly.

'They think it's possible he found somewhere to shelter and got disorientated. There are tunnels beneath the mountain, old mining works. It's possible… well, it's possible. Isn't it?' He looked up uncertainly.

'When do we leave?' Sylvia said.

'I'm sorry?'

She ought to have gone immediately, straight from the school. Wasn't that what a good mother would do? She should be halfway to Germany already, giving impassioned interviews, handing out flyers. *Have you seen this boy?* What was she doing here, serving tea?

'There's no need for that,' the embassy man said, looking alarmed.

'Everything possible is being done.'

'Then why are you here?'

In the silence, she thought she could smell her mother's perfume; the overpowering scent of violets and a cold hand pressed against her forehead. She stood up, feeling weightless, and went to the desk by the window. Arthur's old desk; it was still filled with his letters and papers. She kept it locked now, ever since Cyril – but it was too late for that now, she thought, thinking of his face in the kitchen doorway, the paper in his hand. Stupid, so stupid, not to have locked it before.

A silver frame on the desk held a photograph of Cyril that had been taken last September, on his first day of the new school year. He was wearing a jumper that was far too large for him, and she could remember thinking it would last him for the whole year – however much he grew, he'd still be wearing that jumper by the following winter. Around his neck, he was wearing the green scarf she'd knitted him for the cold months to come. It had been warm that day, she remembered, but he'd insisted on wearing it anyway.

She opened the back of the frame and removed the photograph, holding it out to them.

'That's alright,' the policeman said gently. 'You keep it.'

'Or should I give it to the papers?' she said aloud. 'The German papers. Someone might see him...'

She felt her knees buckle as the policeman took a step towards her. Ruby reached her first and Sylvia leaned against her, feeling Ruby's arm around her shoulders. 'You don't need to worry about any of that,' the policeman said, in the sort of voice someone might use to speak to a child, or a person who was very ill. Someone who was dying. 'I promise, everything that can be done...'

She couldn't remember the men leaving. Ruby was busying herself in the kitchen while she sat staring at the wall, the evening drawing in around them. Sylvia listened to the loud ticking of the clock in the hall, counting the seconds as they passed in her head and wondering how many of them a child could survive for, in the cold, in the dark. A thousand? Ten thousand? How many minutes were there in a thousand seconds? How many had passed already, before anyone had even known Cyril was missing? She looked down at the bundle of thread in her hands, the hem of her skirt hanging ragged, and pulled harder, until the thread snapped.

'I'll make more tea, shall I?' Ruby called out.

Sylvia opened the lid of the teapot and peered inside. She hadn't put any leaves in. A trace of clear water lay at the bottom of each cup. She couldn't even remember making the tea, but she did remember pouring out the cups, how no one had said a word as she'd handed them over.

A pile of cards lay on the mat in the hall. Kind notes from neighbours, requests from reporters; she stacked them up neatly on the side table. She dreaded the first sight of a black-edged card; already she could see it in people's expressions, in the way they couldn't meet her eyes. In

France, each time a new body had appeared in front of her she'd avoided looking at the man's face, focused instead on limbs and skin and blood, the fear of seeing Arthur so vivid she began to imagine him everywhere, in every bloodied face. Each time, when she finally forced herself to look, she'd felt a sharp wave of relief. She thought of the day he'd finally come home. Opening the door to find him standing there in his worn-out uniform, looking exactly the same and entirely different. *We've made it. How about that?* And at the time, she'd really thought they had.

'He is coming back.'

In the silence that followed, she wondered whether Ruby had heard her.

They sat together at the kitchen table. Sylvia caught sight of the outline of her face reflected in the surface of her tea and thought of Cyril's face, staring back at him from some pool of water, a stream, a puddle, a patch of melting snow. Ruby spooned a mound of sugar into her cup and the reflection splintered.

'I got that job, at the lab.'

'Goodness. I'd forgotten…'

Sylvia had forgotten too. When the letter had come she'd assumed it was another well-meaning card, and left it in the hall for hours before finally opening it. She thought back to the rows of benches, the white palettes of blood, the woman's face bent over them. The box of rabbits, squirming and wriggling at her feet. 'It was a strange sort of place. I suppose they'll find someone else easily enough.'

Ruby leaned forwards and took both of her hands. 'Sylv. You have to take this job.'

She shook her head. 'I have to go to Germany.'

'You can ask them for some time, explain what happened.'

'He needs me.'

'He's going to need a life to come back to when they

find him. You've been saying yourself there's not enough domestic work. And anyway,' she added, 'how are you going to afford to go to Germany?'

'I don't know.'

'What about your sister?'

'I can't ask her. I've already thought of that.'

Every penny Julia saved went to charitable causes; she spent most of her weekends distributing food to the homeless or offering her services for free in the poorest parts of the city. Her husband was a Labour Member of Parliament; a career which had taken them all by surprise. He'd been training in medicine when Julia met him, at the hospital where she and Sylvia had both done their nursing training. Unlike Sylvia, she'd carried it on after the war, rising to the rank of matron at the women's hospital in Clapham, whilst resolutely refusing to countenance the idea of children herself. *The work is what matters.* They saw each other once or twice a year, awkward meetings in tea shops or parks where Julia would avoid asking after Cyril, and Sylvia, in turn, would avoid any talk of work. Held up opposite her sister, Sylvia feared her life looked like a failure.

Ruby offered to stay, but Sylvia sent her away. In the silence of the empty house it was easier to imagine Cyril somewhere in another room, every noise from outside a sign that he was about to appear beside her when she stretched out an open hand. *Do you think he's still alive,* she'd asked as Ruby was shrugging on her coat. And, even though Ruby had said all the right things – *Of course, love, of course* – Sylvia had seen the half-second of hesitation in her eyes, the doubt, and something inside her had given way. Finally alone, she'd pressed her face into a cushion and allowed herself a single, animal howl.

Hours later it was dark, and she was pacing the living room with the empty photograph frame from her husband's desk in her hands. A long time ago it had contained a photograph of Arthur, until the day Cyril, three years old, had picked it up and waddled into the kitchen where she was frying chops on the stove.

'Who's this?'

'What?' She hadn't even turned to look. Behind her was a pile of other people's sheets waiting to be ironed. Her back was aching, her fingers raw from the washing she'd already done.

'In the picture.'

Arthur was standing in front of the house in his uniform, beaming into the camera, and Cyril was staring back at him with a look of such intensity that Sylvia already knew she couldn't just explain the photograph away.

'That's your daddy.'

'Where is he?' He'd looked over his shoulder, as though Arthur might have just walked into the kitchen.

The chops were burning; an acrid, bitter smell spread through the kitchen and into her throat, making them both cough. Sylvia turned off the stove and, sitting at the table and pulling Cyril onto her lap, she began to make up a story.

Chapter Ten

Keith was woken by the sun streaming through a gap in the curtains, falling across his face in a warm, comforting blade of light. For a moment, he thought he was still in the inn in Hofsgrund, the muffled voices of the villagers echoing below him. Then he felt the soft sheets around him, the scent of jasmine from the vase on the small table beside the bed, the sound of the sea beyond his window.

He hardly recognised the man he'd been then, although it was only a few days ago. He thought with shame of how they'd pulled him from the snow, how he'd sat mute and stupefied, unable to answer any of their questions. It had been the same in the hospital, then the police station afterwards, they'd spoken his name and it had sounded like a stranger's.

He sat up, arching his back and stretching out his limbs. There was a glorious anonymity to hotels; perhaps that was why he'd come. Here, he could be anyone he liked, shed the man from the mountain from his body like a snakeskin. But as he cast his eyes about the room, he saw someone had placed a pile of newspapers on a table by the door. He turned away, imagining the headlines. *Teacher fails his students; fatal catastrophe. Keith Hughes: murderer. Keith Hughes: coward.*

He'd intended, of course, to go straight back to London. *Face the music,* his mother would have said. He hadn't even written to his parents yet – they could read all about what had happened in the papers, after all. It had been a passing comment from Kurt Runde, the Nazi official who'd looked after him in Freiburg, which had put the idea of Bournemouth in his mind. They were being driven around the city in an open-top car, cameras flashing and reporters fighting each other to get a look at him. *This is only the start of it, my friend*, Runde had said, patting him genially on the back, *they'll be camping out for you back home.*

Keith hadn't quite known how to take that remark, *camping out for you back home.* It conveyed at once an image of young people queuing outside a theatre, hoping to catch a glimpse of Noël Coward, and an angry mob. His father had been at Mosley's meeting at Olympia two years before, and the way he talked about it made Keith's skin crawl. *Amazing what you can achieve, if you get enough people with enough strength in their convictions together. Look at Mussolini, look at those Germans, look at what's happening!*

Runde had been there when he'd first woken in the hospital. There were cameras then too; flashing and popping as he opened his eyes. Runde had shaken his hand; the image had been on the front pages of the local Freiburg newspaper the next day, and some of the nationals too. 'Local Hitler Youth leader Kurt Runde with Keith Hughes, recovering from his terrible ordeal.' Those headlines had been alright; vague allusions to an English calamity, terror on the slopes, calls for mountain patrols, refuges, clearer storm warnings. After a few days, the pictures of Keith had been replaced with smiling German boys in smartly pressed uniforms that made them look like tiny soldiers. There they were, sitting alongside his own boys at the hostel they'd been taken to afterwards. There they were again, playing games of tennis together. There they were waving his boys away on a train bedecked in flowers. Keith was in that one, standing in the background, his image blurred and indistinct. Then, there they were in a chapel in Freiburg, standing soberly beside four small coffins, Nazi

Party flags draped all around them. 'Hitler Youth honour their fallen comrades', the headlines all read, or some variation of it; Keith had stopped reading them after a while.

He was late for morning coffee. The waiters were already beginning to lay out the lunch things in the hotel's lounge as he settled himself into a wicker armchair in a large bay window. The sea, grey and restless, heaved beyond it. Two tall palm trees had been placed on either side of his table, as though he was supposed to imagine himself on a tropical island. Keith winced as he lowered himself into the chair; his limbs still ached and a stiffness seemed to seize him whenever he tried to move. There was a shout from across the room and he looked around warily, but it was just two ladies greeting each other in the doorway. The press hadn't found him here yet, but it was only a matter of time.

A waiter brought him a menu, then deposited a pile of newspapers on the table next to it which Keith swiftly handed back. Was it really so difficult to avoid newspapers, just for a day or two? He could see they were everywhere now, dotted on other people's tables and piled up on the reception desk. His own face, no doubt, staring out from them, next to all those foreign leaders his father was so fond of. He turned and focused instead on the gulls circling above the bay, the white foam tips of waves as they broke against the rocks. The beach was almost empty, but for a few hardy swimmers fighting their way back and forth amidst the waves. He watched them beating their way across the bay and felt a stirring of panic, the feeling of helplessness as the snow held him frozen in place, however much he tried to free his limbs. It felt like the last, lingering memories of a nightmare.

He couldn't recall now how he had left the mountainside. He could dimly remember a man's face leaning over him, anxious eyes. Strong arms lifting him. The tolling of the bells growing more distinct in the distance as he felt his whole body returning from the comforting numbness he had been searching for for so many years. *I can be anyone now,* he had thought, waking in the hospital in Freiburg to the sound of all those cameras flashing, *I don't have to go back.* He pictured his old self still lying on the mountainside, buried in snowdrifts, icicles settling on his eyelashes, the tips of his fingers. He would be found in the spring, a perfectly preserved cast of himself, while this new Keith carried on with his life without looking back.

In the corner of his eye, he sensed someone looking at him. A man was sitting at a nearby table, peering at him over his *Times*. He was younger than Keith, perhaps in his early thirties, with dark brown hair and blue eyes; he looked a little like a film star, Keith thought, he looked like Noël Coward. Incongruous, in this shabby, old-fashioned hotel with its elderly ladies knitting in armchairs and young families tearing about.

He looked again, and Noël Coward darted his expression away. Was there something about Keith in his newspaper? Was he looking between the man and the photograph, drawing conclusions? Keith shifted uncomfortably in his chair. But when he looked back, Noël Coward was turning the pages of the paper, seeming uninterested. He had, he felt sure, imagined that alarming stare, its intensity increased by the man's deep blue eyes and serious expression. People stared at strangers all the time, didn't they? Keith did himself, often enough.

He finished his coffee and was on the point of leaving when the silence of the lounge was broken by a loud cry.

'It's him! It *is*, darling!'

A smart couple were standing opposite him, peering as though he were an exhibit in a museum. The woman was wearing flowing white beach pyjamas and a broad-brimmed hat which shadowed most of her face; she slid onto the chair opposite him and leaned forward, taking his hand. Sincere, wide eyes. Keith immediately stood up, alarmed.

'You're the teacher, aren't you?' she said in an awed voice.

'Those children, in Freiburg? I'm sure of it – I've been reading about it in the papers. What a tragedy.' She drew out the vowels of the last word, savouring it on her tongue.

Keith stammered something awkwardly.

'Will you sign my newspaper?' she asked, thrusting it into his hand. He almost dropped it in his surprise, then forced himself to look.

The front page showed an image of him sitting in a car with Runde, being driven through waving crowds in Freiburg. Below it, there were photographs of the lost children, but it was the headline that arrested him. 'Heroic struggle in the Black Forest: Britain and Germany, united in grief.'

Heroic struggle.

He felt someone taking his hand; the man was shaking it enthusiastically. 'Extraordinary, what you did, sir,' the man said stuffily.

'Extraordinary,' Keith repeated dumbly.

'Those boys should be given medals. Helping their comrades like they did.'

'And the German boys too!' the woman exclaimed. 'Standing vigil over the coffins like that. Little soldiers, they are over there. Wonderful.'

Keith recalled again that image of an anxious face staring down at him, arms reaching around him. He'd been carried, he remembered now, the slow crunch of snow under someone's feet as he held on tightly. Then the inn, a woman bending over him, asking questions. He hadn't answered most of them, had barely said a word. He'd sat there with a blanket draped over him, whilst they all sprang into action around him.

Had it been heroic? He didn't remember it that way, but he was hardly the best judge, after all. Hadn't men come back from the war with their memories all shattered and fragmented? Hadn't they been unable to speak about what had happened to them, unable to recall things clearly? He'd been with Clayton at the end. He did remember that: Clayton's bright green scarf wrapped around his face, vivid against the snowstorm, getting farther and farther away from him. Clayton, who hadn't come back.

'Anyway,' her husband broke in, 'it was marvellous. Absolutely marvellous.'

Keith stared at them both blankly. There was a pen in his hand; mutely, he scrawled something on the paper and watched them leave. He could feel the room's attention drawing itself towards him and felt himself sitting taller in his chair.

For the third night, he didn't sleep. When he closed his eyes, all he could see was Cyril Clayton standing on a mountain ridge, that green scarf like a beacon against the snow. He'd told the boys to wait in pairs; the younger or weaker, those who were struggling, accompanied by a stronger one. But there hadn't been anyone with Clayton. He'd been alone, and now… He pushed the thought away. No point in looking back.

'We had no warning,' he whispered to himself fiercely, knowing now he wouldn't be able to sleep before morning. 'We had no idea a storm was coming.' He reminded himself of the couple in the lounge, of the headline, 'Heroic struggle in the Black Forest'. Heroic struggle. And why not? 'Heroic,' he whispered to himself as he closed his eyes and tried to shut out the sounds of a storm raging at the edge of his mind, the tolling of bells somewhere far away, Clayton's voice calling to him through the dark. Heroic, heroic, heroic.

Chapter Eleven

'Let me see if I understand you.'

Eileen Foster, as neat and disapproving as she'd been on the day Sylvia had first met her, was peering at her over her glasses. Sylvia swallowed hard; she had tried to explain things in a calm, rational way, but the panic that lay beneath everything was threatening to rise to the surface. Four days had passed – how many seconds now, how many hours? How cold was it at night on the mountain? She gripped the arms of her chair and offered Eileen a weak, uncertain smile.

'I realise it's very inconvenient.'

Outside, in the street, a child let out a sharp cry and she flinched. The engine of a passing motor car covered the sound, and when it had passed, she couldn't hear the child any more.

'I read about it in the papers, of course,' Eileen said stiffly, as if to say, *it's alright. I don't think you're making up stories.*

Sylvia thought of the last headline she'd seen. 'Heroic struggle in the Black Forest'. She thought of Keith Hughes, sitting at her kitchen table a few days before the trip to Germany, his shoulders shaking. She'd put out a hand and touched his shoulder, and he'd flinched as though she was attacking him. And then—

'I'm very sorry, Sylvia. It must be a terrible time.'

'I would just need a week or so. Maybe two. Three, at the very most. There's an aeroplane leaving in two days. I know it's a lot to ask.'

'I'm sorry, Sylvia. It simply isn't possible.'

In the five, perhaps six minutes they had been sitting there, an avalanche could have begun. A trickle of snow at first, building to a rushing torrent, swallowing everything it encountered as it thundered its way towards level ground. Were people found in avalanches? Or did they wait until the spring? Until the snow had melted away and new shoots were pushing their way up from underground, and they could lift out the bodies, perfectly preserved, as though they'd been sleeping in the ice.

'Perhaps, if I found the money elsewhere—'

'We can't spare the help. I'm sorry, Sylvia, I really am.' She leaned forward, removed her glasses and met Sylvia's eyes. 'If you want to keep this job, you'll need to be here.' She hesitated, as though hearing the words, how they sounded. 'I'll pray for him,' she added.

Sylvia almost laughed. Perhaps Eileen Foster's prayers could stop an avalanche in its tracks. Cause it to splinter, divide, dissolve, whenever a child appeared in its path. *Was he buried in the snow?* Cyril had asked her matter-of-factly, the day she'd made up a story for him about Arthur. *Did he fall into the sky?* She reached out a hand to the empty space beside her and felt the shock of his absence again, had to wrap her arms around herself to keep from crying out.

She looked up at Eileen's expectant face, and drew a deep breath.

'I can start now, of course.'

Eileen nodded briskly, as though she had known this would be the answer, all along.

'Well, in that case, you're rather late. I would prefer you to work early, or wait until the staff have gone home. But since you're here…' She sighed. 'Just, do try not to get in anyone's way.'

Sylvia dipped the mop into its bucket of soapy water and began to move it in wide, sweeping arcs across the parquet floor of the main corridor, thinking back to her days of training at the hospital, when she'd often done the same. More and more staff were being sent overseas and those who remained were left filling in the gaps. It was how she'd met Arthur; he'd been wheeling a ward carriage in the opposite direction and they'd edged awkwardly around one another, Sylvia trying not to laugh as the carriage slid away from him, until he was smiling too. They passed each other so often that she began to notice the days when they didn't; the first conversation they'd had was after several days of his absence, and she hadn't been able to hide her relief.

'I thought you must have been sent out.'

He'd stopped, about to walk past her. 'You've got a feather for me too, I suppose.'

'No! I didn't...' Only then did she notice the bruise over one of his eyes. 'I'm sorry. I didn't mean that.'

'It's useful work. Hospital porter – it's not like I'm shirking, is it?'

'No, of course not.' She hadn't known what else to say. The only reason she was there, all of her training, was so that she could be sent out. 'As soon as I'm 23,' she'd written to Julia, 'as soon as they let me, I'll be out there with you.' She couldn't imagine wanting to stay behind.

Later, they'd walked together to her bus stop. She hadn't wanted to bring up the subject again, but he'd done it for her. 'My father was part of the Peace Society,' he'd told her. 'He's dead now, but he'd never forgive me.'

'What happened to your eye?'

'Just some children. Looking to let off steam, I suppose.'

'Looks worse than letting off steam. Are you sure I can't—'

'No, really.' He smiled at her. 'It's nearly healed.'

That evening, she'd asked the girls she was lodging with what the Peace Society was, but they'd only rolled their eyes. 'Just another excuse for cowards to hide behind,' one of them had muttered, and Sylvia had decided to try to forget the hospital porter with the kind eyes, the gentle smile. *After all,* she'd thought, *he won't be here for much longer, not if things keep going as they are.* It was 1915, and already conscription seemed inevitable.

She reached the door to the director's office and hesitated, the mop still in her hand. The alarm bell which had begun the night she'd been taken to the school was still ringing in her head, growing louder each time she thought of the Schauinsland. She laid one hand on the office door, imagining him inside, seated at his desk. She would go in, mistakenly assuming the room to be empty, and he would see the expression on her face, the red eyes and the skin pale from lack of sleep, and ask her what was wrong. She would tell him, reluctantly, apologetically, and he would be outraged, he would march her right back to Eileen's office and demand that everything possible be done, without delay. She would go immediately to buy her ticket, and in two days' time she would be in Germany, she would be on the mountain, and some innate instinct, some internal motherly ability she hadn't even known she had, would lead her right to Cyril, sheltering beneath some tree or in some abandoned mountain hut, he would reach out his arms to her and they would go home—

'He isn't here.'

'What?' She turned around. The young woman she'd seen working in the laboratory on the day of her interview was standing behind her, her head on one side.

'He doesn't often start before ten,' she said briskly, continuing along the corridor. 'He keeps strange hours. You'd do best to start with his office so you're out of the way.'

There was a heavy, thick atmosphere in the director's office – last night's cigarette smoke and not enough air. Sylvia pushed opened a window and the sounds of Gower Street traffic rushed in with the sharp morning breeze.

The walls were lined with books and file boxes; she dusted carefully around them, taking in their gilded titles: *On the Origin of Species, The Science of Man, Hereditary Genius*. The last was authored by Galton himself; she took it from the shelf and flicked through the first few pages.

'I propose to show in this book that a man's natural abilities are derived by inheritance, under exactly the same limitations as are the form and physical features of the whole organic world.'

'Do you believe in inheritance?' she'd asked Arthur, on one of their walks to the bus stop. 'You know – Charles Darwin, Francis Galton.'

She hadn't read either of them, only overheard the doctors discussing it. Arthur had looked at her blankly and she'd felt guilty; she hadn't meant to make him feel slow.

'You pass things about yourself on to your children,' she'd said, wondering why she'd brought it up, embarrassed now.

He'd looked at her for a moment which went on for so long she wondered if she really had offended him.

'Yours will be something special then,' he'd said as her bus drew up, then leaned forward and kissed her quickly on the cheek. She'd hugged her handbag to her chest all the way home.

She flicked quickly through Francis Galton's book, as though some answer to her fears for Cyril might be found there, but it was difficult to focus on the words over the ringing in her head, her pounding heart. She put the book down and began searching through a pile of papers on the desk, weighed down with a small plaster bust of Charles Darwin. Where were the headlines and questions, the same as those she'd read in the papers? 'Insanity in the family: should you marry?' 'Sins of the father and the mother – do we need pre-marital health screenings?' Surely, if the answer was anywhere, it should be here, where the research was actually happening, where the answers might actually be found? She stared into Darwin's cold, pale face as though he might speak to her. *Is my son broken? Is he coming back?* She rifled through the papers, then turned back to the bookcase, taking in the titles, pushing the books aside, looking for anything that might have been hidden between them, suddenly forgetting why else she was here, that she wasn't alone—

'Can I help you?'

She spun round; a man was staring at her from the doorway. His dark hair was slicked back against his skull and he wore glasses on a chain around his neck. For a moment, she couldn't speak.

'Sorry. Sorry, I'm just... I'm the new charwoman. Sylvia.'

'It's alright.' He winked at her conspiratorially. 'I won't tell.'

She let out a breath. 'You're not—'

'The director? Goodness, no.' Of course not, he looked far too young, she saw now, perhaps no older than thirty. He deposited a pile of papers on the desk. 'I'm just dropping these off. Dieter.' He held out a hand.

She recognised the German accent then, almost hidden behind the English vowels. He could see that she had, and smiled.

'Berlin,' he said, then added in an exaggerated whisper, 'I'm a fugitive.'

'A fugitive?'

'You've been reading Galton,' he said, ignoring her question, looking at the book lying open on the table.

'Oh – I... I was just interested. I suppose because the place is named after him.'

He picked it up and leafed through it quickly before replacing it on the shelf. 'What did you make of it?'

'I don't know. I suppose I wondered...' She paused. How to explain? 'I wondered how they can be sure. That blood is inherited. That everything in the parent is passed down to the child.'

'You're thinking about your son.'

Her eyes widened.

'Or daughter, or nephew, whatever. Everybody does.'

'Oh, I see. Yes, I suppose I was.'

'You have a son?'

She nodded, swallowing hard. 'Cyril. He's twelve.'

He smiled. 'Look, I know what they write in the papers. What half the people here say. They'd have hereditary health courts, same as in my country, if they got their way.'

'You don't agree?'

He shrugged. 'It's not that simple, that's all. Of course, for some traits it is, but… people aren't just blood and bones. Your son isn't just blood and bones. Is he?'

'No.'

'Be careful with those,' he said, indicating the pile of papers as he turned to leave. 'The governor doesn't like things being moved around.'

She left later than she'd planned; the work had been harder than she'd expected. The building was a warren of nooks and crannies, and people were continuously coming and going, spreading evidence of the wet weather across her polished floors. More than once, Chi-square had appeared at the end of a corridor and padded muddy paws across her work.

She'd half hoped that Eileen would catch her on the way out, would apologise and offer her the money, after all, or even just the time away. *Of course you must go, what mother wouldn't, what mother could possibly do anything else? Of course, we understand.* She'd hoped to run into Dieter again, to ask him more about inheritance, perhaps even broach the subject of Arthur. She'd caught a glimpse of him at one of the tables in the serology laboratory and, remembering Eileen's directive to keep clear, had moved quickly on.

She spoke to no one else as she went about her work. No one seemed to notice her as she made her last pass of the hallway with the vacuum, replaced it in the cleaning cupboard and hung her apron on its hook. No one spoke to her as she made her way down the winding stairs and back through the old museum space, squeezing between the laboratory benches.

Before she left she paused there in the semi-darkness, surrounded by computing machines, trying to imagine all the skulls, skeletons and skins Eileen had told her about, listening instead to the low, insistent hum of centrifuges and fridges. She could feel the boy from the field tent in France watching her, his eyes following her across the room, his hand tight on hers. Above the chaos and the shouting, someone behind her was saying, over and over, *Blood, we need more blood.* The boy's face, visibly paler with every passing second. The doctor who had visited Arthur, as she'd sat in the bedroom stroking the contours of her stomach, whispering to the child she hadn't yet met. *It's possible it was in him all along, Mrs Clayton. These things can lie dormant for years. All it takes is a trigger, and this has been a big one...*

The air outside was cold and damp; she pulled her coat tighter around her shoulders as she closed the door behind her and paused on the steps for a moment, breathing in the icy air. Had she been right to come to work as though nothing had happened? She reminded herself of what Ruby had said, *He's going to need a life to come back to.* It made sense, of course it did, and perhaps it was this that made her a good mother, more than anything. But all morning the seconds had continued to tick by, and she had done nothing with them but the polishing of floors, the wiping of surfaces, the erasure of other people's footsteps.

The sun dipped behind a cloud as she reached the end of her road. She stopped on the street opposite and held her breath; there was a figure sitting on the steps outside her house. Her pulse quickened; somehow, by some miracle, he'd been deposited on her doorstep, he'd found his way home. She clenched her fists. As the man stood up and took a few steps towards her, she had to bite her lip to hold in a howl of disappointment.

'Mrs Clayton?'

She readied herself, trying to imitate Ruby's terse, clipped tone. 'I'm not interested. Thank you.'

'Just a few words about Cyril?'

He was young; perhaps in his early thirties, with a prim, public school demeanour which, she supposed, was partly an affectation to put her at ease. It had the opposite effect; she felt herself bristling, the pain of her disappointment quickly turning to anger.

'I'm sorry,' she said. 'I've had so many cards, people ringing at the bell.'

'It must be awful.'

Then why are you here? She thought of Ruby's voice in the kitchen, as the cards continued to slide through the letter box. *Vultures. Don't you give them an inch.*

'I've got to get inside,' she said.

'Aren't you angry with him?'

Sylvia stopped, one hand on the door, and turned around. 'With who?'

'The teacher.'

'It was an accident.'

'Was it? Don't you think it's strange, all the reports talking about him like he's a hero?'

She felt herself breathing harder, the cold air scratching at her throat. *Of course I'm angry with him,* she wanted to say, and imagined the story this man would write if she did. *Hysterical mother condemns hero teacher.*

'There isn't much about Cyril in the papers,' he said carefully. 'I thought it might help to get the word out. So people know his face, something about him.'

She hesitated, feeling again the pull at her insides. Was

this what a good mother would do? All this time, she'd been imagining travelling to Germany, finding Cyril herself, but perhaps, all along, she should have been focused on this. She flinched at the thought of all the reporters at the door she'd ignored – it had been nearly five days now, five days where Cyril's face could have been everywhere, on everyone's lips. And then another thought struck her – it wasn't impossible, was it? Newspapers flew people to other countries all the time.

She turned back, pushing the door open and stepping to one side, forcing herself to smile.

'Would you like to come in?'

Chapter Twelve

A fight had broken out in the bay. Keith watched from his window as two boys wrestled in the sand, rolling over and over as though the wind were teasing them. It was a damp, grey day. He had woken to a storm rattling trees against windowpanes, the sea being whipped up relentlessly in the bay. On his first morning at the hotel he had loved to lie and listen to the sea, but now it made him feel restless.

He watched as a small crowd gathered around the boys in the sand, shouting and cheering them on. He was reminded of two dogs his father had brought home, years ago when he and Jack were children. A present for each of them, but they had felt more like a punishment, the way they snapped and snarled. *Teach you how to stand up for yourselves*, their father had said with a satisfied smile on his face, as though children ought to learn their strength from animals. His older brother had watched, fascinated, as they went for each other, but they had always made Keith feel uneasy.

He reached for the papers. The German ambassador in London had died; there was a full page spread in the *Illustrated News*. Nazi Party flags, all the way along Pall Mall. Keith wondered what his father would have to say about that, imagining the old man allowing himself a faint smile as he turned the pages; a hopeful vision of things to come.

There was another article about the mountain; four

photographs of the fallen boys, accompanied, this time, by another depicting Cyril Clayton. He flinched at the thought of the boy, still out there somewhere on the mountainside. Should he have stayed in Germany, helped more with the search? They had told him there was nothing more he could do, but didn't they always say that? Proper heroes were people who ignored all that, who went against advice. He thought again of those final moments, turning to look back at Clayton, standing alone on the ridge. The German woman's face, close to his as he sat on a cold stone floor, blankets draped over his shoulders. *We need to know if there's anyone else out there. We have to know if we should go back.*

He looked down at the notepaper in front of him; 'Dear Sylvia', an expanse of white space beneath it. What on earth could he say?

He looked out of the window again. One of the boys had almost won; he had the other pinned against the sand. Some innate excitement began to heat the blood in Keith's veins as the shouting reached a higher pitch; if the boys were dogs, this would be the time to go for the throat. Their own dogs had been sent away in the end; after weeks of watching them try to tear each other to pieces, his father had lost his nerve. Keith had been relieved; he and Jack had each chosen a favourite, and he had been terrified one of them would eventually win. Afterwards, though, he had regretted the loss. The dogs had drawn some of his father's attention away from his sons, at least for a few weeks, which had been enough time for most of their bruises to heal.

He took a sudden step back from the window. Surely that had been Noël Coward, the man from the hotel lounge, standing on the street outside? He'd been looking up at Keith's window, or at least it had seemed that he had. Keith felt a ridiculous urge to drop to the floor, as though he were under heavy fire. Hesitantly, he approached the window again and looked down. The man was still there – he was sure it was the same man – but now he was staring intently at a street map, as crowds on their way to the beach streamed past him.

By mid-afternoon, Keith was standing amongst the crowds at the station waiting for the London train. There had been more headlines in the afternoon papers – mainly about the search for Clayton, a few more photographs of the surviving boys returning home, the German children waving them off with a parade of Nazi Party flags and flowers thrown onto the tracks. He wasn't afraid of the newspapers now; they all seemed completely on his side. The man on the street, though; he wasn't keen on staying behind to find out who he was, or what he was after. On his way to the station he'd woven through the streets in an irregular pattern, feeling ridiculous even as he glanced behind him, checking for signs of being followed. He'd go back to his parents' house, no one would think to look for him there.

He tried not to look out of the window on the journey back to London. He found that the more he stared out at the rushing countryside, the more he felt his mind going back to Germany, to Freiburg and the mountains, what was left behind there. He reached into his pocket, feeling for the cold edges of his medal, pressing it into his palms and thinking of the night before the trip, when Sylvia had taken it from a drawer in her kitchen and handed it over to him.

'I'm sorry,' she'd said, not looking at him. 'Cyril... he likes hearing about the war. Things like that. I suppose he just wanted to look at it more closely. It was wrong of him, obviously.'

'It's quite alright. I should never have shown it to them.'

Why had he? The boys had been restless, fractious. Prendergast had been teasing Clayton, the scholarship boy, and all of a sudden one of the other boys was standing on his desk, egging him on. How had he lost control of them so completely? He'd heard his father's voice in his ear, *Coward, show them who's boss,* and another voice too – his own, perhaps – *How will they cope out there? How are they ever going to survive?* His father used to force him and Jack to take baths in cold water, to prepare them for winters in the trenches. The beatings, too, were meant to inure them to the greater violence that was, surely, destined to come. He knew he should be using the cane more than he did, but something in him cringed at it, at the sound of it tearing through the cold air of the schoolroom, the snap against fragile skin, the yelp a boy would try to suppress.

So he'd taken out his medal instead. Told them stories of being fired at in the trenches, of watching boys not much older than they were shattered by shrapnel, choking in gas. Told them stories about what real life, real death, was like. Eventually, they'd fallen silent and listened, none more so than Clayton, who'd stared at him with a kind of fascinated awe. It was a feeling Keith had never experienced before, so much rapt attention focused on him, the fear, the respect in their eyes.

He hadn't noticed the medal was missing until the last of the boys had left and he'd packed up his things. He'd left it out on his desk without thinking – the first time in years he hadn't kept it close to him. He'd known it was Clayton. Something about the way he'd stared at it, long after the other boys had lost interest. He'd never suspected the boy of being a thief, but you never knew with children; traits could lie dormant for years, before suddenly springing to the surface. He knew he shouldn't have gone straight to the house – had it even been ethical to look up her address in the school records? But he needed the medal back, he needed to know where it was.

He'd felt Sylvia's fingers brush against his as she handed it to him. 'I found it in his school bag. I really am very sorry. Embarrassed—'

'Please. There's no need...' And he'd taken a step towards

her. The moment was so brief it might never have happened, but she'd taken a step back in turn, and both of them had looked away.

'My husband was at the Somme,' she'd said unexpectedly. 'He didn't get a medal. I've never seen one before. You must have been very brave, I suppose.'

'Everybody was—'

'Oh yes, I know that's what people say. *Everyone* was brave. It's not true, though. Some people don't have the stomach for it.'

Was she talking about her husband? Keith had never heard anyone talk about a soldier that way. It made him feel uneasy, as though he ought to come to the man's defence.

'What happened to your husband? I mean, he is…'

'Cyril's father? Oh yes. He came back.'

'Well then.'

She'd looked at him, eyes narrowed, as though she was expecting him to say something else. But what else was there to say? Plenty of men hadn't come back, she was luckier than most. But then, where was he now?

'Tell me about your medal.'

He flinched. But after all, she'd seen it now. No going back. 'I got it for sniping.'

'What happened?'

He sighed. 'We were trying to advance the line, heavy fire. It was in Lille; we were holed up badly, running out of supplies. I found a good position. That's all, really. Just luck.'

'You had the stomach for it.' She was looking at him strangely.

'I suppose so. You don't really think about it, at the time.'

He stared down at the medal in his hand as the train flew on towards London, towards the real life he would have to finally face. He thought of Jack, holding the medal up to the firelight, all those years ago in his rooms at Cambridge. The look on his brother's face, the edge to his voice. *It doesn't mean anything, you know. Just the luck of the draw.* He'd known then that he'd carry it with him always, not to show people, just to keep in his pocket, a talisman to hold on to whenever he felt afraid or uncertain. A reminder of his own strength. He tried to draw on that strength now, as he stared at the blank sheet of paper in front of him. 'Dear Sylvia'.

He'd tried to leave, that night in Sylvia's kitchen. He'd made a move towards the door, but something in him had given way. Perhaps it was exhaustion, apprehension about the trip, the responsibility. Or was it simply that he'd said so much out loud? He tried not to speak about the war, but the words, the stories, seemed to spill from him when he expected it least. Whatever it was, he'd felt himself swaying.

She'd eased him into a chair, and he'd found he was suddenly breaking down in front of her, muffling the sobs in the sleeve of his jacket. He'd pressed the medal tight between his palms, and he'd felt her hand tentatively resting on his shoulder, squeezing it gently. He hadn't meant for anything to happen, but when he'd turned his head she was staring into his eyes, so intently he'd tried to look away. She'd taken his face in her hands and, as he'd half stood up, clumsily, stumbling, she'd pressed her mouth against his.

He'd pulled away almost at once. Until then, neither of them had noticed the child standing in the doorway, not making a sound.

They were saying Clayton might still be alive out there. Hiding out in the mining tunnels, or perhaps somewhere deep in the forest. Keith wondered if all his stories of war would be a comfort to the boy now, if he really was still alive. If he lay awake in the dark thinking of that medal, the possibility of survival. Or was he thinking of that night when he'd stood in the doorway to his kitchen and watched two strangers, one of whom had looked exactly like his mother?

He looked down at the sheet of paper, the intimidating white space. 'Dear Sylvia'. He began to write.

Chapter Thirteen

By the fifth day the ice had, at last, begun to weaken, and the search moved underground. With the dwindling resources, most of the mining works under the mountain were closing, leaving behind a complex web of shafts and pathways; perfect for hiding, so the rumour went, a child could get lost for days. How could a child eat, Hilde wanted to ask them, how could a child live, how could anyone possibly find him? No one seemed to have the answers to her questions, but the theory persisted anyway, fuelled by a mythical mountain king, a vision of an army of children rising up from beneath them.

Hilde was on her way back from the fields when she saw them: a long line of men stretched out from the mouth of one of the tunnels, lifting out crates of soil and rock. She stood watching, thinking of the days following the cave-in, when she and her mother had gone down to the mineworks and watched the search, waiting to recognise Hilde's father amongst the faces of men being hauled out of the earth, ashen with rock dust and shock. Hilde remembered approaching one of the men and asking him whether he'd seen her daddy, and he'd stared back at her with eyes so wide and blank that, for days afterwards, she'd convinced herself he must have been a ghost, his own body still buried in the earth. When they'd come home, the radio was still switched on. *Adolf Hitler has been declared führer und Reichskanzler,* a clipped voice was saying. *He promises to restore Germany to the power and respect it commanded before the devastations of the Versailles Treaty.*

She saw Hans Huber amongst the men; he straightened and waded through the snow towards her, wiping his hands on his trouser legs.

'Hilde! I hope you weren't thinking of trying to lend a hand?' He smiled at her, and she instinctively took one step away from him.

'They really think he could be down there?'

Hans shrugged. 'No stone unturned. It's the right thing to do.'

She tried to make out faces amongst the men emerging from the tunnels. 'What about the teacher?' she asked, half expecting to recognise him among them. 'What did he have to say for himself?'

'No more than what's in the papers. It was a terrible accident, nothing more.'

Hilde hesitated, and saw him notice.

'What is it?' he asked.

'Just that – he must have known about the storm. It was obvious even in the morning that bad weather was coming.'

'In Freiburg, perhaps not.'

'No, perhaps not. But surely someone must have said something.'

'It's all been gone into thoroughly, Hilde.'

'He told me they were all accounted for. He must have lied—'

'It was a misunderstanding, nothing more. He was confused, in shock.'

She thought back to that night, to the man's blank, staring eyes. It was possible, of course it was possible. He hadn't seemed to be with her in the room. And if it wasn't deliberate, or shock, then the only other possibility was that she had been mistaken. That it was all her fault.

'He said something else, though. Something that—'

'What?'

But she hesitated, unsure of herself. What could it possibly have to do with all this, after all?

'What matters now is making sure we've done everything we can. By the way,' Hans added, turning back to her. 'Your sister, Anna? My son asked if he could call by. He tells me she has a cure for headaches, better than the doctors have in Freiburg.'

Hilde stared at him, unsure of what to say. Hans had four children, all of them girls but the oldest, Paul, a tall, serious-faced boy who sometimes helped them move hay into the barn or repair storm damage. She'd noticed him stealing glances at Anna in church but never thought anything of it; he must be three, four years older than her at least. He attended meetings of the Hitler Youth whenever he could be spared from the farm; she'd seen him in his uniform, heading out on the long walk to Todtnau, the town just south of Todtnauberg, where the nearest meetings were held.

'I'll bring it to church on Sunday,' she said.

Hans smiled. 'I think he'd like to collect it himself.'

'She's fourteen years old, Hans.'

'It's just the headache cure he's after.'

'Is it?'

He held up his hands. 'Of course. Just children, both of them. I'm sure there's nothing in it. So...'

'No,' she said, feeling her anger build, the same anger she'd felt outside the inn after the police had questioned her. 'If Paul wants the medicine, tell him I'll bring it to church on Sunday.'

Anna was kneading dough in the kitchen. Hilde stood in the doorway watching her: the curve of her neck where her hair fell forward across her shoulders, her fists pummelling the dough, the frown on her face, a sheen of sweat on her forehead. She thought of the night of the elections, Anna running out to cheer the parade, the bright costumes, the display of lights. The day Fritz had brought her back, the day their father—

'Leave the bread,' she said, resolve tightening her jaw. 'We're going out.'

'What?'

'We're going out to look for that missing boy. Come on.' She held out a hand. 'The bread can wait.'

The sun was high, melting the last of the snow which ran through the village in tiny rivulets, filling the air with the constant sound of rushing water. The Party flag that flew in the square was hanging limply from its flagpole. Back when it had first appeared three years ago, it had occasionally been torn down, discovered in pieces throughout the village, but it had been a long time since anyone had dared. The last time, the sexton at the church had been accused and taken away. To Dachau, Hilde assumed, although no one knew for sure.

'They died, didn't they?' Anna said as they climbed the hill above the church. 'Those children – why didn't you tell me?'

'Four of them did.'

'You didn't tell me. I'm not a child any more.'

At the top of the ridge, they turned and looked back across the village. The sloping roofs of the farmhouses were nestled amongst a patchwork of vegetable and herb gardens, a few clumps of snow still dotted between them. The beaten path through its centre wound its way in a ribbon towards the square, branching out towards the church in one direction, the inn in another. A few carts were being pulled along it, but mostly people were keeping indoors, fearful of a sudden relapse in the weather.

'I didn't want you to be upset,' Hilde said carefully.

'I was going to find out.'

'I know. I'm sorry, it was stupid.'

'How on earth could we find him anyway, when a whole search party haven't? When none of you did,' she added, an accusatory edge to her tone.

'We did our best, you know. In the dark, the storm—'

'Yes, I know.' Anna's face softened, and she slipped a hand in Hilde's. 'I didn't mean – of course you did.'

They climbed on towards the treeline, winding their way between the low-hanging branches of pine trees clinging to the steep slopes. Hilde found herself imagining children in the dark shapes of the trees, the shadows they cast against the snow. At times, she thought she could hear a child's voice in the birdsong, in the running water, even in the tread of Anna's footsteps next to her, her heavy breathing as they pressed on through the trees.

'Look!' Anna stopped ahead of her. She was pointing towards a clearing; at its centre was a low-roofed shelter, half hidden amongst branches and moss which had been piled up on its roof of corrugated iron. Anna took a few steps forwards and peered into the entrance, crouching low against the ground. 'It's where Fritz found me, that day.'

'The day you went missing?'

Hilde joined Anna at the entrance, where the remains of a fire were evident. Inside, a camp bed almost filled the space; a few tins of food were lined up against the far wall.

Anna nodded. 'His painting lodge. That's what he calls it; I suppose he doesn't use it much any more.'

Hilde crawled further in; it was damp and cold, the air heavy with moisture. 'It doesn't look like anyone's been here for months.' She examined the camp bed, the tins, looking for signs that any of them had been recently moved. Beneath the bed she found a wooden box; it contained a few tubes of paint and some brushes, bound together with twine. 'If the boy found this place...' she began.

Anna, still crouching at the entrance, looked up at her. 'Then why isn't he still here?'

Fritz came by that evening; it was a weekly custom they'd kept up since their mother's death. They sat in the *Stube* and Hilde brought in the stew she'd had bubbling on the stove all day, ladling it out into small bowls and hoping their size would disguise how little of it there was. The last of the daylight fell in an orange glow across the flagstones, illuminating the print of the Virgin Mary her mother had hung on the wall years before, whose corners were beginning to peel.

'Ah!' Fritz beamed when Anna told him about the painting lodge. 'I haven't been there in so long. I can't sleep on that old camp bed any more.'

'We were looking for that boy,' Hilde said, staring into her bowl, the thin broth and slices of vegetables she'd taken from the garden that morning.

'The whole village seems to be doing the same. It's a wonder any work's being done at all.'

Hilde put down her spoon. 'Don't you think we should do everything we can?'

'Of course, of course.' Fritz held up his hands. 'But we have to carry on with life, don't we?'

'They think he's in the mines,' Anna said in a low, quiet voice. 'That's the worst thing in the world, don't you think? To be buried underground.'

She waited for Anna to go to bed before she told him about the conversation with Hans.

'Oh, Paul Huber's harmless,' Fritz said as she poured him out a glass of schnapps. 'A little stupid, perhaps. But he's a nice enough boy.'

'He goes to Hitler Youth meetings.'

'Most boys do, Hilde. It doesn't mean they believe all of it.'

She sighed, leaning her forehead on her hands. There was so much she wanted to say to Fritz, about the Party, about her father. It was only fear that stopped her; the fear of having misunderstood him, of giving too much away. You couldn't trust anyone, that was what she had learned in the three years since the elections. She'd heard of neighbours reporting neighbours; family, even, handing over each other's secrets, conversations they'd overheard. It was their duty, they were told constantly on the radio, in the newspapers, to be vigilant.

'Did you know Hans is trying to start up a local Party branch?' Fritz said.

'What?'

'Tired of being the only one, I suppose. There'll be brownshirts patrolling the streets if he gets his way.'

'Do you think he can?'

Fritz shook his head. 'There's not enough of us. Oh, he might manage a few meetings, a rally, even. It won't come to anything more. Anyway, I don't think you need to worry about Paul. He's got a head on his shoulders.'

'That isn't the point! I don't like him thinking about Anna that way.'

'What way?'

'I don't know.' Hilde was still thinking about the men at the inn, how they'd looked at her as she stood in front of them answering their questions. *You haven't thought to marry?* 'I want to leave, Fritz. I want to take Anna and go.'

'Where to?'

'Freiburg, I suppose. My aunt lives there.'

Hilde had only met Else a few times, but the thought of her, of the life she must lead in the city, always produced a little spark of excitement. The last time she'd seen Else had been at their mother's funeral; Else had arrived late and stood at the back of the church wearing a black lace veil, a ghost hovering just out of sight. Afterwards, she'd hugged them both and Hilde had felt it was like holding on to a skeleton or a rose bush, all sharp angles and thorns. Whenever the subject of Else had come up, Hilde's mother had sighed an exasperated sigh; there was an unspoken agreement that Else, with her life in the city, no husband or children to be seen, was no good. *Oh Else,* she'd sigh, whenever anyone mentioned her. *Oh, Else.*

But Hilde had always felt differently. 'She's a nurse,' she said now. 'That must be wonderful, mustn't it? Spending every day helping people.'

'I suppose it takes a lot of training.'

'I suppose it does.'

The spark dimmed a little, and Hilde forced it back into life. Each time she imagined Else's life in Freiburg she embellished it a little more – a beautiful, elegant house by the river, high ceilings and chandeliers, parties where women wore silk dresses and drank tea from china cups. A life with enough food, her own bed; Anna might even go to school again. When their mother had still been alive it had been unthinkable, to abandon the farm. But now...

'It must be possible, though, if I worked hard enough. If she did it, why not me?'

'And you think in Freiburg, things are different?'

She looked up at the print on the wall. 'People might not look at us like we're cattle on their farms, for a start.'

Fritz held out his empty glass. 'Well, you'll find plenty of brownshirts, I promise you that,' he said as she refilled it. 'A thousand Hans Hubers, just waiting to make your acquaintance.'

Anna was still awake when Hilde crawled into bed beside her. She wrapped her arms around her sister, trying to block out the hunger which was settling in the pit of her stomach.

'Fritz looks older,' Anna mumbled. 'Don't you think? Since the winter.'

'Maybe. Anna, what do you think about going away?' She'd suggested it before, in a half-hearted, imaginary way, like a fairy tale, but now she began to see it clearly. 'I mean, really away. Going to Freiburg. Or somewhere else.'

'We can't,' Anna said simply. 'Mother and Father are here.'

'You mean their things?' They had kept everything in boxes in the basement; Hilde had never been able to summon the courage to sort through it all. It was underneath them, hidden away, except on those occasions she had to go down there for tools or supplies, when the memories rushed in at her, threatening to unbalance her.

'No, I mean them. *They're* here.'

Hilde closed her eyes, thinking of the stone slab outside the church, which Fritz had helped them to pay for. 'Hannah Meyer, 1888-1935'. And then the imagined, dark place where her father lay, somewhere unmarked beneath the mountain, deep below their reach. 'They'll be here forever,' she said. 'We can come back and see them whenever we like. There's a whole world out there,' she added, thinking of the postcards Else sometimes sent them from Freiburg, the streets filled with people, vast squares that made Hofsgrund's meeting place look like nothing more than a beaten patch of earth. Streets lined with market stalls, the cathedral spire reaching to the clouds. She imagined herself there in a nurse's uniform, walking briskly along corridors, giving and receiving orders, knowing the answers to impossible questions. 'Don't you want to see it?'

'You're being silly,' Anna said in a matter-of-fact voice that reminded Hilde of their mother so much, she clenched the blankets with her fists. 'We can't just start up somewhere else. There's enough world here, isn't there? And anyway.' She rolled onto her side, and the rest was muffled by her pillow. 'What about Gretel? What about the pigs?'

Chapter Fourteen

'So.' The journalist clasped his hands in front of him and leaned forward across Sylvia's kitchen table. 'Tell me about yourself.'

Sylvia was standing at the stove, waiting for the kettle to boil, her face turned away from the kitchen door. Each time she looked at it she saw Cyril standing there, his little fists curled around the piece of paper, his cheeks red. Why hadn't she run to him then, why hadn't she put her arms around him and held on to him? The next day, when the car came to take him to Germany, she could have kept him with her instead, kept him close. What had she been thinking, letting him go so far away?

'Mrs Clayton?'

It had been a mistake to let the man in. When he'd slid his card across the table, 'Ronald Lane, *Daily Sketch*', there had been an eager, hungry look in his eyes, as though Cyril was the prey and he the hunter. And what did that make Sylvia? *I've lost my boy,* her mind screamed at him. *I've lost Cyril. What else do you need to know?*

'What do you want to know?'

'Well, perhaps we should start with your husband.'

There was a silence.

'I don't see what that has to do with my son.'

'Readers like the full picture. Family life, all that.' He waited, and when she didn't speak he smiled a tense, polite smile.

'So it's gossip you're after?' she said coldly.

'He isn't here then? Your husband?'

She took the kettle from the stove and poured water into the pot. In the cupboard beside the teacups, she found a tiny wooden figure; a man carrying a backpack and a thick wooden staff, and her throat closed up. He hid his toys in strange places and waited for her to find them. Her fingers clenched on the countertop.

'You should know,' Ronald Lane was saying, drawing in a long breath, 'that the absence of information can be more damaging than the truth. People imagine all sorts of things in the spaces—'

'Tell them what you like. I don't care.'

'Mrs Clayton, if you're having second thoughts—'

She closed her eyes, swallowing down the panic that was threatening to break through to the surface. *Just ten minutes. Five, even.*

'He likes explorers.'

'I'm sorry?'

'Cyril. He likes reading about mountain climbers. His father was a climber, he used to go away to climb mountains sometimes.'

'Really?' The sound of a pencil scribbling quickly. 'Which mountains?'

'I don't know which mountains,' she snapped. 'He didn't tell me. It's what he did, to get over…' She hesitated. 'To get over what happened.'

'The war?'

'Yes, the war.'

'Did he win any medals? Anything notable we can say?'

She reached up and took the wooden figurine down from its shelf, placing it on the table for Ronald Lane to see. 'Cyril hid these around the house for me to find. In cupboards, on the stairs. Climbers, you see?'

'Yes, I see.'

Another silence.

'It must be difficult, raising a child by yourself.'

'We're fine. We don't need – we didn't need...'

She turned to the wall, breathing hard. When was he going to leave?

'Do you remember the last thing you said to him?'

She wanted to scream. She realised she'd been wanting to scream ever since it had happened, at policemen, at Ruby, at strangers in the street. *I've lost him, I've lost him, don't you care?*

'I told him I loved him.'

Had she told him that? She'd had his things ready, and he'd not even looked at her as he'd picked up his case. She'd stood between him and the door, determined not to let him leave like that, terrified of his anger, of this side of him she'd never seen before. She'd searched desperately for something to say, but what on earth was there? Had she said anything? Had he?

'He's coming back,' she said loudly. To herself, she thought, *What if that was it? The last time I'll ever see him.* When she turned around, Ronald Lane was staring at her with such pity in his eyes she wanted to slap him.

She sent him away with the photograph of Cyril she'd taken out of its frame. The frame sat empty now on the desk, a grey rectangle where an image of her son used to be and, before that, her husband. Ronald was right, what he'd said about people filling in the gaps for themselves. That was why she'd done it, all those years ago when Cyril had come to her in the kitchen and asked her about the man in the photograph, what had happened to him. There had been a newspaper open on the table in front of her, and she'd glanced at a headline. 'George Mallory: Everest Hero'. Someone had written a biography, only three years after he'd been lost. 'His last hours on Everest will always be among the mysteries, and we can only speculate...'

We can only speculate. Cyril wriggled restlessly on her knees. His question – *Where is he?* – hung in the air. She had to tell him something. Something which would leave Arthur lingering between myth and reality, out of their reach but still present, still tangible, half formed. Something which would take away some of the pain of carrying on without him.

He climbed a mountain, she thought, suddenly seeing Arthur as she never had before, striding out into densely packed snow. *That's right. He climbed a mountain, and he never came home.*

A few hours later she was sitting in the dark, clutching Cyril's toy climber tight to her chest, when she remembered the postcard. She'd had it in her pocket when she went to the school. She could remember pressing her fingers against its sharp edges as the headmaster gave them the news. Where was it now?

Her coat pockets were empty. She searched them again, increasingly panicked. 'Dear Mum'. What else had it said? She hadn't even read it. His last words before the storm, and she didn't even know what they were.

When Ruby let herself in the next day, Sylvia was sitting on the floor, surrounded by piles of papers fanned out around her.

'Sylvia?'

She looked up, surprised by Ruby's voice. She hadn't brushed her hair; she was wearing one of Arthur's old jumpers, full of moth holes and worn at the elbows. She felt light-headed, staring up at Ruby, and realised she hadn't eaten since the previous day. Arthur's desk lay open; she got up hurriedly and gathered up the papers, pushing them back in the drawers before Ruby could see.

'What are you doing?'

'How did you get in?'

'You gave me a key.'

She didn't remember doing that. There were a lot of things

she didn't remember – the two men leaving the house, how she'd got home from the school that night. The last thing she'd said to Cyril.

'He sent me a postcard from Freiburg. It was in my pocket...' She turned back to the room, as though she expected to see it sitting neatly on the coffee table, where it had been all along. 'I can't find it.'

'Come on, love. You need to eat something.'

She stared at the empty photograph frame. It hadn't been a lie, Arthur in the snow, not completely. He'd always talked about it. Those early days at the hospital, walking each other to the bus stop, he'd been full of stories of the pioneers of the Alps, Edward Whymper, Albert Mummery, Oskar Schuster. How one day, even Everest would be conquered. She'd had all that to draw on, when she whispered her stories to Cyril. After a while, that was all they were, bedtime stories which he'd begged her to retell as she put him to bed, tales of his brave, absent father who one day – who knew? – might come back to them. They'd moved to a new part of London by then, and she'd hoped that would be enough to stop the endless gossip around them, the speculation. The stories were a secret, she'd told Cyril, terrified that the telling of them might cause someone else to find out the truth.

And then he'd come to her with news of the trip to Germany, begging her to let him go. She felt now, with a horrible certainty, that it was her fault he'd wanted to go so badly. What little boy didn't want to follow his father?

Ruby took her to a tea shop near the station. They'd passed it before but never been in; Ruby would joke about the prices and the type of women they could see through the misted-up windows. *Too much time on their hands,* she'd mutter as they passed, *must be nice having a man at home who pays the bills while you sip tea, eh?* But today, she steered Sylvia inside and sat her at a table, accepting two menus from a waitress wearing a neat white apron and matching hat.

'Teacakes,' she said, after Sylvia had stared in bewilderment at the menu. 'For two. And a pot of tea.'

'You don't have to do this, really,' Sylvia said weakly. 'Where are the children?'

'With their dad. He wanted to take them on an outing. Feels guilty, I suppose, for – well, we don't need to talk about him, do we?'

'If you like—'

'How are you?' Ruby leaned forward and put a hand on Sylvia's. She nearly pulled it away; the only way she could be around other people was to exist in a state of numbness, which the touch of Ruby's hand threatened to dissolve. She wondered how she could do it, if there was something wrong with her; perhaps she was missing some vital, heretofore undiscovered organ in the body which dispensed emotions like the liver dispensed bile. She kept her hand in Ruby's, waiting for her resolve to break, but instead there was only the softness of Ruby's fingers, the slight cold which still lingered from the outside, the hard chair beneath her.

'It's my fault,' she said.

'Oh, Sylvia—'

'No, it is.' She couldn't explain to Ruby why. She couldn't tell her about all the stories she'd told Cyril, tales of his father's heroism. They hadn't felt like lies at the time. They'd been necessary fictions, to make both of their lives easier – sometimes she'd even forgotten herself they weren't true. Was all this punishment for what she'd done?

The waitress returned and Sylvia watched as Ruby spread butter across the teacakes and poured out the tea.

'I spoke to one of those journalists' she said, accepting her cup and saucer.

Ruby's eyes widened.

'Ruby, what if that's how we find him? We get his face into the newspapers, his story.'

Ruby let out a sigh. 'They don't want to help you, love. Don't be so naive.'

'And I thought—'

'What?'

Her voice was small. 'I thought they might be my way to get to him. To get to Germany.'

Ruby put her face in her hands.

'He's going to do a profile.'

'In Germany?'

'No, not yet. But they might – soon.'

'Or he's just telling that to keep you on the hook.'

'I have to do something, Ruby.'

'Well, you know what I think about it.' Ruby took a bite of teacake, as if silencing herself before saying something she'd regret.

When it came time to pay, Ruby reached for her handbag, swatting Sylvia away from hers.

'My treat.'

She began pulling things out of the bag, searching for her purse: a hairbrush, a compact mirror, a lipstick. A pile of papers, bright yellow, with bold print, the words arranged in a sort of flow chart with arrows linking them together. Sylvia reached for one, reading aloud.

'Live, love... marry wisely... result: sound children. Where did these come from?'

Ruby looked up at her sheepishly. 'The woman who gave that talk at the Guild the other day. After you left.' She paused, embarrassed. 'We got to talking. She was interesting. She's given me pamphlets to read.'

'I thought it was all nonsense? You said—'

Ruby shrugged. 'I thought it was too. But she made a lot of sense. Did you know there was a committee a couple of years back? A proper parliamentary one, they said making sterilisation legal would be a good idea.'

'Kids are born how they're born. That's what you said—'

'I know, but the way she explained it – she made it sound different. It's about freedom, isn't it?'

'It doesn't sound like freedom.'

'Well, anyway, nothing's been done about it.' Ruby stuffed the flyers hurriedly back into her bag. 'It wouldn't be such a bad thing, though, would it? I mean, Christ, the idea of having more kids!'

A look of horror crossed her face and she put a hand up to her mouth. The waitress came for their bill and they sat in uncomfortable silence as she counted out the change.

As soon as she was home, Sylvia remembered the jewellery box. It had been a present from Arthur, a few weeks after they'd first started walking together to the bus stop. He'd handed it over shyly: a small carved wooden box with a pattern of leaves and roses on its lid. She'd stopped in the street and held it in both hands, momentarily lost for anything to say.

'Did you make it?'

'It's only birchwood. I didn't have anything nicer.'

She'd stared up at him, still searching for the right words, when the bus pulled up beside them.

She'd used the box for keeping treasures in; not the glittering jewels she'd dreamed of as a child, but small things: a daisy from the first posy he'd given her, pressed between two ticket stubs from the bus. The notes he left in her coat pocket on days they didn't see each other. Later, a lock of their son's baby hair, folded up in an envelope.

And the postcard Cyril had sent her from Freiburg. Of course she'd put it there, in those first, bewildered hours, of which she'd retained barely any memories.

She laid it on the bed, taking in the words, Cyril's handwriting, in pieces, hearing his voice as she read.

'Dear Mum. Today we climbed the big tower and I saw a great big bell ringing. It was very loud. Mr Hughes says we are to cross the Schauinsland to Todtnauberg (they have such funny names) tomorrow. Mr Hughes says there will likely be a storm, and it will be a good test of our blood to get through it. I have bought you a snow globe with the cathedral in it. See you soon, Love Cyril.'

She read it again, imagining him sitting at a desk in some hostel, frowning at the card, Keith Hughes standing over him and correcting his spellings. Was the card intended as a sign he forgave her, or had he been made to write it? She tried to detect some deeper message hidden in the words, but couldn't. She read it a third time, and that's when she felt it. Something was very wrong. Something… she read it again and her hands began to shake. She thought of the news reports, which she'd only been able to glance at in pieces. She'd kept them all; they formed one of the piles in the living room, pages torn from the papers. She took the postcard downstairs and laid it next to them, fanning the newspaper articles out around her, searching for the quote she thought she remembered.

'Recalling the disaster, Mr Hughes stated, "We couldn't have known there was going to be a storm. It was unusual for the time of year."'

She looked from it to the postcard, and back again, searching through more of the articles for the same quote, repeated over and over in smudged ink. She looked up and spoke Cyril's words out loud to the empty house, feeling a bewildered rage rising up hot in her throat.

'Mr Hughes says there will likely be a storm, and it will be a good test of our blood to get through it.'

Chapter Fifteen

It was nearly dark by the time Keith reached Chiswick and his parents' road: a street of identical terraced houses of red brick and peeling paintwork. The houses must once have been relatively grand; he could imagine Victorian gentlemen on their way to jobs in banks and legal firms – not the top men, not by far, but respectable enough in their smart suits, a couple of servants back home, a nursery maid, someone to do the cooking. Now, the houses were split into upper and lower flats, and the elegant plasterwork was beginning to crumble.

His parents occupied one of the upper flats. There had been a time, not so long ago really, when Keith had thought he would never come back here. His mother still kept a room for him; the same room he and Jack had shared as children, tucked away in the eaves. It had been a servant's room, no doubt, and as a child he had liked to lie awake thinking of how lucky he was, never having to rise early to sweep out chimney breasts or collect bedpans. Back then, he'd thought he would go on to have someone to do those things for him: a wife, or a servant, it didn't really matter which.

He stood on the pavement opposite, looking up at the familiar windows. A light was on in the sitting room; his heart beat a little faster. His father would be sitting in his armchair, perhaps even looking out across the street, a newspaper balanced on his knees. He hadn't warned them he was coming; he should have done, he supposed. He still hadn't written since the accident. The whole thing had been such a rigmarole, so many parades and questions and, before that, those first few bewildering days in the hospital. He'd gone to Bournemouth because he needed a break from it all – they would understand that, surely.

He rang the bell, listening for sounds of movement inside. At first he heard nothing; then the familiar shuffle of his mother's footsteps on the stairs.

'Keith!' She was wearing her cooking apron, her face flushed and damp. Keith could smell the aroma of boiled meat and gravy clinging to her. 'Where on earth have you been?'

He paused, unsure what would be the right thing to say. 'I just had to get away for a bit,' he said slowly. 'I'm sorry – I should have written.'

'We've had the police here – you've no idea, Keith!'

'Listen, is it alright if I stay? I can't go back to the flat.'

He didn't offer a reason why, and she didn't ask, only assented with a non-committal grunting sound he had heard often enough to interpret correctly. He followed her up the stairs, still thinking of his father in the armchair above them. His hand gripped tightly to the stair rail as he approached the entrance to the flat.

'Mum, could I...' But she wasn't listening to him, had already shuffled back to the kitchen and left him alone in the hall. She came back with a cup of tea, pressing it into his hands.

'We had the police here, asking questions. And your headmaster came looking for you.' She said it as though the two were of a similar degree of seriousness. 'Broken, he looked.'

'Alright, Mum.'

'He said you've to go and see him about it.'

'Right.'

'I told him you'd be there if you'd be there.'

'That's alright, Mum. Of course I'll go.'

'Keith, what *happened*?'

'I – can we talk about it another time, please? I've just got back. I'm alright, though. That's good, isn't it?'

There was a long silence.

'Is he here?' Keith said at last, nodding at the sitting room door.

'Go in and see for yourself.'

Keith stood for a moment in the doorway, folding his coat over his arm. His father's armchair was turned towards the window; he could see only one arm holding a newspaper, the crown of his head, grey-brown wisps of hair. He looked around the room; a chaos of books and piles of old newspapers, in even more disarray than when he had last seen it. The pile closest to the armchair was largely back issues of *The Blackshirt* and *Action*, which he and his mother were forbidden from using for kindling. *They'll be in the history books one day*, his father would mutter if anyone suggested it. *They'll be... artefacts.* The day of the Olympia riot, he had hung a photograph of Oswald Mosley above the mantelpiece, carefully cut from the issue reporting on the day's events. He hadn't gone himself. *That's a young man's game,* he would have said, something like that. But he had read the reports avidly, pausing to read some aloud to Keith and his mother, licking his lips as though he could taste the blood himself.

Keith looked up at the photograph of Mosley, his tiny handlebar moustache, a slightly ill-fitting suit. Beside it, there was a photograph of Jack in his uniform, beaming proudly. Sometimes, Keith looked at the picture and wondered if there was some hint of what was coming in his brother's eyes. But how could there be? None of them had had the slightest idea.

'Dad?'

The newspaper moved, and Keith instinctively flinched and took a step back; old wounds reopening.

'You're back then?'

'Yes. I'm – I'm sorry.' Why had he said that? 'I mean, sorry for all the trouble it's caused.'

He stood up slowly, peering at Keith over his spectacles. He was wearing a grey double-breasted suit; he hadn't worked for years, but he stuck rigorously to his routines nonetheless. 'You'll want to apologise to the kiddies you lost, not to me.'

'Yes.'

'What?'

'Yes, sir.'

'A tragedy.' He shook his head. 'Though, most of them likely to be gunned down in a few years anyway, if this lot don't get a grip.' He waved his copy of *Action* in the air. Keith could just make out the headline, 'To Hell With Government Liars', above the fold.

'I told him about the police.' His mother had carried in a plate of biscuits. 'Coming round here, asking after him.'

'What did you say to them?' Keith asked, suddenly afraid.

'What do you think we said?' his father spat. 'We'd heard nothing from you, we didn't know where you were.'

'For all we knew you might have been dead in that snowstorm!'

'There were newspaper reports, Mum.'

'Expecting his mother to read about it in the papers,' she exclaimed. 'The papers!'

'Cowardly, that's what it is. You're a bloody coward, Keith Roger Hughes.'

'That's enough now,' his mother said softly, and Keith knew what was coming, just as she did. His father's fingers were flexing, and Keith backed away towards the door; he wasn't a child any more.

Up in his room, he dropped his bag on his bed and sat down, running his fingers along the quilt which had been there since he was a child. Jack's bed was made up too, identical to his. He could hear the muffled sounds of his father's raised voice, his mother's pleading. But for Jack's absence everything felt exactly the same: the room, the dust motes hanging in the air, the way he tried to breathe quietly, tried to calm himself down as the fear rose in his stomach. When the shouting didn't stop he gave in to instinct and pulled a chair over to the window, opened the sash and climbed up, leaning out into the cold, filthy air.

It was harder to pull himself onto the roof without Jack; they had always helped each other. When he reached out his arms, he expected to have to strain to make contact with the guttering, forgetting his arms were longer now, his body capable of strength that he hadn't known back then. *Reach your arms up,* he heard the doctor from his conscription examination saying. *Over your head, like this. Mobility good.*

Gripping the edge of the tiles he lifted himself up onto the sloping roof and slid down to the valley between each apex. The sun had sunk behind the house and he shivered, wishing he'd thought to put his coat on before climbing out. In the old days he and Jack had kept things up here: blankets and magazines, sometimes half a pound of toffee, wrapped in a tarpaulin they'd borrowed from a neighbour, telling him it was for a fishing trip. When their father had come back half-cut, or they'd sensed his temper rising, this was where they'd hidden themselves, sometimes for hours, sometimes until the first hint of daylight had appeared over the rooftops and the birds had begun their screeching.

He reached into his pocket for the medal, rubbing his forefinger and thumb against it. What would she be doing tonight? He pictured her sitting at the kitchen table, a stack of newspapers in front of her. No note from him; he'd lost his nerve in the end, hadn't been able to think of a single word. And what about him? The boy standing in the doorway. They'd sprung apart as soon as they'd seen him there, and the boy had stood still for a moment, eyes wide, and all Keith had wanted was for him to yell, scream, anything but that silent, accusatory stare. The way Clayton had looked at him, on that long, tedious journey to Freiburg. The way Keith had caught Clayton's eye when he least expected to, and felt the boy's disgust radiating from him, until he began to fear it would be impossible for everyone else not to see it too.

They were talking about the tunnels beneath the mountain now; he'd read rumours in newspapers that they were being searched, that there was a maze of underworld passages in which a boy might lose himself. He tried to remember what he'd said to Clayton, those last words shouted through the storm. *You go on ahead. The others are waiting for you.* And then, opening his eyes to that woman's face peering over him. *We need to know if there's anyone else out there. We have to know if we should go back.* What had he said back to her? He'd known, he must have known – he couldn't have known, he told himself. The cold, the shock, the dark.

He leant back against the tiles, trying to banish the thought of Clayton from his mind. He thought instead of his brother. The last time they'd sat out on the roof like this was just before Jack had been sent out. Keith, still too young to follow him, could remember feeling excitement alongside the fear, his whole body fidgeting and animated, his fingers flexing as though he were the one about to hold a gun.

Do you think you'll kill anyone?

Of course, Jack had said, *of course, isn't that the point, after all?*

The horror of the idea, the thrill of it, had flashed through Keith's mind in a rush. Would he really? Could he? And what would he do, when his own time came? Slowly, he had raised his hands, leaned forward on the rooftop and squinted at some imaginary enemy below them, holding his breath, his whole body still until, with a quick puff from his nostrils which tinged the cold air around them like smoke, he had let the bullet fly.

Part Three

Chapter Sixteen

By the time Hilde went out searching again, nearly a week had passed. She hadn't meant to leave it so long – hadn't imagined the boy could be missing for so long – but the farm had consumed nearly every hour of the day, leaving her only the evenings which, despite the thaw, were still bitter and dark.

She went out early, before most of the village was awake. The sun was bright, warming the back of her neck as she climbed the slopes behind the house to the ridge that ran around the village on three sides, sheltering it against the mountainside. She turned to look back across the valley, seeing no sign of the line of figures that had been sweeping across it for days now. For most of the village, enthusiasm for the search was beginning to fade; the drama of the missing child had been replaced with the excitement of newspaper reporters, some from as far away as England, interviewing and snapping photographs, traipsing through the village as its inhabitants peered at them through shutters, or followed at their heels. Those who had come from England spoke very little German; their conversations were brief and awkward, barely more than an exchange of uncomfortable silences and staccato bursts of tense laughter.

Hilde tried to ignore the reporters; it felt ghoulish, picking over the story before they even knew how it would end. The official search party had dwindled in size until only the most determined were left, five or six men led by Hans Huber, who went out at odd hours of the day and returned with grim faces. They didn't invite Hilde to join them.

She tried as far as she could to copy the route they'd taken on the night of the rescue, remembering the huddled figures they'd found clinging to each other, the piles of clothing and belongings, half buried in the snow. As she walked, she kept one eye out for anything Anna might be able to use for her concoctions – pine cones, wild garlic, chickweed – gathering it up and filling her pockets.

What was she looking for? She had dreams where, on a day like this, she would duck beneath a branch, wander into a clearing, and the boy would be right there, sitting in front of her, smiling up at her as though he was expecting her. More likely, she knew, he'd be found at the bottom of a cliff, in a river, a cave, his body broken and unrecognisable. She preferred her imaginary scene. It was the way she thought about her father: not dead, not transfigured, just temporarily somewhere else, somewhere she would eventually stumble upon and there he'd be, smiling up at her.

She was high above the village now, climbing the ridge that led to the summit, pushing her way through thick pine branches, their leaves crunching underfoot. It was some distance from where they had found the children that night, and she was on the point of turning back when a flash of something bright caught her eye. She looked up; the sun was streaming through the pine leaves, casting a green-gold pattern across the sky. Was that the glimmer of green she had seen? She strained her eyes, and saw something moving in the trees. Carefully, testing each branch with her weight as she climbed, she hauled herself up into the tree, reaching up until her fingers caught hold of a piece of fabric, hanging like lichen from one of the branches. She slid back down and held it out in front of her. It was a scarf, matted with mud and damp. She ran her fingers along the fabric and found a label, stitched into one corner. A name had been written on it in ink, long since blurred by snow and rain.

By the time she returned, the scarf stuffed in her pocket with the treasures she'd brought back for Anna, the village was awake and busy with life; carts rattled through the uneven streets and a few people gathered together in the square. No one met Hilde's eyes as she passed among them; she was bad luck, an ill-fated charm. Two parents gone and a dwindling farm, and doing nothing to help herself either. To associate with her was to risk bringing all that bad fortune down upon yourself.

'Is that you, Hilde?' Anna's voice sailed in from the kitchen as she opened the front door.

'It's me. Is that Fritz in there with you?' She could hear the sound of farm tools being sharpened by the open side door. He uttered a monosyllabic greeting in reply, as Hilde bent to pick up the newspapers which had been pushed beneath the door.

She spread them out on the table in the *Stube*. Their usual *Freiburger Zeitung* bore a photograph on its front page of the inside of a small chapel, adorned with a British flag and a swastika, side by side. Four wooden coffins were lined up beneath the flags, and boys in Hitler Youth uniforms stood solemnly alongside them, their faces grave. The headline read 'Hitler Youth stand vigil over fallen English comrades'. Alongside it was a photograph of the boys and their teacher, standing outside a building in Freiburg, ready for the climb. She leaned closer; one of the children, the one still missing, had been marked out in the photograph. Most of the children looked as though they were dressed for a summer picnic; only this one, Cyril Clayton, had a scarf around his neck.

She turned the page; there was a spread covering the upcoming Olympic games, full of images of youthful Germans in the midst of running, throwing javelins or holding medals aloft. On the next page, she read about a woman in Freiburg who was being recognised for giving birth to her eighth child. A photograph showed her beaming with joy, three children gathered around her. 'Frau Meinlinger has borne eight healthy Aryan children in as many years: a credit to the German nation.' Hilde stared at the photograph, at the children who ranged from a tiny baby to a little boy dressed in the uniform of the Hitler Youth. Motherhood. She tried to imagine it, waiting for the twinge she was supposed to feel, the inescapable, inevitable pull at her heart.

There was a flyer with the paper, a heading which proclaimed, in bold letters, 'German Mothers, German Children'. The flyer bore details of a Women's League, promising classes for prospective brides and mothers, tutorials on how to make butter, bread, how to mend clothes. Had Reiner pushed it under the door? More likely Hans Huber, she thought; hadn't Fritz said he was trying to establish a local branch of the Party? She looked at the flyer again, then up at the walls of her farmhouse, still standing. She'd begun to feel as though they were doomed to fail, that there was no possible way they could continue this life without Hilde acquiescing to marriage, then children, additional pairs of hands. And yet, she thought, smiling slightly, there were women in Germany who required tutorials on how to make bread.

The third item was a copy of *Der Stürmer*. Hilde took a step back. Who had delivered it? The front page of the paper bore a lurid caricature of a group of Jewish men, their features exaggerated and grotesque; her stomach lurched. The last time she'd seen a copy of the paper was two years ago, and she could still remember the image on its cover. Two Jewish men holding up a bowl, into which the blood of children was draining. It had been so shocking that somehow everyone in the village had seen a copy; at the inn, Gertrud had been so furious she had burned it in the fireplace in front of them all. She remembered a story they'd broadcast on the radio, not long after the elections. *They collect the blood of children, bake it into their bread.* She thought of the missing English boy, the newspaper reports, the way they seemed to delight in the mystery of it all, the suspicion, the veiled accusations, the fear in her neighbours' eyes. Was this why the newspaper had been delivered to them?

On the radio, she'd heard men from the Party saying Jews were no longer citizens. There had been laws passed that forbade them from marrying non-Jews, from working for the government, even from flying the Party flag. *German blood must be protected.* She thought of her father that night in their room, holding them close. *Remember you're no better than anyone else. No worse, either.*

'What are you doing in there?' Anna shouted through to her from the kitchen. Quickly, Hilde tore the paper into sheets and pushed it with the flyer into the box by the stove with the rest of the kindling.

'I brought you these,' she said, emptying her pockets onto the kitchen table.

Anna was at the table, plucking the carcass of a chicken she'd slaughtered that morning; Hilde looked away as one dull, glassy eye met hers. Leaving the chicken, Anna picked through the spoils, exclaiming over the chickweed and the garlic, carefully arranging them in the jars she kept on a shelf by the stove.

'And I found this.' Hilde held out the scarf to Fritz, who turned it over in his hands. 'Well?'

Fritz shrugged. 'It's just a scarf.'

'A child's scarf – it might have been his! That boy—'

'You want it to be. There's no reason it should be, Hilde.'

'He's wearing a scarf in the photograph, look.' She held out the copy of the *Freiburger Zeitung*. 'This one must have been lost after the storm, or it wouldn't still be there. I found it on a tree branch, it would have been blown down.'

'That doesn't follow.'

'Why are you so determined he won't be found?'

Fritz sighed. 'I want him to be found, of course I do. I just think it might be safer for us to stay out of it.'

'What on earth do you mean?'

A sharp note rang through the air as Fritz, saying nothing, ran a blade along the scythe. Anna had settled herself at his feet, leaning her head back against his knees the way she used to do with their father when she was a child. Hilde stood in the doorway, feeling suddenly alone.

'Do you think he's been taken?' Anna said, looking up at Fritz. 'By the mountain king, I mean.'

Fritz smiled. 'You're too old to believe in fairy stories, Anna Meyer.'

'That's not true. You believe in them, don't you?'

'Do I?'

Anna grinned. 'Yes, you do. You used to tell me all sorts of stories. And you keep that old tin soldier in your pocket.'

'Georg? He isn't a fairy story.'

'Isn't he?'

'You know he isn't.'

Anna sat up, staring up at him expectantly, waiting for the story they'd heard so many times before. Fritz let out a long sigh, leaning back in his chair.

'He was my best friend in the war,' he began, as Hilde slid into a chair to listen too. 'One day, we were trapped in a dugout, just the two of us. I'd been hit by shrapnel, and things were looking pretty bad. All we had was a box of grenades and a rifle with two shots left. He took the rifle, left me with the grenades and ran across an open field to find help.'

'And you were saved?'

Fritz nodded, smiling. 'I was. They shot him twice while he was running, but he made it. God knows how.'

'And then he—'

'Died. Two days later, in a field hospital.'

'He was a hero.'

'Yes, he was.'

'And he gave you—'

'Yes, he gave me this.' Fritz reached into his pocket and took out the tiny tin soldier, holding it out to them. 'I keep it with me, to remember him. The bravest man I ever met. Apart from your father, of course,' he added quickly, smiling up at Hilde in the doorway.

'Our father wasn't brave,' Anna said, in a bitter, angry voice.

Hilde felt stung. 'He was, Anna,' she said. 'Why do you say that?'

'Fritz knows,' she said coldly.

Hilde turned to him, but he was still staring at the tin soldier, cradled in his palm.

'Anna, what are you talking about? He fought in the war too. Doesn't that make him brave?'

Their parents' story had been told and retold as many times as Fritz's tales of the war. Walter Meyer, invalided to Todtnauberg, who had met Hannah Hermann on her way to the market. Eventually he had been declared too injured to return to the war – he had walked with a limp all Hilde's life – and the two of them had settled in Hofsgrund. Hilde had been told the story so many times it had become a fairy tale itself, as though it was always meant to happen, he was always meant to be shot in his leg, always meant to meet a woman on the road from Todtnauberg, as though she and Anna had always been meant to be born. It was easier to think about life that way, less a series of random chances, more a pattern: complex, intricate, destined to be followed. Who was Anna, to question that now?

But Anna only shrugged and, taking up a carving knife, began hacking at the chicken carcass in strong, determined strokes, the last of its feathers flying up around her face.

Hilde looked down at the scarf in her hands. The men from Freiburg who had questioned her were long gone, and the nearest police were in Todtnau. The investigation seemed at an end; only Hans and his search party were still half-heartedly making their way out every day.

'Anna,' she said, deciding. 'Do you have any of that headache medicine?'

'Of course.' Setting the knife aside, Anna reached into a dawer and handed her a small glass vial.

The Hubers' farmhouse was at the other end of the village, close to the inn. Hilde hadn't visited since she was a child; she gave the Hubers a wide berth, especially now that Hans was a Party member. But when Alice Huber, a large, red-cheeked woman with smiling eyes, came to the door, Hilde remembered her kindness; she'd brought them food and supplies after their father had died, and again when they lost their mother. She'd sent Paul to help with the farm. As Alice drew her inside and put an arm around her shoulders, Hilde wondered if she'd been right to stay away for so long. Then she remembered Paul, and Hans' ideas about Anna, and felt her fingers clench around the glass bottle in her pocket.

'Is Hans here?' she asked Alice.

'Of course, he's in the *Stube*. Come in – it's been too long, Hilde, too long.'

The rest of the Hubers – Hans, Paul and his three younger sisters – were gathered around the table playing cards. Hilde stood in the doorway, watching as Alice rejoined them, remembering the long, cold nights when her parents would teach her and Anna card games, or read to them from books of fairy tales as the wind rose outside. She felt a longing to be part of a family again, so sharp she had to turn away from them and blink away tears.

Hans came over to her.

'I brought Anna's headache cure,' she said, holding out the vial.

'Oh, I thought—' Alice began, but Hans interrupted her.

'Thank you, Hilde. That's a kind thought.' He slipped it into his pocket.

'Could I speak to you about something else?'

'Of course. We can go into the kitchen, if you like.'

They sat on either side of the fire, the sound of the children's card game filtering through the open door as Hilde handed him the scarf, watching as he inspected it closely.

'I found it in the branches of a tree. I thought – well, it can't have been there before the storm.'

'No, I see that.'

'It was far away from where we found them that night. If you're still searching, perhaps...' She trailed off, waiting for Hans to say something. For a long moment, they were silent. Then Hans looked up.

'We aren't still searching, Hilde,' he said simply. 'We're calling it off.'

'What?'

Hans shook his head. 'He can't possibly have survived for this long.'

'How can you be so sure? You said yourself – the tunnels—'

'We've spent nearly a week searching the tunnels.'

'We can't just abandon him!'

Hans sighed heavily. 'There are other things to focus on.'

She stared at him. 'What do you mean?'

'Nothing. Nothing in particular.'

'The newspapermen are still here. They must think there's hope.'

Hans frowned. He leaned forward, handing the scarf back to her. 'It was good of you to go out looking for him, Hilde. It's appreciated. And this – even if it did belong to the boy, I don't see how it helps us now.'

She didn't know what to say. All she could think of was her father – it had been nearly two years, and she still hadn't given up, not entirely. How could they give up on Cyril Clayton, when so little time had gone by?

On her way out, she glanced at a poster hanging in the hallway. 'Unhealthy genes enter a village', the bold print read, and beneath it was a diagram, set out like a family tree, a series of faces growing increasingly infirm with the introduction of one pale-faced, sickly-looking member, whose descendants mingled until each one of them was blighted. She looked back into the *Stube*, where the children still sat around the table with Alice, laughing and smacking their hands on the piles of cards. Then she thought of Anna, back in their own *Stube*. The newspapers that had been slid under their door, the flyer, 'German Mothers, German Children'. She shut the door behind her and stood for a moment on the steps outside, breathing heavily in the chill night air.

Chapter Seventeen

A blinding light flashed in Sylvia's eyes. She blinked, the insides of her eyelids briefly seared.

'Just one more,' someone murmured, and she felt the tickle of a powder puff on her face, fingers pressing into her cheeks.

'Do we have to—'

'Nearly done.' She heard Ronald's voice beside her.

'Open.'

She opened her mouth as someone leaned closer.

'We'll lead with a quote, I think,' she heard Ronald mumbling to someone else. 'Heartbreak and pride, the usual sort of thing. We'll get a spread, if we're lucky.'

She began asking about the article, about what it would say about Cyril, then felt fingers rubbing against her lips, silencing her. The sickly scent of vanilla and coconut clouded around them.

'Alright,' the make-up artist said, her tone clipped and distant. 'I'm ready. That's enough.'

She'd forgotten about the photographer. She'd agreed to everything Ronald had said without really listening; all that mattered was Cyril, making sure his face was known, his name was still in print, still remembered. Whatever it took, she'd told herself, but she hadn't imagined she would need to be packaged up herself, presented alongside him, mournful and elegant, wearing make-up she couldn't ever have afforded, feeling like a stranger to herself.

Ronald was in front of her now, leaning in close. 'You alright, Sylvia?'

'I'm fine. There's something else I wanted to tell you.'

'The article's already written.'

'Yes, I know, but I found something. Cyril, he wrote me a card—'

'Sylvia.' Ronald put a hand on her shoulder and smiled at her; it was a strange, affected smile, as though she were a child or an invalid. 'You don't have to worry about anything,' he said slowly. 'We've got plenty of material for the article. Let us take care of it, alright?'

She nodded mutely, watching the photographer and the make-up artist packing up their equipment, sitting in silence as they closed the door behind them.

The policeman who'd visited the day after it happened had left a card; as soon as the newspaper people had gone, Sylvia took it to the telephone box at the end of the street. By the time the call connected, her fingers were shaking.

'I need to speak to...' She checked the card. 'Sergeant Cooper. It's very urgent.'

There was a long pause, during which she thought she could hear the sounds of a busy office, typewriters and the murmur of voices. When a voice sounded over the hum, it was small and far away.

'It's Sylvia Clayton.' She paused. 'Cyril's mother.'

'Of course. How can I help?'

She leaned her forehead against the glass of the telephone box. She hadn't prepared what she was going to say. The postcard was in her pocket; by now she had the words memorised, could hear them in Cyril's voice, imagining the mountain, the impending storm looming over him.

'I found something. A postcard from Cyril.'

There was a pause. 'Oh yes?' Did he sound weary, or was it simply the effect of the line, the faded tone of his voice?

'He knew there would be a storm. The teacher – Hughes – Cyril says so, quite clearly. He knew, and he took them on the hike anyway.'

She waited for a reply, trying to picture him – she could barely remember his features, anything about him at all – holding the telephone to his ear, patiently waiting for her to continue. Was he expecting more? Wasn't this enough?

'I'm saying he put them at risk. Deliberately. Or – negligently – I don't know the right words. But he needs to be – I don't know what you call it. Investigated, I suppose. Arrested,' she added, thinking of him being marched into a prison van, handcuffed, his head bowed low. Standing in a dock, twelve pairs of eyes assessing him. 'He killed four children,' she added, as if she hadn't already made herself clear. 'He lost my son.'

At the other end of the line, Sergeant Cooper sighed a heavy sigh. 'We're not investigating Mr Hughes, Sylvia.'

'Well, I'm asking you to.' She could hear her sister Julia's voice as she said it. It was the sort of demand Julia would make without thinking; I want it to be so, therefore it will be.

'There isn't – we haven't – this is a matter for the German authorities.'

'How on earth do you expect me to contact the German authorities?'

'I don't. I'm sorry, Sylvia, there's nothing I can do for you. We'll contact you, of course, if there's any news about the search.'

'I want him arrested.' She could hear the slight tremor in her voice. How could she expect him to take her seriously, when she sounded so weak, so on edge? 'It's a crime, what he's done. That's obvious.'

'I'm sorry.' She thought of the moment he'd put his hand on her arm, the day they'd come to the house. Had it been real, that expression of feeling? Had he simply been playing a part? 'If you like,' he said wearily, 'I can take down the information. If it ever... becomes relevant. To an investigation.'

'So you can file it in a cabinet somewhere? I won't go away, you know.'

'Look, Sylvia, I have to go. We'll be in touch if there's any news.'

She hung up the receiver and stood still for a moment, watching as cars and bicycles edged their way past the telephone booth. She thought of the banner she'd made with Ruby for the anti-war march. 'I could lose my son'. Imagined painting another, holding it up high, attaching it to the side of her house, or printing it on flyers to scatter throughout the city. 'Keith Hughes lost my son. Keith Hughes: murderer.'

She took the bus to the laboratory. She'd agreed with Eileen that for a few days she would go in after hours, instead of first thing, without telling her the reason why. She had a feeling Eileen would disapprove of the publicity. She imagined her pressing her lips together and declaring, like Sylvia's mother might, that Sylvia was making an exhibition of herself.

After a few stops a woman sat down opposite her with a child on her knees: a boy of three of four years old who was staring out of the soot-smeared windows with his hands pressed up against the glass. Sylvia watched as he waved to people on the street, shifting his body a little so that he could lean his face closer to the window. A pain rose up in her chest so acute she had to stand up and move away. When she looked back, the mother was eyeing her suspiciously, drawing her arms more tightly around her little boy, and Sylvia wondered if somehow what had happened was written on her face. *It's not my fault,* she wanted to scream back to the woman, to everyone on the bus, to the street outside. *I didn't mean to, please, I want him back.*

She'd expected to find the building empty, but as she passed through the serology laboratory she recognised a single figure sitting at one of the long benches. The room felt damp and cold; Dieter was bent over a microscope, a scarf around his neck. He looked up, startled, as she passed him.

'Sorry. I thought you heard me come in.'

He smiled at her. 'We haven't scared you off then?'

She shook her head.

'Are you alright? You seem—'

He was staring at her so closely she had to turn away, pressing her nails into her palms. She didn't want kindness, not here. She just needed to get through the day.

She heard him shuffling back to his work, the *click click* of the microscope as he focused.

'What are you working on?' She thought of the book in the director's office, the bust of Darwin, the answers she hadn't been able to find. *Your son isn't just blood and bones.*

'Do you want to look?' He indicated the microscope.

'I should really get on.'

'Come on. Everyone's left, they won't know.'

Tentatively, Sylvia bent forwards and squinted, waiting for the image through the lens to resolve itself. She stood again, turning to him.

'What is it?'

'Blood. It's from a patient at the hospital.'

'But it's so…' She leaned forwards again to look. The dish under the microscope was covered in tiny dark spots, like seeds scattered across its surface.

'It's agglutinated. Clumped. It clumps up when something gets added to it and they don't get along.'

'What did you add to it?'

'In this case? Blood from the rabbits.'

She stared at him. 'Why on earth would you want to do that?'

Dieter sighed, and she knew what he was thinking. *It's complicated, it takes time to explain.*

'I used to be a nurse,' she said, aware of the defensive tone in her voice.

'Well, you know about blood types then – A, B, O, all that.'

She nodded.

'It turns out there's more of them – we don't know how many. The one I'm looking for, we call MN.'

'How do you look for it?'

'Well, we've inoculated the rabbits with human blood. Then we split the rabbit blood – take out the red cells, end up with just the antibodies and the plasma. Then the real fun begins.' He winked at her. 'We pop the rabbit serum – that's the bit with the antibodies – back into a human sample, and see what happens.'

Sylvia stared at the slide again. She'd never seen agglutination up close before, but she knew what it meant. That boy in the field hospital, the way he'd gripped her hand. The wrong blood in the wrong arm – she didn't know what sort of blood that boy had had, or what sort was in her syringe. Only that they hadn't been the same, and his body had filled with those tiny seeds, flooding his veins.

'Now it's clumping up,' Dieter said, scribbling a note on his pad, 'that means our chap's an M.'

'But what does it matter what type of blood he has?'

'Oh, it doesn't matter on its own. Our man's suffering from a mental disease, that's what's important. And even then, he doesn't matter on his own. What really matters is testing enough of them. Then we might see if there's some link between the disease and the blood. Say they all come out M, something like that.'

'Then what?'

He sat back, staring up at the ceiling and stretching out his arms, rolling his neck. 'That's not really my business. I just test the blood, tell them what I find. The director, all those men in committees and medical councils, they decide what to do with it all. They want a way to map it all out – illness, disease, weaknesses, all that. For years we didn't know where to look. Then we found out about the blood. It's inherited, you see. Those types come from your parents' blood, and their parents' blood. It's all linked, just like the diseases are linked.'

'But you said...' She hesitated.

'What?'

'The other day, in the director's office. You said people aren't just blood and bones.'

'Well, of course that's true. But the science is still so young. Who knows what links we might find?'

She felt disappointed, as though he'd taken away some of her hope. It was silly, she knew, to connect Cyril with theories, especially those which hadn't even been proven. But wasn't that what the papers were doing every day? 'So anything can be inherited?' she pressed. 'Not just physical disease? Anything at all?'

Dieter shrugged. 'Who knows what's controlled by genetics? That's what they think, anyway. Some of them think we could find a link to alcoholism – it does seem to run in families, after all.'

'How would finding the link change anything?'

'Like I said—'

'Not your department.'

But she thought of Ruby, her flyers, the sterilisation bill, the woman at the Guild meeting with her petition. She felt a sudden chill at the idea of it; some committee assessing Arthur, assessing her. Declaring them unfit. Declaring Cyril... But it was just research, she reminded herself. Weren't they just trying to understand people better?

'And you learned this in Germany?'

'They're miles ahead over there. Your lot had no idea, ten years ago. You're still catching up.'

'And you're helping? That's why you came?'

'Not exactly.'

He reached into his jacket and pulled out a photograph, handing it to her. It was blurred and unfocused: a man standing in front of a shop window filled with stacks of books. He wore glasses and a smartly tailored suit, and was staring uncomfortably into the camera lens with arched brows and a sceptical smile.

'My father,' Dieter said. 'I haven't been able to get him out yet.'

'Out?'

'He's still in Berlin. I got over here through this work, but it's not so easy for him.'

It took a few seconds for Sylvia to understand, and when she did she felt foolish. What had he said, that day in the director's office? *I'm a fugitive.* She'd thought at the time he'd just been making a joke she hadn't understood.

'It's ironic, really, that he's the one left behind. I'm not even a practising Jew, I suppose I might have been alright.' He took the photograph back from her and stared at it for a moment before replacing it in his pocket. 'He's very devout.'

'It's really that bad over there?'

He looked at her, and she found it hard to read the expression in his eyes. *I read the papers,* she wanted to say, *I do my best. It's so hard to know what's true any more.*

'It might be,' he said.

She looked harder at the face in the photograph, trying to see Dieter in his eyes. 'What will happen to him?'

'I don't know. His shop – that's his bookshop, in the picture – it's been boycotted a few times. Looted. But nothing worse than that. I don't even know if he'd come, if we could get a visa for him.'

'What will you do?'

He shrugged, bending again to his work. 'Hope it all blows over, I suppose.'

Chapter Eighteen

'Will you smoke, Keith?'

The headmaster was sitting back in his chair, a pipe in its rest in front of him. Keith hesitated in the doorway, unsure what to say. He had never been invited to smoke in the school before. Certainly not in the headmaster's office. He shook his head dumbly.

'Alright. Sit down then.'

There was an uncomfortable silence. Keith wondered if he was supposed to say something; perhaps offer up an apology, some sort of explanation. He would lose his job, that was clear, and perhaps after all it was for the best. The thought of coming back to the school every day, seeing the empty chairs in his class—

'How are you?'

'Fine, sir.'

'Recovered?'

'Wasn't anything serious, sir. Just the cold. A bit of shock.'

'To be expected. I know all about that, God knows.'

'Of course, sir.'

'I wanted you to hear it from me first, Keith.' He drew in a deep breath. 'There's going to be an inquiry.'

Keith stared at him, at a loss for what to say. What did Franklin mean, an inquiry? All he could see were images of a trial, the headmaster wearing a white wig, the school governors lined up like a jury. Parents, glaring at him where he sat in a dock.

'I'm sorry, Keith. There's no avoiding it.'

'Yes. I mean, I understand, sir.'

Keith looked around the room, taking in the books which lined every inch of the walls, their glossy spines plump and shining in the light from the window. It would be drawn out then, this firing. The inquiry first, and then – what? Newspaper articles, the assassination of his character. But of course, they were saying another war was coming. Perhaps, in the end, that was a mercy. It would eclipse his own shame, make it seem petty and small in comparison.

'I need to know, Keith, that you've told me everything.'

'How do you mean, sir?'

'There will be press interest, of course.'

'Naturally.'

'I don't want there to be any surprises. For the school.'

'What sort of surprises?'

Franklin leaned suddenly forward, his face eager, his eyes wide and questioning. 'No one understands how it can have happened, Keith. I mean – how – what – how did it happen?'

Keith looked away. He'd explained so many times, to so many different people. Something in his explanation never seemed to convince them; they continued to ask, over and over, as though he didn't know his own mind. And now this inquiry, and they would ask him all over again, and what would he tell them? He'd tried, ever since he'd come back, not to think about that night on the mountain, to press it to the back of his mind, and why should he have to dredge it all up, after all? He was in shock – he must be, after what he'd been through. A kind of shell shock, like all those men after the war who'd had to go into sanatoriums. Some of them had never come out, and perhaps that was because people kept on at them, bullying them into thinking too much about the things they couldn't change.

He looked up. The headmaster was still staring at him, expectant.

'I suppose,' he began. 'I suppose I thought it was safer to go on than to turn back.'

Franklin frowned at him. 'But the storm, Keith. The dark – their *clothing*.'

'With respect, sir, their clothing wasn't my affair. The school—'

'Yes, of course.' Franklin turned his gaze away, staring blankly out of the window. 'That will all be gone into,' he said softly.

'At the inquiry.'

'Exactly. At the inquiry.'

There was a long silence. Eventually the headmaster turned back to the room, taking in a deep breath as though returning himself from somewhere distant.

'And what about these Germans?' he said.

'Germans, sir?'

'Yes, the boys who helped with the rescue. I've had a letter from someone over there. Something or other Runde – the local youth group. He says – wait a moment…' He pulled a letter from a large pile at his elbow. 'He says he is happy that the boys of the Third Reich were able to save so many of ours, and he believes those who died did so for the cause of furthering the understanding between our two nations.' He looked up. 'Well, what do you make of that?'

Keith shook his head. 'There weren't any German boys, sir. Only the men and women from the village.'

'You're sure of that?'

'Absolutely.'

Franklin shook his head, staring at the letter in his hand. 'I'll have to reply to this,' he said. 'It could be very awkward, if… if…' He frowned, seeming to forget Keith was sitting opposite him until he stood up to leave.

On his way out of the school Keith paused in front of the trophy cabinet in the main corridor, his eyes running over the names etched into silver plates and cups, the photographs of smiling boys holding cricket bats, polo mallets, tennis racquets. At the edge of the bottom shelf, half obscured by more recent triumphs, was a photograph in a wooden frame, a boy posing with a cricket bat, squinting into the sun, a faint grin on his face. 'Jack Hughes', the gold lettering on the frame read. 'Captained the first eleven to three interschool-victories, 1914–16.' Jack's name was on three of the silver cups too; fencing, boxing, swimming. They'd said he would play for England at Lord's one day. He remembered Jack, one night on the roof, swinging his bat and sailing a pebble all the way over to next door's back garden. *I'll do it to him one day, Keith. I'll swing it right in his face, you'll see.* Keith raised a hand and pressed it against the glass.

Outside, London was patterned with pools of sunlight, the last remnants of the previous night's storm no more than patches of rainwater warming in the sun. Keith made a path through them towards the bus stop, feeling the heat on the back of his neck, the headmaster's words following him from the school, ringing in his ears. *I don't want there to be any surprises.*

Surprises. He thought of the man they'd encountered on the road from Freiburg that day, who'd been so insistent they go back. He wished now he knew who that man was, how to ensure no one else knew about him. Would the boys say anything? Probably not, he thought, they hadn't heard any of their conversation. To them, he'd just been a German peasant, pausing to pass the time of day. And then there was the woman at the inn, after they'd been rescued. She'd asked him, over and over, if there were any more boys out there. And there was something else too, something he'd felt sure he'd whispered to her when she found him in the snow, half mad with cold and exhaustion. What had he been thinking? He couldn't take it back now, and what if she'd heard him, what if she'd told someone?

His thoughts were interrupted by someone tugging at his arm. He turned to find a young, smartly dressed woman at his side, smiling brightly. A white poppy was pinned to her jacket and a satchel, heavy with papers, bounced at her hip. Keith blinked at her as she pressed a leaflet into his hand. 'PEACE PLEDGE' was printed in bold writing across the top, and beneath that, 'SIGN TODAY'.

'What's this?'

'You tell the government,' she said fiercely, 'when the war comes, you'll refuse to fight.'

Keith stepped back, alarmed. 'What war?'

'All you have to do is sign the paper and send it to them – the address is already printed, look.' She turned the paper over. 'If enough of you do it, they won't have a choice. They'll have no one to send.'

'I'm not a coward.'

'It's not cowardice,' she said quickly, 'It's bravery, standing up for what you believe in. No one can call you a coward for doing that. It's *principled*.'

'I...'

'Another generation of young men, lost to the altar of war. And what would be the point of it all?'

He stared at her. She meant it, he could tell. He could remember feeling the same, last time all the talk had been of a coming war, of the destruction and chaos that would come with it. It had been his brother who'd convinced him otherwise. Jack had been longing for a war to fight his whole life, before he'd even known what war meant. He'd spent his life protecting Keith, their mother, and then the opportunity had come to protect the whole world. How could he have turned it down?

'What if there's another conscription?' he said, considering whether to take out the medal and wave it in her face. 'What if men don't have a choice? You're asking them to break the law?'

People in the street were beginning to look over at them now, no doubt wondering if they ought to intervene.

'It's not cowardice,' she said stubbornly, pushing the

leaflet back into her satchel. 'It's the bravest thing there is, to defy the law for your own principles.'

He watched her walking away, thinking of Jack, one night on the roof, talking excitedly of a war that hadn't even begun yet. It was a clear, bitingly cold night, fierce with stars. Their father had come back particularly late and been particularly brutal, and they'd climbed out as soon as they'd heard him on the stairs. Never mind that it was November, never mind that they had examinations the next day.

The tiles were icy as they slid themselves down into the valley between the rooftops.

'You'd really go?' Keith had asked, wide-eyed.

'Wouldn't you? Better than all this.'

'Maybe.' Keith hadn't been able to imagine it. All he knew of war was his picture books and magazines; men on horseback holding long spears, their faces hidden beneath pointed helmets. His father had never been, on account of his heart. That's all Keith knew, some vague allusion his mother had made once to a heart that wasn't strong enough to fight. He'd been beaten, the one time he'd asked about it.

'It's going to be glorious,' Jack had said, wrapping an arm around Keith's shoulders. 'You'll see. It'll be the making of us.'

'I thought this was the making of us.'

Jack pulled him closer. They sat there until they felt sure their father must have gone to bed, and for a while the icy air had seemed a little less bitter, a little less real.

Chapter Nineteen

In the *Stube*, in the half-darkness, Anna was sitting with Gretel, dangling a piece of string in front of her paws. Hilde sat watching them, the green scarf still in her hands. Night was drawing in around them; she thought of the Hubers, gathered together in their *Stube* around a warm fire. The missing child – if he was still out there – shivering somewhere in the dark.

'How is your headache?' Anna said, looking up at her.

'What? I don't have a headache.'

'You asked for the medicine.'

'Oh. It was for Hans. He wanted it for Paul.'

Anna frowned. Beside her Gretel reached out a paw, dabbing ineffectually at her sleeve. 'But I already gave some to Paul.'

'When?'

'He was here. Earlier, when you were out searching.'

They fell silent again. Hilde wanted to say something; wanted to demand to know why Paul Huber had come to her house and no one had told her. She knew that's what her mother would have done. Before she was ill, anyway; she would have driven Paul out with a firm hand and a stern word. How was Hilde failing so badly? And if she couldn't look after Anna, how could she hope to look after her own children, the children which the state told her must, without question, come?

She stood up and went to the window, opening the shutters and looking out at the moonlit street. In the distance she could just make out the lights of the inn, flickering against the grey shadows of the mountains. It would be busy now; newspapermen as well as the locals crowded in the half-light. Gertrud had been exclaiming over the windfall, as though she'd forgotten the cause of it all. Hilde turned back to Anna, who was dozing now, her head tilted backwards, Gretel asleep in her lap. She pulled on her coat and slipped out of the house.

In the inn's main parlour, the air was thick with cloying woodsmoke, mingling with smoke from pipes and cigarettes. A steady hum of chatter dimmed slightly as Hilde stooped under the low doorway. As she approached the bar she felt the eyes of the room following her; women didn't come here often, and hardly ever alone. Even so, amongst the groups of men drinking and playing cards, there was another woman by herself. She was sitting at a table by the fire, a jug of wine at her elbow and a large satchel on the table in front of her. As Hilde watched she scribbled something in a notebook, frowning slightly before taking a sip of her wine. She was perhaps the age her mother would have been now, Hilde thought, but she was dressed in the way she imagined Else in Freiburg – a smart tweed jacket, tan trousers and thick, sturdy boots.

'The holidaymakers are coming early this year,' she said to Gertrud at the bar, but Gertrud only offered her a tight smile in return. 'Are any of the newspapermen still here?'

Gertrud gestured to a small table close to the door, where two men were sitting with their heads bent close together. They were both young, thirty perhaps, and their neat dress and clean fingers would have given them away if Gertrud hadn't already done so. A few men like that had come in the days after the cave-in, and Hilde had occasionally caught sight of them approaching men in the village, notebooks tucked under their arms, or knocking on those doors which had black ribbons hung above them.

'What are you up to, Hilde Meyer?' Gertrud asked with narrowed eyes.

'Nothing,' she said, 'nothing at all. I wanted to tell them what I saw, that's all. I was there that night, wasn't I?'

'You and everyone else in the village.' It was true, almost everyone who was able to had gone out to help that night. Those few who hadn't had begun to claim their own share of the story, until it had become difficult to tell what was real and what wasn't. The way Gertrud said it made Hilde almost question herself. *I really was there,* she wanted to say to Gertrud, *don't you remember? It's not just a story, it's what really happened.*

The two men were deep in conversation; Hilde approached them without giving herself time to question what she would say. They looked up together and one of them, bright blue eyes and a shock of yellow hair, offered her a quizzical smile.

'You're with a newspaper?' she said, hearing the querulous tone in her voice.

She hadn't thought the next part through – should she sit down, should she offer to buy drinks for them? Should she have a drink for herself? She could feel the eyes of the room on her and wondered what they thought she was doing, introducing herself to two strangers, late at night.

'I found something,' she went on. 'On the mountain. I think it belonged to one of the children who got lost.'

The other man, who up until now had been staring fixedly into his drink, raised an eyebrow.

'Do you know what's happening?' She was speaking more quickly now, anxious to get the encounter over with. 'Are they still searching?'

'We're not supposed to talk about it,' the first man said.

'Everyone's talking about it.'

'They'll be packing us off soon enough.'

'You don't think he'll be found?'

There was a long silence. Hilde shifted uncomfortably from one foot to another.

The blonde man was looking up at her, smiling now. 'Look,' he said. 'We've spoken to everyone we need to. But don't go.' He pulled out a chair and waved a hand in the direction of the bar. 'Let us buy you a drink.'

For a moment, she hesitated. Looking over her shoulder, she could see the woman by the fire watching them, her pencil stilled. She felt the rest of the room growing silent, and imagined them all turning towards the three of them, whispering behind their hands. Slowly, she slid into the chair.

'I'm Stefan,' the man said, edging a little closer to her. 'That's Karl.'

Hilde laid the scarf on the table. 'It's too small to be an adult's,' she said. 'And – in the pictures – he's the only one wearing a scarf. The boy who's still missing.'

Stefan took a long sip of his beer. 'You'd be amazed, the artefacts we've been shown,' he said. 'Belt buckles, shoelaces, handkerchiefs. The ice is melting, that's all. It's all coming to the surface.'

'I found it in a tree. Resting on a branch – I don't think it can have been there before the storm. And it wasn't close to where we found the rest of them.'

'Forget about that.' He looked up at Gertrud, who had brought over a glass of water which she set down pointedly in front of Hilde. 'This must be a lonely place to live in.' He put a hand close to Hilde's, their fingers just touching.

'There's something else.' Hilde spoke quickly, but she didn't move her hand away. 'The teacher, that night. He told me all the boys were accounted for.'

'Well, he must have been confused. The cold.'

'I asked him more than once. Once when we were here, in this room. He had time to check, to look around at them. He said they were all here, he didn't say anything about one of them being missing. Doesn't that seem strange?'

'Not particularly.'

'He told me something else as well. When I found him in the snow – I haven't told anyone else.'

'Well?'

'You tell me what you think about that scarf first.'

'Oh, she's making bargains now.'

Stefan grinned at Karl, who still hadn't looked up. Hilde began to feel a creeping sense of shame; her face felt flushed in the heat from the fire. She took a sip of water and felt Stefan's weight shift in his chair, their knees pressing together.

'You haven't told us your name,' he said, and she could smell the tang of his breath, an intimacy which somehow heightened her shame.

'I don't – I can't—'

'Let's take a look at this scarf then.'

'There's something written on it,' she said hoarsely, 'on the label.'

'Yes, look, Karl, she's right.' He held it up close to his face. 'It says, go back to your kitchen.'

Across the room, a group of three men burst into laughter, high and sharp. Hilde felt Stefan's hand on her knee and she wanted to stand, to move away, but something kept her frozen in place as she felt his fingers pressing into her skin. Then a woman's voice behind them, in a heavy accent, spoke sharply.

'You're drunk, Stefan Schulz. Go to bed.'

Someone leaned forward and took the beer mug from Stefan. Hilde looked up; the woman who had been sitting by the fire was standing over them, Stefan's drink in her hand. Stefan stood up, and seemed about to speak before, thinking better of it, he staggered towards the stairs. Hilde watched him go, still feeling the imprint of his fingers on her skin.

'Sorry about him,' the woman said, turning to Hilde. 'Men are pigs. Come and sit with me?'

Hilde wanted to go back to the *Stube* and bury her face in Gretel's fur, forget the boy on the mountain, the newspapermen, the shame which seemed to follow her through the village like a cloud. But the room had stilled now to watch her, and instead of leaving she allowed herself to be led to the table by the fire.

'What's your name?' the woman said as she resumed her seat. 'Mine's Katherine – Kit. Ignore them.' She looked back at Stefan, now sitting alone. 'Nothing to do for days, I think it sends them a little crazy. Well?'

Hilde felt herself relenting. There was a warmth to the woman, an openness, as though they were conspirators together and the rest of the room, the rest of the village, were on the outside. She seemed like someone used to asking for things, to politely giving orders, as though she would usually be found in far more expensive places – the sort of places Hilde imagined Else visiting, dressed in elegant furs and drinking wine from crystal glasses.

'Hilde Meyer,' she said.

Kit held out a hand and they shook, the formality of it making Hilde smile.

'So?' Kit said, sitting back in her chair. 'Tell me about this scarf you found.'

Hilde hesitated. The room was quietening down now, everyone slowly turning back to their drinks as the excitement died away.

'Are you – sorry – on holiday?'

'On holiday! I wish.'

'You're a reporter?'

'Don't look so surprised.'

Hilde hadn't known there were such things as women who worked as journalists; she stared at Kit with a new fascination, taking in the silver locket around her neck, the notebook in front of her filled with scribblings and sketches.

'I came over from England a few weeks ago. Started in Berlin, then thought I'd give Freiburg a go. And now I'm here.'

'Your German is very good.'

'Yes, that's why I came. I thought I might be able to – well, never mind about that. Let me see the scarf.'

Hilde handed it to her and she inspected it with close attention.

'Tell me about the teacher. You said there was something he told you, that night? I was listening in,' she added with a quick wave of her hand. 'Sorry.' She didn't sound sorry at all.

'He told me all the children were found. It wasn't true.'

'You think he lied to you? On purpose?'

Hilde considered. Did she think that? She hadn't really thought about the teacher since it happened; not as a real person, anyway, as someone with anything to lose. If she was wrong, what might happen to him?

'There's going to be an inquiry at the school,' Kit said. 'If what you say is true…'

'It's difficult to say,' she said quickly. 'It was confusing – so many people coming and going, so much noise.'

There was a gust of cold air as the door opened and Hans came in, accompanied by a man in Party uniform. The two of them stood at the bar, Hans' companion surveying the room with hawklike eyes.

'But it could be true?' Kit pressed.

'It could be. It could be. Yes.'

'Can I keep this?' She was already stuffing the scarf into her satchel. 'There was something else, wasn't there?' Kit went on. 'Something else he said, something you were going to tell those men…'

Hilde hesitated. She turned her head slightly and met Hans' eyes. Gertrud was watching them too; it was no good, she thought, talking about anything in public, you could never be sure who was watching and listening. Why should Hans care what she said to this woman, why should the Party care? She was only trying to find out what had happened.

'Who are they?' Kit asked, looking over at the bar.

Hilde shook her head. In the warmth of the fire, the woman's close attention, she felt her courage returning. 'Tomorrow,' she said. 'Meet me here at noon. We can go for a walk, and I'll explain.'

Chapter Twenty

'You read it. I can't.'

Ruby pulled the newspaper across the kitchen table towards her. Now that it was here in front of her, Sylvia didn't want to look; she couldn't bear the thought of seeing Cyril's face in stark black-and-white, the bare facts of what had happened laid out in print. Ruby flicked through the pages, pausing at one and drawing in a sharp breath.

'What is it?'

'Nothing.' Ruby held up a hand. 'Just let me...'

Sylvia watched her eyes dart across the page. When she looked up, Sylvia could tell from her face that something was wrong. 'Let me see.'

'Oh, Sylvia. I'm not sure—'

'It's alright. I know it won't be exactly what – it's so I can get to Germany, Ruby. If this goes well he'll want to do another piece. The paper might send us out there together.'

Ruby tried to stop her, but she pulled the newspaper across the table. Her own face stared back at her, barely recognisable, filling nearly a quarter of the page. Her eyes were staring blankly into the distance and her skin was a cold, pallid shade of powdery white. She looked like a woman from the kind of films they showed at the theatre at the end of her road; a woman who was about to commit a terrible act, or be attacked by a vampire killer. The headline, stark and unforgiving, read 'First she lost her husband: now her son'.

She stared at the page, unable to take in the words. There was no detail about Arthur, other than a brief mention of the stories she'd told about his climbing, about how he had inspired Cyril. Nothing about what had happened to him – just that she was a single mother, the whereabouts of her husband unknown. Unknown – that was almost worse than the truth. The fictions people would be dreaming up, the scenarios they might be imagining. It was what she'd been warned about, but alongside the headline they seemed to be implying his absence was somehow her fault. At the bottom-most corner was the photograph of Cyril; so small, it was barely possible to make out the details of his face. She felt tears rising and blinked hard, trying to take it in.

'Vultures,' Ruby muttered. 'I did try to tell you.'

'I didn't lose them,' she whispered. She felt Ruby's hand on her arm. 'It was him. It was Keith Hughes who lost the children. And Arthur... Ruby, I didn't lose them.'

She felt the newspaper sliding from under her hands as Ruby took it from her and tore it into pieces.

The doorbell sounded just as Ruby was pouring out tea. Sylvia's first thought was that Ronald had come back, eager for a second interview, a further intrusion.

'I'll throw the furniture at him,' she said out loud, and heard Ruby giggling from the kitchen. Or could it be Keith Hughes, finally showing his face? She'd expected something from him; a letter at the very least. She'd assumed he would try to speak to her to get his story straight, even attempt a stumbling apology. But she hadn't heard a word from him since the night he'd come for his medal.

She wished now she hadn't given it back to him. What was it called? Blood money. A murderer, compensating for his crime. She could have taken it to a silversmith, had it melted down, turned into something new. Or a pawn shop, and used the money to have the boys' names etched onto the wall of the school. How much would something like it be worth? And how much blood and sweat would have been shed, just to scrape that small scrap of silver out of the earth?

Instead, she found Cyril's headmaster on the doorstep. She hadn't seen him since the night in the gymnasium two weeks earlier, and for a moment she wasn't sure what to say. He was wearing a double-breasted tweed suit, his greying hair swept back to cover his growing bald patch, and he looked a little nervous, shuffling from one foot to the other.

'I'm so sorry to bother you so early, Mrs Clayton.'

She took a step back and watched as he strode into her hall, pausing briefly to take in the low ceiling, the papers still scattered on the floor of the living room, the teacups she hadn't cleared away. He took a seat on the settee and she perched on a chair opposite him, before remembering her manners and springing up to offer him tea.

'That's quite alright,' he said quickly, 'I'm not staying long. Must get to the school before nine.'

'What can I do for you?'

He swallowed, looking increasingly uncomfortable. When he spoke, he didn't meet her eyes. His gaze darted from the mantelpiece to the window, to the door to the hallway and back again.

'I've been speaking to the police, obviously,' he said. 'They've been keeping me informed about the... ah... the search.'

'Of course.'

'I'm so sorry,' he added, and she felt a flicker of rage in the pit of her stomach.

You sent him out there. You let that man take them. I didn't lose him.

'One of the officers mentioned a postcard you've found. A postcard from Cyril.'

She stared at him, surprised. 'Yes, I telephoned about it.'

'May I see it?'

'It's upstairs.'

'This is very awkward.' He coughed. 'We're conducting an investigation into Mr Hughes' conduct. It seems that… well, it seems his account of that day might not be entirely accurate. Your postcard seems to confirm that.'

'They told you what it says?'

He nodded. He removed his glasses and polished them on the sleeve of his jacket. She noticed beads of sweat gathering at his hairline and wondered if she ought to offer him a glass of water.

'I'm so sorry,' he said again.

'What sort of investigation?'

He looked up at her. 'There will be an inquiry. In front of the parents, the school governors. We're gathering as much information as we can.'

'And you think the postcard could help?'

'It's the only evidence we have, that his story might not be the whole truth.'

She sat back. The thought of an inquiry, in front of everyone – it wasn't a trial, but it was the next best thing.

'What would happen if he was guilty?'

'It's difficult to predict outcomes, obviously. But I'm sure there would be a suspension. At the very least. Perhaps even permanent—'

'He'd lose his job?'

He looked at her. 'I think it's very likely.'

'And it would be in the newspapers?'

'We would make the outcome public, of course.'

She nodded, taking in a deep breath. 'What do you want me to do?'

'That's why I'm here. I've come to ask if you would lend us the postcard. Just for the duration of the inquiry. A few weeks at the most.'

'Oh, I don't think…' It was still under her pillow. She felt for it every night before she went to sleep, the hard edges against her fingers. She woke every morning afraid it would be worn to pieces, the writing blurred and unreadable. 'Would it be enough to take down a copy of what it says?'

'I'm afraid not.'

She thought of Ronald Lane, her plans for Germany. She hadn't shown him the postcard yet, but without it, would she be able to persuade him? And did she even want to? The thought of more articles which spoke of Arthur, which made her look like some sort of... But it was for Cyril, she thought fiercely. All for Cyril.

'I may need it back sooner than a few weeks.'

He nodded. 'I'm sure we won't take that long.'

'Even if you could just loan it back to me for a day or two. It's very important.'

'Of course. Whatever you think, Sylvia. It's important you're comfortable with whatever you decide.'

She took in a few deep, long breaths, listening to Ruby clattering about in the kitchen. What would she say? *Forget the newspaperman, they're all vultures, bloodsuckers, he doesn't want what's best for you, love.* And hadn't Professor Franklin always done his best for Cyril? It wasn't his fault, if he hadn't known what Hughes was capable of.

'Alright.' She stood up, steadying herself and feeling a new determination growing in her. 'I'll get it for you now.'

Chapter Twenty-One

At noon the next day Hilde walked to the inn, hoping to find it empty. It was rare for anyone to be there before evening, with so much work to be done outside. She'd rushed her morning tasks, feeling guilty as she left Anna in the kitchen baking bread, mumbling an excuse about a new buyer for the calves they were expecting any day. Anna hadn't answered her and she'd slipped out without waiting, unsure whether her sister had believed her.

She'd lain awake half the night, and spent the rest of it dreaming of a child in the snow, a flash of green around his neck. As she walked through the village she imagined the article Kit might already be planning, the search party's renewed efforts, Hans Huber proved wrong. She imagined herself, strolling through the streets of Freiburg wearing clothes like Kit's, full of plans for the future. Things were going to happen.

But when she reached the inn there was no sign of Kit. Instead, she found Karl, the man who had barely spoken the previous evening, standing alone by the fireplace. He was smoking a cigarette, staring through the window at the street outside.

'Where's Kit?'

'Who?' He turned around, looking her up and down. 'The girl with the scarf,' he said, realising. 'I'm sorry about my friend yesterday.'

Hilde said nothing.

'He's not here' Karl added quickly. 'Gone out for a walk.'

'The English reporter. I was supposed to meet her here.'

'Foreign press,' he said, lighting another cigarette. 'They've all gone.'

'Gone?'

'Yes, they weren't...' He paused, searching for the right words. 'They weren't falling in line.'

'What about you and Stefan?'

'We have to fall in line. It's the law.'

'How is it the law?'

He sighed wearily. 'They decide what we can report. They choose who can write, and who can't. Don't you know?'

It made sense, Hilde thought, when they controlled so much else. And, when she thought of what she was reading in the newspapers now, she realised she must have known all along that they were managing it all, that they had been for years. She thought back to all the articles about the accident she'd read since it happened. There was very little coverage of the missing child in the larger papers – they all carried images of the Hitler Youth children, standing vigils by coffins and entertaining the survivors. It was only the smaller papers, like the one Hans Huber had put through their door, that seemed interested. Those which carried lurid cartoons and speculative headlines – were Karl and Stefan working for one of those? She didn't want to ask.

'But they can't tell foreign papers what to do, can they?'

'Of course not. They just tell them that if there was an incident – if they were attacked, they mean, that's always what it means – there wouldn't be any resources to protect them. Look, I shouldn't be talking to you about this. We'll be clearing out ourselves soon enough.'

'But they haven't found him yet. Why would you leave?'

He shrugged. 'They don't want us covering it. Makes them look bad, I suppose. Loose ends, unfinished business – it's not meant to be like that.'

'Who do you mean? Who told the foreign papers to leave?'

'That man. He was in here last night, with Herr Huber. Runde.'

She remembered him, the way his gaze had swept across the room, how she'd felt unable to carry on talking to Kit in his presence. 'Where is he now? Runde?'

He was staring at his feet now, shifting his weight from one to the other, avoiding her eyes. 'You need to be careful, Hilde.'

'Is he with Hans?'

'It isn't worth the trouble. This will all be over in a few more days.'

'So you're happy, just writing what he tells you to write?'

He took another cigarette from his pocket; she shook her head as he offered her the case. 'I'm happy to have a job,' he said, striking a match against the mantle. 'I'm happy just getting by. You should be too,' he added, touching the match to his cigarette and taking in a long breath.

Hans came to the door himself; he looked unsurprised to see Hilde on the threshold. He stepped back, and she saw the man from the previous evening, Runde, was sitting at the table in the *Stube*.

'I came…' She hesitated. Why had she come? 'I came to ask about the search.'

A weary look crossed Hans' face, but he covered it quickly with a smile. 'Come in, Hilde. Alice will get you some milk. Or a glass of water?'

She shook her head. Runde stood up, standing stiff and upright beside his chair. She stared at the swastika armband around his forearm, the same design repeated on the cap he had placed on the table in front of him.

'Hilde Meyer, this is Kurt Runde,' Hans said. 'He's come from Freiburg, to enquire about the accident.'

'I thought you were finished investigating,' Hilde said curtly. 'They've all gone home, haven't they?'

'Herr Runde isn't part of the police investigation.'

'You might remember me,' Runde said, holding out a hand. 'From the night of the accident.' He smiled apologetically as she stared back at him. 'Of course. It was dark, and all the confusion.'

'I remember it all clearly enough.'

There was a brief, uncomfortable silence.

'Herr Runde is the local Hitler Youth faction leader,' Hans said hurriedly. 'I'm sure you saw, in the newspapers.'

'Yes, of course.'

The vigil in the chapel, games of football with the surviving boys. Quite the performance, she thought as she looked at Runde, who was studying her with narrowed eyes.

'Shall we all sit down?' Hans gestured to the table.

The two men sat opposite her. She felt trapped, suddenly, unable to see the way out, obscured by Hans' body and the shadows gathering in the corners of the *Stube*.

'She was at the inn yesterday,' Runde said, as though Hilde wasn't there. 'Talking to the English woman.'

'What were you talking about, Hilde?'

'She was just asking for directions. She was leaving, I think.'

'And?'

'What do you mean?'

Hans raised an eyebrow. 'You were talking to her for a while, weren't you?'

'Of course, I asked her if there was any news.'

'You know, you can ask me that, Hilde.' Hans sat up a little taller in his chair. 'If you have any questions about the search, the investigation. Why would you not come to me?'

She wanted to tell him he wasn't the mayor, he wasn't the local police. He didn't know everything, and he couldn't tell her what to do. Instead, she only smiled. 'Of course, Hans,' she said. 'I would always ask you first. She just happened to be there. And,' she was warming to her theme now, 'it's so interesting, isn't it? Meeting real reporters.'

'You should be careful,' Hans said. 'They're all liars and charlatans. Aren't they?' he said, turning to Runde.

'Not any more' Runde said. 'We've taken them in hand.'

'Yes, yes, of course.'

'You mean the Party?' Hilde asked. She regretted the question at once; there had been an edge of distaste in her voice she had meant to conceal. Had Runde detected it? He didn't seem to react, only smiled slightly, as though her naivety amused him.

'We're preparing a news release,' Runde said, 'about the night of the accident. You say you remember it clearly – your impressions would be helpful.'

'A news release? Why aren't you looking for the missing child?'

'It's impotant to clarify the order of events. And to ensure some good comes of such a tragedy.'

'How can anything good come from it?'

There was a heavy silence. Hilde felt a prickling sensation along her spine. She thought of the rasping sound of the scythe, knives cutting into the pigs' throats as Anna looked on impassively. She forced herself to look up; from a distance Herr Runde had appeared to be relatively young, but now she could see dye on his temples, the lines around his eyes. He was older, she thought, than he wanted people to realise. Less sure of himself too. It was noticeable in his discomfort, his uncertainty in how to respond to what they had said, to look them in the eye.

'Not everyone is aware, *Fräulein*, of the role my boys played that night.'

It took a few seconds for his words to make sense.

'Your... boys?'

'Yes, we heard of an English group in difficulty. It was really a miracle we were able to be there in time to help.'

'Yes, it was.'

He was looking at her expectantly now.

'I'm sorry,' she said, meeting his eyes. 'I don't remember any boys, except the English.'

'You deny that they were there?'

'Not at all. I simply don't have a memory of them being there.'

'Well,' Hans said brightly, 'it takes time for memories to come back sometimes. Doesn't it? I remember the night my boy was born, waking up the next day with nothing, absolutely no memories of it at all!' He laughed uneasily, but Runde was peering at her closely.

'What did you say your name was, *Fräulein*?' he asked.
'Meyer?' He looked at Hans. 'Walter Meyer's child?'

Hans nodded.

'Well then,' Runde said slowly. 'Well then. It's hardly a surprise.'

In the *Stube*, Anna was sitting at the tiled stove, a torn sheet of paper on her knees. Hilde stood in the doorway, her fists tightening and her breath catching in her throat.

'What do you know about Pa?'

'What?' Anna looked up, wide-eyed.

'You said something yesterday, that he wasn't brave. What have people been saying about him?'

'Did I?'

'You know you did, *Liebling*. What are you looking at?'

Anna's expression was suddenly guilty. She tried to screw up the paper and hide it in her fist, but Hilde snatched at it, then held out her hand until Anna reluctantly passed it to her.

The cartoon, creased and lined, was even more distorted now. The men's faces were leering masks, staring up with crazed, bulbous eyes. Hilde scrunched it into a ball again and threw it onto the fire.

'You're not to read this filth, do you understand?' She pulled the rest of the pieces of newspaper, Hans Huber's flyer, from the kindling box and burned them too.

'They're saying that boy was killed. They're saying those boys from the Hitler Youth tried to save him, but it was too late.'

'I know what they're saying. You're not to read it.'

'I can read what I like. You're not my mother.'

Hilde stared at her, open-mouthed. 'What did you mean yesterday, about Pa?' she asked again.

Anna stood up; Gretel, curled up beside her, sprang away in alarm. 'Why? Why do you want me to tell you? You only ever want to hear good things about him! You can't even look through his things in the basement, in case you find something you don't like. That's why it's all still there, isn't it?'

'What are you talking about?'

'You never want to know the truth – haven't you heard the things people say? Can't you see what they all thought of him?'

'Anna, what are you talking about? Since when did you care so much what people say?'

Anna knelt and scooped Gretel up, pressing her face into her fur.

'Maybe it matters, what people say,' she said, her voice slightly muffled. 'Maybe you should start listening.'

Hilde stood on the front porch, taking in deep lungfuls of fresh air. From farther along the road she heard a stirring: children shouting excitedly and barked orders. She walked towards the sound; a crowd had formed around the square, spilling out onto the road. At its centre, Kurt Runde was standing with a few boys of about fifteen or sixteen, all dressed in military uniform, brown shorts and shirt, swastika armband, leather belt and shoes. As she watched, they raised their hands in the Nazi salute and the crowd of villagers returned it, cheering and waving. She recognised Paul Huber amongst them, his eyes bright and a broad smile across his face. Above them, the flag flew proudly, the huge black spider positioned at its centre like a target, the red canopy rising and falling in the breeze, cutting into the clear blue sky.

Chapter Twenty-Two

They walked to the Guild meeting together, arm in arm. Sylvia hadn't wanted to go, but Ruby had insisted she leave the house for something other than work. For days now, she'd been expecting a knock at the door, a grim-faced stranger with news, but there had been nothing but silence after the article was published. She could feel the world moving past what had happened, people forgetting, and felt powerless to pull them back. Sometimes she wondered if it would have been easier with Arthur around – there would have been two of them, in it together, a mirror for each other's pain. Even Ruby seemed less willing to talk about it.

A woman holding a basket of white poppy pins approached them; seeing Ruby's pin, she smiled and raised a hand. Sylvia reached in her coat pocket for her own and hastily attached it to her blouse.

'Why don't you wear that all the time?'

'I don't know,' she said, turning to Ruby. 'Sometimes people say things – doesn't that happen to you?'

'Of course. Wouldn't be a statement if it didn't make some people angry, would it?'

'I just felt – I didn't want Cyril to feel…' She stopped, unsure how to explain. She thought of the first time Arthur had told her about the Peace Society, the day they'd first walked to the bus together. *You've got a feather for me too, I suppose.* In the months that followed she'd seen people handing him white feathers herself. Women, sometimes girls, would stride up to him purposefully, reaching into their handbags, and she'd learn to recognise the look in their eyes, to anticipate the feather before it came. She'd hated those women, how they could interrupt the few moments she and Arthur had alone together and fill them with shame. He would take the feathers silently, never complaining, never talking back. The woman would hesitate for a moment, clearly anticipating a fight, then disappear into a crowd.

She'd known he was wavering, even before the rumours of conscription began. There was a change in him she couldn't quite describe in words; he was more withdrawn than the man she'd first met in the hospital corridor, as though his mind was forever elsewhere. Even so, she couldn't help wondering afterwards whether he would have done it, if it hadn't become clear that before long, the choice would be taken away from him.

Once, when she hadn't seen him all day at the hospital, she'd gone to the common room she knew the porters sometimes used. It was the end of the day, and the room had seemed empty before she'd seen him sitting in a chair in the corner, his knees drawn up to his chin. He was crying, rocking himself back and forth rhythmically, and she'd wanted to go to him, put her arms around him, but instead she'd backed out of the room, hoping he hadn't noticed her there.

He'd enlisted the next day. Three weeks later, they'd announced the conscriptions.

'What is it today?' she whispered as she and Ruby slid into their seats in the hall.

Ruby consulted her flyer.

'Eugenics Society again. Voluntary sterilisation of the unfit.'

Sylvia's heart sank. 'Good grief,' she said, trying to sound dismissive, shooting Ruby a smile. But Ruby only frowned at her, raising a finger to her lips as a stern-looking woman took her place at the lectern. It was always women, Sylvia thought, why was that? Over the years they had listened to talks on an endless list of subjects, from animal husbandry to the evolution of man, and the speakers had always been men, looking out across the sea of women with benevolent, patronising smiles. When it came to questions of genetics, blood, birth and inheritance, why should it be any different?

'Ladies, thank you for your attention.' She beamed at them. Something about her reminded Sylvia of a headmistress, and she felt herself sitting straighter in her chair.

'I saw her speak last week,' Ruby whispered. 'She's absolutely marvellous.'

'Consider the racing pigeon,' the woman said, smiling at them as though the instruction were the most natural one in the world. 'Each one bred over generations to be perfectly adapted to its task.'

Sylvia leaned over to Ruby, ready to say something disparaging, but she could see in Ruby's face now that there wasn't any point.

'Imagine if we were able to do the same for ourselves. Imagine if all the traits which cause us grief – mental illness, disability, alcoholism – all of it could be eradicated. We have the power to ensure that no child in the future is born defective. We can improve the genetic quality of our race, not by using conflict or violence, but with science.'

Before Arthur was sent out, she'd realised with some surprise that she wanted a child. It didn't fit in with any of her other plans, becoming a scientist, making a difference, but she'd wanted it anyway. She'd never told him. There hadn't seemed any point; there had hardly been time to say goodbye, to hold on to him and cry into his collar, to promise him she wasn't far behind. She hadn't been able to imagine anyone not wanting to enlist, but now that it was happening, now that he was really going, she couldn't imagine being without him.

'The effects of the last war were devastating, particularly on those in our population with the strongest genetic make-up.

Young, healthy, brave individuals were selectively removed from the gene pool, whilst those genetically unfit to fight stayed at home, and survived.'

She'd seen more feathers being handed out, after conscriptions had started. The women who did it became more organised; there were rumours they'd formed themselves into brigades, a campaign to shame men into service. Sometimes, the men they targeted were on leave or home wounded, and she'd watch as they waved their pay-books angrily, shouting about the things they'd seen. Once, she'd seen a man hold out an arm which ended in a twisted stump, and the woman holding the feather had burst into shocked tears.

She'd wondered why Arthur had finally volunteered after holding out for so long, and concluded that, in the end, the shame must have hurt more than the thought of going. But only just, she'd thought later, remembering that day she'd found him in the common room. Only just.

'It's 1936. Only eighteen years since Armistice, and yet we are facing the prospect of another, even greater conflict. Meanwhile, those with the most desirable genetics choose their careers, their luxuries, their own selves, above the needs of their country. Birth rates among the poor continue to increase. Sterilisation offers these people freedom from a lifetime of burdensome responsibility, at the same time as improving the genetic stock of the country. Because,' the speaker spread out her hands in appeal, 'if another war is coming, how can we be expected to survive it?'

There were more questions than usual after the talk. Most were about the science, some about the medical procedure itself. One woman asked about what was happening in America – they were already doing it, she'd heard, and they didn't need anyone's permission for it either. Prisoners, people in institutions, the poor. *One step at a time,* the speaker said gently. *When it comes to new laws, the best thing is to take things one step at a time.* Would the operation be free of charge, they asked, how can I get it, do I need to prove I'm defective, can I simply add my name to a list? Sylvia closed her eyes, trying to block out the sound of their voices, the memory of Arthur in the common room all those years ago, wondering if, even then, she ought to have known.

Their wedding was held the day before she was finally sent out to France. Arthur was back on leave and they'd made their plans in hurried letters which Sylvia had written at odd hours of the night, unable to sleep for worrying about him. Arthur's parents were dead, and they hadn't told Sylvia's. Only her sister, who by then was posted to Italy. They'd asked two of the girls Sylvia lodged with to be witnesses, and Arthur had pulled a man from the street to be best man and carry the rings. Afterwards they'd all gone for a drink in the Red Lion over the road and she and Arthur had held hands across the table, both of them dazed at the speed of it, at how little time they had left. They'd spent the night in a hotel, and the next morning they'd boarded separate trains.

Part of her, as she'd sat on the train that day, had hoped they'd done enough on that one night together to give her the child she'd been imagining. The thought of it terrified her, and something else – after her years of training, finally being able to do her bit in the war, did she really want to be sent straight back home again? She couldn't deny that, despite all her plans, it would have been a relief. And she'd felt, as she stared out of the window at the grey smog of the city fading into the soft greens and browns of the countryside, that any child they'd conceived in those stolen few days couldn't help but be born with bravery running through its veins.

When her blood began flowing a week or so later, she'd almost forgotten the quiver of hope she'd felt on the train. She'd only torn up some bandages and pressed them quickly into her underwear, moving on down the line of stretchers without pause.

After the meeting, as they gathered at the back of the hall, Ruby handed her a printed card.

'They asked me to give it to you, after the last talk. I wasn't sure – but it's important, Sylvia.'

She looked down at it.

'We, the members of the Islington Branch of the Women's Co-operative Guild join with the Eugenics Society in calling on the government to enact the recommendations of the Brock Report and to legalise voluntary sterilisation of the unfit.'

'Have you signed it?'

'Everybody has.'

She looked up. 'We used to laugh about it, Ruby. All their genetic stock nonsense, all that talk about racing pigeons and spaniels.'

Ruby breathed a heavy sigh. 'If there is something,' she said slowly. 'Something in our blood, or whatever – if we'd pass it on to our children. Wouldn't it be better to know? All those diseases – what if they didn't have to happen?'

'Knowing's one thing. Doing that – it's different, isn't it? Sterilisation.' A long, cold word; she said it slowly, testing it out.

'Not a lot of point knowing and doing nothing about it. Anyway, seems to me at the moment it's only rich women who can do anything about it. That hardly seems fair, does it?'

'You think people already are—'

'Of course!' Ruby scoffed. 'You can get anything with money, can't you? Why have kids if you don't have to? At least this way, it's the same for everyone.'

'It's not the same for everyone!'

She hadn't meant to raise her voice; a few of the women gathered around the tea urn glanced over at them, exchanging whispers. Sylvia looked down at the piece of card in her hand.

'You're really going to vote for it, aren't you?'

Ruby shrugged. 'At least it might give us a choice.'

She walked home through a heavy, damp fog that fell from nowhere like a mesh around the city. She was thinking about the woman at the podium; how simple she had made it all seem, how easy it was to slide into agreement with someone who presented their arguments so persuasively. Whatever they told you, if they said it with conviction, made your old ideas suddenly seem meaningless and small. Was it a surprise that Ruby, that any of them, had been so swept along?

She'd realised, standing there in the hall, how little they really knew each other. Ruby never talked about her life, the husband and three children at home. Sometimes, when she was late to meetings, she looked as though she'd been crying. Once, she'd turned up with a bruise over one eye, carefully covered up with powder but visible all the same. Sylvia had felt resentful, all those years with Arthur and no one offering help, but had she ever offered any to Ruby? It wasn't what people did, looking into each other's lives, asking what they needed. And what would Sylvia had said, if anyone did? That it was her own fault, what had happened. That she should have known, right from that day she'd found Arthur crying in the common room. She should have realised the path that was laid for them and found a way to avoid it, before the choice had been taken away.

When she reached home, she found her sister waiting on the doorstep.

'Julia.' She stopped dead, taking her in. Julia was dressed in a prim, plum-coloured suit, her hair done up in that irritatingly neat way Sylvia had never managed to imitate. She was sitting on the step smoking a cigarette, like a schoolchild who'd found herself locked out. How long had they left it, this time? Months, Sylvia thought, perhaps even a year. For a moment, she didn't know what to say. Then Julia looked up, her face softened into a smile and the tears Sylvia had been working so hard to hold back came all at once, as her sister stood up and put her arms around her.

Julia set to work immediately. She put the kettle on the stove, tidied away used plates and cups, swept the kitchen floor and wiped down surfaces while Sylvia sat slumped at the kitchen table, wondering why she had been so afraid to tell her sister what had happened. She'd read it in the papers, of course – Sylvia flinched at the thought of Julia and Charles opening their morning paper and finding her mournful face staring back at them.

'I've brought – it's not much.' Julia held out a paper packet. 'Just some cuts we didn't need from the butcher.'

'Thanks.'

'Charlie's doing everything he can. He's asked for a meeting with the new ambassador to Germany. And the foreign secretary. He won't get them, obviously, but someone ought to do something. They haven't even questioned that teacher, as far as I can tell.'

'There's going to be an inquiry, at the school.'

'An *inquiry*,' Julia repeated with distaste. 'And God knows what the German authorities are doing out there.'

'Their best, I'm sure.'

'It's outrageous. There should be a delegation, some sort of—'

'He's just one boy, Julia. We can't expect them to drop everything. Especially now.'

'Well, I don't know how you can be so calm about it. Oh, Sylvia, I just can't imagine.'

Of course you can't. Julia had always been open in her disdain for the idea of having children. *Work is what matters*, she always used to say when the topic had been tentatively raised between them, *you can't have both. If you have brains, you have a responsibility to follow it through. Imagine, being stuck at home washing napkins and wiping up sick when you could be actually doing things, making a difference.* At the time, as lowly trainee nurses, Sylvia had wanted to point out that that was exactly what they were doing – were their own hypothetical children less worthy of it than these strangers? But she'd known Julia wouldn't understand. *We owe it to the future,* she'd say, *we owe it to other people's children to make something out of ourselves.*

And then Cyril was born, and it was as though Sylvia had betrayed some ideal she had never fully understood. What would that woman from the Eugenics Society have had to say about it? Quite the opposite, she felt sure – *If you've got the brains, it's your duty to reproduce them. Enough rotten babies being born into the world, it's our job to balance the scales.*

She looked down and realised her hands were shaking. It had been happening in waves ever since Cyril had gone missing – convulsions which spread to the rest of her body, until her teeth chattered and she had to wrap her arms around herself to try to keep still.

She wondered, in a dull, detatched way, if she might be going mad. Once, a few months after Armistice, she'd woken to find Arthur sitting in the bed beside her, his face turned towards the door and his whole body shaking so badly she could feel the bed move a little beneath her. She'd said something – about the milk delivery, about her plans for the day, she couldn't remember now – and he hadn't responded. She'd given him a little tap on the shoulder and still nothing. She'd got up, made them breakfast, and when she came back to the room he was still sitting there shaking, staring at her in the doorway until she'd turned, convinced there must be something appalling taking place just over her shoulder.

Julia reached out and held both her hands tightly, until the shaking subsided. 'We're going to find him, Sylvia. I promise we will.'

She wanted to believe Julia so badly. Julia, who always

insisted on being right about everything. She leaned her head forward into Julia's shoulder and let out a sob, felt her sister's hand on the back of her head, holding her tight, and willed her to be right this time.

'There's no details in that article,' Sylvia said later as they sat together in the living room. 'I didn't tell them anything about Arthur. They don't know anything.'

'We agreed. Didn't we? For Cyril's sake.'

'I know we did, but this is different. I did it for him, to get his name out, his face.'

'It hardly mentions him. It's all about you.'

'I didn't know it would be like that!' She felt a familiar surge of anger at the way Julia always seemed to blame her whenever something went wrong. Did she blame her for what was happening now? She'd been surprised by how kind Julia was being, how she'd allowed Sylvia to sit and cry without trying to interrupt or offer advice, but now she wondered if Julia's silence was hiding a condemnation she didn't want to speak out loud. 'I lied to him, Julia. Cyril, all those years—'

'You were just doing your best for him.'

'Julia, did you ever...' She stopped, but it was too late now, the question was half spoken and Julia was staring at her questioningly. 'I mean, have you ever—'

'What?'

'Made a mistake. With work, I mean.' She paused, feeling the tremor beginning again in her fingers, spreading to her palms. 'There was a boy, in France, and I think – I think...'

I think I killed him.

'Of course I have,' Julia said briskly, 'all the time.' And Sylvia knew she hadn't done anything like what had happened to that boy, that she would never understand.

Julia got up and began tidying the living room, patting at cushions and gathering up newspapers and more empty teacups.

'What's this?' she said, holding up a piece of paper. Sylvia had left the pledge from the Guild meeting on the table with her keys, still undecided about whether to sign it.

'"Voluntary sterilisation". Good God, is this what they're spewing at those meetings now?'

'It makes sense, in a way,' Sylvia said uncertainly, trying to think what Ruby might say.

'What? Forcing people to—'

'It's not forced! People would have to agree with it.'

'And what do you think would happen to those people who aren't able to agree? Someone will decide for them, and then how is it different? I can't believe you'd be so naive, Sylvia.'

'I thought you hated the idea of children.'

'I hate the idea of it for myself. I would never support something like this.'

'You mean Charlie would never support it.'

'I'm still capable of having my own opinions. Are you saying you would? You're not going to sign this?'

'No! I mean – I never said – it's just a petition, a campaign. It's not like it will ever actually happen.'

Julia held out one of the newspapers. 'Nazi health law kills thousands'.

'Oh, for heaven's sake. It's hardly the same.'

She read the first few paragraphs anyway. 'Experts estimate the number of deaths following sterilisation operations at five per cent.'

'It's not like that here,' she said uncertainly. Wasn't it paranoia, assuming the worst of everyone the way Julia did? 'People just want the freedom to choose, that's all. Anyway,' she said, looking at the newspaper again, 'isn't this all a bit…'

'What? Exaggerated?'

'Well! Newspapers don't always tell the truth, do they?'

'My God, Sylvia, are you really so ignorant?' She snatched the paper back. 'Do you know what they said in our Parliament, the last time this whole thing got so far as that? Those people who wanted what they call voluntary sterilisation? It was only five years ago, Sylvia.'

She waited, and Sylvia felt her cheeks flame with anger and shame.

'They called it "merely a first step"' Julia said. 'A first step towards compulsory sterilisation. That's what they really want.'

'You should go.'

Sylvia stood up, folding her arms. She could see her sister attempting to come up with a reply; it wouldn't be an apology, she knew that.

'Really, Julia, you've done enough,' she added, trying to make her voice sound measured and calm. 'Thank you for coming.'

They stared at each other for a moment. She thought Julia might refuse, insist on staying to make them dinner, perhaps take Sylvia out for a walk. They could go to a tea shop, even to the cinema on the corner, they could talk, make a plan for how Sylvia would survive the next few days, weeks...

She watched as Julia began gathering up her things.

'You'll want to cook that meat in the next couple of days,' she said coldly as she shrugged on her coat. 'Put it in a stew, or something.'

Julia left the newspaper on the table, still open to the article. After she'd gone, Sylvia tore it to shreds, pushing the pieces into the box of kindling by the fire.

Chapter Twenty-Three

Hilde stood at the top of the stairs leading down to the basement, staring down into the dark. It had been so long since she'd opened the trapdoor, she hadn't been sure of where the key was; she'd found it in an old water jug high on a shelf in the kitchen.

Was Anna right? Had she been afraid to look at her parents' belongings for fear of what she might find? She'd never thought so, but now she was standing here, she felt unease creeping across her skin. Within the early morning silence she could hear the wind moving in the eaves, the slow creak of the house as it shifted around her. A breeze was lifting from the darkness below, as though another world existed down there, its air colder than that of this one.

She paused, listening for Anna, but the house was silent. She reached for her oil lamp and slowly descended the wooden staircase, forcing herself to keep her eyes open, to take everything in.

The boxes were lined up against one wall, three or four high. Much of the rest of the space was taken up by barrels, which once would have been filled with grain and livestock feed from previous harvests. This year, they were empty – after the hard winter, just the two of them, they hadn't built up enough supplies to need the extra storage space. She tried not to think about that, about their future, pushing her fears away as she turned to the far end of the room.

Two wooden sledges were leaning against the opposite wall, broken beyond repair. Their father had made them one winter, years past, and as yet she'd had neither the skill to mend them nor the heart to turn them into firewood. In the far corner, a metal contraption like a mangle was pushed against the wall. She remembered her mother complaining: *It takes up so much space, Walter, is it really worth keeping?* And her father's reply, always the same: *I didn't pay that man double his fee to drag it up the mountain, only to pay him again to come and take it away.* He had worked for a printing company in Freiburg before the war; this smaller model had been destined for the reclamation yard before he had offered to take it off their hands and mend it himself. On quiet evenings, when a storm was brewing and the rest of them sat contentedly by the stove, he and Fritz would disappear to the basement, sometimes for hours, tinkering away at it until long after the rest of the house had gone to bed.

Eventually they'd suceeded, and Walter had used it to print seed packets which he'd tried to sell to local farmers, or to businesses in Freiburg; he would travel to the city himself, trying to encourage them to make orders. Hilde had never been quite sure how many had come, but he would still print them, packing them up carefully into boxes and loading them onto the cart which took him to the city. *It's a pipe dream,* their mother would mutter as they watched him depart, *he didn't have to be a farmer, did he, but now he's chosen it, it's never good enough for him.*

After the cave-in, Hilde's mother had burned the remaining seed packets in the yard by the side of the house, throwing them into a large metal barrel, her face hard and expressionless. Hilde had managed to keep one, at the last moment, when her mother's back was turned. She'd taken one of the seed packets from the pile and, later, hidden it under a floorboard in the tiny room she shared with Anna. A little piece of her father, hidden carefully away.

She lifted one of the boxes onto the floor. It was lighter

than she'd expected; when she opened it, she found it was filled with dried flowers, crumbling together into a grey-pink dust. She remembered now, all the bunches of flowers he'd presented their mother with, not on birthdays or festivals, but just in ordinary, unexpected moments. Their mother had kept them all, drying them from the rafters in the kitchen until there were so many, they'd had to be moved to make way for curing meat. After she'd died, Hilde had found them all over the house: lying on shelves, tucked into spaces on the windowsills, pushed into empty cups and tankards. She pushed her fingers into the box, feeling the contents dissolving between her fingers.

The next box was heavier; it was filled with papers. Hilde sat on the floor and spread them out around her, feeling apprehensive as she sifted through them. The first few piles were relatively mundane: bills, letters, old receipts and credit notes. The papers grew gradually more worn and yellowing as she continued to look through them; the corners were torn and ragged, the ink beginning to fade. At the very bottom of the box, she found papers from her father's regiment; his conscription papers, his face staring solemnly out from a faded photograph, younger than Hilde could ever have imagined him being. It was in a folder, bundled together with other army documents, most of which looked technical and uninteresting, until she found a small folded sheet among them, on which her father's name was written in curling script. 'Walter Meyer. Notice of dishonourable discharge.'

'What are you doing?'

Anna was standing on the stairs in her nightgown, blinking at Hilde in confusion. Hilde turned, feeling inexplicably guilty.

'What does it look like I'm doing?'

'It's the middle of the night.'

Hilde shrugged, and felt a shiver run through her. She hadn't noticed, while she was sorting through the papers, how cold it had grown.

'I'll be done in a minute. Go back to bed.'

'It's because of what I said, isn't it? You're looking for something – what?'

'I don't know,' Hilde said, slumping back against the wall.

Anna came down the last of the steps and knelt beside her, taking the paper from her hands.

'You know something, don't you?' Hilde said. It didn't make sense, how could Anna know when she didn't? Was it really just village gossip, had she really just closed her ears to it? Anna hugged her knees to her chest, leaning back against the wall beside Hilde.

'I didn't want to tell you, because you think so much of him. You're always saying—'

'Anna, what is it?'

Anna sighed. 'He was a deserter. There, now I've said it.'

There was a long silence, while Hilde listened to the sound of the wind in the eaves above them, the creaking and sighing of the house, Anna's soft breathing.

'What do you mean, a deserter?'

'Exactly that.'

'But he was discharged – 1918, that's what Ma always said.' She scrambled to remember the scraps her mother had told her; he had never talked about it himself, but that wasn't unusual, hardly any of the men did. Only Fritz, with his stories about his friend, about how he'd come so close to dying and been saved. 'He came to Todtnauberg to convalesce, and that's how he met her. He decided to stay here instead of going back to Freiburg, because he loved her.'

'Because it was safer than going home. He was on leave, Hilde. He was supposed to go back and fight.'

Hilde shook her head. The boxes around her seemed suddenly gigantic, towering over her, threatening to fall. What else would she find in them? She hadn't even started opening them, and already things were tumbling out that she didn't want to see. 'How do you know all this?' Her voice sounded small; wounded.

'Paul Huber told me.'

'And what does Paul Huber know about it?'

'He doesn't know. He only told me what the rumours are. And I overheard them talking about it myself once. *I did it for you,* Pa said, and she said she never asked him to, and if she'd known she wouldn't have let him. That's what they were talking about, what else could it have been?'

'It could have been all sorts of things,' Hilde said slowly, but she already knew Anna was right. The way he'd avoided talking about the war, about what had happened afterwards. All Hilde knew about it, she'd heard on the radio: angry tirades about how the settlement had been too punitive, how the French and the British had weakened Germany to the point of collapse. How, now that Hitler was in charge, everything was going to turn around. The names of the men from the village who hadn't come back were etched on a plaque in the church; Fritz would stop and bow his head each time they passed, but her father had walked past without pausing.

'Paul says it's men like him who lost us the war,' Anna said. 'Not the army, not the people who were actually dying. It was people like Pa, and the people at home who didn't even go.'

'What?'

'He says it was Jews and socialists. He says they were plotting against the army and that's why we lost.'

'Anna, what on earth—'

'Pa was a socialist, wasn't he? That's what everyone says. Paul says he was...' She paused, recalling the phrase. 'An *enemy of the people*.'

'You're not to speak to Paul Huber any more, do you understand?'

'You think it's true, that's why you won't answer. Don't you?'

'Of course it's not true!'

Anna stood up, wrapping a shawl around her shoulders and shooting Hilde a hard, defiant glare. Hilde stood up too, feeling anger flooding her veins.

'Anna, what has he being saying to you?'

'Nothing they're not saying on the radio. Nothing I don't see in the newspapers, every day.'

'Well?'

'They're saying the Jews aren't citizens any more. They're saying the socialists, the Jews, they're the reason the country's been in so much trouble, they're why there's not been enough money, that—'

She raised a hand and struck Anna across the cheek. She was so shocked, after she'd done it, that she burst into tears. When she looked up, Anna wasn't crying with her. She was staring back at her with a hard, cold expression that filled Hilde's chest with fear.

Part Four

Chapter Twenty-Four

Sylvia arrived early to the inquiry. Ruby had agreed to come with her, and gripped her hand tightly as they approached the crowds surrounding the school gates, reporters and onlookers struggling with each other to get a decent view. They were stretched along the street outside, leaving no space to pass through; as they got closer, Sylvia heard Ruby take in a sharp breath.

'Are you sure—'

'Of course,' she said quickly, squeezing Ruby's hand. 'I've got to be there, haven't I?'

She hadn't slept much the previous night. Several times, she'd felt beneath her pillow for Cyril's postcard and remembered it wasn't there. She'd given it to the headmaster, she'd trusted him to make the most of it, to see that Keith was punished. When she closed her eyes, all she could see was that night in her kitchen, Cyril standing in the doorway looking up at them both, Keith's hand still on her wrist, his eyes staring into her eyes. The desk, open behind him. It was what she'd always feared, Cyril seeing something he wasn't meant to see, the truth rising to the surface. She'd been afraid of what he might find out for so long, of what he would think of her when he did. She was still afraid, even now, with her son miles away from her and the world believing he would never come back.

'Mrs Clayton!'

People began shouting as they came closer, stumbling

towards them. Ruby took her arm and pushed through the crowds towards the school gates, as she tried to block out the voices rising around them.

'Is there any news of Cyril?'

'Could you spare a moment to talk to us about your son, Mrs Clayton?'

'Sylvia!' a woman's voice rose above them. 'Can I speak to you about Cyril? Can I speak to you about your son?'

She turned briefly towards them, bewildered by the crowd of faces. The last voice had come from a woman wearing a mustard-coloured jumper over tan trousers; quite apart from the fact that she was a woman, she looked far too young to be a news reporter; her small frame was nearly obscured by the men struggling to push their way forward around her. She was holding something up, something green which flashed against the sky – before Sylvia could make out what it was the woman had vanished among the crowds.

The gates swung shut behind them and Sylvia leant against them, breathing hard.

'Good lord,' Ruby muttered. 'I've never seen so many of them all together like that. One's quite enough, isn't it? Come on, love.' She took Sylvia's hand. 'Let's get this over with.'

They filed into the gymnasium, where rows of chairs had been set up to face a lectern. The Prendergasts were just ahead of them; Roger Prendergast looked calm and upright, dressed in a dark suit and holding his wife's hand. Sylvia recalled him sitting suddenly on the gymnasium floor, his gasping sobs. The chair, sailing silently through the air. She put a hand on his arm and he turned around.

'Sylvia. How are you?'

'I – you know. It's been difficult.'

Mary Prendergast nodded, and moved a little closer to her husband. *I'm not going to eat you*, Sylvia thought loudly, and almost said it.

'Any news?' he asked gruffly, and she shook her head.

Mary leaned closer. 'Did you know he went to a hotel in Bournemouth, afterwards? As though he was on a holiday!'

'No, I didn't know that.'

'We hired a private investigator,' Roger said, without any outward signs of shame. 'Followed him around for a few days. No one knew where he'd gone.'

'Lounging about by the sea,' his wife said, an edge of bitterness in her voice.

'Anyway, today we'll see a reckoning, if there's any justice at all. He should be behind bars.'

'We saw your piece, in the paper,' Mary said, a flicker of distaste on the corners of her lips. 'We've been asked, of course. All sorts of requests. We didn't think it would be right.'

'They wanted us to talk about those Hitler boys.'

'To thank them – imagine it!"

'We're very grateful to the people who went out and tried to help, of course we are,' Roger said, 'but we don't want anything to do with those German children. Stomping around like they're saving the damn world. Well, my son's still dead, isn't he? He's dead, and those German boys did nothing to help him!'

'Alright, love.' Mary put a hand on his arm and led him quickly away. Sylvia watched them go, feeling suddenly furious, though she knew they didn't deserve it. They knew what had happened to their child, they had answers. They didn't have to lie awake in the night and wonder.

They took their seats. A hum of anticipation rippled through the gymnasium as everyone stared at the empty lectern, the row of chairs behind it. When the doors finally opened, Sylvia half expected to see a man in a white wig and a black gown, a gavel in his hand, a black cap ready. But it was only the headmaster and the school governors, who filed in slowly and took their places, their faces grave and solemn. One of the chairs was still empty; the spectators were leaning forwards now, straining to see – what if he didn't come? What if he'd... what was it called? Made a run for it. Done a bunk. Absconded. Deserted. Absent without leave.

When a man in the front row of the crowd stood up, no one noticed him at first. Perhaps it was because his image – hero, villain, victim – had been so inflated over the past days that they'd ceased to think of him as simply an ordinary man. Keith Hughes, dressed tidily in a neatly pressed grey suit, his shoulders bowed and his head down, took a seat among the governors, staring resolutely at the floor.

Sylvia forced herself to look at him. For some reason she'd imagined he would be wearing black. Most of the people in the room were dressed sombrely, and so was he, but that grey, somehow, affronted her. She glanced at Roger Prendergast. He was dressed as though for a funeral – perhaps it was the same suit he'd worn for his son's. He was holding a photograph of his boy, and she wished she'd brought one of Cyril, then remembered that her favourite, the one she'd tried to give to the police, was still with that journalist. She'd tried to contact Ronald a few times since the article was published, but all of the calls she'd made had gone unanswered. And Cyril's postcard – she glanced over at the headmaster, sitting amongst the governors. Did he have it with him now? Or perhaps it was locked up somewhere, like a precious bar of gold. The proof, the irrefutable proof, that Keith had lied. 'Mr Hughes says there will likely be a storm, and it will be a good test of our blood to get through it.'

The governor was speaking in a low, monotonous voice, summarising what had happened, the stark details, as though they were an academic paper, and then he called on Keith to stand. She felt the room tense as he took his place at the podium. The silence was total. He gave a nervous, echoing cough, and blinked at them all as though he had no idea of why he was there.

'Mr Hughes, can you give us some background – what was the purpose of the trip to Germany?'

Keith stared blankly at the governor for a moment, then drew in a deep breath. When he spoke, his words sounded measured, as though he had been carefully preparing them. 'The boys were studying German culture, as well as the language. We wanted them to gain an understanding in person, not just from books.'

'And can you give us a brief overview of the itinerary?'

'We took a boat to Calais, then a train which brought us to Leipzig. Three days there, then we travelled by train to Freiburg. I gave the boys talks on the local customs, the flora and fauna, that sort of thing.'

'And didn't it seem rather a strange time for a visit? Given' – the governor coughed nervously – 'given the current political climate?'

'You mean Hitler?'

The room stirred.

'He seems alright to me. He sent condolence cards.'

More murmurings from the crowd. The governor was on his feet now, trying to regain control. 'Moving on to the climb itself,' he said in a louder voice.

'Hike.'

'I beg your pardon?'

'It was a hike. We never intended such a difficult climb. We had no idea how the weather would turn.'

Chapter Twenty-Five

He wakes early – too early, he thinks as he stares up at the whitewashed ceiling. He's barely slept, and his head aches. Too much whisky; he can see the near-empty bottle on the floor. Today's hike across the Schauinsland to Todtnauberg is a long one; stupid, to have got himself into such a state.

The previous night comes back to him in awful, jagged pieces. Clayton, sitting opposite him by the fire, his eyes wide. His own voice, on and on, why didn't he stop talking, why didn't he stop drinking? And now it's done, and he'll have to decide what to do next.

He runs through the route in his head. Challenging, but manageable. A good day's walking; enough, he hopes, to tire the boys out before they're at their next hostel. It takes them over the Schauinsland mountain – he wonders briefly if the boys can manage it, and shakes the fear away. The things people have been saying – he can't listen to all that talk. They shouldn't either.

He drags himself out of bed and peers out of the window. Rain is beginning to fall. Some of the boys, the more eager, have already assembled in the courtyard outside, chattering and playing an impromptu game of football with someone's cap. He has them in full uniform today; they're marching through the streets of Freiburg, representing their school, their country. He wants these Germans to know that English boys have discipline, that they can't be walked all over.

He rouses the stragglers from their beds, grumbling and muttering. 'These rooms are prison cells,' Tom Carter mutters when he thinks his teacher has left the room. He looks for Clayton, but he must already be waiting in the street. He allows himself to hope, for just a moment, that Clayton won't appear at all. That he's ill, perhaps, or even that he's run away. He isn't thinking about what the consequences of either would be, just that he finds it difficult to imagine looking Clayton in the eye. But outside, there he is, standing alone at the edge of the group, his hands thrust firmly in his pockets.

'Good morning, Clayton,' he says, standing next to him.

'Good morning, sir.'

'Hope you're feeling up to the day's task. Listen…' And he lowers his voice, leaning closer to the boy so that the rest of them won't overhear. 'Listen, whatever I said last night – best you just forget it, eh? It was nonsense, really. I must have been tired. Anyway, we'll keep it between us, alright?'

'Of course, sir.' The boy glances up at him, and Keith doesn't like the look in his eyes. It makes him think of that night, with Sylvia – but he can't, he won't think about that now.

He distributes a roll and some cheese to each of them and then carries out a headcount, all thirteen of them present and correct, lined up neatly like a small army ready for a march. He checks their kit, water bottle, handkerchief, sketchbook and pencil, that each of them has their shoelaces tied, then gives what he hopes is a rousing speech about honest toil, fresh air, tells off some of the boys already grumbling about the weather.

Freiburg is barely awake. The boys huff and stamp their feet, their breath misting in the air as the sun rises too slowly ahead of them, lighting up the cathedral spire. Snow begins to fall as they trudge through the city, clinging to cobblestones and settling in the water in the Bächle running alongside the streets. Someone had told Keith on the train that if he put his foot in the trenches of water accidentally, he would marry a Freiburger and never go home. *Only accidentally,* he had quickly replied, *doesn't it work if I do it on purpose?* He had laughed a little too loudly, and the woman on the train had looked at him strangely.

They take the south road out of the city. It begins as a wide, paved street, space enough for cars to pass each other. A few vehicles do pass them, open-topped, men in uniforms and swastika armbands eyeing them curiously as they drive by. The boys stare back, unsure what to make of it all. One of the boys raises his arm, begins a salute which Keith quickly stops with a look.

The road is lined with tall, elegant trees of deep green and yellow, fields of wheat and the occasional small dwelling like a stone nestled in a verdant stream. They must look like a long line of persecuted heretics, he thinks, leaving the city for sanctuary, heads bowed as the cathedral bells ring after them. The air is cut with frost, though the sun is shining brightly enough, and his fingers tingle with the cold. Ahead of them the mountains slope towards the sun, their gentle, tree-covered flanks topped with a surprising amount of snow. *Still,* he thinks, *why shouldn't we go on, what's stopping us? They don't look so bad from down here.*

Even so, he can't quite shake the warnings he received at the tourist office, the previous day. The woman behind the desk, shaking her head at him, jabbing her fingers at her own map, which somehow looked completely different to his. It was all nonsense, of course, all folklore and superstitions. *There's a sleeping king under that mountain,* she said, as though anyone had asked her. She grinned so widely he could see the rotten black tooth at the back of her mouth. *Waiting to assemble an army. You mind you don't wake him, you and your boys, he'll have England in ruins.* And then she stopped smiling and peered at him closely, as though checking to see if he was the sort who might actually do it.

They make good progress for most of the morning. On occasion they stop for a brief lecture on the flowers, the landscape, the shape of the hills and the impossible, ancient forces that have sculpted them. Keith has got it all from books he's borrowed from his father. He's terrified, as they advance towards the mountain, of dropping one of them in a muddy puddle, or lending it to a boy who'll lose it on the slopes, tear pages from it to wrap his lunch in.

By mid-morning the boys' grumblings have risen to a constant: complaints that it's too far, that their provisions aren't enough, their feet are damp, their feet are aching, their feet are numb. He feels the same dread he has been feeling now for months – how will they ever survive a war when it comes, how will they manage? He can't help thinking of men cowering in trenches, bullets flying overhead, their next meal still hours away. All the hardships they've never known before. He wants to shout at them, but instead he distributes oranges, one between two, the peeling of which keeps them occupied for a time. *Grit your teeth. Haven't you ever taken a hike before?* It is true, the mountain seems to be getting no closer to them, however far they walk. Then he feels the first ominous kiss of snow on his eyelids, the back of his neck. He dismisses it at first, just a quirk of the weather, a brief break in the sun.

There are fewer people on the roads now; earlier they passed the occasional farmer at work in fields, or cart on its way towards Freiburg, but now he feels isolated, as though the rest of the world could have vanished while they weren't looking. They reach a thick line of trees at the foot of the slopes and begin to push their way through, the boys laughing and squabbling as the light dims and green shadows cross their path. Keith thinks of all the fairy tales of his youth: 'Hansel and Gretel', stories of being lost, of wandering in dark, canopied places. All the creatures that might be stalking them in the undergrowth.

There's a crack of footsteps ahead and he stops, suddenly

afraid. The boys stop with him, whispering and joking to each other. There might be snipers, Keith thinks, suddenly imagining his brother leaning across a rooftop in the dark, there might be enemies disguised under rocks and in rivers. They might be laughing, right until the moment a bullet hits them between the eyes.

It's snowing properly now, silent gusts which sting his eyes. It's settling fast; he looks down at his feet and finds they're already half buried in a drift.

A man's figure resolves itself against the snowfall and trees, coming closer.

'Excuse me!' he shouts in German, then, as he comes nearer, repeats himself in English. 'Excuse me. What are you doing?'

'We're hiking,' Keith replies pointedly in German as he studies the man; his face is hard to make out behind layers of scarves and a hat pulled low over his eyes. His leather boots are half hidden in the snow. Keith wonders how much of their conversation the boys can follow; less than they ought, if last week's grammar test is anything to go by.

The man is shaking his head. 'This weather will only get worse. You should go back to the town.'

'We're heading to Todtnauberg.' Keith frowns at the shadow of the mountain in the distance. 'Perhaps you can advise us…'

He shakes his head more vigorously. 'You won't manage it. It's practically sheer, the climb, you'd have to go around, and that might take hours. Really, you must turn back.'

Keith bristles at that, at being ordered about by a stranger. He strikes his stick against the snow. 'You're out here,' he says pointedly. 'If it's so dangerous, what are you doing?'

'I'm heading to Freiburg. I deliver the mail.' He glances at the empty satchel at his side. 'And I don't have children with me.'

'They're not children. They'll be men in a few years.' Outrage is prickling along his spine. Who is this man, a peasant practically, to tell him his way? He's brought maps, he has a compass, he has youth and vigour on his side. *In a few years*, he thinks, *these boys might be aiming a gun at you.* 'We can manage very well. Thank you for your concern.'

He turns to his boys, who are standing, confused and expectant, whispering amongst themselves.

'Come on, lads,' he says, still in German. 'A few more miles that way.' Keith points towards an expanse of white-grey sky through the trees.

'It's too dangerous,' the German man says, a tinge of irritation in his voice.

'They can stand anything. That's what I've taught them.'

They stare at each other. Keith's outrage is being replaced now by another, more primitive feeling. Who knows they're out here, whom has he told? The woman at the tourist office, the man at the hostel. No one else, no one who would be near enough to help. This man might be a murderer, a criminal, a soldier for the enemy. He can't read the look in his eyes.

'It's what I've taught them,' he says again. Even in the time they've been standing here, the snow has thickened and the wind is rising. They need to press on. 'Well, thank you for your help.'

They watch the man continue on through the trees. Keith stares after him, waiting for the anger to dissipate. When it doesn't, he turns to the boys.

'What did he say, sir?' Prendergast asks, looking up at him expectantly. 'He sounded angry.'

There is a silence as he stares back at them. He's already decided, in his own mind, not to turn back. And what would be the point of giving them cause for fear? Better to know as little as possible of your enemy, when you've no choice but to face him anyway.

'The usual nonsense,' he says, grinning at them. 'He told me English boys aren't strong enough to climb German mountains. And what do we think?' He looks up at the ridge ahead of them, the incline the German man had warned them against. It doesn't look so difficult. Hardly a long climb, at any rate.

There is an outraged murmur amongst the boys, the rising sound of discontent and determination; it's what they'll need, he thinks, it will make them stronger.

'This way then!'

The light is fading now, the snow falling faster and with a vicious, biting edge to it that gets into the bones. It begins to settle in great drifts up to their ankles, banked against trees, hiding roots and branches which pull at them as they walk. A horrible silence settles over the boys; the grumbling has stopped, replaced with a grit Keith has long encouraged in them, but which frightens him when it finally comes. The only sound is an occasional muffled grunt as a boy stumbles, lies for a moment in the snow, then eases himself out of it and carries on.

When they reach the steepest part of the climb, he looks up uncertainly. It's steeper than he had imagined, from a distance. But then, he supposes, most mountains might seem like that up close. What worries him more is how hard it is becoming to get a grip on the path; their shoes slide back on layers of pine needles and wet leaves packed deep beneath the snow.

'Alright, boys,' he says over the cold silence as they stare at him. 'Now for the real climb. Time to show each other what you're made of.' He feels his toes curling tight in his boots. They press on, faces pale and seemingly translucent as the snow begins to fly upwards, sideways, biting at their faces, pricking at their eyes. At first he thinks they might be doing alright, carving out trenches of snow which shelter them from some of the storm, but perhaps by then he has already begun losing his sense of time and space; when he looks around him he finds he can't see all the boys any more, and it's much darker, much colder than he had realised. He puts his hands up to his face and finds he can't feel anything, and through his fingers he catches sight of a shape ahead of him, a child lying prone, cold and white and dead as a marble statue in the snow.

Chapter Twenty-Six

'This man you met on the road.'

'He was delivering the post, I think.'

The governor nodded. 'What did he say to you?'

Sylvia could feel everyone in the room leaning forward a little in their seats. There was a shifting, then a stillness in the air. She wondered if the reporters, still gathered outside, could feel it too. She took Ruby's hand, pressing it tightly.

'Just some nonsense about how German mountains are too much for the English. The usual guff. I kept it from the boys, I didn't want them to doubt themselves.'

'He didn't make any attempt to encourage you to turn back? To return to Freiburg.'

'Certainly not.'

'He didn't tell you there was a storm approaching?'

'He did not.'

'What has confused this panel, Mr Hughes, is how you came to take the route you did. According to the maps we have here, it was the steepest possible ascent. A seventy percent gradient.'

'That wasn't shown on my map.'

The governor's eyebrows rose.

'The map you – the school – gave me,' Keith went on. 'It wasn't any good. It didn't show the contours.'

Someone stifled a cry. Sylvia felt herself stiffening.

'But surely this man would have known for himself how dangerous the route was?'

Keith shrugged. 'He was just an ordinary German peasant. Not too bright, I suppose.'

'There was talk of clothing – the boys were well prepared?'

'They were prepared for a hike in springtime. We couldn't have foreseen the snowstorm, of course.'

'So you weren't warned about it? At the hostel, or—'

'No. It took us completely by surprise.'

She gripped Ruby's hand harder.

'You've mentioned a visit to the tourist office, prior to the climb – they didn't warn you about the snow?'

'No.'

'Can you speak up, please?'

'No, sir, they didn't. There was no information at all.'

'So, to be clear, you started out without any knowledge of an impending storm?'

'That's right.'

'And what did you do when it struck?'

'Well.' He took a sip of water from the glass that had been placed beside him. 'We did our best, I suppose. To get on.'

'To... get on?'

'Yes. I tried to encourage the boys, tried to keep their spirits up. Some of the older children helped the younger, I paired them up and sent two on to reach the village. We could hear bells...' He stopped, his face suddenly contorting.

'Mr Hughes?'

'Sorry. We heard bells, but we were turned around by then. Two of the boys ran on ahead to get help.' He spread out his hands. 'That's all. I must have lain down in the snow, or – I don't know. The next thing I knew, someone was carrying me to the village.'

'And what about the missing child?'

Keith raised his eyebrows in a question.

'Do you recall the last time you saw him?'

'I've told all this to the police in Freiburg. It was dark, I couldn't really make out individual faces.'

She stared at him, willing him to meet her eyes. The longer

the questioning went on, the more the nervous anticipation was building in her; soon, they would bring up the postcard, and what would he say then? It was clear he had no idea it was coming.

'I didn't see him being separated from the group. We were scattered by then, confused. I'm...' He paused, as though short of breath. 'I'm very sorry that he hasn't been found.'

'You say you arranged for the boys to wait on the mountain in pairs.'

'That's right.'

'There were thirteen boys, Mr Hughes. Which of them did you leave alone?'

'I don't – I mean – I suppose I sent three to the village then.'

'It certainly sounds like you're confused about the details.'

There was a long silence. Sylvia stared at him; he seemed to be working something out, his eyes darting quickly around the room.

'Perhaps I am confused,' he said at last. 'Perhaps – well. Perhaps the experience was more traumatic than I've allowed, so far.'

'Traumatic, sir?'

'It brought back... memories.'

'Memories of what?'

She watched him take a deep breath. She knew what he was going to say. She was thinking of that night in her kitchen, his shoulders shaking, and how he'd reached for her hand—

'Of the war, I suppose. Look,' he said firmly, 'what happened was an accident. A terrible tragedy of weather. But perhaps, if my recollections are a little unclear, that might explain why. It's well known,' he added, a little defensively. 'Situations like that – they can dredge things up, I suppose.'

'You're talking about shell shock?'

'Oh, for heaven's sake,' Ruby muttered, shaking her head. Some of the parents turned around, stared at her, whispered amongst themselves.

Keith sat back in his chair. The governor sat down too,

looking uncomfortable. He leaned over to the rest of the board and a whispered conversation took place, whilst the room sat in silence, straining to overhear. Sylvia felt breathless; it would be now, this was the moment someone would stand up, read the postcard aloud.

'Well, Mr Hughes,' the governor said at last. 'Thank you for your time, and for such a complete account of events. This concludes the meeting. We'll produce our report in due course.'

'That's it?'

She hadn't meant to speak aloud. A row of faces turned towards her; she felt her face growing hot, her breath quickening.

'This concludes the meeting,' the governor repeated nervously.

'He killed them!' She stood up, feeling Ruby's hand slip from hers. Her whole body was shaking. 'He killed those children! He lost my son!'

'Mrs Clayton, perhaps we can talk about this another—'

'He knows!' She pointed to Professor Franklin, who was still seated amongst the governors. 'Cyril wrote a postcard – I gave it to him. Tell them,' she added pleadingly, trying to meet Franklin's eyes. 'I don't give a damn about his war service, about his trauma! He can't just…' She turned to Ruby, tears running down her cheeks, holding out a hand as though there was something Ruby could do. 'He can't just…'

Ruby looked stunned; as Sylvia stared at her she gathered herself, standing beside her. She began trying to usher Sylvia towards the exit; Sylvia shook her off.

'Tell them!' she shouted again. 'Don't just sit there, say something!'

She stared at the professor; it was as though something in him had shut down, he wasn't even looking at her. What was happening? He couldn't have forgotten about the postcard, he had come to her specifically, he had promised her. Would he even give it back to her, now? And without it, what did she have of Cyril's? What did she have to make anyone listen to her?

'You should have helped him,' she wailed as Ruby put an arm around her. She felt limp and exhausted now, allowing herself to be led towards the end of the row of people, towards the exit. She turned back to stare at Keith, who was looking away from her too, as though he was somewhere else, as though none of it was happening. 'You didn't help him,' she hissed. 'You left him there. You – you lost him.' She shook Ruby off and stood firmly facing him. 'I hope they send you back out there, when this war comes,' she said, her voice calm and measured now. 'I hope they send you out there, and I hope this time those Germans do their job properly.'

Outside the school, she leaned against a wall, taking in deep, shaking breaths. Ruby had a hand on her shoulder. When she righted herself, the sun seemed too bright, the air too sharp as she leaned her head back, blinking away fresh tears.

She looked at Ruby. 'You think I'm crazy, don't you?'

'Why should I think that?'

'I don't know. Because I'm...' She held up her hands, indicating her body, her dishevelled hair, her smeared lipstick, her shaking hands. 'Because I'm like this.'

'I think you're exhausted,' Ruby said. 'I think we should go home. Come on.'

She took Sylvia's hand. As they began to move along the street Sylvia heard a woman's voice, calling her back. They stopped and turned; the woman from the crowd of reporters was running after them, calling out her name.

'Ignore her,' Ruby whispered, pulling Sylvia forwards.

'What's that she's carrying?'

'Come on – that's our bus.'

'Wait, just a minute. She's carrying something – she had it before too.'

There was something green, trailing behind the woman as she ran.

Ruby sighed with frustration. 'Sylvia, have you forgotten

what happened last time you spoke to one of them? I don't imagine you're likely to hear from him again, either. All those promises he made.'

The bus was easing to a halt now, the stop just a few paces ahead of them.

'I just want to know what it is, that's all. It looks like – but it can't be—'

'Sylvia.' Ruby dropped her hand and pulled away from her. 'I know how hard this is, I know you've been through a terrible time. But talking to another of those vultures is not going to help.' She held out a hand. 'I'm getting on that bus. You can either come with me, or…'

She turned. The woman following them had stopped now a little way along the street, waiting. She looked back at Ruby, who was fishing in her handbag for change.

'Thanks for coming with me. Really, I couldn't have gone without you.'

'Sylvia—'

'I'll just be a few minutes. I'll see you later. It'll be alright, Ruby, I promise.'

She took a few steps along the pavement, staring at the object the woman was holding. It was a piece of green material; a dark, mossy green that seemed so familiar. She reached out a hand for it instinctively as she came closer. The woman held it out to her, and when she took it, she felt a shiver running through her body, heard herself uttering a strange, strangled gasp.

'Where did you get this?'

They stared at each other for a moment. The woman was younger than Sylvia, with an air of assured authority which made Sylvia feel momentarily unbalanced. She held out a hand and Sylvia took it, feeling dazed as she heard the bus pull away behind her.

'I'm Kit,' she said. 'Shall we find somewhere to talk properly?'

Chapter Twenty-Seven

'Hilde.' Fritz's eyebrows rose in surprise as he opened the door. He was wearing an apron, his fingers streaked with paint.

'Can I come in?'

'Of course, *Liebling*.'

Fritz's *Stube* was filled with woodsmoke and the scent of smoking meat in the rafters; it was smaller than Hilde and Anna's farmhouse, and sparsely furnished, just two chairs on either side of the stove, a small sideboard and a table pushed up against the wall. A canvas on an easel was tilted towards the window: a half-painted expanse of snow dotted with farmhouses and cattle beneath a grey-blue sky.

'Is it a commission?'

He nodded. 'From Freiburg. My first in a while, it was a relief when it came.'

She stared at the painting. The Schauinsland dominated the background, its peak blotting out most of the sky. The snow was a stark, bold canvas; she leaned closer to see how he'd done it, made something so plain and pale look deep and textured, a multitude of colours glistening beneath a painted sun.

Fritz poured out two mugs of beer from a barrel by the door and handed her one. She sat down heavily in a chair by the fire, resting her head in her hands. He took a seat opposite her.

'Well?'

'Anna told me something about Pa. It's not true, I'm sure it's not true.'

There was a long silence; she couldn't say the words.

'She's been meeting up with Paul Huber,' she added.

'I see.'

'The way she's started talking, Fritz. You wouldn't recognise her.'

'Paul's harmless enough.'

'You always say that! You said it about Hans, and look what's been happening. Those flyers, the newspaper – that rally in the square.'

'It will blow over.'

'How do you know?'

'It always does.'

She drank her beer in quick gulps, trying to steady her hand on the mug. When she looked up Fritz was staring at her, his head on one side.

'What did she tell you about your father?'

'She said Pa was a deserter. You knew him, Fritz, he couldn't have been. Why would she say something like that?'

'Ahhh.' It was a long, low sound, rattling in his throat. He sounded relieved, as though he had been waiting to hear her say it for a long time.

'It isn't true?'

Fritz sighed heavily. 'It's... more complicated than that. Much more complicated than Anna knows, I'm sure.'

'How could he never have told me?'

'It's a difficult thing to say out loud.'

'Anna says half the village knows! Shouldn't he have been arrested, or even...' She couldn't say the rest of it, what she was imagining. Her father standing against a wall, his head bowed, the shot ringing out...

'It doesn't matter what should have happened,' Fritz said. 'He kept his head down, made a new life.'

'And that's why he came here. I always thought – my mother—'

'It was for her too, *Liebling*. As I said. Complicated.'

'I don't understand.' She sat back in her chair and closed

her eyes. She could hear Fritz shuffling slowly around her, refilling their glasses and tidying up his painting things. When she opened her eyes, he was staring at the painting. She looked too, the pale expanse of snow shifting and moving in the corners of her eyes. There was a dark shadow towards the base of the picture that she hadn't noticed before; for a moment she imagined it was a small, faint figure outlined against the snow.

'Do you think he's still out there?'

'Hm?'

'Sorry.' She shook her head and turned away. A shadow, perhaps, or just a flick of paint gone astray. 'I was thinking about that boy. I can't stop thinking about him, Fritz. If he really is in the mines—'

'He isn't. That's just talk, superstition.' He was sitting opposite her again. He leaned forward and took her hand. 'You have to forget it, Hilde. You did the best you could. We all did.'

'Perhaps.'

'Are you still thinking of leaving?'

She nodded. 'You know some of the cattle traders, don't you? Can you help me find a buyer? There's the pigs as well.'

'I can, if it's really what you want.'

'We can't stay here.' She felt more certain as she said it. 'Something's happening to Anna, Fritz. It's this place, something in the air, it's not right. If we can get away, if she can see there's more to life—'

'You think it's different somewhere else?' He sighed. 'I know terrible things have happened to you here, Hilde. Terrible things happen everywhere.'

'They asked me to lie, Fritz. About that night.'

'Who asked you to?'

'Some official from Freiburg. Haven't you seen him with Hans?'

Fritz shrugged. Hilde wanted to get up and shake him; didn't he care about what was happening, couldn't he see?

'He told me the Hitler Youth children were at the rescue. That they organised it – can you believe it?'

'Of course I can.'

'Aren't you angry? It was us, Fritz! We saved them!'

'Of course it was us. They aren't going to give us any medals for it, Hilde. Let them say what they want.'

'But...' She hesitated, unsure what else to say. She thought of all the times she'd overheard him talking with her father, all their discussions about politics, about how the Party would never get anywhere, it would all blow over, even the boycotts would come to nothing in the end. She'd always thought Fritz was on her side, but now – he seemed so calm, so unconcerned. 'Don't you believe in telling the truth?' she said at last.

'I believe in staying out of their way.'

She stared at him. She couldn't believe this was the same man who'd sat up for long nights with her father, setting the world to rights, ranting about the importance of truth. Was she being naive, to still cling to the truth as though it meant something? She imagined, for a moment, taking Fritz's advice. Forgetting about that night on the mountain, allowing this new reality to take root. Forgetting what she'd learned about her father; returning to the comforting fiction – the war hero, his triumphant return, the romance of his decision to stay with her mother.

'I can't,' she said heavily, and Fritz breathed a long, defeated sigh.

'I know what you're thinking,' she said. 'Anna thinks it too. She says I always make things difficult.'

'What sort of things?'

She shrugged. 'I turned Reiner Haas down. Even though he has a horse, even though he could help us with the farm.'

'Those aren't the only things.'

'I don't want to have children.' She turned her face away, the shame washing over her as the realisation landed. 'That's not right, is it? I mean, it isn't normal. I should want to, shouldn't I? Isn't it – I don't know – in my blood, something like that?'

'I don't know.'

'I think there must be something wrong with me. I don't feel anything. I think about it, getting married, having children, and I don't feel anything.' She pressed her face into her hands. 'I wish my mother was here.'

She hadn't known how much until she said it. It had only been six months, and she was beginning to forget her mother's face. Since their father's death she'd seemed to fade away, becoming more and more distant until Hilde barely recognised the memory of her. When the fever had started, she'd tried for weeks to hide it from them. Hilde had found her one morning in her bedroom, leaning forward on her knees and shivering so hard Hilde had had to wrap her arms around her to hold her still. And somehow, although it was terrible, although it was shocking to witness, she hadn't been surprised. *He takes the strongest, leaves no one behind but weaklings like you.*

'Anna will be alright,' Fritz said, draining the last of his beer. 'But Hilde, you have to try to keep your heads down.'

'What does that mean?'

He sighed. 'This business with the English children. It isn't over. There'll be more questions. Difficult questions. I know what you're like, Hilde. For Anna's sake, for your own, please just try to stay out of it all, alright?'

Chapter Twenty-Eight

There was another storm that night. Nothing like the one that the English children had been caught in, but still, enough to keep Hilde sitting up through the night by the *Stube*, Gretel curled on her knees, waiting for a summons which she prayed wouldn't come. She could hear the cattle, restless and agitated through the walls, and imagined, as she always did on storm nights, the whole house kicked into splinters, the rain rushing into the rafters, the basement, her parents' belongings lifted and spun in the air until they were torn to pieces and scattered across the mountain.

She got up and went through to the kitchen, where the side door was rattling against the latch. She opened the door to the tiny space, barely larger than a cupboard, where she and Anna had once slept as children. She hadn't thought about her father's old seed packet since she'd hidden it there, not until she'd opened those boxes in the basement.

Now, the space was filled with storage barrels and boxes; she moved them aside and stared down at the floorboards, trying to remember which one it was she'd pulled loose. Was it still there? She knelt to pry it up, but in the darkness, the only light a flickering candle which was down to its last stub of wax, she hesitated. What if it wasn't? Wasn't it easier to go on thinking she still had it, without looking to be sure? It had been nearly two years; damp, or insects might have long since dissolved it. Wasn't her own, imagined memory of it – of him – enough?

There was a crash as something outside was flung against the side of the house and she stepped back, alarmed. Picking up her candle, she went back to the *Stube*, where Gretel was chasing her tail, her body spinning and tumbling across the tiles. She sat back by the stove, closing her eyes to the sound of the wind screaming against the eaves, shaking the shutters, only easing as the first hint of daylight began to creep across the flagstones towards her.

She opened the shutters and peered out, afraid of what she might see. But there was no visible damage to any of the neighbouring houses, and on stepping out onto the porch, she could see no damage to her own either. When she went back inside Anna had appeared in the bedroom doorway, bleary-eyed in her nightdress.

'You'd sleep through the end of the world,' Hilde said, smiling.

'It wasn't so bad, was it? I hardly heard a thing.' She wrapped a shawl around her shoulders and padded through into the kitchen, pausing to give Hilde a quick hug. Hilde, sitting back in her chair by the stove, felt a wave of relief; perhaps things were back to the way they had been before. As though the first storm had upended everything, and this second one had set it right again.

The knocking started as they were preparing to go out: Anna to tend the vegetables, Hilde to lead the cattle out to the fields. It was heavy and insistent; most people simply tapped once and walked in, but something in the knocking felt more formal than the usual neighbourly visit. Hilde wiped her hands on her skirt and went to open the door.

'Hans. What a surprise to see you so early.'

Kurt Runde was with him, dressed in his immaculate uniform. She moved to one side and they strode into the *Stube*, suddenly taking up all the space, making her feel small and trapped. They seated themselves at the table; Runde sat back in his chair, spreading his hands out on the polished wood.

'How can I help?' she asked, taking a seat opposite them. 'I'm sorry, I wish I had tea to offer, or – it's a little early, I suppose…'

Hans waved his hand. 'It's a very brief matter.'

'A formality,' Runde added, not looking up at her. He took a sheet of paper from his jacket and laid it on the table, smoothing down the edges. Printed text, several signatures beneath it. He turned it towards her.

'We can summarise, if—'

'I know how to read.'

She bent to the page.

'We, the undersigned, affirm and acknowledge the aid of the Freiburg Hitler Youth, on the night of 16 April 1936, in the rescue of a party of English children and their teacher on the Schauinsland mountain. We offer our sincere thanks for their leadership and bravery, which saved lives and ensured the continued friendship between our two nations.'

'There's been some confusion about the details,' Runde was saying. 'We wanted to make sure they were clear.'

'They're clear to me.' She looked up. 'What about the children who died? What about the one who's still missing?'

They said nothing.

'You're asking me to sign it, I suppose?'

'It's simple enough.'

'Well, I can't. I'm afraid I have no memory of any German children.'

'Hilde.' Hans reached across the table and tried to take her hands; she flinched away from him, folding them in her lap. 'Everyone understands what a difficult time you and your sister have had. I've been explaining to Herr Runde—'

'Difficult?'

'The loss of your parents. Some... uncertainty, over your future, the future of the farm. And then the storm, those children dying so tragically. It's perfectly understandable.'

'What is perfectly understandable, Hans?'

'That you're confused. Unclear about the details. Anyone would be.'

She drew in a deep breath. She hoped her voice sounded calm, firm, assured. Because inside, despite herself, despite her own memories, she was beginning to feel unsure.

'There were no children on the mountain that night. None, except the English boys. They weren't at the inn, afterwards, and they weren't there the next day.'

Hans took a copy of the *Freiburger Zeitung* from his jacket and slid it across the table. The article to which it was folded read, in bold text, 'Exclusive: Hitler Youth came to aid of English schoolchildren'. She recognised Stefan's name beneath the headline.

'It's in the newspapers already, Hilde. You'll only be corroborating what's already been reported.'

She scanned the text quickly; no witnesses were named, no evidence given.

'Just because others have lied, it doesn't mean I should too.'

From nowhere, Kurt Runde slammed a hand on the table. The sound echoed through the *Stube*; Hilde wondered if Anna could hear it in the kitchen, if she felt the same tense fear, spreading through the walls. All the warnings she'd been given about staying quiet, not saying the wrong thing. *Dear God, make me dumb...* Surely there weren't punishments for refusing to speak a lie as well?

I could run, she thought, *before they have time to stop me. I could take Anna and run. All the way to Freiburg, if we have to.* They could go to Else, she would know what to do, how to keep them safe. Else, in her elegant flat by the river; they would drink tea from china cups and eat sweet cakes and sandwiches, and Else would speak soothing words to them, make everything alright. Did Else know about Hilde's father's desertion? Her own brother – Hilde had never thought about it before now. She hardly knew anything about her aunt, her beliefs or opinions. For Else, his desertion might have been the decision to leave Freiburg in the first place, to choose a life on the mountain and give up all the comforts they must have had in the city. What must she have thought of them all, on the few occasions she had visited? Small, provincial people. Their horizons were so narrow. Hilde drew herself up; she wouldn't be made to feel like that by anyone. Especially not by these men, sitting uninvited at her table.

'We rescued them,' she said slowly. 'Fritz, Reiner, me. The men and women of this village. It was us. Only us. You weren't even there yourself, Hans.'

There was a long silence. 'Come on, Hilde,' Hans said at last, trying to sound conversational again. 'You must admit, it seems unlikely. The men and women of this village are resilient, yes. Strong, able to withstand physical trials. But this—'

'It's what happened.'

Runde leaned forward. There was a warm, conciliatory smile on his face, but when he spoke, his voice was cold. 'This would have taken coordination,' he said. 'Precision. Discipline, of a military nature. All these things, my boys have.'

'No one has said they don't.'

Runde slid the paper towards her and took a pencil from his jacket pocket. 'That is exactly what you are saying, by staying silent.'

Hilde looked down at the paper, at the names who had already signed it. 'Hans Huber'. 'Paul Huber'. Neither of them had even been there. 'Reiner Haas'. 'Gertrud Braunling.' She shook her head. And then – there at the bottom, the most recently added, in his familiar, scrawling script.

'Fritz Feldberg'.

Chapter Twenty-Nine

There was a tiny restaurant at the end of the street, all clean white tablecloths and polished silver cutlery. Sylvia had never been inside before; it was the sort of place she could never have afforded, and she felt nervous as Kit led her in and they sat at a table by the window. The staff clearly knew Kit; the waiter flashed her a quick smile as he handed them their menus.

'I hope you don't mind,' she said. Her confident, well-enunciated tone, as well as her immaculately made-up face, reminded Sylvia of her sister. 'It's a little shabby, but the veal's good.'

'How did you find this?' Sylvia was still staring at the scarf in her hands. It was Cyril's scarf, she knew it was. The label she'd sewn on to it before the trip was there, the writing on it faded and smudged, but she recognised the stitching, the places where she'd broken the thread and begun again, the faded blue ink. 'Did he leave it at the hostel?'

'Let's order first, shall we?'

The words on the menu blurred in front of her eyes; she allowed Kit to order and sat in dazed silence as the waiter poured out two glasses of wine.

Kit watched him leave, then leaned forward, her glass in one hand. 'I've just come back from Germany,' she said. 'From Hofsgrund.'

'You've been there?'

'I've been there.'

'And the scarf—'

'It was on the mountain. At least, she said it was. And then I saw the photograph of Cyril in that article – it looks exactly the same.'

'She?'

'Sorry, I'm doing this all wrong, aren't I? I'm nervous, to be honest.' She took a long sip of wine and shook her head, the way a dog might shake off water. 'It was my first try at – well, I thought it would be easier.' She smiled. 'I don't know why. I don't know what I expected to happen. They'd welcome me with open arms, I suppose. Offer me an exclusive, and I'd send it back to *The Times*, get my own byline. Ridiculous.' She shook her head again, then looked up at Sylvia. 'Sorry. Sorry, I know you're not here to listen to me feeling sorry for myself.' She took another sip from her glass. 'A woman in Hofsgrund gave me the scarf. She said she found it on the mountain, she thought it might be important. They laughed at her. The other journalists, the police too, I suppose. They all just laughed.'

'Do you think it's important?'

'I don't know. I don't think it tells us very much on its own, does it?'

Sylvia shook her head. 'I'm glad to have it, though. Thank you.'

'What matters is what we do now.'

Sylvia stared down at the scarf in her lap, thinking of all the hours she'd spent sewing it, thinking of the rest of the clothing she'd sent Cyril out with. Why hadn't she questioned the school more, before the trip? Just a few woollen jumpers and his everyday coat, how had she not seen what was coming?

'Did you see the search?' she asked.

Kit nodded.

'And are they...' She swallowed hard. 'Are they still looking for him? I can't get any information here, they just tell me they're doing all they can. I want to go out there, but...' She hesitated, not wanting Kit to think she was asking, although she was asking, of course she was. 'It costs money,' she said finally. 'And things aren't – my friend Ruby says I should concentrate on work, make sure there's something for him to come back to. But how can I just sit around, waiting? How could anyone?'

'Of course you can't. You're his mother. Of course you want to do something.'

She could have cried with relief, that someone else saw it too.

'I'd still be there now if I could be,' Kit said. 'I had to leave. If things were different, I'd try to help. I'd try to find your boy, Sylvia.'

'What happened?'

Kit shook her head. 'I should have known, I was warned. Everyone I know who's been out there warned me.' She looked up. 'They don't want people reporting out there. Of course they don't, not unless it's a story they've invented themselves. I thought, the mountain, it was remote enough that – well, I thought perhaps they wouldn't care.'

'What happened?' she asked again.

'Oh, it was nothing obvious. They're cleverer than that. No public beatings in the square, nothing like that. He simply told me, it isn't safe, and if anything were to happen, I can't guarantee we will have the resources to help you. I knew what he meant, of course.'

'What who meant?'

Kit pulled a newspaper from her bag; the headline read 'Hitler Youth came to our brave boys' aid'. Below it was a photograph of a man in uniform, sitting in an open-topped car beside Keith. It must have been taken shortly after the accident; Keith was staring down at his feet, his face half hidden from the camera whilst the man beside him beamed at the crowds.

'Runde – he's the local youth leader.'

Sylvia drew the newspaper towards her. 'I don't understand,' she said, staring at Runde's face. 'Why would he care about it?'

The waiter returned and placed two plates in front of them. Sylvia stared at the veal, feeling her stomach lurch.

'They don't want to make a fuss,' Kit was saying. 'All this talk of war – it would be the worst time for it, any sort of dispute. Worse, anything criminal. It's the same here. Much better to pass it all off as a marvellous show of solidarity. And of course, they get to make a show of strength themselves, at the same time.'

She gestured to the newspaper again. Above the photograph of Runde and Keith in the car, there was another of the Hitler Youth children, standing in their full uniform on the side of the mountain, their faces raised to the sky.

'They look like soldiers,' Sylvia said, trying to imagine Cyril dressed like that, standing in formation alongside his classmates. 'Like little soldiers.'

'Anyway, I didn't want to write about that. So now I'm here.'

'What about this woman who found the scarf?'

Kit waved a dismissive hand. 'Just one of the villagers. She said she helped with the rescue, but they're all saying that now. Hard to tell, really. But she was there alright. She'd spoken to Hughes.'

'Spoken to him? What did he say?'

'For one thing, he told her all the boys were accounted for. Obviously they weren't. Whether that was just shock and confusion, hard to say. But there was something else as well. Or she said there was. I didn't get to ask her about it before we had to leave.'

She took a bite of her veal and sat back, chewing thoughtfully. Sylvia cut a piece from hers and held it up suspiciously; she had never eaten veal before, but it smelled good and she was, she realised suddenly, starving. She wasn't eating properly; Ruby kept telling her as much. It was the thought of cooking for herself alone that she couldn't face. She was surviving on quick, snatched meals taken at odd times; a slice of bread before bed, an apple in the middle of the morning. The meat Julia had brought her was still sitting in the larder, untouched. She chewed quickly, and took another bite.

There was a long silence. Eventually, Kit said, 'What do you think of it? All the reporting, I mean.'

'They haven't said much about Cyril.'

'They haven't said much about anything. Not your son, not the teacher. Just vague references to heroism and sacrifice. It feels like—'

'It feels like being in a play.'

'Exactly! And now they're saying the German children helped with the rescue.' They both stared at the headline. 'Hitler Youth came to our brave boys' aid'. Kit shook her head. 'It's all wrong, I can tell it's all wrong.'

'How do you know this isn't true? I know they exaggerate, but this – they wouldn't lie so openly, would they?'

'Of course they would. Don't you know they control the press over there? Can't publish a thing unless the führer's people agree.'

'What are you going to do now?'

'I can't go back without a paper to back me. It isn't safe. In the meantime, I'll try to talk to Hughes, I suppose. I imagine that inquiry didn't lead to anything?'

'Shell shock,' Sylvia said quietly.

'What?'

'That's what he told them. Why he got in such a state. Listen, if you do talk to him, will you ask him…' She hesitated. 'There was a postcard. Cyril wrote it, before the climb. He said his teacher knew there would be a storm. Will you ask him about that?'

Kit leaned forward eagerly. 'Where's this postcard now?'

'I gave it to the headmaster. I don't think…' She sighed heavily. 'I don't think I'll see it again. I suppose he'll deny ever having seen it now, won't he? If what you say is true, if all they want is for everyone to get along.' She took a tentative sip of wine and felt its warmth surging through her, emboldening her. 'We could confront him?' she said. 'The headmaster, I mean – threaten to expose him, something like that?'

Kit shook her head, staring into her glass. 'They'll only deny it. It wouldn't be hard to discredit you. I don't mean to be – I just mean, it always is, isn't it, with women?'

Sylvia thought about her outburst at the inquiry. If anyone who had witnessed it was asked, what would they say, except that she was unbalanced, crazed with grief? And who would she have to speak up for her? She hadn't shown anyone else the postcard. She'd only spoken of it to Ruby, to the police. Ruby, they'd dismiss along with her, and the policeman – she thought of the cup of tea she'd poured for him, that first morning. Just hot water, and he'd sat calmly and drunk it without saying a word.

'I shouldn't have given it to him,' she said miserably. 'I should have...' What should she have done? She'd tried everything she could think of, and Cyril was still gone, and she was still here.

The waiter took their plates and Kit ordered them both coffees; Sylvia was already nervous about the bill. Perhaps Kit was paying it, but how could she be sure? And if she did pay it, did that mean Sylvia owed her something? But she didn't want to leave. Kit was the first person who'd listened, who'd understood her need to go to Germany, to find answers.

'There was something,' she said, sipping at her coffee, 'at the inquiry. He said there was a man on the road from Freiburg – a man delivering the post. He spoke to them. Perhaps he said more than Hughes is letting on now?'

Kit frowned. 'It's not much, is it?' She sighed. 'What I really want to do is speak to that hostel, the tourist office. Find out what warnings he was given. And that woman in Hofsgrund – what was it Hughes said to her?'

'You'd go out there again?'

'If I can find a paper to back me. That's not exactly easy.'

'Why did you go in the first place?'

Kit sighed. 'It was stupid really,' she said. 'I was hearing stories, from Germans in London, people who don't like what they're doing over here. They said civilians were being arrested for protesting. Peaceful protest, sharing pamphlets, things like that. I thought if I could witness it happening, if I could write articles about that, people might take notice.'

'But you didn't see anything?'

'Oh, I saw plenty.' She looked away. 'I saw people being beaten in the street, I saw Jewish shops being vandalised. I just couldn't get anyone back here to care.'

Sylvia stared at her, thinking of all the times she'd doubted the rumours, even what Dieter had told her about his father. There was nothing in the newspapers, and wasn't that a measure of what was happening? If she didn't have that, what else was there? 'Someone must be writing about it,' she said, aware of how naive she sounded. 'Perhaps it was… could it have been—'

'Because I'm a woman? Maybe.' Kit sighed. 'Probably. I don't know. It's not like they're publishing much from anyone else. Anyway, I heard about the accident, and I thought: there. That's news even they ought to care about. I went to Hofsgrund to try and find out what had happened, but even that – they didn't want anything except those pictures of the children playing football together, the heroic stories. They didn't even want to hear from the locals, the people who actually helped.'

'What if you told them I'd go there with you?'

She could hear Ruby's voice, loud in her ear, whispering a warning as the image of the article in the *Sketch* rose in her mind. 'First she lost her husband'. *It's not like the last time,* she wanted to whisper back, *it's not the same. This time, everything will be different.*

'Wouldn't that make a difference?' she said. 'Especially now we have the scarf. His mother, Cyril's mother, out there helping with the search? Wouldn't they want those pictures?'

Kit stared at her. 'Listen, Sylvia. About the search, you should know—'

'We could do it together! I could tell them the scarf was

his, that I believe he's still out there. I could say...' She was excited now, perhaps it was the wine, perhaps it was her mind lying to her, telling her there was hope. 'I could say I can sense it, some maternal instinct, I could say I know he's still alive, that it takes a mother to know. Don't you think it does?' she added, wanting, wishing it to be true.

Kit studied her over her cup, then replaced it carefully on her saucer. 'I could try,' she said slowly. 'I can't promise anything – it's not going to be *The Times* or anything. But I could try.'

'That's all I want,' Sylvia said, feeling more animated than she had done for days. 'All I want is to try.'

Chapter Thirty

Fritz was chopping wood outside his porch; Hilde marched up to him in full view of the men who were gathered in the square, engaged in their daily ritual of exchanging news, discussing the price of wheat, the latest political upheaval. Since the German forces had entered the Rhineland almost two months ago, breaking the treaty that had been imposed on them for nearly twenty years, the talk had been of nothing but war. *We're reclaiming our status in the world*, Hans would declare to anyone who cared to listen. *We've had a boot in our face for far too long. This is only the beginning.*

'Hilde!' A voice carried across the square towards her. She turned and saw Reiner walking quickly in her direction.

She froze, feeling suddenly trapped.

'I've been hoping to catch you.'

'I've been in church every Sunday,' she said, raising her eyebrows.

'Yes I know. It's – well, I've been building up the courage. Silly, I know.'

'Reiner, if this is about—'

'Of course not!' He smiled at her. 'All that's done. I know that.'

Behind him, she could feel the men's eyes on her; *Hilde the strange one, her sister's a witch, you know, what do they do in that house, why don't they sell it? She broke Reiner's heart, you know.*

'I heard about the statement. That you haven't signed it, I mean.'

'And who told you that?'

'It's none of my business, I know. But I think you're confused, Hilde. Don't you remember, at the inn that night – there were Hitler Youth children there, I'm sure of it. I remember them sitting by the fire.'

'I don't.'

'What harm is there, though, in saying so? If I remember it, if Gertrud does, if Fritz does?'

'I would be lying. I don't have any memory myself.'

Reiner's face became harder, a frown crossing his brow. 'I'm trying to help you,' he said. 'I don't understand why you won't make things easy on yourself, Hilde.'

'Are we still talking about the statement?'

'Perhaps we aren't. Hilde, no one would think less of you.'

'I would think less of me! I would! Isn't that enough?'

Fritz had come over to them now, the axe still in his hand. He said nothing, standing silently behind Hilde.

'There's still time,' Reiner said falteringly. 'You can still help yourself. You can still let us help you.' She saw, for the first time, the Party badge on his collar. When had he joined? Since the accident, or had he simply not been wearing his membership openly? Over his shoulder she saw Hans Huber staring at them. Wondering, no doubt, what sort of hex Hilde Meyer was casting on her neighbours, what new trouble she was about to cause.

'I thought...' she began, thinking of all the times she'd heard Reiner mock Hans for his dogged devotion to the Party, his idealism. He followed her gaze to the badge and turned slightly, adjusting his collar nervously.

'Please, Hilde,' he said. 'Be sensible.'

She took a step closer to him; perhaps it was Fritz, standing behind her with the axe in his hand, that emboldened her. But then, hadn't Fritz signed that statement too? 'I'm not interested,' she said slowly. 'I'm not interested in you, in signing that paper, in—'

'In what? In the Party, that's what you were going to say, isn't it? Do you know what happens to people like you, Hilde? They get sent to Dachau, that's what.'

'I can look after myself.'

He shook his head. She heard her own words, how naive they sounded, how childish. Looking up at Reiner, she was shocked to see tears gathering in the corners of his eyes.

'I'm sorry for you then,' he said, putting a hand on her arm which she shook quickly away.

'Come on,' Fritz said behind her. 'Come inside, it's going to rain.'

It was dark in Fritz's *Stube*; he had drawn the shutters and lit lamps in every alcove. The painting was nearly finished; the expanse of snow had been widened, and it seemed to glitter now in the painted light that shone from behind the mountain. Hilde peered closer; the tiny shadow she thought she'd seen last time was gone, only fir trees and farmhouses breaking up the landscape. Or perhaps it had never been there.

'It's lovely, Fritz.'

He shrugged. 'It's not what I wanted. But it will do, I think. I should have gone out to the cabin, seen the early morning light on the snow. Ach, I'm too old for all that now.'

'You're not so old.'

As she said it, she studied his face as she'd studied the painting; the lines and creases across his forehead, around his eyes. His body, slightly hunched, but still strong. Still able to ski across the mountain in the dark, to raise an axe. He'd held Anna on his shoulders once, on outings to the summit, or on their way to the fields to meet Hilde's father. But it was true, if she looked at him with the eyes of a stranger she would see age, weighing him down as though something under the earth was slowly pulling him back to itself.

'My father would never have signed that statement,' she said quietly. Fritz sighed, easing himself into his chair by the fire and indicating the other. 'Why did you?' she asked bitterly as she sat down.

But Fritz didn't reply.

'Is this what you meant?' she pressed. 'You told me we should keep our heads down – is this what you meant?'

'I didn't know what I meant. But I'm not surprised.'

'They weren't there, Fritz. I know they weren't there.'

'It doesn't matter.'

'Of course it matters.'

'No, it doesn't!'

She looked up, surprised; she'd never heard Fritz raise his voice before.

'They've decided those boys were there,' he said wearily. 'So they were there.'

'Don't you care about…' She hesitated, unsure of the right words.

'About what?'

'About truth. My father would have wanted us to tell the truth. Even though – he wouldn't care about getting along with powerful people, about saying the right things. Fritz, what he'd think of you—'

'It's not always that simple.' Fritz leaned towards the fire and pushed another log into the flames, then looked up at her. 'Did your father ever tell you how we met?'

'He said you went to the farm, asked him to print some of your designs.'

'We met years before that. Before I came to Hofsgrund, before this new government.'

She looked up, surprised. 'I didn't know.'

'No one does. We met in Freiburg.'

'When he lived there? But that was—'

'Before the war, yes.'

'That's years before he said.' She stared into the fire. She was struggling to reconcile her image of her father, a man who cared so much about truth, with the man she was learning about now. How could he have hidden so much from her?

'I did some printing work with him once. As an artist – it was a long time ago. He used to come for dinner. His sister – your aunt – she was great friends with my wife.'

Hilde didn't know what to say. Fritz had never mentioned a wife before. She'd never thought much about his family at all; he'd always been alone. She looked at him, trying to imagine him as a younger man, back in Freiburg with her father, working at the printing press. The two of them sharing jokes at the end of the day, walking home through the city, past cafes and restaurants and bookshops, all of it images derived from her aunt's postcards, no more vivid than paper cut-outs. She tried to cast him in the world she'd already imagined for Else, elegant parlours, cocktail parties and trips to the theatre. A whole life, a whole world she'd never seen.

He got up and opened a drawer in the sideboard, taking out a bundle which he upwrapped slowly on his knees. Inside was a silver photograph frame which he handed to Hilde. It was a picture of a couple in wedding dress. A woman with dark eyes and a quick, amused expression as she looked up at the man who, Hilde saw now, was a much younger, more upright version of Fritz, his arm around the woman's waist.

'Ada.'

'What happened to her?'

There was a silence as she stared at the photograph. 'She died,' he said. 'A few years back, before I came here. That's not why I mentioned Freiburg, anyway.'

'Why did you?'

Fritz was staring into the fire now, as though he was unsure how to go on. Eventually, he said, 'Look at the photograph again'.

'What am I looking for?'

'You don't see it? Not Ada and me, what's behind us.'

The picture was grainy, faded, but Hilde could make out

brickwork and an arch behind them. She looked closer and saw what Fritz meant: a five-pointed star, inlaid into the stone.

'It's a synagogue,' she said, looking up at him. 'She was Jewish?'

'She was. I am.'

She stared at him. 'But you come to church. Every Sunday. Why, Fritz?'

But she saw why, or thought she saw. What had he said to her, just a few days before? *The important thing is to keep your heads down.* She thought of the cartoon Anna had found, the daily vitriol they heard on the radio. The laws which had been passed a few months earlier. Jews were no longer citizens, no longer afforded the protection of the state. They were Untermensch. Subhuman.

'What happened?' she said, feeling her mouth growing dry, her heart beating fast.

'We had a business selling cloth. My wife ran it; I used the room above it to paint. Society portraits, things like that. Nothing like these,' he said, glancing at the painting on its easel. 'We were doing well, until he became chancellor, that's when it started. Just boycotts, at first – we survived those, most people didn't seem to care. We still had friends. It just got worse.' He looked away.

'So—'

'Your father was a friend. He came to the shop sometimes. We used to meet in the square, drink coffee together. After Ada died, he visited more. So he saw. He saw what it was like. How it wasn't going to get better.'

'What was it like?' She knew, she knew what he was going to say. So why was she making him say it?

'They spat on me in the street. I could take that, but they were just getting bolder. I was attacked, more than once. The shop was looted. Well, that didn't matter so much, I was winding it down, I couldn't keep it going without her. But it was my home too. Your father came to see me one afternoon.

We went for a walk, and when we came back, there had been a fire. The whole place, it was burning.'

Hilde felt too ashamed to look up at him now. She sat with her hands pressed between her knees, blinking furiously to stop the tears falling.

'I still had friends, they helped me find somewhere to stay. And then your father found this house was for sale. He helped me arrange it. I changed my name. In Freiburg, they'd just assume I'd left the country; enough people had by then. I thought, if I came here, I could be someone else. Get away from all that madness. But now—'

'Now it's here too.'

She held out the photograph and Fritz took it, wrapping it up again in cloth and placing it at the bottom of the drawer. How long would it be, Hilde wondered, before that hiding place wouldn't be enough?

'So, you ask me why I signed their bit of paper. Why I don't throw up my hands and make a fuss. It will change nothing, Hilde. It will stop nothing. It will only make them angry, and they'll turn their anger towards me, and then who knows what else they'll do? What they'll find out? I've managed this far by keeping my head down, pretending to be someone else. Is it brave? Perhaps not. If you ask me, there's a thin line between brave and foolish. A very thin line.'

She stared at her feet, lost for anything to say. She'd read so much in the newspapers about what was happening, but she'd never thought about the reality. What would have happened to Fritz, if he'd stayed? What could still happen to him now? She wondered suddenly about that sexton, the one who'd torn up the flag. It was more than a year ago; where was he now? Was he even still alive?

'I'm sorry,' she said at last. 'I didn't know. He never told me.'

'People don't have to tell you everything, Hilde.'

She nodded, still unable to look up.

'He was a good man, your father. He may not have told

you the truth about everything, but that much is true. I would have done the same for him.'

Hilde walked home through the rain with Fritz's words ringing in her ears. How could she have been so stupid, how could she not have seen? She had assumed the only risk in Hofsgrund was for a citizen who said the wrong thing, was too critical of the regime – *so I won't to Dachau come.* She'd never imagined all the rest of it could stretch this far, as far as Fritz, who was practically a father to her and Anna. *You can't tell anyone, Hilde,* he'd said before she left. *I'm trusting you with this, you can't say a word.*

Back home, she went straight to the basement and sorted through the papers she'd found until she had the one she was looking for. 'Walter Meyer. Notice of dishonourable discharge.'

The rain was falling harder, clattering against the thatched roof, the windows as she climbed back to the kitchen and knelt in front of the stove. *I won't,* she thought fiercely as she took one final look at the paper. *I won't say a word.* She pushed the paper into the flames and watched its edges curl and flare, thinking of her mother's hard, determined face that day she'd burned the seed packets, her father's letters. Why hadn't they ever destroyed this, the evidence of the secret he'd been running from for so long? And how long would it be before Fritz would have to light a fire of his own, watch his photographs, his old life, disappear in the flames?

I won't say a word, she promised Fritz as she watched the paper burn, listening to the rain hammering harder against the walls. She knew how to keep a secret as well as he did. She'd keep him safe, just as she would keep Anna safe. As for the rest of it – well, she'd follow Fritz's advice. Keep her head down, her mouth shut, her eyes closed. *Dear God, make me dumb.*

Chapter Thirty-One

She had only been inside Ruby's home once before. As she stood on the doorstep, where they'd met many times to walk to Guild meetings together, Sylvia felt suddenly nervous. Until what had happened to Cyril, until the last few days, they'd kept their inner lives carefully separate. She knew no more about Ruby's life behind that door than Ruby knew about Arthur.

She heard footsteps in the hall and took in a breath.

'Sylvia.' Ruby was still wearing her dressing gown. She looked as though she was halfway through her morning routine; half of her hair was pinned, the rest hanging in curls. 'Sorry, I've only just got the kids out.'

'I'm too early. I'm sorry – I just wanted to apologise. For yesterday.'

'Oh, don't be so silly. Come in.'

Ruby lived in a narrow terraced house a few minutes' walk from Sylvia; the walls were so thin Sylvia could hear the neighbours rowing as they went through to the kitchen. The surfaces were covered with unwashed crockery and piles of papers; she paused in the doorway, unsure if Ruby wanted her to continue.

'Sorry, we're not very on top of – Reg had to leave very early – I'm about to go to work myself—'

'Please don't go to any trouble.'

They sat at the table. Ruby cleared a pile of papers away, but not before Sylvia saw the words 'issued by the Eugenics Society' in tiny print.

'More flyers?'

Ruby shrugged. 'I know what you think about it all.'

'Do you? I'm not sure myself.'

'We deserve the right to choose, don't we?'

'Ruby, that's not what…' The motion at the meeting had only talked about voluntary sterilisation, it was true. But she couldn't shake what Julia had told her. *Merely a first step.* And even if it never became compulsory, there would always be people unable to consent, and what would it mean for them? 'It's not just going to be offered up to whoever wants it. They choose, Ruby, not us. They decide who they think should have children, and who shouldn't.'

'Well, maybe that's not such a bad thing.'

'You can't possibly think that.'

Ruby looked around her at the chaos of her kitchen, the unwashed dishes in the sink. 'What government would say I was doing a good job?'

'It's hardly their business!'

'Well, maybe it should be. Maybe we need them to help, sometimes. Maybe we need…' She slumped forward, resting her head in her hands. 'I don't know. I'm tired, Sylvia. I'm so tired. If I had been offered a choice, it wouldn't have been this.' She looked up. 'I love my children. But it wouldn't have been this.'

'What about me?'

Ruby stared at her. 'What do you mean?'

'Nothing,' she said quickly. Ruby had never asked about Arthur, and Sylvia didn't want her to now. Had she been offered a choice, when Arthur came home? It hadn't felt like it at the time, but now she wasn't sure. All she knew was that she'd been expected to be happy, to recognise the gift they'd been given, and that, once he'd stepped through the door, no one had wanted to hear about what happened afterwards.

'Remember what Keith Hughes said at the inquiry? About having shell shock?'

Ruby snorted. 'Convenient enough story. I can't stand it, how they make up such nonsense. There's enough men came back without making a fuss about it. Reg never says a word.'

Sylvia swallowed hard. 'But what if it's real?'

'You don't want to go believing in that nonsense, love.'

There was a shout from the other side of the wall, and a woman's voice cried out. Ruby flinched, her fingers tightening on the plate she was holding.

'I don't know,' Sylvia said. 'People don't always act how you expect, that's all.'

'Well, I don't see how it would make him take a group of kids on a dangerous climb, in a storm. I don't see what imaginary condition would do *that*.'

'A lot of them kill themselves.' She picked up one of the flyers, absently folding it into smaller and smaller pieces. 'Did you know that? The men who came back with shell shock – I know you don't believe in it, but it's true. A lot of them die.'

'All sorts of people kill themselves.'

'I know, but—'

'You think – Sylvia, that's a funny way to kill yourself. And to risk the children like that – ach, you're just imagining up stories.'

'Maybe that's what he was doing. Maybe he was thinking of what's coming for them.' She fingered the white poppy on her blouse. *Mr Hughes says there will likely be a storm, and it will be a good test of our blood to get through it.*

She could see the face of that boy in France so clearly. The first boy she hadn't been able to save. There had been so many others afterwards, but his was the face that had lingered. Pale blue eyes. Sometimes when she woke up he was standing by her window, looking out at the cold haze of morning light, and when he turned to her now, it was Cyril's face staring at her, Cyril's eyes blinking back snow.

She thought of the photograph of Keith in the papers, sitting in the back of a car, a German official beside him. The dead, blank look in his eyes. She'd seen that look so many times – in Arthur, in Ruby, Julia – anyone who'd endured those long, terrifying years. People must see it in her, she thought. All those times people asked her what nursing had been like, what she'd done, trying to drag it up from the place she'd kept it so safely buried.

'Look, I know you think he made it up. But it's real, Ruby. I know it is. I've seen it before.'

'In your patients?'

'Maybe. No, not really. That was all bullet wounds and shrapnel, blood and bones. The shock doesn't come until after. Years after, sometimes.'

'Then—'

'I saw it in Arthur.'

There was a long silence. Eventually, Ruby put down the plates and sat opposite her. Sylvia glanced down at one of the flyers on the table between them. 'Insanity in the family? Should you marry?'

'I didn't know,' she said softly. 'You never said.'

She took a deep breath. 'When he came home, it wasn't really him. I mean, of course it was, but it felt like a stranger had moved in with me.' Ruby was still staring at her, but it wasn't really Ruby she was telling anyway. It was Cyril; all the things she should have explained to him long ago.

She remembered waking alone on their first morning back together and finding Arthur in the kitchen, standing by the open back door. When she tried to speak to him he couldn't move. It was like that for weeks; the more she tried to reach for the person he'd been before, the further away he seemed. They hardly spoke, and she began to feel resentful of his silence. *I saw things too*, she wanted to say, *didn't we all have it hard?* At night, he curled himself up on his side of the bed while she lay awake thinking of the child she'd been imagining – half fearing – for so long, who now seemed no more real than her dreams of becoming a doctor, of doing her own research, of making sure what had happened to that boy, the wrong blood in the wrong arm, never happened to anyone else. She'd thought, after the war was over, there would be opportunities waiting for her, but there no longer seemed to be a need for nurses who'd only been volunteers, whose training was only half finished. And there was no money to complete it now. Arthur was barely able to work and she was supporting both of them, taking in other people's washing and cleaning their houses.

Then there were the fits, which usually came at night. She'd be woken by screaming, his body flailing against some imagined enemy, and she'd have to leave the room to avoid being caught in its wake. *It's normal*, friends told her, *you have to be patient,* and eventually she stopped talking about Arthur, stopped seeing anyone, ashamed of their inability to put the pieces back together again.

'There were good times too,' she told Ruby, 'it wasn't all...' She fingered the pale skin of her forearm, the places where his fingers had marked her skin. Afterwards he would cry, too ashamed to look at her, and she would put her arms around him and tell him she understood, that she knew he hadn't meant to do it, it hadn't really been him.

Ruby took her hands and she closed her eyes as a wave of grief passed over her.

'What happened to him?' Ruby said. 'Arthur – what happened?'

Sylvia thought about telling her. Saying the words out loud for the first time. She should have told Cyril, she knew that now. She shouldn't have made up her stories, tales of a heroic climb, his father disappearing into the mist, just to save them both the pain of the truth. She saw Arthur's face suddenly, sitting across from her at the Red Lion, reaching for her hands and smiling, and she tried to hold onto it as her own hands tightened around Ruby's, as she pushed away the memory of what came after.

Dieter wasn't in the lab the next day; the only staff member Sylvia encountered as she went about her work was Eileen, who offered her a brisk nod as she entered her office. No one had asked her about Cyril, although they must have realised by now, her face had been in the newspapers, she had – what would her mother have called it? – *made an exhibition of herself.* As though she was an exhibit in a jar, a skull laid bare in the museum which had been carefully dismantled.

She wanted to tell Dieter, wanted to ask him what it meant. Did blood really dictate everything, the narrative of a person's life? When she dreamed about her son, he was crawling on his knees on the side of the mountain, searching for shelter somewhere, in a barn, amongst trees, the tunnels under the mountain, and sometimes he had Arthur's face, sometimes shots were being fired as he dodged his way between the trees. People continued – in letters, in casual conversations, when they recognised her – to reassure her that he was still out there somewhere. That he'd found that shelter, that someone had taken him in, he'd forgotten his own name, perhaps, didn't that happen to people who'd suffered a trauma, wasn't it normal? He'd come back again, and everything would be alright. She couldn't tell them what she really feared. *That doesn't sound like my Cyril, that doesn't sound like something he could do. You don't know everything about him. You didn't know his father.* She thought of his wide, frightened eyes, the night he'd found her with Keith. Tried to imagine him curling up beside an animal in a barn, somewhere on a mountainside in Germany, using its warmth to keep himself alive. Later, coming home to her and picking up the pieces, carrying on. *A test of our blood.*

When she finally reached home, aching and exhausted, there was another pile of cards on the mat. She sifted through them, separating out the notes from journalists, the cards from friends which, increasingly, were beginning to resemble condolences. At the bottom of the pile was a telegram; a single line.
    'CALL AT ONCE. KIT.'

Chapter Thirty-Two

Hilde was in the kitchen kneading dough, listening to a rainstorm outside and pretending not to hear the pounding at the door, the shouts from outside. Anna had gone out early; to collect herbs for her concoctions, she'd said, but Hilde wasn't sure if that was true, there'd been something in Anna's eyes, she hadn't looked Hilde fully in the face. It was late afternoon and she hadn't come back; Hilde was trying to tell herself it was normal, Anna was nearly a grown woman now, there was no reason to be afraid.

'Hilde Meyer? We need to come in.'

'Open the door, Hilde, please.'

The pounding grew louder and she thought of Fritz, in his house by the square. Each time there was a hammering on the door like this, men in uniform on the other side of it, the fear that must wash through him, the effort it must take to keep calm, to seem unafraid.

Hans and Paul Huber were on the porch, both in uniform, with three brownshirts Hilde hadn't seen before. She stepped back, saying nothing as they fanned out through the house.

'Hilde, I'm sorry,' Hans began, as his son went through into her kitchen and began opening drawers.

'What are they doing?' The house seemed suddenly smaller than ever, filled by the men's bodies and the smell of damp sweat and cigarettes. From the *Stube* she heard a heavy thud as the men rifled through cupboards and drawers, rolled back the carpet. There was a crash from the kitchen; something broken. The men didn't pause; the footsteps carried on, crawling through the life she and Anna had barely managed to rebuild for themselves. She thought of Reiner, standing in the square. *Do you know what happens to people like you?*

'What is it you're looking for?' she asked Hans. 'Perhaps it would be quicker, if—'

There was a terrifying blank look in his eyes, as though he didn't know her. A thought struck her – it was absurd, but she asked it anyway.

'Is it the child? The missing child – because I haven't seen anyone else's houses being searched?'

Hans didn't answer. They stood together in the hall, silent and unmoving as the chaos continued around them. She heard them open the trapdoor to the basement, clattering down the stairs, and then one of them gave a shout, and Hans went to join them.

Hilde followed, watching as they carried boxes from the basement, the dust of a hundred dried, crushed rose petals trailing after them. Her eyes flickered briefly to the stove, thinking of the paper she'd burned just a couple of days earlier. Surely they couldn't still care about that?

'My parents' things…' she began, but they didn't pause, their footsteps echoing in the bowels of the house. 'Hans, what is this?'

'Is this all of it?' Hans asked, impassive. 'Is there anything else of your father's in the house?'

She stared at him. 'I don't understand. Hans, if you could just tell me what you're looking for—'

He shot her a look, and she hesitated.

'No,' she said, thinking in a rush of the seed packet, hidden beneath the floorboards. She would still have that, anyway. 'There's nothing else.'

One of the men gave a shout and brought something to Hans:

some of the sheets of newspaper she'd torn up for the fire, clearly identifiable as *Der Stürmer* by their cartoon images, the vitriol of their headlines. She'd thought she'd burned all of them.

Hans took the papers, slowly turning them over in his hands. 'You tore this up?' he asked, looking up at her.

'Just for kindling. I always use newspapers.'

'No other reason? It wasn't, perhaps, because of the content?'

'No, I—'

'You don't have a Party flag displayed.'

'On the house? Hardly anyone does.' It wasn't true, she realised. They'd been appearing during the past few days like buds bursting from the earth; splashes of red and white and black all across the village, visible from high up on the ridge above the church. She hadn't wanted to see, hadn't looked up as she'd passed them. She didn't want one for their house, but increasingly the lack of one, rather than its presence, was conspicuous.

Hans gestured to one of the brownshirts, who held a bundle out to her. 'I expect to see it displayed in your window by this evening,' he said, and she found she was nodding mutely, holding it to her chest.

'Hilde, what happened?'

Anna was standing in the kitchen doorway, a basket in her hand filled with plants and roots. Hilde looked up, seeing for the first time the mess of it all. The kitchen table had been upended, crockery smashed and strewn across the floor. The dough she'd been kneading was trampled against the flagstones; a heavy boot print pressed into its surface. The trapdoor still lay open, cold air rushing up from the empty basement. Only the printing press and the two sledges remained, alongside the empty storage barrels.

She was sitting on the floor, staring at the stove, at the flames dancing against the glass door. Anna knelt beside her, putting her hands on her sister's shoulders.

'What happened?' she said again.

'Your friend Paul,' she said. 'And Hans. And others, I don't know who they all were. Brownshirts.'

'You must have done something. Why would they...' She paused, dropping her hands and staring at the floor. 'It's that statement, isn't it? The one you won't sign.'

'How do you know about that? Paul, I suppose. Anyway, it wasn't that. They were asking about Pa. They took away his things. They're all gone. Did you tell them something, Anna?'

Anna fetched the broom and began sweeping up the broken crockery and spilled food. 'I haven't told them anything,' she said. 'Why don't you just sign it, Hilde? What can it matter? Fritz has – everyone has. Why do you always—'

'What? Always what?'

She paused and looked up. 'Why do you always choose things that make us stand out?'

'You're talking about Reiner, aren't you? You said you didn't mind.'

'Well, maybe I do mind. Maybe I'll marry Paul. Maybe I understand you have to think about other people sometimes, not just yourself.'

'Anna!'

'I'm sorry.' She did look sorry, Hilde thought. But there was something else in her expression as she stared at Hilde – a contempt, a disappointment, as though Hilde was a poor crop, a lame cow, a day of bad weather that set back the harvest.

'They did come to ask me questions,' Anna said quietly. 'The other day, when you were with Fritz. They had a woman with them.'

'What woman?'

'She said she was from the social services. In Freiburg.'

A cold, hollow feeling filled Hilde's stomach.

'She wanted to know what it's been like, since our mother—'

'What it's been like?'

'Whether you look after me. Whether there's enough food.'

'Anna, my God. Why didn't you tell me this?'

'I didn't want you to be angry. You've been so angry.'

Hilde put down the broom and went to sit opposite Anna at the stove. The sun was setting outside: a blaze of pink and orange silhouetting the trees through the open side door.

'We've been alright. Haven't we?'

Anna shrugged, looking away.

'What did you tell her? I'm sorry I've been angry, Anna. I didn't mean – I'm sorry it's been so hard.'

'They asked about Pa too.' Anna looked up, and the expression on her face filled Hilde with more fear than the men had that afternoon, spreading out through her home and ransacking her belongings.

'Anna, what did you say?'

'It was after what you said about Paul. About how I shouldn't talk to him. I was angry with you. I was angry with him, for leaving us. I didn't mean it.'

Lying awake that night, Anna shifting and sighing beside her, Hilde realised she'd eaten nothing that day. Somehow, with the upheaval, with the work that had had to be abandoned, she'd forgotten, and now she felt a gnawing, angry emptiness spreading through her bones. Had Anna eaten? Probably not, she thought, unless she'd found a meal somewhere else. With Paul Huber, perhaps, in their well-ordered, well-stocked kitchen, enough children to share the workload, a good-sized portion for everyone, a proper German family. Was that what Anna had told the woman from Freiburg? *I go for days sometimes without food. She doesn't even think of it, there isn't enough to go around anyway. She turned down Reiner Haas out of spite, just to prove to everyone she doesn't need his help, that she doesn't need anyone. He could have saved us, and she turned him away, and now there isn't enough to eat. She doesn't want children, did you know that? She doesn't want to help Germany rebuild, take back its place in the world.*

239

Could they take Anna away? She'd never considered it before, that the life they were building was so fragile, so easily threatened. She'd not considered it when she'd said no to Reiner, when she'd refused to sign the statement. She'd only thought of herself. Was Anna right? *You have to think about other people sometimes, not just yourself.* If she refused to agree to a lie, was that where it would end?

Nonsense, she thought, turning over and burying her face in the pillow. They were going to leave, go to Freiburg, where no one would care about such small, petty things. There were bigger things in the world, more important things, than two girls and the fragments of a life they were trying to piece back together. In Freiburg, they could disappear. Else had managed it well enough, hadn't she? Hilde had written to her, a tentative suggestion of a visit, nothing more permanent, no suggestion that they might need more of her help than that. She was still waiting for a reply.

She thought of the day Else had come to their mother's funeral, even though they'd hated each other, even though, any time Else was mentioned, Hilde's mother would roll her eyes and sigh heavily, as though Else were a family curse, better left unnamed. *Oh, Else.* Else had asked about Hilde's parents' belongings that day, so casually Hilde had forgotten until now. Affronted, Hilde had told her everything had been burned, all of it destroyed. She hadn't been able to read Else's expression; was it relief, or disappointment? Had there really been something of value in those boxes? Something her aunt wanted, something Hans wanted? Was that what the men had come searching for?

She shook her head; it was nonsense, a fairy tale. There was nothing in those boxes for Hans to find, nothing but rose petals, papers and dust. Fragments of a life she couldn't get back, however hard she tried.

Chapter Thirty-Three

Sylvia went to the telephone at the end of the street, took out the card Kit had given her and dialled the number with shaking hands. It rang five or six times before a terse, clipped voice answered.

'Hello?'

'Hello? It's Sylvia Clayton. You sent me a—'

'Sylvia! Yes. When can you be ready?'

'What?' She put one hand over her ear, straining to hear. The sun through the window of the call box was in her eyes, blinding her as she took in Kit's tinny, distant voice.

'For Germany. You do still want to come, don't you?'

For a moment, she couldn't say anything. It had been so long, so long since anyone had offered her hope.

'Of course I do.'

'Well then. I found a newspaper willing to back us.'

'Are you sure? To join the search party? To say he's still alive, like I said?'

Later, trying to remember the conversation, she thought she'd heard some slight hesitation in Kit's voice, a pause before she answered. It had been difficult to hear; a crowd was gathering at the other side of the road, men and women with placards raised, shouting over the noise of the traffic. Sylvia thought at once of Ruby's flyers, the petition – had it come to this already, were they marching in the streets?

'Yes, like you said. We can start in Freiburg, ask some

questions. And then we can go on to the village. We can find Hilde.'

'And we can join the search?'

'Yes, yes, we can do all of it. Listen, Sylvia, there'll be some other things. Photographs, some ceremonial nonsense. That's all secondary, though. We're going to find the truth. We're going to find out what happened, what Keith Hughes really did that day.'

'And Cyril?'

There was a silence at the other end of the line. She looked up at the crowds massing at the end of the street. They seemed to have materialised from nowhere, all of them wearing the same dark uniforms, shirts and trousers or neatly pressed black skirts. They were moving closer, surrounding her in the call box as they flowed past her and she realised as she read the words on their placards that it wasn't anything to do with Ruby's flyers, that it was something quite different. 'KEEP OUT ALIEN JEWS.' 'MOSLEY FOR PM.' 'BRITAIN FIRST.' A woman in the crowd caught her eye for a moment and smiled, as though beckoning her towards them; Sylvia turned away and, when she looked again, the woman had melted into the crowd.

'Sylvia? Are you still there?'

'I'm here.'

'Well? Will you come? I need to let them know now.'

She waited for the crowd to pass on, but more and more of them seemed to be joining in, swelling their numbers, as though, all along the street, people were being roused out of their everyday lives by some larger, irresistible force.

'Of course. Of course I'll come.'

She dropped the telephone and sank to her knees, closed her eyes and tried to shut out the sound of them, rising higher and higher until it filled her head, rang in her ears, pushing out thoughts of Germany, of Cyril, of anything except a crowd united in a common anger.

Chapter Thirty-Four

Keith stood in front of the mirror in his childhood bedroom, straightening his tie and frowning at himself. Was this what Jack would look like now? They had always looked similar, but there had been a mischievous, rebellious twinkle in Jack's eyes that Keith had never quite been able to imitate.

Sounds of the street waking up filtered through the shutters; cats scrapping and the rumble of the first bus rolling past. He looked over at the clock; still two hours until he needed to leave. Was he really going through with it? Each time he felt certain, something else made him waver. Now, it was nothing more than the warmth of his own bed, the memory of his brother, the familiar way the first morning light picked its way along the carpet.

He pulled a suitcase from under his bed and began folding clothes into it, counting out socks and underpants, jackets and woollens. There was space for a few books; he picked up his copy of *Grimms' Fairy Tales* and laid it on top of the pile. The cover showed two children holding hands, about to enter a dark, dense forest. He leafed through the pages; more forests, mountains, menacing doorways. When he picked up his hiking boots a shower of mud and pine needles fell from them and he jumped back, staring at the fragments of the mountain scattered across the carpet.

'What are you doing with that suitcase?'

He blinked at his mother, standing in the doorway.

'Keith, did you hear me?'

'Just taking a little trip.'

She was beside him now, smelling of bacon and shedding flour all over his shoes. He didn't trust himself to look at her, but he held her hand briefly, her palm surprisingly soft, and squeezed it tight.

'You'll be alright, won't you?'

'Of course I'll be alright. There's a woman here to see you.'

'What? What woman?'

'How should I know? She's pretty, I'll say that for her.'

He wondered what sort of woman his mother would consider 'pretty.' A terrible idea struck him.

'It's not one of the parents?' He should have written that letter to Sylvia, he should have gone round, even. What must she think of him?

'Of course not.'

'Well, didn't she say what she wanted?'

'It's not my job to be questioning your callers, Keith Hughes. Go in and ask her yourself.'

She turned on her way out, seeming to take in the room for the first time.

'It's nice, seeing you back here,' she said. 'Almost like – almost as though...' She left the sentence unfinished, closing the door behind her.

The woman was sitting in his father's chair. He flinched at that – instinctively wanting to move her, to smooth out the cushion and erase all traces of her. His mother had been right, she was pretty – she had dark hair and eyes and a quick, intelligent expression. She was wearing a tweed skirt and jacket, her hair pinned back; she had made an effort, he thought. As Keith watched from the doorway, her gaze settled on the photograph of Mosley and he felt the familiar flush of shame. Sometimes, when his father was out, he thought about taking the photograph down. Hiding it, and denying all knowledge if he was asked. But even if he did, there were still the newspapers, the volumes on the shelves. Fascism oozed through the flat; it wasn't so easy to make it go away.

'Can I help you?'

She stood up, and he knew at once why she had come. He couldn't say why, but there was an edge to her, a resolve which made him instantly nervous.

'I suppose Mum didn't imagine you could be a reporter,' he said. 'She's very old-fashioned.'

'I told her I was a friend of yours.'

'She's desperate to marry me off.' He had meant it as a joke, but it came out awkwardly, made things even more uncomfortable. Avoiding each other's eyes, they both glanced up at the photograph of Mosley above the fireplace. Beside it, Jack's face smiled down at them, frozen in place, his chin raised.

She handed him a card. He glanced at it – 'Katherine Harris, reporter' – and resolved to say nothing. Though she didn't seem to be waiting for his permission. She sat down in his father's armchair again and he nearly cried out.

'How on earth did you get this address?'

She shrugged, as though the question was a meaningless one. He couldn't help it, part of him was impressed. He'd managed to avoid the reporters for so long, and this one had simply rung the bell and walked in.

'Why aren't you at home?' she asked, and it was Keith's turn to shrug. 'I heard you went to the seaside.'

'It's a free country.'

'Oh, I know. It just looks bad, that's all.'

'Bad? I'm not being accused of anything.'

'Of course.' She stared hard at him, and he felt himself blushing.

'Well, I'm not saying anything. So you may as well leave.'

She didn't move. He wouldn't tell her a thing, she couldn't make him.

'I'll call the police,' he said impulsively. 'I have a perfect right—'

'I've been to Hofsgrund. Spoke to a woman there.'

He looked up at her; he hadn't been prepared for that. He wondered what on earth he'd been thinking, coming back to London. That man in the hotel lounge, and then again in the street – it was paranoia, that was all. Ridiculous, now he thought back on it. He could have stayed there, played the hero, let them all crowd in close and hidden amongst them.

'She told me you didn't notice one of the boys was missing. Is that true?'

'I was confused. That's all been gone over now.'

'I know what else you told her.'

He wouldn't sit down. If he sat down, it would feel like giving in. He could feel his legs beginning to shake. This was how they got to you. He might confess to anything, he thought, just because of how she was looking at him, as though she could see inside his head.

'I don't know what you mean.'

'Are you going somewhere?' She nodded to the suitcase in the hall.

'That's none of your business either.'

'I'm working on an article' she said. 'It would be easier if you gave me your side of things now. What you told Hilde—'

'I didn't tell her anything. I don't know what you're talking about.'

Why had he done it, what had he been thinking? How could he take it back? This was just one of their tricks, fishing about for weaknesses, intimidating people into admitting to things they had no business asking about. He spread out his hands. *I don't know what to tell you.*

'I've seen a postcard,' she said. 'Written by one of the boys, before the climb.'

He raised his eyebrows. *And?*

'It says you warned him about a storm.'

There was a long silence. Eventually, pressing down his

growing fear, Keith said, 'Let's see it then. This postcard. Where is it now?'

She smiled. He smiled back, feeling as though he'd won a tiny battle.

'And what about the German boys?' she said.

'The – who?'

'The Hitler Youth. It's all over the German papers. They helped with the rescue, they're saying.'

He stared at her. 'Of course,' he said, 'I've seen what they're saying.'

'You must remember yourself if they were there?'

'I've explained already. My memories are – fragmented.'

'Shell shock,' she said, and he looked at her strangely. He'd said that to the inquiry, but nothing had been published yet. How could she know? He wished he hadn't seen the articles. He wished he'd kept up his policy of not reading the papers at all. Since those first positive reports he'd begun devouring everything he could find, cutting out the clippings and keeping them in a drawer by his bed, rereading them whenever he felt the first wave of a panic washing over him. Each time he read a new article he felt his memories shifting and changing, until he couldn't be sure what was real and what was only a suggestion. Had they been there? It was possible, he thought, of course it was possible. 'And you don't know what happened to the missing child?'

'Of course I don't know. Don't you think I would have said something by now, if I did?'

After she had gone he sat on the stool opposite his father's chair for a long time, staring at the slight dent in the cushion she'd left behind. He'll know, Keith thought, when he comes back. He'll know someone's been in his chair. He was glad he hadn't moved the photograph above the mantelpiece; he'd know about that too.

I know what else you told her. She was just bluffing, he

knew that, but still it had made him feel uneasy, as though something inside him was written on the outside. He felt stripped down, that feeling of standing naked in front of the doctor for his conscription examination, every inch of his body inspected and recorded. *If you could just cough for me. Now, read the words on this card. Vision, excellent.*

She'd asked about Cyril Clayton. That was a bluff too, it must have been. She didn't know anything about Keith's last image of him, standing alone on the ridge, his green scarf bright against the snow. Didn't know, either, about the night before the hike. Clayton, sitting opposite him by the fire, his feet barely touching the ground in the youth hostel's big, overstuffed armchairs. Keith, talking and talking like he always did. How had it happened? Whisky, probably, and the exhilaration of being away from everything, the loneliness of sudden freedom. But there was something about Clayton too, something that persuaded you to keep going, to share things you didn't intend to. He could still see the boy, his eyes wide as Keith talked on, talked more than he had for years. It had been such a rush, a relief. And then afterwards, waking to the shame of what he'd said. Things that no one knew. The fear which had rushed at him, almost knocking him sideways.

On the bus, he stared fixedly out of the window, still unsure if he was really going through with it. He could simply go to the station, watch the train pull out and then go home. There was no call to do anything more. They'd slowed to a halt in a queue of traffic, and on the river, three swans were gliding effortlessly away from the bank. He clutched his duffle bag to his chest, the sharp edges of the books pressing into his knees.

He had paused, back in his room, at one page of *Grimms'* in particular. A grainy picture of mountain cottages, their sloping roofs like sails pinned to the mountainside, women in aprons milking cows, men chopping wood. In the background, the forest grew denser and twisted goblins and witches emerged out of thickets, looming from dark shadows. His memories now were slowly merging with those pictures, as though everything that had happened had been something from a storybook. The bells of Hofsgrund, chiming far off, and the wind in his ears screaming a warning. His own voice, thick and muffled in the snow. A woman bending over him, pouring ice-cold water between his lips and whispering to him, wearing the same apron as the women in the drawings, the expression on her face the same expression, the cows in the barn the same cows. He struggled to pull his memories free; they'd been real, those people on the mountain who'd rescued him, the man who'd held onto him as he was carried across the ice, the woman who'd spoken to him at the inn. They weren't a drawing in a storybook, they'd really been there. *How many are out here, how many children?*

'Sorry, folks.' The driver's voice brought him back to himself; they'd stopped with a sudden jolt. Ahead of them the road was thick with crowds, leaving no way for the bus to get through. He watched as they inched closer, the driver cursing as people began running past them, knocking against the side of the bus.

'What's happening?' Keith peered around the driver, but he couldn't make out the words on the signs they were holding up.

'I'm sorry, there's no chance of getting through.'

'I need to get to the station by four o'clock.'

'No chance. You're better off walking.'

Sighing heavily, Keith got out and shouldered his bag. The noise struck him first: the roar of crowds calling out chants he couldn't make out, the shouts of onlookers as they pushed their way through. It took him a while to realise the meaning of the crowd of people; he walked towards them, hoping to find a way through on foot, and only as he came close to those at the back of the march did he see the placards, the black shirts, and realise what was happening.

'You'll want to clear out of here,' a man close to him said, glancing back over his shoulder. 'Unless you're here to join in?'

Keith stared at him. He was dressed in black, holding a cardboard sign above his head on which his slogan, 'Britain First', was drawn untidily in red paint. As he stared, drums started up somewhere in the distance and the crowd began to move with more purpose, advancing along the street with a terrifying, relentless purpose that made him back away onto the pavement.

'You seen this?' a woman said, pushing her way towards him. She was dressed in black too, a sash across her chest. Behind her, a sign held up high read 'On to Fascist Revolution'. She pressed a newspaper into Keith's hand, open to the central pages; he looked down and saw Cyril Clayton's face staring back at him.

'It's from Germany; they tell the truth over there.'

He stared at a photograph of the Schauinsland, another of the Hitler Youth boys standing guard over the four coffins. She pressed another edition of the newspaper into his hands and he took in the cover: a lurid cartoon of two men standing with their mouths hanging open, the blood of a child, suspended above them, dripping onto their lips.

'You see?' she said, thrusting the newspapers again as Keith backed away. 'They know how things are over there. It's Jews that killed that boy, I'm telling you.' She tapped the side of her head knowingly. 'They take the blood, they—'

'Stop it!'

He stepped further back as more people turned towards him. They only looked for a moment; there was too much fervour, too much noise in the street for anyone to pause for long. The woman had been swept away by the crowd now; Keith stood by the side of the street staring after her at the seething mass of people, their uniforms binding them together into one organism as though there was a pattern to their movements, a meaning only they could see.

Part Five

Chapter Thirty-Five

Sylvia was standing beside the largest bell when it began to stir. It started with a slow, mechanical whirring, a faint *click click* which made her turn towards it, holding her breath as though anticipating an explosion. They called the bell Hosanna, an aged guide had told them as she and Kit climbed the agonising flight of stairs to the bell tower. She watched Hosanna ease herself up, her bulk teetering in the stillness, ready to fall, and thought of Arthur and the little he'd told her about France. The earth exploding from beneath him, the silence before and afterwards.

In a sudden, arching rush, Hosanna fell and a deep, heavy tone flooded the air. Kit gripped her arm as the first toll rang out, shaking the stones of the tower. Other visitors laughed and spun around, and more bells began to sound, each peal preceded by the grinding of wood and steel. Two children were running from one side of the wooden platform to the other, shrieking as the sound shook the tiny space, their cries emerging from between the dense chimes which filled Sylvia's head until there was no room for anything else, not doubt or fear or loss. She put a hand against the stone to brace herself, closed her eyes and allowed her mind to empty until there was nothing left but the slow, deep ringing, making her skin shake, her fingernails vibrate, her whole body welling with a peace she hadn't felt since Cyril went away.

At the top of the cathedral spire, a few more flights of stairs above the bells, a brisk wind stung their faces. Arches met above their heads in a crown against the blue sky. Freiburg looked minute below them; rooftops and cobbled streets spiralling out in a web, disappearing into forests shadowed by the dark shapes of mountains in the distance. The square below them was busy with market stalls, their brightly coloured awnings jostling for space as tiny figures moved amongst them and the rows of cars and carts from which supplies were being unloaded. Groups of people sat clustered on benches alongside the stalls, or gathered together beneath the arches of a building painted a deep, brick red and flanked with twisting turrets. Above them, the flag of the Nazi Party hung from a balcony, obscuring most of the building from view; Sylvia watched as the tiny figures passed beneath it without looking up.

Kit was leaning her elbows on the edge of the tower, looking out towards the mountains on the horizon while Sylvia traced the carvings on the red stone of the tower walls; precise, elegant script made by long dead hands. Strange names; 'Elias', 'Friedrich', 'Georg', 'Alise'. More recent ones, 'Hannah and Reiner, 1934'. She thought again of the postcard – 'Today we climbed the big tower' – and found she was searching the walls for Cyril's name, following the maze of letters with her fingers, imagining his fingers doing the same, the ghost of him standing beside her. From below them the bells rang again, Hosanna's heave and thrust reverberating through her body.

'That's it, over there.' Kit, a map in one hand, pointed and they looked out across a series of hills stretching back to the hazy distance, brilliant green slopes dimming into grey. Sylvia had brought the wooden figurine she'd found in the kitchen; she took it from her pocket and held it out against the mountain's shadow as though it was a faraway figure, silhouetted against the sun.

'It doesn't look like a mountain.' She wished she had a pair of binoculars, then berated herself for the foolishness of it; as though she would hold them up to her eyes and there he'd be on a hillside, waving back at her.

They climbed down in silence and sat at a shaded table in the square drinking strong, small coffees while they waited for the tourist information office to open. They had been in Freiburg for less than a day, and already they'd visited everywhere they could think of: the hostel where the boys had stayed; the tourist office, where they'd been turned away until later; even the post office, hoping vainly to find the man Keith had met on the road from the city. At the hostel, a low-roofed, whitewashed building surrounded by cobbled streets, they'd got nowhere. The proprietor, an elderly man who wore spectacles and a nervous, suspicious expression, was reluctant to answer any questions about the school party. They'd sat together in a small, cluttered lounge, on overstuffed armchairs surrounding a cavernous fireplace, as a group of young girls clattered up and down the stairs and he shook his head sternly.

'He did know there would be a storm,' Kit had said afterwards, translating, 'but he can't recall if he warned them. He does recall that their bill is still unpaid,' she'd added, as they hurriedly left.

She was quiet now as she stared down at her coffee cup. Sylvia looked up at the mountain in the distance, feeling suddenly further away from Cyril than ever. This had been her goal, and now that she was here, she had no idea how to find him. She tried to focus her thoughts on the search party that must, even now, be scouring the mountainside, calling out his name. And soon, she and Kit would be joining them.

'Why didn't they find the scarf?' she said aloud.

'Hm?'

'The search party. Or was the woman who found it part of the search party?'

'No, I don't think so.'

'So why didn't they find it themselves?'

Kit sighed. 'I don't know, Sylvia. I've already said, I don't know anything about the search party.'

'Are you alright? You sound – I don't know.'

'Tired. I'm just tired.' She leaned her head in her hands as she stared down at her cup. Sylvia studied her, wondering, as she had wondered since agreeing to the trip, why she had decided to trust her, to come to Germany with her, when she barely knew anything about her at all. 'It's strange,' Kit went on, picking up a bread roll from the basket between them and juggling it between her fingers. 'I was only here a few weeks ago, and already it feels different. People are – don't you feel it? They're nervous. No one wants to talk.'

'Do you blame them? I imagine Germans in London are getting strange looks as well.'

'We're not at war.'

'No, I suppose not.' But it was beginning to feel like it. Before she'd come away, Sylvia had removed her white poppy from her blouse and placed it carefully in a drawer.

The bells began again, pealing across the square. People stopped mid-stride and stared up at the spire, eyes wide until they stilled and conversation slowly resumed. The last of the roll fell apart in Kit's fingers and she flicked it across the square, where a flurry of pigeons appeared from nowhere, swooping and bustling as they fought to get close to it.

'This newspaper you're working for—'

'The *Post*.'

'The *Post*. What do they want?'

'I told you. An interview, photographs, that sort of thing.'

'That's all?'

'That's all.'

'It's just…' Sylvia hesitated, unsure how to phrase what she was thinking. 'Why you? Sorry – I don't mean – I just – there are so many other—'

'So many men, you mean.'

'Well…'

Kit smiled at her, a sly, sideways smile. 'The feminine angle,' she said. 'I told them you wouldn't talk to anyone else.'

'Kit—'

'It's alright, it won't be like that article in the *Sketch*. No mournful photographs, nothing like that.'

'You promise?'

'Of course. I'm not interested in all that.'

'What are you interested in?'

'I told you. I want to know the truth. And I suppose...' She smiled, lifting her chin. 'They tried to intimidate me. Those men on the mountain – they tried to make me feel afraid. I want them to know it didn't work. Come on,' she said, standing up and draining the last of her coffee. 'The tourist office should be open now.'

It was a few streets away, a modern-looking building on the corner of a busy road, gleaming with fresh white paint. They ducked under a low doorway to find a woman behind a desk, half asleep. She wore a heavy woollen jacket, a deep shade of olive green, and glasses that had slid down her nose, rising and falling slightly with her breath. A framed photograph was on the wall beside her, a group of boys in uniform, flags of the Nazi Party surrounding them as they smiled widely into the camera.

Kit coughed, then again a little more loudly.

'*Verzeihung.*'

She repeated the word and the woman sat suddenly upright, shuffling some papers as though she hadn't paused in her work. She slid her glasses back up her nose and peered at them both, then beckoned Kit closer, apparently struggling to hear.

Kit glanced sideways at Sylvia before pulling a photograph from her bag. 'Do you know this man? *Hast du ihn schon gesehen?*'

Sylvia looked over her shoulder at the photograph. Keith

was sitting for his portrait for the school, upright and stiff in a chair, his face solemn. The woman nodded at once.

'*Ja.* Yes. *Der unglückliche Engländer.*'

'The unfortunate Englishman – yes, that's him. The schoolteacher.'

'Yes. I know his face,' she said, bursting suddenly into English. She snatched the photograph from Kit. 'I see it in the newspapers.'

'Oh – he didn't come in here himself then?'

'Of course. Visitors always come here first,' she said proudly, sitting a little straighter in her chair. 'I remember him. I remember all of them.'

'The children?' Sylvia felt a jolt of excitement.

'Do you remember speaking to him?'

'I showed them maps. Maps of the mountain.' The woman smiled. 'He was handsome, I thought,' she said slowly. 'But very rude. He was in a hurry. He wanted books about the flowers, history, that sort of thing.'

'Yes, and did he take any maps?'

'I always give them maps. Always, if they are climbing.' She pulled some sheets from under her desk and laid them out, running her fingers across them affectionately. 'Schauinsland,' she said, as proudly as if she had built the mountain herself. She was pointing at a place on her map where contour lines gathered and bunched themselves together as though someone was sketching a warning there. Small numbers printed between the lines indicated the height of the land, and beyond the maze of contour lines, a tiny black dot marked out Hofsgrund.

'Did he take any maps?' Kit said again, the frustration beginning to show in her voice.

'He didn't want them. English maps are better, he said.' She beat her fist on the desk, smiling and shaking her head at the memory. 'He should never have climbed, that day,' she added.

'The storm – did you know it was coming?'

'Of course.'

'You warned him?'

She nodded fervently. 'Of course, I told him it wasn't safe to climb.'

'And what did he say?'

The woman closed her eyes, remembering. 'English are not afraid of the cold,' she said slowly. 'That's what he said. *We're not afraid of the cold.*'

There was a long silence. Sylvia felt her hand moving towards the photograph of Cyril in her pocket. *He was here, you must have seen him, do you remember? Would you know him again? Was he happy?*

'Those boys were lucky,' the woman said suddenly, folding her own map away.

'Lucky?'

'They had our boys there to save them.' She raised a hand and brushed her fingers against the photograph of the children in uniform on the wall beside her. 'Our good German boys.' She smiled widely, her face transforming into lightness as she laid her fingers reverently on the glass. 'The best in the world. They saved your boys. Found them all, kept them safe. Very soon, they will save the whole world.'

Chapter Thirty-Six

Hilde woke early with a feeling of foreboding rising in her stomach. Anna was gone again without explanation; all night she'd dreamed of crawling through tunnels beneath the mountain in search of a missing child, finding Anna instead, curled up foetus-like at the feet of a king so terrible and great that no one could look up at him.

A red glow suffused the air in the *Stube*; for a moment she felt panic, before she remembered the flag Hans had given her, that she'd hung in the window. The light was streaming through it, casting a red stain across the flagstones. There wasn't a house in the village without one now; some had three or four, draped in every window, across the doors. A few nights earlier, the Hitler Youth had lit a bonfire on the Schauinsland's summit and paraded through the neighbouring villages; though they hadn't passed through Hofsgrund, Hilde had seen them, a long, snaking line of light in the distance, and heard the far-off sound of drums beating, as though an army was advancing across the valley. All the talk now was of war, how it was inevitable, how Hitler had to finish what he'd started, restore Germany to its proper place in the world. *A just war*, they whispered in the square, *a righteous war, we've waited long enough already.*

After seeing to the cattle, Hilde walked in the direction of the inn, where she had arranged to meet Fritz. He'd been making inquiries about the sale of her animals, and the closer Hilde came to making leaving a reality, the more hopeful she felt. She was excited, for the first time in months. She'd still had no word from Else, but she was already imagining herself and Anna walking by the river in Freiburg dressed in furs, whilst people sat at tables in elegant restaurants, glasses of wine clinking and laughter rippling across the squares. She might go back to school, train for nursing, even. Anna could have the proper education Hilde had never had, she could do anything she wanted. They were still citizens, they still belonged in this new Germany. She felt a pang of guilt at the thought of what Fritz had told her, at the idea of leaving him behind. But after all, what could she do about it? Was she wrong to still have hopes, when such things were happening? Was she wrong to feel thankful there were no laws against her, against Anna?

She found a crowd gathering in the square; something was being constructed, and the streets rang with the sound of hammering and shouting. The sun was bright enough, but a sharp breeze cut through its warmth and had the onlookers huddling in their coats, rubbing their hands together and hunching their shoulders. Hilde stood a little apart from them, watching as men worked on a wooden construction along one side of the square, under the direction of a group of SS soldiers.

'What is it?' she said to the woman closest to her: Gertrud Braunling, the landlord's wife.

Gertrud turned to her, seeming to flinch a little when she saw Hilde. *It's not contagious,* Hilde wanted to say, *whatever it is you see in me, it can't be spread.*

'It's for tomorrow,' Gertrud said curtly. Hilde stared back at her blankly. 'You know, surely?' Gertrud sighed, uttering a little *tsk tsk* under her breath. 'Ask Hans, he'll tell you.'

'Tell me what?'

'Such a lot of fuss,' Gertrud said, shaking her head. 'I

wish...' But she turned away, and whatever she'd been about to say was left unspoken.

At the inn, Hilde sat with Fritz in a corner by the fire. She felt strangely secretive, as though leaving Hofsgrund was a betrayal, a crime in some way punishable. She hadn't yet brought it up with Anna, knowing what her sister's reaction would be.

'You won't struggle to sell the animals, provided you don't ask for too high a price. A lot of people lost cattle in the winter, and pigs are always welcome.'

'How long?'

'A week, maybe.'

'You can't arrange it for sooner?'

'A week is fast, Hilde! And that's just the animals. For the house, we'll need more time.'

'That's alright. We can stay with our aunt for now; sell the house when we can.'

He nodded, looking uneasy.

'You'll be alright. Won't you?'

He reached out and took her hand. 'Just be careful, *Leibling*. Look after your sister.'

They looked at each other. Hilde tried to think of the right words - how could she thank him properly for everything he'd done? But as she began, the door opened and some of the workers from the square crowded noisily in around them, followed by an SS soldier. Fritz stood up quickly to leave. Hilde watched him go, still wondering what they were working on in the square. *Ask Hans*, Gertrud had said, but Hilde had already decided not to. Better to have as little information as possible, to keep yourself ignorant, keep your head down.

When she reached the house, she could hear voices in the *Stube*. Through the window she saw Anna at the table, bent over something. A boy was sitting beside her; as he raised his head Hilde recognised Paul Huber, frowning in concentration.

She stood in the doorway, trying not to make a sound. Anna and Paul were leafing through a series of colourful posters, holding them up against the walls, studying each one intently. There were images of Hitler, of young men in the uniform of the Hitler Youth, standing proudly with their heads held high. Anna read one of the posters out loud: 'Sterilisation is liberation, not punishment.' On it was a photograph of a child, its eyes screwed shut and its mouth open in a scream. Another depicted a family tree; it was the same poster she'd seen in the Hubers' house, images of family members growing gradually distorted along a branching line, until they were hardly human any more.

'They're to go in the square,' Paul was saying. 'For tomorrow. But you can keep this one.' He held up the portrait of Hitler, a photograph of him standing proudly in his uniform, with rows and rows of boys in the background, their arms raised in a salute. Anna spread it out against the wall and took a handful of pins from her pocket.

'What are you doing?'

Her voice was loud in the still, quiet air of the *Stube*. Anna turned around, and for a second she didn't look like a child, like Hilde's sister. Her face was a stranger's, staring at the doorway in mild surprise, as though Hilde had walked into someone else's home.

'Paul was just—'

'Take that down, at once.'

'Why?'

Hilde checked herself, remembering Paul's connections, the risk of speaking out. They trained them at meetings, she'd heard, from when they were children, to denounce their neighbours, to listen out for signs. She smiled at them both, feeling her hands shaking. 'The wall – you'll damage it. We can find a proper frame, perhaps.'

When Paul had gone, she sat at the table, where he'd left the posters in an untidy heap. She wanted to tear them up, to burn them in the stove. What would happen to her if she did that? She couldn't look at Anna as she sat down beside her.

'He was only showing me some of the posters they gave him at the Youth meeting. There's no harm in it.'

'I don't want him in the house. Not when I'm not here, do you understand?'

Anna shook her head. That same indifference Hilde had seen on her face was in her voice too, a quiet calm that was more unsettling than her anger had been. 'You're not my mother. Or my father, are you?'

She reached out and took her sister's hand. 'What's happened to you, Anna? Why can't we talk any more?'

'I want to join the League.'

'What?'

'The League of German Girls, it's the same as—'

'I know what it is.'

'Paul says they meet at the same time as his group, we can walk there together.'

Hilde slumped back in her chair. From her place by the stove, Gretel picked her way over and leapt into her lap; she leaned forward and buried her face in Gretel's fur, feeling her warm body vibrating against her cheek. She felt exhausted, suddenly, all the energy leaching from her body. How had they managed it, these people whom Anna had never met? Just a few pictures in the newspapers, a few words on the radio. How had they captured her so completely, when Hilde couldn't reach her any more?

'What do you think Pa would say about it, Anna?'

'He'd want me to be the best German I can be.'

'And he'd want you to think Jews are inferior, would he?

That anyone who believes something different, anyone who has an illness they were born with, who looks different, who wants to vote for a different party—'

'There are no different parties! It's an emergency, Hilde. These aren't normal times. Those people with illnesses – there's barely enough money in the country as it is. Do you know how much it costs to keep someone in a hospital, their whole life? You don't know, because you haven't spoken to the people I've spoken to, you don't read the articles. We can't expect things to carry on as they are. We might be alright here, in this safe little world, but there are bigger things happening.'

'What people?'

'What?'

'What people have you spoken to?'

Anna hesitated, looking away. 'I went with Paul to some of his meetings. I couldn't go in, of course, but he let me talk to some of the speakers afterwards.'

'So that's why you've hardly been here.'

'They're good people, Hilde. They just want our country to be safer. Happier.'

She looked up. Anna looked so certain, so optimistic, she almost wished she could believe it with her.

'And what about the Jews?' she said slowly.

'They don't want what's best for us.'

'And what about Fritz?'

Anna looked confused. 'What about him?'

She couldn't help it, she couldn't stop herself. For once, she was the one who knew a secret. 'Did you know he's Jewish, Anna?'

Anna stared at her. The expression on her face, her mouth set into a hard line, reminded Hilde of something she couldn't quite place.

'Our father knew. He helped him find a home, to get out of Freiburg. All that bile, all those things Paul's told you. All this.' She picked up the posters, tossing them into the air. 'They're about him too. Our friend. Who we *love*.'

She waited for the realisation to appear on Anna's face, the certainty that she'd been wrong. The momentary satisfaction Hilde had felt at her victory, the triumph of an argument that couldn't be denied, was replaced with guilt; she had promised Fritz, she had promised herself. Then, just as quickly, alarm, as she saw that Anna's expression hadn't changed. Hilde wished she could take the words back, stuff them into her mouth, swallow them up.

'Anna, you can't tell anyone that. I mean it. You know what can happen.'

Still, Anna said nothing, just stared back at her with that strange expression on her face. It was her mother, Hilde realised. The look she would give them if one of them confessed to losing a calf in the snow or forgetting to lock up the barn. *There will be time later for anger*, it seemed to say. *For now, there is work to be done.*

'You know what can happen,' Hilde said again in a childish, pleading voice, looking at the pile of posters between them and realising that she herself had no idea at all.

Chapter Thirty-Seven

As darkness fell Sylvia and Kit walked back to their hotel through cobbled streets, crossing a road busy with cars and horse-drawn carts until they reached a brightly lit square. Ahead of them, the black steeple of the cathedral rose above the jumble of rooftops, its steep sides filigreed like shadowed lace, and the bells began to sound, the city seeming to pause to listen.

Sylvia felt restless and impatient now that they were so close to their goal. It had taken more than a week to organise the trip; more time for Cyril to fall further away from her, for her imagined avalanche to gather pace. Tomorrow marked a month since the accident, and they would be in Hofsgrund, joining the search party. She would see for herself, and she would finally do her best for him, she would finally be the kind of mother everyone expected her to be, the kind he needed.

'Imagine if we did find him,' she allowed herself to say aloud. She knew how it sounded. But she'd been devoid of hope for so long. 'Imagine if, somehow, my being there is what makes the difference. It could be, couldn't it?' She could feel all the doubt which others had laid on her – Julia, Ruby, Eileen, even Dieter with all his talk of inheritance – lifting away. Kit said nothing, and even that felt like a silent agreement.

One side of the square was dominated by the City Hall, from which hung the largest swastika flag they had seen so far, almost covering the entire building. They stopped beneath it, stunned into staring up at this marker of a new era, a regime which seemed to be moving faster than anyone could comprehend.

'It's something, isn't it?' Kit said, her eyes wide. 'You should see Berlin.'

'Where did you learn to speak German? It's much better than mine.' Sylvia had learned a little German during her brief medical training, but it was slow and cumbersome. Kit, on the other hand, spoke fluently to everyone they came across; staff at the hotel beamed at her as she slid easily into the language.

'My father was German. From Munich.'

Sylvia turned to look at her. 'But—'

'He came to England years ago. Met my mother. They told everyone he was Dutch.' She smiled. 'Just easier, that way.' She took off her locket and, opening it, handed it to Sylvia. Inside was a photograph of a middle aged man with a neat moustache, the image cut in a jagged oval to fit the frame. It was so small, Sylvia could barely make out the bushy eyebrows, the stern, frowning expression, the square jaw. 'He was a printer. He used to bring home bits of newspaper sometimes, he knew I liked the pictures. Then I started reading the words. I wanted to do it myself, but of course that wasn't on the approved list.'

'What was?'

Kit smiled grimly. 'Oh, the usual. They expected me to marry, bring up children. I was allowed to go to university, but only so I could meet someone suitable. My mother was the money,' she added, answering Sylvia's unspoken question. 'She died before I left school.'

'My mother was the money too,' Sylvia said, thinking of the hours she and Julia had spent learning deportment, manners, poise, all the useless, tedious tools with which to navigate a particular sort of life, a life in which their only task was to continue the family bloodline. The dreams she'd had – the dreams she and Julia had both had – of becoming a doctor one day. They hadn't ever known what sort of inheritance they could expect; only that, after enrolling in nursing training, they'd been told there would no longer be anything for them at the end of it. *So much for your career,* her mother had said when she'd held Cyril for the first and only time, and there had been an edge of grim satisfaction in her voice, that things had come to this, after all Sylvia's talk.

Julia had tried to audit medical classes, and had come home talking of not being allowed to sit in the lecture theatre, of having to position herself by the open door, straining to see over the heads of rows of men. Being mistaken, over and over, for a cleaner, a tea lady, a secretary. *But we have to try, Sylvia. It's our duty to try.* And Sylvia had, and then, so suddenly it felt like she had slid into a dream, she had found herself there, in the field tents of France. Young men, bleeding so quickly she could see their faces change colour in front of her.

She closed the locket and handed it back.

'It bothers you, doesn't it?' Kit said.

'What?'

'I know that look, Sylvia.'

'What look?'

'You're thinking, *she's not one of us, she's been hiding in plain sight all along.* I'm English. I've never been anything else.'

'I hadn't – I didn't—'

'They locked him up during the war.' Kit's expression was suddenly hard and angry, as though Sylvia had done it herself. 'They were so frightened he would side with Germany – with his old life. They put him in a camp. Alexandra Palace – they have concerts there now, don't they? They're going to broadcast the BBC. He was there for four years.' She looked up again. 'In *England*,' she said fiercely, and Sylvia didn't know what to say. 'So I know how people feel about us. *Us* – I've hardly even been to Germany, just a few holidays when I was young. But I know what it's like. If it happens again—'

'If there's another war, you mean?'

Kit shrugged. 'Well, anyway, I don't suppose they'll be interested in locking me up, will they? They're not afraid of women that way. All the same, I'd rather not have to answer a lot of questions.'

'Sorry. I'm sorry.' She thought. 'Kit, if he was locked up in the war, and your mother…'

'I was in boarding school.' She offered Sylvia a weak smile. 'It wasn't so bad, it was the same for everyone else. I just couldn't go home for the holidays.'

Sylvia didn't know what to say. Cyril had asked once if he'd be sent to boarding school; he'd looked terrified, as though it were akin to being sent to a war. She'd taken him to Alexandra Palace once. The two of them had lain in the grass watching workmen crawling over the building, their tiny figures dark against the sun. It was impossible to imagine people imprisoned there, beneath that huge expanse of sky.

'People didn't get over it, you know?' Kit said. 'There wasn't enough food – they came home different. Older.'

'You really think it would be like that again?'

There was a long pause, before Kit turned her face away from the flag. 'Come on,' she said quietly. 'We'll need to start early tomorrow.'

As they crossed the square, there was a shout from inside one of the buildings and men in Party uniforms began to spill from it, fanning out and pushing people back. Kit and Sylvia jostled their way through the crowds to try to see; a man was being marched out of the building, flanked by Nazi officers, struggling as they wrestled him towards a car.

'What are they doing?' Sylvia whispered.

A woman in the crowd in front of them turned around. 'He'll be a communist,' she whispered in English. 'Or an anarchist, or just doesn't know when to shut his mouth. Might even be resistance.'

'Resistance?'

The woman leaned closer, lowering her voice even further. 'They don't want to admit it still happens, but I've seen the flyers they leave around. Encouraging people to resist, to join their networks. Resist what? That's my question. Prosperity, better lives, enough food to go around. Who resists that?' She shook her head.

Sylvia stared as the car drove away and the officers shouted for people to disperse. With the crowds thinning, she could see the woman more clearly now; she was young, pale blue eyes and blonde hair escaping from beneath a headscarf, a baby wriggling in her arms.

'Where will they take him?' she asked as the car moved away. She reached into her pocket and found the toy climber there, rubbing her finger against the rough wood.

The woman shrugged, adjusting the baby on her hip. 'Who knows?' she said. 'Some people say they get deported. Some people say there are camps.'

'Camps?'

She nodded, lowering her voice yet further. 'Camps, where they put you to work on something useful. Something better than dreaming up revolutions that won't ever come.'

Chapter Thirty-Eight

For a moment after he woke, Keith didn't know where he was. The air was heavy with silence, and a draft had seeped in through the shuttered windows, bringing with it the scent of manure and woodsmoke, mingling with the smell of fresh bread from somewhere below him. It came to him: arriving at the inn in Hofsgrund late the previous evening, after a long, winding drive from Freiburg, where he'd been met by a Nazi Party official, on through farmlands towards the wooded slopes of the Schauinsland. The road, increasingly narrow and rough, had brought them past farmland and small clusters of houses, which grew increasingly sparse until they began to climb higher, eventually opening out into the valley that brought them to Hofsgrund.

He hadn't been sure he'd come. Right up until the moment he boarded his train in London, he hadn't been sure. The summons – because that was what it really was, a summons – had taken him by surprise. After the inquiry, after the endless questions and accusations, the newspaper articles and the notes through his parents' door, he'd thought it might finally be over. It was only fitting, he supposed, that it should end here.

They'd spent most of the journey in silence. Keith had tried to match the landscape with what he remembered from the hike, but everything was brighter, sharper, the thick covering of snow replaced with brilliant green and colourful splashes of flowers along the verge. He felt he was experiencing everything for the first time; the little houses nestled against the slopes, the dirt tracks, the cows ambling slowly across fields, the smell of their manure lacing the air with a sweet, heavy warmth. Only when he saw the church on a ridge above the village was he able to orient himself – somewhere along that rise was where he'd stopped to send on two of the boys, where he'd last seen Cyril Clayton. It had seemed so much further from safety then; he hadn't known how close they were, how nearly he'd avoided disaster.

He could hear voices downstairs; the inn was already busy, despite the early hour. From outside, the sounds of banging and sawing echoed across the square. A wooden platform was being hastily assembled; he'd seen it last night as they'd arrived. Through the window, he could see Party flags flying high against the sun.

Keith straightened the collar of his shirt and held up his medal to his chest. Looking at himself in the mirror on the wall beside his bed, he felt as though he were staring into the past, at a version of himself – or was it Jack? – which he had almost forgotten. He smoothed down his hair and fiddled with the pin on the medal, attaching it a little crookedly to his jacket. For a moment he contemplated wearing it openly, this signifier of the death of Germans, of the destruction that had been wrought in his country's name. He imagined it, standing up on the platform in front of crowds of people and cameras, the medal in full view on his chest. Then he undid the clasp and slid it back into his pocket.

Downstairs, platters of food and supplies were being carried in and out of the kitchen, and women and boys wearing aprons were pushing past one another amongst the tables. A fire was struggling into life in the grate, and he took a seat at a nearby table, pulling his chair as close to its warmth as he could. One or two patrons turned and stared at him; did they recognise him from news reports, or was it simply that he was a stranger? He felt himself sitting up a little straighter, pushing out his chest.

The Hitler Youth boys were sitting at a table near the kitchen, eating bowls of porridge. Their uniforms were neat and pressed; light brown shirts and shorts, a sash across their chests. From across the room, Keith studied them, trying to match their faces with his memories of that night. Had they really been there? It was possible, he supposed, and after all, why not? It was true what he'd said at the inquiry, about how memories could be muddled and changed. He'd heard some soldiers had gaps from the war which lasted hours, or even days. Gaps which, years later, had never been filled in.

The door opened, bringing with it a new rush of cold. Kurt Runde, dressed in his own uniform, approached the table of boys, who stopped their conversations and gazed reverently up at him as he issued their instructions. Then, seeing Keith at his table by the fire, he came over, removing his hat and laying it on the table in front of him.

'Good of you to come, Keith.'

'I wasn't sure I would.'

'Well, you're here now. Everything's ready for this afternoon.'

'Is she here yet?'

Runde looked over his shoulder at the window, through which the men working on the stage in the square could be seen, hauling planks of wood and hammering at them. 'Not yet.'

'But she'll come?'

'She'll come.'

He had no idea how they'd managed it. They had ways, these people, of convincing you to do things without your meaning to, or even knowing you had. How else had he been persuaded to come himself? The chance to be a hero, Runde's invitation had said, imagine it, all those people shaking your hand, applauding. It's not just for them, it's for you too. Don't you deserve that, after all you've been through?

'Listen,' he said to Runde, looking over his shoulder at the children. The porridge bowls had been cleared away and they'd begun a noisy game of cards, their hands slapping hard against the table. 'Your boys. That night on the mountain – how on earth did you get to us in time?'

Runde stared at him. Keith was already regretting the question, but he couldn't stop himself now.

'It's just, if I'm going to do this, I'd like to know.' He leaned forward. 'They were there, weren't they? I mean, this is all... real?'

There was a long silence. A young woman appeared beside him and laid two bowls of porridge on the table with a heavy crash. Keith looked up; he didn't recognise her. He hadn't yet recognised anyone from that night, which, he thought, only made his theory more plausible. His memories were gone, or changed, or faded – it didn't really matter. What mattered was that he'd made a choice.

'The boys are looking forward to meeting you,' Runde said at last, as though Keith hadn't said anything at all. 'We'll take some photographs later. Make sure we commemorate everything properly.'

He sounded certain, and Keith, in turn, felt more certain too, that he'd done the right thing in coming here, that it was going to turn out for the best.

Some of the villagers had already claimed a space in front of the platform in the square; one or two families were sitting resolutely on the ground in semicircles, waiting for something to happen. They were bringing people in from the surrounding villages, Runde had told him; carts had been sent to transport them across the valley. Keith wove his way amongst them, standing back to view the platform from a distance. It was a clear day, and the summit was visible behind it, seeming suddenly innocuous behind winding dirt tracks and the blue haze of sky. He felt ashamed, now that the weather was milder and the sky no longer threatening, that this mountain should have beaten him so badly.

Some empty crates had been stacked at the edge of the square and he perched on one of them, noticing, opposite him, a tall, broad-shouldered man doing the same, his arms wrapped around him against the cold. He looked up, meeting Keith's eyes, and Keith felt a strange sensation, as though the ground beneath him was shifting, as though he might fall.

'It was you,' he said in German.

A memory stirring: the face looking down at him, reaching to lift him out of the snow, carrying him back to the village. Thick white eyebrows. A gentle, reassuring smile. It was him.

The man walked over to him and held out a hand. He was wearing a dark green knitted jumper, badly mended at the elbows, and a heavy dark wool coat, its collar pulled up high around his face. He was older than Keith had originally thought; his face was lined and his eyes looked weary.

'I'm right, aren't I?' Keith said nervously as they shook hands. 'You rescued me that night? The children on the mountain.'

'I remember you. Yes, I remember you.'

He swayed and nearly fell; the man put out an arm to steady him, as though Keith was the elder of the two of them.

'Sorry,' Keith said, 'sorry. It's just – I thought I knew, and now – and now you. Sorry.'

'You were half frozen when we found you.'

'Yes. I suppose I was. Thank you,' he added, taking the man's hand again. 'Thank you so much. What you did—'

There was a loud bang; behind them one of the flags had fallen with a hollow crash. Two men, shouting curses, ran towards it.

'What's your name? Will you have a drink with me? I'm staying at the inn, we could—'

'No. Thank you.' He took Keith's hand and shook it. 'Fritz Feldberg. I'm glad to see you again.'

Keith watched Fritz walk across the square towards the upper slopes of the village, wondering what the strange look on his face had meant. He hadn't had the chance to say his thanks properly – it had been inadequate, that short, stumbling speech, it wasn't half of what he'd intended to say. He looked back at the platform, the flags, the men in uniform. What had he been thinking, handing them his memories like that? He'd felt so sure – it was something, the way they could convince you of whatever they wanted. He thought of the portrait of Mosley on his parents' wall, his father sitting beneath it amongst his piles of newspapers, telling stories about the Olympia riots. All those people who'd been persuaded to act, to commit violence when they might have gone on quietly through their whole lives, no one noticing them, no one being hurt. If you believed in something enough, could you make it real?

Chapter Thirty-Nine

A trap came to collect them from outside their hotel, drawn by a tired-looking horse and driven by a boy who looked barely older than Cyril, perched like a fisherman in the driver's position with a long, thin rod held out to the animal's flank. They loaded their bags onto it and sat uncomfortably on a wooden bench as they were driven through the city. As they passed beneath the great red and black flag hanging from the town hall, Sylvia thought of what the woman in the square had said. *Some people say there are camps.* Was it really true? She thought of Dieter at the laboratory, trying to bring his father to England. Kit's father, spending years as a prisoner in London. Had she even known, all those years ago, that things like that were happening? Did the people they were passing in the streets now know? They couldn't, Sylvia thought, and it couldn't really be true. They'd be tearing down that flag, storming the building, if it were.

'They know we're coming,' Kit said. 'We're due to meet some of the local officials, that sort of thing. Tedious, I know,' she said, making a face, 'but it can't be helped. The paper arranged it for us. They're having some sort of ceremony – I said you wouldn't mind.'

'Mind what?'

Kit shrugged. 'I'm not sure exactly. To commemorate what happened somehow. The good news is, they're letting me cover it. I'm the only foreign journalist, that's what they said.'

'Because of me?'

'I suppose so, yes.'

'And then we can help with the search? We can talk to the woman who found the scarf?'

'Of course. Whatever it is they're planning, it won't take long.'

Sylvia could feel a growing unease spreading between them. Kit was avoiding her eyes, and she wanted to ask her why, to understand what sort of trap she had somehow negotiated herself into. She wanted to know, but more than that, she wanted to preserve the image of her son, standing on the side of the mountain, waving back at her. An absurd image, impossible, but it was all she had.

They crossed a narrow bridge; on the other side, the houses were smaller, more closely packed, and the stench of manure and something else – sweet and rotting – rose up from the street. Two tiny children were poking sticks at the mud by the riverbank; Sylvia turned to watch, and one of them looked up and stuck out his tongue at her as the trap bounced past.

The roads slowly changed from wide paved streets to dirt tracks, then all of a sudden the city fell away and they were travelling between fields of wheat, still green and fresh, and beyond them the grey shadows of mountains cutting into the sky. As soon as they left it behind it was easy to imagine that the city had never been there; the air was clear and silent, smelling faintly of pines and recent rain. The road was growing steeper and more uneven now, fields and clusters of houses giving way to thick groves of trees and wild, uncultivated land. The trap began to judder and skip between stones and potholes; the boy, who hadn't spoken a word since they left Freiburg, cursed at his horse in sharp whispers and a flick of the whip.

After an hour or so the horse let out a strange, guttural whine, and they pulled up abruptly at the side of the road, its verges thick with foliage. The boy turned in his seat.

'Lower station,' he said, gesturing to a low brick building surrounded by concrete.

Behind it, a series of wires and pulleys stretched high into the hills, wooden carriages like dull-coloured bird cages suspended above them, vanishing into the mist. He must have known it was here, she thought, picturing Keith Hughes at the tourist office, in the hostel with his maps and plans. Why hadn't he chosen this way?

They purchased their tickets and settled themselves into a car. There were no other passengers, save two young men dressed for climbing who waited for the car before theirs, hauling their equipment in after them. They heaved and swung their way through the air, the car creaking slightly as it lifted them on up the mountain. Kit, pale and silent, was staring blankly out of the windows, gripping the small blankets which had been laid across the seats with both hands. Sylvia, too, found she was holding on to the edges of the wooden seat, as though it would save her if they plummeted down through the trees.

The journey took longer than Sylvia had been expecting. She stared out at the slopes below, trees packed close, their fine needles knitted together as though they might be enough to break a fall. At times they were low enough against the mountain that she felt she could have touched the tips of the trees, and she felt glad that the children hadn't come this way, that the cable cars hadn't been visible to them as they struggled against the snow. She pictured Cyril suddenly, looking up and catching her eye from high above, imagining herself staring down at him from a warm, safe cocoon – a traveller from another place.

'My husband wanted to be a climber,' she said, thinking of the man he'd been before the war, always making plans, poring over photographs in newspapers of snow-covered peaks, men wearing crampons and heavy packs, squinting into cameras, the wide vista of a mountain stretching high behind them. Later, long after the war was over, reading the reports about George Mallory, the newspaper shaking in his hands.

'I remember, from the article. What did he climb?'

'Nothing. He never went,' she said. 'It was just a dream he had, and then, after the war…' She stopped herself.

'They were wrong then, in that piece?'

'I probably made it sound like more than it was.'

They were silent for a moment, listening to the slow rattle of the machinery above them.

'What happened to him?' Kit asked.

Sylvia shook her head. The truth was, she didn't know. There wasn't any story to tell. She had nothing left, except the shame of what she'd done.

'I lost him,' she said with an air of finality. 'I made a mistake, and I can't take it back.'

They sat in silence until the car began to swing wildly and they looked about them, momentarily panicked, wondering if another storm had come or if the ropes were about to snap; then they were twisted suddenly to the right and found there was solid ground, a wooden platform beneath them, a man in the uniform of the cable car company reaching out to open the door and help them out.

Kit, at Sylvia's insistence, showed him the photograph of Cyril, Hughes' portrait, eliciting nothing but a brief nod of the head and the now familiar '*Der unglückliche Engländer*' as he pushed the photographs back again.

The upper station was small, just a low concrete building where the cable cars turned in a slow circle. They stepped out into a cold, blinding sun and climbed towards the summit through densely packed trees, their low-hanging boughs stretching across the path like a series of stiles. Emerging into a clearing they stared out at the sudden expanse of sky, the trees giving way to a pattern of farmland, sweeping down into slopes that stretched into the distance, disappearing into a veil of cloud behind which, Sylvia supposed, must be the village.

A small pile of stones had been gathered at the crest of

the slope. A metal plaque loosely attached to them read 'Schauinsland, 1,284m'. Close by, a huge, uneven pile of wood had been built into a pyre. They stared at it, as Sylvia traced the plaque with her fingers.

'They never came this high, did they?' she said. 'They were somewhere that way...' She gestured towards the clouds, imagining, four weeks ago, her boy somewhere behind them. Her hand found the toy climber in her pocket and she squeezed it tight.

As they watched a figure did appear, climbing up from the direction of the village, then two more, walking towards them.

'Here they are,' Kit murmured.

Sylvia watched as the three men came closer. Two of them were dressed in the brown shirt and trousers of the Nazi Party, the swastika bands around their arms bright in the sunlight. The other was carrying a camera, raising it to his face as they came closer, scoping them out like a hunter. She felt herself backing away. There had been something wrong since they came to Freiburg, she knew it now, and from the edge in Kit's voice she knew there was no avoiding it any more. She looked back towards the cable car station, hidden amongst the trees; began calculating how long it would take if she ran, how quickly she would be able to reach a car, whether she could descend the mountain on foot and run back to the city. Would it be an advantage, to know the patterns of the tree trunks, the curve of the paths, would she be able to outrun someone who wasn't so sure of the way? Why did she suddenly feel so afraid? Hosanna was tolling beside her again, her ears full and ringing, the warning reverberating through her body as the three men came closer.

'What's wrong?' Kit turned to her with an anxious expression.

'Nothing. Nothing. Let's just get this part over with, I suppose.'

The camera flashed and she put a hand up to her eyes. One of the men came forward and held out a hand, beaming, and when Sylvia shook it she felt him turning at an angle, smiling towards the photographer, ensuring that both of their faces were in view.

'Mrs Clayton,' he said in clipped, careful English. 'Kurt Runde. It was extremely good of you to come.'

She looked helplessly at Kit, who had drifted away from her now, standing alone by the pile of stones.

'I'm here for my son,' she said, meeting the man's eyes. He looked weary, behind the stiff uniform and the carefully slicked-back hair. She recognised him from the newspaper articles, the photograph of him with Keith in an open-topped car. 'I'm here to find Cyril.'

She could feel every muscle straining to keep herself still, to not cry. *He's here,* she screamed silently, *he's close to me now, what have you done?*

'Of course.' He glanced at Kit, a brief flash of confusion in his eyes. 'We are all praying for his return. Let's show you to the village, get the two of you settled in.' He nodded towards their cases, and the third man hurried to pick them up as they turned towards the path.

As they walked down the slope towards the village, the man with the camera turned to take more photographs, walking backwards ahead of them. All the time, navigating a narrow, weed-strewn path, Sylvia could feel Hosanna's warning toll, the shock ringing through her body, an explosion of fear and surprise.

'What is this?' she asked Kit.

'I told you. Some formalities. A ceremony of some kind.'

'What sort of ceremony?'

'I don't know, I didn't ask. It was a condition of our coming.'

'And you didn't ask them what it was?'

'Do you want to be here or not, Sylvia? There's always something. What matters is what we can get out of it.'

'If it was a condition of our coming—'

'They want me to send back a report, yes.'

'About the ceremony? And you didn't ask them what it was?'

There was a silence as they continued along the path. Kit looked uncomfortable now, looking back towards the summit, then ahead, where the village was appearing below them, a long, winding street dotted with fields and clusters of houses. It was built so close to the mountainside that the houses might have been cave formations or natural hollows, until they were close enough to make out thatched roofs and tilled earth. A large wooden stage had been built in the central square, draped in Nazi Party flags, the sudden flash of red and black shocking against the dull greens and browns of the mountain. The photographer paused, his camera still snapping. Party flags had been hung in the windows of the houses, more draped over doors and windowsills. The fields were largely empty; tools stacked against fences the only sign of work that had been abandoned for the day. People were beginning to mass in the square, gathered in front of the platform where, they could see now, a row of chairs had been assembled. On a board at the edge of the square, various posters had been pinned: pictures of the SS, of Hitler. As they passed, she read a third, 'Bad genes enter a village', and thought of the newspaper Julia had shown her. 'Nazi health law kills thousands'.

'I came to find Cyril,' she said again, but Kit was staring at the ground now, digging the toe of her shoe into the rough soil. 'Kit, this isn't why we came. We came to join the search, to talk to Hilde.'

Kit, still staring at her feet, shook her head. 'I'm sorry,' she said in a voice so quiet Sylvia could hardly hear her. 'I'm so sorry.' She looked up, and her eyes were full of tears. 'There isn't any search. They gave up, weeks ago. Sylvia, no one's looking for him any more.'

Chapter Forty

Hilde knew, when they knocked, why they'd come. She was in the bedroom when she heard them; the cattle dealer was coming tomorrow and she'd begun folding clothing and packing up their belongings, hoping Anna wouldn't notice until the last possible moment. All that was needed was a cart to take them to the road, then transport to Freiburg, directions to their aunt's flat. She was so close to getting Anna out, to starting their new life. If not Freiburg, then they would keep going, until she found somewhere where Anna could be safe, herself again, where everything that had happened – since the elections, since the night their father hadn't come back from the mines, all of it – would be a distant dream.

She opened the door.

'Can I help you?' Paul Huber was standing in the doorway, dressed in his Hitler Youth uniform, several more boys behind him. The sun was falling below the line of hills over Paul's shoulder, casting their long shadows across the threshold.

Anna came through from the kitchen and stood beside her.

'Paul? What is it?'

'You're required in the square. You received a notice.'

'We didn't. Did we, Hilde?'

She'd burned it as soon as it had come. At some point, over the last few days, she'd decided that was the only way to keep them safe. Pretend she hadn't seen the notices, the demands, the attempts at control. She hadn't imagined they would come knocking on doors.

'Some misunderstanding, perhaps,' she said. 'I'm afraid we're too busy today, anyway.'

'You received a notice,' Paul said again, seeming suddenly unsure of himself. 'You're required to attend.'

She felt Anna flinch beside her.

'What can possibly be so important? Everyone has work to do. I'm sure you do yourself, Paul.'

'Please, Hilde…' For a moment he sounded like himself again, uncertain and hesitant, just a child. She thought of all the times he'd helped her with the harvest, with hauling hay into her loft, hanging meat to dry in the eaves. One of the boys behind him took a step forward and took Hilde by the arm.

'Paul…' She heard Anna say, as she closed her eyes.

The first blow wasn't hard, but it took her by surprise. She hit her head on the door frame as she fell, and when she opened her eyes she saw specks of blood on the flagstones, slowly sinking into the ground. Anna was screaming; her voice sounded far away. Her cheek was cold, and though she felt no pain she knew it would come, once the shock had run through her. She tried to stand and felt something on her arm, pressing her down. A boot, polished leather, the laces neatly tied.

'Will you come now, please?'

'Hilde, please.' Anna's voice was pleading and small. The boot was removed, and for a moment, Hilde thought about standing up. Going quietly. Then she thought of Fritz, the flames rising from his house in Freiburg, a house she'd never known existed. Her father, standing on the street beside him, holding his hand.

'No.'

The boot landed heavily in her side. Over the buzzing in her ears, she heard Anna start to cry.

'Please.'

Hilde turned her head and looked up, and there she was.

Her sister, just a child, her eyes red and puffy, her hands held out. She reached up and took one of them, allowing Anna to pull her to her feet.

'Alright. Alright, Paul, I'll come.'

She put an arm around Anna as they walked together to the square. Her whole body ached. Drumbeats sounded ahead of them, and bonfires had been lit above them on the mountainside. The uniformed children walked on either side of them, their arms swinging smartly by their sides. She pulled Anna closer. 'It's alright, I'm alright.'

'They didn't need to do that,' Anna whispered. 'They didn't need to.'

'I know. It's alright, *Liebling*.'

The rest of the village was streaming towards the square, emerging from their houses, from the inn, from carts which had come from further along the valley. Party flags were swinging above them, held aloft by boys in uniform marching in perfect unison. Anna pressed herself closer to Hilde, and as they reached the square she began to say something which was drowned out by the drums, by the voices all around them as they were pressed forwards by the crowds surging towards the platform, where a row of SS officials were lined up. Hilde saw the English teacher among them, looking stronger and taller than he had seemed on the night of the accident. How had they persuaded him to come back?

'It will be alright' Anna was saying. 'Won't it?'

Hilde turned and saw Fritz pushing his way closer to them, and relief surged through her; he had always made her feel safer. On her other side she found Gertrud Braunling, and as she looked up, Gertrud offered her a quick, uncertain smile which Hilde returned, surprised to find Gertrud's hand in hers, squeezing it tight. Anna was still murmuring something under her breath; Hilde strained to hear, but the crowds were too loud now, pressing in around them, faces she'd never seen before amongst those she'd known all her life. And then, as Runde took his place at the podium and the crowds begun to quieten, she didn't want to hear; she turned away from Anna, closing her eyes and allowing the sound of the drums to fill her head until there was no room for anything else.

Chapter Forty-One

A scattering of rain had begun to fall. Keith stood amongst the SS officers on the platform, still and upright as the Hitler Youth boys gathered in the square. They didn't flinch as fat drops of rain blurred their eyes and ran down their necks. Behind them, spectators were being herded in by officers, the square so full they could hardly move, surging forwards as one as they gazed up at the men on the stage, holding raincoats over their heads.

He watched as they tried to persuade Sylvia to step onto the platform. She was shaking her head, as the woman with her pleaded and gestured. She looked up and met his eyes, and he felt shame washing over him, a shame so acute he had to look away. And then she was standing beside him, as another woman holding an umbrella hurried onto the platform and began daubing her face with brushes and powder, running her fingers through Sylvia's hair, her mouth stopped with a collection of hairpins which she inserted one by one with delicate precision.

He thought of all the blank sheets of paper he'd thrown away, and couldn't come up with anything to say.

'I shouldn't have come,' he whispered.

She turned to look at him. Her face was heavy with powder, a white pallor clinging to her skin which made her look ill. The flash of camera bulbs began to hum through the square as the crowds quietened. He could hear her breath, quick and light.

'I came to find Cyril,' she said, and there were tears in her eyes. 'They're not even looking for him any more.'

He reached out for her hand and pressed it between his.

Kurt Runde stood at the centre of the stage and spoke into a loudspeaker, his voice echoing tinnily around the square.

'We are here to honour the five British children who were lost on this mountain on a night of terrible weather. Their sacrifice, which has furthered the cause of friendship between our two nations, will never be forgotten.'

He motioned to the side of the stage. One of the Hitler Youth boys stepped up, carrying a wreath of greenery and pine cones, tied with red and white ribbons. He crossed the stage and handed it to Sylvia, a broad smile on his face which she did not return as she took the wreath and cradled it to her chest.

'We honour, too, the best and the strongest of our nation. The boys of the Freiburg Hitler Youth, who so nobly risked their own lives to lead the rescue operation, and afterwards paid their respects to their fallen comrades. Their efforts are proof that, whatever struggles are yet to come, the youth of Germany is fit to meet them.'

Keith looked down at them, gathered at the side of the stage. Some of them looked younger than the boys he'd brought to the mountain; others, almost men. He knew the truth now. They had never been there. It was a fiction, forced bluntly into reality, and he had done nothing to stop it. Had he known all along? Of course he had, but something had persuaded him to doubt his own mind. And now he was here and it was too late, far too late, to stop it.

Another of the uniformed boys, the tallest, climbed the steps towards them, saluting smartly as Kurt Runde handed him a medal. The photographer crawled closer, crouching below them as though he were poised in the trenches, an umbrella held awkwardly over his head. Runde returned the salute, and then the boy turned to Keith, and raised his hand again.

Keith stared at him. It wasn't his symbol, this flattened, outstretched hand. It meant nothing to him. In another world, it might have been a symbol of peace; an offering – *My hand is empty,* it might be saying. *Look, I have nothing to hide.* In this world – he thought of his father, all his newspapers, all his talk. How easy it would be to agree with it all, to shield himself from any more punishment. How afraid he had been, all his life, to tell his father what he really thought of him.

There's still time, he thought to himself as he faced the child. I could turn to them all, now, and tell them the truth. There were no German children on the mountain, only the men and women of the village, only these people, standing anonymously in the crowds. I could tell them the rest, tell them everything, speak it out loud just once and it would be done. There were reporters here, photographers, it would all be printed on ink and paper, no one would be able to deny it.

He looked up and noticed Fritz Feldberg in the crowd. Beside him, a young woman was gazing up at him. Keith met her eyes and took a step back, almost losing his footing. The memory of a voice, speaking urgently, arms on his shoulders. *We need to know if there's anyone else out there.*

It came to him in a rush. What he'd told her, the truth he'd spoken out loud for the first and only time. How had she done it, how had it happened? And who had she told? The fear, the shame; his whole body shook with it. The boy was still standing in front of them, his hand raised in the salute, and Keith felt himself giving way. Instinctively, his hand began to move, before Sylvia took hold of it and held it tight.

The camera whirred beneath them as, slowly, the boy moved away.

Chapter Forty-Two

After the speeches, Hilde thought it was over. Her head and side ached; she put a hand to her temple and felt dried blood clinging to her hair. Fritz was still beside them; Anna was holding tightly to her hand, her eyes wide as she stared up at the SS officials, who were gathering now at the centre of the platform. Kurt Runde approached the loudspeaker and she felt a hush descending again on the square.

'I'm sorry, after such a joyful occasion, to have to deliver the news we've just received.'

Anna was pulling at her arm. 'Let's go,' she whispered. 'They won't notice now; let's go home.'

Hilde turned to look back – the crowd behind them was packed in tightly; they would have to push their way through.

'It's nearly over,' she whispered back. 'I promise, we'll leave when it's over.'

'It is proof,' Runde continued, 'that we must continue to be vigilant. Our enemies are within, as well as without.'

'Please, Hilde.'

'There is a Jew living among you. Hidden in plain sight. A cuckoo in the nest.'

All the blood seemed to drain from Hilde's body. She felt herself falling, the mountain hollow as air beneath her.

'A non-citizen, enjoying your rights, stealing from your land.'

I didn't tell anyone, I didn't say a word.

'And a child has not been recovered.'

He left a long silence then. Enough space for the crowd to draw their own conclusions. A British child, an Aryan child. Hilde felt Fritz's breathing growing quicker beside her as the panic rose in her throat. All those cartoons in the newspapers, the disfigured faces turned upwards towards a child, blood dripping onto their lips. *I didn't...* and then she remembered. She did. She had. She'd told Anna, and as soon as she had she'd known, deep down, what would happen.

'The purity of German blood is the essential condition for the continued existence of the German people. I quote directly from the laws passed in Nuremberg only a few months ago. We cannot tolerate defilement, concealment. You all know what those laws say. Jews enjoy no protection from the state.'

She turned towards Fritz, held out a hand, and suddenly he was running. It happened so quickly that no one reacted at first. Hilde had turned too slowly to catch his eye, in time only to see him pushing his way through the crowd. On the stage Runde was saying his name, over and over, and someone else was running too, reacting almost as fast as Fritz had. It was the English teacher, tearing after him, past the Party flags and the boys lined up beside the platform, forcing his way through the crowds as Runde stood still. What was he running for? Hilde waited for Runde to react, to order his men, but he stood silently. She realised why as some among the crowd of villagers, slow to respond at first, began running too.

'Stop!' she heard herself shout. 'Leave him alone, stop it!' Could anyone hear her? Could Fritz? She wanted him to know that none of this was what she wanted, that she hadn't let him down. *I didn't, I didn't.* She pushed her way through the crowds, adrenaline forcing her on before she could think about the consequences, and pulled herself up onto the stage. She turned to face the crowd, her voice hoarse now with shouting. 'What has he done to you? Stop it, for God's sake!'

She felt hands on her arms, pulling her back, but she carried on screaming, doubling over as the first blow met the back of her head. Looking up, she saw her sister in the crowds, almost disappearing among them. Hilde knew what had happened. That afternoon with Paul, the posters, their heads bent together. Anna flattered, eager to impress. She had always enjoyed showing off. What had their father said? *They're inside our heads now, they don't even need to pass laws, we'll do anything they ask of us.*

She opened her mouth to speak and was struck in the face, closing her eyes against the blow. When she opened them again, she turned to look for Fritz, but he was too far away from her now, hidden by the rushing crowds. About a third of the people in the square had run after him; the rest had stayed, staring up at the platform, at her. Runde was in front of her, looking at her with cold, indifferent eyes.

'Do you have any family in the village?'

She shook her head.

'Friends? Sympathetic friends, I mean.'

She stared back at him, unsure how to respond.

'Your sister will need to be taken in.'

He said it so casually. Slow to come, the realisation fell heavily, winding her. *Dear God, make me dumb, so I won't to Dachau come.*

She tried to form the words. Her mouth was dry, her upper lip swollen and bleeding.

'You'll have to speak up, Hilde.'

'Hans Huber.'

He gave a short laugh. 'You think he will want to be associated with you? Well, I suppose it shows forgiveness. And the sister can hardly be blamed for your failings, after all. Alright.' He turned to one of the men and spoke into his ear before turning back to her. 'Well then. Shall we go? There'll be a delay, I'm afraid. We can't get the cars this far.'

She wanted to ask him about Fritz, but it hurt too much to move her lips and she was afraid of what the answer might be. Only a few people were left in the square now; they were slowly dispersing, back to their houses, or winding their way together towards the inn. She thought of them all gathering in the main room, discussing her downfall over schnapps, shaking their heads at the shame of it all, this final confirmation that Hilde Meyer was no better than her father had been. *Always thought it would come to this. Has her father's blood, doesn't she? Her poor sister, she's always been the best of them, a true German patriot, a true friend to the Reich, she'll go far once she doesn't have that shade hanging over her. It's hardly her fault, after all.*

Anna was still in the square as they led Hilde down the steps. She looked stunned, standing with her hands by her sides. Their eyes met as Hilde was turned towards the road; for a moment she wondered if Anna would cry out, try to stop them, run after her and demand Hilde back. It had all been a mistake, a terrible misunderstanding. *Stay quiet,* she willed her as they passed. *For God's sake, Anna, don't say a word.* As Hilde was led through the square, her sister turned away.

They were taking her towards the inn. A winding, roundabout way, so that they wouldn't meet the crowds already streaming there. When they reached it they led her towards a back door and down into the basement, locking the door behind her without saying a word.

She stared around her at the barrels lined up along the walls, the bottles stacked in alcoves, the sacks of grain. The floor was bare, but for a pile of sheets discarded in a corner. Hilde sat down, reaching for one before she remembered. Four children, carried down in the dark, a storm still raging outside. Upstairs, the hum of activity. Reiner, Fritz, Gertrud, herself, working together with a common purpose, all their resentments and petty disputes, all their grudges temporarily forgotten.

She leaned back against one of the barrels and closed her eyes. Hours seemed to pass; she wished she had a radio, some way to break the silence. She'd had the radio playing the day Anna disappeared, the day they lost their father, to drown out the silence of the house. After the first few frantic hours, their mother had lain down on her bed, still as a marble statue in a tomb. And so Hilde was alone when she'd heard that the president was dead, that Hitler had passed a law, only the day before, which meant he was president now, as well as chancellor. *Führer und Reichskanzler.*

The day of the collapse.

She'd heard the news, and then, just moments after, there had come a knocking at the door and there was Fritz Feldberg, cold and shivering, with her sister in his arms. He'd slumped into a chair as their mother, suddenly more alive than Hilde had ever seen her, beat at Anna's frozen body with a broom, held her tight, and afterwards they'd all huddled together by the stove, Anna chattering away, the radio still playing in the background, a tinny voice that no one was really listening to any more as they waited for her father to come home. Over the sound of the announcer – *This marks a new beginning, our country will at last be renewed* – Hilde watched her mother, holding fast to Anna, rocking her back and forth. Whispering, over and over, *God bless you, Fritz Feldberg. God bless you. An angel sent you here to us.*

Chapter Forty-Three

Sylvia and Kit pushed their way through the thinning crowds in the direction the girl had been taken in. As they ran, Kit tried her best to explain what had happened in the square, why the man had run, why the girl had been taken.

'That was her,' she said breathlessly, 'she found your scarf, talked to the teacher. She knows what happened.'

They were approaching the village inn, where a crowd of villagers had already filled the main bar, their excited chatter spilling out on to the street outside.

'What will happen to him?' Sylvia asked, looking back in the direction the man had run in. 'What will they—'

Kit held up a hand. A crowd of soldiers had massed at a side door to the inn. The two women stopped, breathing hard, both of them staring at the door.

'Do you think she's—' Sylvia said, at the same time as Kit said: 'We have to talk to her.'

They looked at each other.

'I didn't know,' Kit said quietly.

'What will they do to her? What will they do to that man?'

Kit didn't answer. Sylvia watched as she approached the soldiers, feeling despair creeping over her; there was no search party, and the only other person who still seemed to care about Cyril was behind a locked door. She looked back across the valley, at the green sweep of the mountains behind them, imagining every speck and shadow was her son, every variation in the light a message he was trying to send her.

When Kit returned her face was grave.

'They say you can go in. But not me.'

'Kit – how?'

'I told them I wouldn't write about any of it, not unless they let you.'

'Without you, though—'

'No press,' Kit said firmly. 'Just you.'

Sylvia put out a hand to the wall as she climbed down the narrow steps, feeling the rough wood splintering against her fingertips. The darkness was total, until she reached the bottom step and saw the grey shadow of the floor ahead of her, her eyes adjusting to the dim light which was coming from a candle flickering in an alcove in the wall opposite her. Beneath it, a woman was sitting with her knees drawn up to her chest.

'Hilde.'

The woman looked up, wide-eyed, and Sylvia saw she was barely more than a girl. She hadn't seen her clearly in the square. There had been too much noise, too much shouting and clamour, the sun too bright in her eyes.

'Hilde,' she said again, and took a few steps forward. She held out her hands, desperately searching for the few snatches of German she'd thought she remembered from her old life, finding nothing there. 'It's alright. Don't be afraid.'

Hilde didn't move. A trickle of blood ran from her hairline to the edge of her right eye; Sylvia knelt in front of her and used her sleeve to wipe it away. She wished she had her old kit with her, some bandages and antiseptic. She wished she knew enough of Hilde's language to be able to ask her if she was in pain.

'Thank you for finding the scarf. For trying.'

She reached out to take Hilde's hand, but the girl pulled

her own away, suddenly speaking in an angry torrent of words Sylvia couldn't follow, the last work, *defekt*, spat out as though it was a bitter taste in her mouth.

'I wanted to ask you something.' It was pointless now, without Kit. She should leave, it wasn't helping anyone sitting here in the dark. But she had to ask the question anyway. She sat down next to Hilde, the two of them staring out into the dark, damp space. 'What did the teacher say to you, that night?'

Hilde turned to look at her, and for a moment, Sylvia thought she'd understood. But she only said something under her breath, and leaned her head back against the wall, closing her eyes, sounding as though all the energy had been drained from her body.

'I wanted Cyril to come on this trip,' Sylvia said. She could feel Hilde turn to look at her, and even though she knew they couldn't understand each other, there was a relief to speaking it aloud to the dark. 'I encouraged him, actually. I was so ashamed of what he'd seen.' She turned to face Hilde. 'I betrayed him. I betrayed his father. He's never even met his father, and that's because of me as well.'

She'd known, that night before the trip, what was written on the piece of paper in Cyril's hand. What he'd found in his father's desk. It was the letter she'd received from the Ministry of Pensions, ten days after she'd had her husband committed.

'I thought it was for the best,' she told Hilde, unable to stop now. 'I thought they'd diagnose shell shock, that he'd be given a pension, and that would help pay for Cyril. Arthur would get better, and we'd all be together.'

And then the letter had come. 'After consultation with your husband's doctors, we have concluded that his condition is not due to military service, but to a pre-existing feeble-mindedness.'

'You're supposed to believe in people, aren't you?' She stretched out a hand towards Hilde in the dust, and felt their fingertips touch. 'You're supposed to have faith that things can get better. And then they tell you something like that, and you wonder what you've been waiting for, all that time. You think you ought to have known all along that there wasn't any hope.'

The day after Cyril was born, when the nurse had brought him back into the room, she'd felt such a flood of happiness as she held him close that she'd forgotten, just for a moment, everything else. Later, she'd remembered that feeling as she decided that they had to move forward, they had to leave Arthur behind. He was broken, and there wasn't ever going to be a cure.

'He used to write to me all the time. He used to ask about coming home.' She closed her eyes; she couldn't look at Hilde as she said the next part. 'Eventually, I wrote and told him to stop. We didn't want him back. After that, I just burned his letters without opening them. I pretended he didn't exist.'

She closed her eyes and felt tears dripping onto their fingers. Hilde reached out a hand and Sylvia leaned forward, rested her head on the girl's shoulder and cried until her head began to ache. It was a relief, there in the dark where no one could hear them.

'*Defekt*,' Hilde whispered again, putting a hand on her own chest as Sylvia sat up. Tears were mingling with the blood smeared across her face. '*Defekt*.'

Sylvia shook her head slowly. She felt so certain, suddenly. She wanted to tell Dieter, to go back to the laboratory and write it on the walls, scream it from the windows, down to the courtyard below. 'It doesn't mean anything,' she said, 'all that talk. All that about defectives, about not being good enough. *Feeble-minded*. I wish I'd known it then. I thought he'd never get better, I thought Cyril would inherit – whatever it was that was wrong with his father. That his blood was somehow tainted. People kept telling me Arthur could get better and I didn't believe them. Listen.' She turned and put her hands on Hilde's shoulders, desperate for her to hear, to understand.

'They've got it all wrong, in their labs. It doesn't matter where you're from, what kind of person you are. It doesn't matter if you're healthy or sick, if you're the right sort of person or the wrong one, it doesn't make any difference. How can it? People just do their best. You were just doing your best out there.' She indicated the staircase, the outline of the door above them. 'So was I, so was Arthur, so was Cyril. We were all just doing our best.'

She sat back, still gripping tight to Hilde's hand. When the door above them opened, flooding the basement with torchlight, they both put their hands over their eyes, wincing as the soldier at the entrance shouted out an order. Sylvia saw Kit's face staring anxiously down at them, and slowly stood up.

Chapter Forty-Four

Keith moved faster than he knew he was capable of. Why did he do it? Afterwards he wasn't sure, but something compelled him to run after Fritz Feldberg, an urge so strong that he kept going long after he felt his chest begin to hurt, focusing on the figure ahead of him, feeling the crowd surge after them.

He'd always been the fastest runner. He'd tried to explain that to the doctor at his conscription examination, who'd hummed and hawed over his body, turning him to see it from every angle, scribbling notes on a pad. *I can run,* he'd tried to say. *In a fight, if it comes to it, I know how to run. I'm faster than you think.* The one night their father had caught up with him and Jack it had been the same; Jack had whispered *run* and he'd somehow slid past the figure in the doorway, past his reaching, clawing hands, thrown himself down the stairs and out the front door, running along the street without thinking, without stopping to look back, until he was standing in the patch of abandoned scrubland at the end of the road, behind which the railway stretched long and winding, out from the city. Hours later, he'd gone back and found Jack lying in his bed, one eye black and bruised, the other half closed by a cut across his face. The state of him, the mess of him, he hadn't been able to stop staring. They'd always stuck together, he and Jack, and after that, things between them had never been quite the same.

They reached the church. Fritz hurled his body against

the doors but they were locked; behind them, someone threw a bottle which smashed above their heads. He turned and saw Keith for the first time; put up his hands as if to defend himself. Keith raised his own and spoke slowly in German.

'I won't hurt you.'

For a moment they stared at each other; then there was a shout from behind them and they ran together through the churchyard, up towards the crest of the ridge surrounding the village and on towards the darkness of the forest. They could still hear voices behind them as they entered the trees, ducking under low branches, their feet sliding on pine needles and wet leaves until, somehow, the sounds of the chase began to die away.

Keith leaned forwards, his hands on his knees, breathing heavily.

'I think they've given up.'

Fritz shook his head. 'They won't.'

'Well, they can't find us in the dark, not if we stay quiet.'

In the silence, Keith looked up at the web of branches over their heads, a pattern of veins and arteries against the pale darkness. Somewhere below them, down into the depths of the slopes he'd dragged his boys into, an animal of some kind howled and rustled. His father would probably be able to identify the call. All those books he kept pristine on their shelves, they must have been good for something once. Below the animal cry he could hear water, rushing gently away from them. *No one knows we're here,* he thought, and imagined stepping into the dark and letting himself fall. *No one's coming. Not like last time.*

Fritz hadn't spoken again, and Keith wondered if he was in some kind of shock, like the men who'd come back from war, if a part of his mind had fled and taken refuge somewhere else. Was it temporary, that fleeing? Did those men ever really come back? At the inquiry, he'd said that was what had happened to him, and he'd wanted to believe it, he'd wanted it to be possible that his memories were so untrustworthy. He'd only known for certain it wasn't true when he'd seen Fritz in the square that afternoon, and the memory of his face had come back to him so clearly. He'd kept everything. Perhaps he was jealous of those men who hadn't.

'Why did you follow me?'

Keith shrugged; he had no idea, after all.

'Well, you don't have to stay.'

'I don't really want to go back.'

'We'll have to in the end.'

Keith sat down on the damp earth, leaning against a tree and closing his eyes. 'They don't really think that, do they?' he said. 'That you did something to Cyril?'

'Who knows? It doesn't matter.' Fritz sighed heavily.

They could still hear shouting, but it sounded more distant now, as though a barrier had been put up between them and the rest of the village.

'I shouldn't have come here,' Fritz said. 'I should have known you can't just become someone else.'

'Who were you before?'

Fritz eased himself down onto the ground beside Keith. Keith was shivering now; while they'd been running, he hadn't felt the cold, but now it began to bite at him and he drew his arms around his knees, remembering the numbness that had crawled over him that night in the snow.

'I had a wife,' Fritz said. 'A good life. Maybe that's what they didn't like.'

'What happened to her?'

Fritz smiled a fond smile. 'We were married twenty years. It was influenza, in the end. A good end, as far as they go.'

'I'm sorry,' Keith said. 'It's my fault, all this happening.'

Fritz shook his head.

'Isn't it? If I hadn't come here with the boys, none of this would have happened.'

'Of course it would. It's happening everywhere. You don't see it, so far away, but it's true.'

Keith thought of the crowd on Oxford Street, the day he'd

come away. How certain they'd seemed, how determined, how they'd moved as one. 'England isn't so far away,' he said.

'It's far enough, when there's no way to get there.'

'Yes, I suppose that's true.' It would be so easy for him, when the time came. A car to Freiburg, a train to Leipzig, and he'd be leaving it all behind. 'I shouldn't have let them lie like that,' he said. 'In the square, all those boys. They were never there, were they?'

Fritz laid a hand on his arm and Keith looked up, afraid he'd heard something. But there was nothing but the thick darkness of the forest, the black sky above them. *I'm a coward. Always have been.*

'So what really happened?'

Keith pushed his hand into his pocket and felt the rounded edge of the medal, cold against his palm. A child's voice sounded, loud in his ear against a storm long since blown over and finished. *Sir, it's not far. Sir, there are lights ahead. We can hear bells...*He saw them again, two boys running away from him towards the sound of the bells, disappearing suddenly below the cleft of the ridge, leaving him and Clayton alone. He felt again the rush of shame, his body about to give way and somehow Clayton, the only child he hadn't paired up with another, was still so strong, still wading through the snowdrifts as though they were no more than fields of grass and wildflowers. He'd felt a rush of hatred for the boy, so strong it almost overpowered what strength he had left as he'd felt himself sinking into the snow. He'd lost, he'd known it then. There would be no triumphant home coming, no medals and tearful words of gratitude. It was all over.

'I didn't want anyone to find us,' he said to Fritz. 'I wanted to disappear.'

He could remember a sudden silence as the storm briefly paused, and the bells from the village stopped ringing. Clayton, looking about him in panic; Keith had long since lost track of where they were. Each direction had felt very much like any other, and when Clayton asked which way to the village, he'd only waved a hand vaguely in the air. *You go on ahead, Clayton. Go on, the others are waiting for you.*

And then he'd been alone, lying back in the snow as the boy climbed on without him, into the storm, taking Keith's shame with him.

The square was empty when they finally made their way back down the path through the churchyard. Fritz led him beyond it, towards a house surrounded by vegetable patches and an open enclosure with various tools hanging from hooks along its walls.

'You should get back to the inn,' Fritz said, but Keith shook his head.

'I'll see you inside first.'

They entered the house by the kitchen side door. Fritz took a knapsack from a hook and began moving through the house, collecting up belongings.

'You're leaving?'

Fritz continued without speaking. Keith followed him into a living space, the embers of a fire still glowing in the hearth. A painting of the mountain sat on an easel before the fire, the snow covering its slopes brilliant with glistening colours. On the table, a pile of newspapers had been carefully stacked. They were all copies of *Der Stürmer*, the paper he remembered from the Blackshirt march in London.

'What are these?'

'Just nonsense.'

'But why are they here?'

There was a long pause before Fritz looked up. 'They've been delivering them with the mail,' he said at last. 'I try to get up early, take them from people's doorsteps.'

Keith turned over a page and stared at an image of Cyril Clayton, next to a photograph of the Schauinsland. Runde's voice in the square. *There is a Jew living among you. A child has not been recovered.* It was never said, not explicitly. The two facts were simply presented, side by side.

'It's nothing new,' Fritz said. 'They had all this where I came from too. I suppose it will be wherever I go next.' He looked up at Keith. 'People are people, wherever you go.'

'Then—'

There was a crash from behind them. They stood frozen, staring at something which had landed in the centre of the room between them. A window was shattered. Then another crash, and they both dropped to the ground. A sound like rushing water filled Keith's ears, and when he looked up the curtains were alight, the fire already spreading to the rug which lay across the flagstones, across to the barrels lined up along one wall, and the door to the outside was a wall of flame.

Part Six

Chapter Forty-Five

'*Ruhe!*'

Hilde opened her eyes to a thick, blanketing darkness. The voice came closer, but it moved on past her and she heard the heavy clang of a door closing. Then footsteps, disappearing into silence.

She must be in Freiburg, she thought, though it was hard to be sure. She had slept on the journey, and her sense of time was rapidly dissolving. She'd tried, when they'd brought her out of the car, to see something of the streets and houses, to match them with what she'd imagined, with Else's postcards, all her dreams and fantasies, but there had only been a few seconds, and she'd been blinded by the car's headlights.

The room was windowless and small; perhaps half the size of the *Stube*. Besides the bed she was lying on there was a chair, a small table and a narrow slit, high above her, which let in a thin blade of grey light. Sometimes she heard footsteps from above, voices echoing outside. It was too high for her to climb up on the chair and look through, so she imagined scenes instead, straining her eyes at the ribbon of light above her, imagining she could see the city beyond it, all the images from Else's postcards. The cathedral square busy with market stalls, women inspecting fruits and vegetables, turning them in their hands, pressing them against their cheeks as children pulled at their skirts. Above them the cathedral spire, casting a shadow across the square, tiny figures massing at the top of the tower and looking out across the mountains. Else, on her way to the hospital, her uniform pressed and neat, her head held high as she breathed in the scent of pine trees, car fumes, honeysuckle, all the smells of a city in the shadow of the mountains. She wondered if she would ever see it: blossom and cars and the mud and smoke of a city. It didn't seem to matter now, except for Anna. They were meant to come here together.

She pulled an extra blanket over herself and lay back. It had been warm all day; she had sat with the sun on her face for as long as she could, the act of following its passage around the tiny room a way of passing the time, but the nights, wherever she was, were cold. A light flicked on somewhere outside her cell; she was blinded for a moment, then began to make out shapes moving in the corridor outside. Her head ached; already a lump was swelling painfully at her temple.

The door swung open and two men entered. Hilde understood, without being told, that she was to stand.

They sat her on a bench in a tiny room which smelled of sawdust and fresh paint. She tried to focus on the face of the uniformed man sitting opposite her, but there were so many others now; Anna, Hans, Reiner, Paul. The woman in the basement holding her hand, words rushing from her that Hilde couldn't understand. The missing child, lost in the tunnels below the mountain, groping in the dark. And Fritz, running away from the square, the whole village surging after him. What had happened to him? Guilt and shame flared hot in her stomach.

'Are you comfortable?'

Hilde looked up. He was a young man, perhaps in his early thirties, with an open, friendly expression that instantly made her want to talk to him. He might have been chosen deliberately for that reason, she thought. Beside him, a woman in a dark grey suit was taking notes without looking up. Her hair, startlingly pale, was set in waves against her temples.

'Do you know why you're here?'

'You're sending me to Dachau.'

His eyebrows rose. 'Tell me why you think so.'

'Aren't you?'

She wondered, for the first time, what it was really like. For so long it had been a fairy tale, an imaginary place, a bad dream. Did people come back? And if they did, were they ever the same?

'Did you know Fritz Feldberg was a Jew?'

Hilde shook her head, feeling ashamed. She wanted to ask what had happened to him, but didn't dare.

'He never spoke of it? Showed any signs? You were friends, I think.'

'I didn't know.'

'Are there any other undeclared Jews in your village?'

'No.'

'How can you be sure? If you didn't suspect this one.'

'Well, then, I'm not sure.'

'Tell me about your father.'

Hilde stared at him. 'What? He's dead.'

'He had some unusual views, didn't he?'

She shook her head again, thinking of those boxes being taken from the basement, Hans' cold stare. 'I don't know anything about that,' she said, adding, 'I hardly knew him at all.'

He sat back, folding his arms.

It went on like this for an hour, maybe more. By the end of it, Hilde had become convinced within herself that everyone in the village was a Jew, a communist, a revolutionary, that she had known about all of it, kept secrets even from herself. The more she determined not to speak, the more suspicions the man seemed able to plant within her mind. He asked if she had been a member of any of the banned organisations, the social democrats, the communists, and she began to feel that she must have been.

Another man entered the room and whispered in her interrogator's ear; he looked momentarily irritated, then resumed his former benign expression and turned to Hilde, smiling.

'What happens now?' she said.

He shrugged. 'You have somewhere to go?'

'You're letting me go?'

He laughed then, a low, throaty laugh. 'Do you know how much it costs us, to keep people in protective custody?'

'Protective custody – is that what it's called?'

'It's not safe for some people to be among the population. The damage they could do – the damage that could be done to them.'

'I know. I've seen it.'

'Is there someone who can come and get you?'

She hesitated. 'My aunt. I have her address.'

Back in her cell, Hilde wondered if it had been a lie. Were they really letting her go? She thought of the man who'd entered the room, who'd seemed to bring about the end of her ordeal. What had he whispered? Had he been searching through her father's boxes? If so, had he come to say they'd found nothing, or had there been something she'd missed?

She wondered if Else would come. She could hardly imagine Else as a real person, something more than a cut-out photograph. She spent some time practising what she might say. This was their chance, Anna and hers. Perhaps their only one. Had she already ruined it? What would Else think of her now, being summoned to collect her from a police station, what would she say?

The door swung open and Hilde stood up, suddenly

nervous. A woman was standing behind one of the guards; it was too dark for Hilde to make out her face.

'Is that her?' a tired voice said. 'Alright then.'

The guard moved aside and Hilde breathed in a wave of cigarette smoke. The woman in the doorway was tall, wearing a dark blue suit and a shabby, stale-smelling fur coat. She took a long pull on her cigarette, looking Hilde up and down.

'Good God,' she said, her eyebrows raised. 'Hilde Meyer. Has it been as bad as all that?'

Outside, dusk was falling over the city. Overwhelmed by the enormity of it, by the crowds of people and the sounds and smells, everything harsh and bright and loud, Hilde stared at her feet as her aunt led her briskly through the cobbled streets. Wide channels of water ran along their edges; grey and silted, nothing like the clean, clear rivers that ran through the valleys above them. She could feel an impossible number of bodies jostling past her, their sweat leaking through the air towards her. There was so much noise: people calling out to each other through open windows, men selling newspapers crying out their headlines, cars and buses pushing their way through the crowds of people, occasional fights breaking out among groups of young men, mothers shouting after their children. She looked about for silver, thinking of the mines, expecting to find it piled up in great stacks, and saw nothing but manure piled up at the sides of the streets, crumbling pavements and brown, muddy puddles. Perhaps, she thought, when the silver reached the city it was all hoarded away, a cellar somewhere, or vaults beneath the streets; hardly any different from its life under the mountain, after all.

'I should explain,' she said, trying to keep up with Else's rapid pace.

Her aunt held up a hand. 'Don't say anything. Not until we're home.'

Hilde looked up properly then for the first time and saw

the uniformed men, gathered together in groups or standing in shop doorways. She noticed how people slid around them in a wide arc, as though some sort of protective barrier existed between them and the city; they eyed each other with wide, inquisitive eyes. Ahead of them, a huge spire rose above the rooftops; however far they walked it didn't seem to get any closer. The streets were growing increasingly narrow, and the dank, unmistakable smell of sewage was beginning to fill her nose. They'd reached the river; on the other side, a row of tall, elegant houses rose up against the dark sky, ivy twisting around their flanks. Here they were at last then; exactly the sort of houses she had imagined Else living in, that she'd imagined herself and Anna moving into. She waited for them to cross, but Else led her instead further along the dark street and through a narrow alleyway. The smell was everywhere now; a mix of sewage and rotting food which, to Hilde, was not so different to the barn when she'd been slow to clean it out. When she turned around, she couldn't even see the beautiful spire any more, only the maze of rooftops that surrounded it.

They stopped in front of a tall, narrow building of grey stone. Hilde looked up; a few twisting metal balconies ran along each floor. A woman was sitting on one of them, a flurry of feathers rising from her fingers as they worked at a chicken carcass. By the entrance, two children were sitting on a step, a cap laid out in front of them, one or two shiny coins glinting within it. She looked at her aunt, who was fiddling with her keys, and saw her as though for the first time.

Oh, Else, she thought, as her dream of Freiburg, of the elegant life that was waiting for her here, slid quietly away. *Oh, Else.*

Chapter Forty-Six

Keith woke with the fire still in his lungs. He could smell it, feel the ash floating in the air around him. He lay still, testing the ache in his limbs until he heard the loud crack of flames licking wood and sat up, terrified.

'It's alright.'

Fritz was handing him a cup of water. Behind him, a small campfire was spluttering into life outside a low doorway.

'Where are we?'

He was sitting on a camp bed, a rug stretched over him. He could hear rushing water somewhere close by, and behind it an empty silence which brought everything into closer focus. It was quieter than he could remember any place ever having been; he thought the completeness of it must have been what had woken him, the absence of sound becoming its own sound.

'My cabin. I used to come out here to paint.'

Keith looked up and saw the view in front of them: the sweep of the valley through the trees, the open sky. He held up his hands and saw the blisters, the broken nails where he'd scratched at the window ledge, the floor. He tried to think back to the fire, and all he could remember was Fritz pulling him into a side room, giving him a reassuring look, running his hand across the beams of the kitchen wall, confident and slow, *the timber is proofed, it's alright.* Then the realisation that there was something in the room with them, something more than flames. They could smell it, acrid and poisonous, and as he smelled it he thought of France, the final moment, a bullet soaring and time seeming to slow. Jack's voice in his ear: *Run. Run now.*

He remembered looking at the piles of newspapers, the vile cartoons already beginning to curl at the edges as the heat spread. Then at the open door and the darkness of the forest beyond it; a darkness that was suddenly welcoming. He couldn't do it. He was a coward, he always had been. He would stand staring stupidly at the flames until they began biting at his ankles, or until the crowd outside found them and pulled them into the fire. He could hear the conscription doctor's voice, indifferent and brisk, *Just walk to the end of the room and back again, nice and slow. Now, a little faster, that's it.*

Run. It had been Fritz shouting it then, seizing his hand. Keith realised the kitchen had filled with a suffocating, foul smoke which had stopped his throat, and he was on his knees, crawling without knowing which direction to go in. *Run, Keith.* Someone had seized his collar and begun dragging him along the floor, which was somehow, inexplicably, still cold against his cheek.

He looked up at Fritz, poking at the small campfire which was flickering indifferently into life. His home was gone, his safety, his neighbours. Where would he go?

'We can't stay here long,' Fritz said, 'I've got a few cans of food, not much.' He looked back at Keith. 'You should go back to the village.'

Keith joined him and held out his hands to the flames. Around them, pine trees were knitted together beneath a clear, pale sky. He tried to imagine it: going back, facing the school again, his parents, all the parents of the boys he'd lost. He tried to imagine pushing away the memory of Cyril Clayton, that last image of him standing at the top of the ridge, a dark shadow against the snow until the storm swallowed him up. *You go on ahead.*

'What about you?' he asked. 'Where will you go?'

'I don't know.' Fritz turned his face away.

'She told me they've stopped searching for the boy. Is it true? They've given up?'

'Yes, they've given up.'

'What do you think really happened to him?'

Fritz looked up, over the line of trees towards the mountain ridge, half hidden in haze. 'These mountains used to be mined for silver,' he said. 'Miles and miles of tunnels underneath us.' He stamped a foot against the turf. 'Most of it good for nothing, any more. The silver's long gone. The lead too. The midwives use the tunnels to get between villages, sometimes.' He blinked and turned back to Keith. 'He's dead, I suppose. How can he not be? Sometimes, though. Sometimes, I find myself wondering...' He stamped a foot again, as though he was trying to call something up from beneath them. 'They say a king is sleeping in the mountain. They say he's gathering boys for an army, that he'll come back some day and fight a great war.'

'That sounds like nonsense.'

'Yes, just a story. But there is a war coming. Isn't there?'

'I don't know.'

'You'll have to fight it, when it comes.'

Keith shook his head.

'You would, I am sure of it.' The old man smiled as though the thought of it amused him. 'They might have us both, before it's over. All men will have to prove themselves. You're – what are you? Forty? Ach, it won't be as bad as you think.' He shook his head, and Keith found himself wondering, suddenly, how many Englishmen Fritz Feldberg had killed.

Keith leaned back, closing his eyes. 'I can't go back,' he said.

'You want to – what? Desert?'

'Perhaps I would, if it came to it. I'm a coward, really.'

'It isn't cowardly. Desertion.'

'Isn't it?'

Fritz shook his head. 'I knew a man once – well, you don't

need to hear about that. Here.' He held something out. 'This must be yours, I think.'

Keith stared down at the medal. It looked suddenly small and dull, sitting there in Fritz's palm. It must have fallen from his pocket, some time during the fire, or while they were running. 'I don't want it,' he said. 'You might as well keep it. Really,' he pushed Fritz's hand away. 'It doesn't mean anything. Just the luck of the draw.'

'Alright.' Fritz put his other hand in his pocket and held out something else, dropping it into Keith's palm. 'You can have this, in return.'

It was a toy soldier, old and faded, a crude face painted onto the metal and a gun so worn down it was barely visible over the man's shoulder.

'What is it?'

'Just something I found once in the mud,' he said. 'Back there, back in France, lying in some field. Some child must have dropped it. I was hiding in a dugout. My friend was with me – he wanted to make a run for it, but I couldn't do it. We split the supplies between us, wished each other luck.' He shrugged. 'Could have been me they shot,' he said, shaking his head. 'Just the luck of the draw, in the end.' He looked up at Keith. 'How do you make sense of something like that? I made up a story afterwards, said he'd done it to rescue me.' He gave a low, quiet laugh. 'They just didn't find me, that's all. Which of us was the braver? I don't know.'

'Why did you make up a story?'

'I don't know. People love stories, don't they? They wanted me to tell them what it was like, fighting a war, and I didn't know what to say. So I made it up. Told them this is the last thing he gave me, before he ran to get help.'

Keith nodded. 'I make up stories too,' he said. 'I tell them about hiding in an apartment building with a sniper rifle. Taking men out from a distance. It's lies, all of it.' He gestured to his medal, still in Fritz's palm. *For bravery in the field.* 'Read what it says, around the edge.'

Fritz held the medal close to his face and read the inscription around its narrow rim. 'J R Hughes,' he said out loud. He looked up.

'Jack. My brother. He didn't come back.' He felt suddenly calm. At last, he had told someone. 'He's still out there somewhere, I suppose. Underneath some field somewhere.'

'And you did come back.'

'No,' Keith said, almost laughing now at the relief of it. He'd held on to his lie for so long. So long, he had begun to forget the truth. 'I never went,' he said. 'Haven't stepped foot out of England, my whole life.'

'Until you came here.'

'Yes. Until I came here.'

Chapter Forty-Seven

The fire is sputtering out; he looks around for someone to stoke it, but the boys have all long since gone to bed. Why has he chosen a youth hostel for this portion of the trip? They are almost a week in; he's growing tired of thin mattresses and poor food. He should have planned for something better, just for a couple of nights. God knows, most of the parents can afford it. The climb to Todtnauberg across the Schauinsland is tomorrow, the least he could have done is given himself the chance of a good night's sleep first.

He reaches for his whisky glass. Finding it empty, he pours himself another. Why not, when there's no one here to see? He brought the whisky with him on the train, secreted in his luggage, and he has been thinking about it all the long, wearisome day. Thinking about the moment he'll be able to retrieve it, the moment he'll finally be done with the boys and all their chatter.

The pain comes in a rush, without warning. It's so sudden, he finds he is shouting, screaming for help. It happens like this sometimes. Creeps up on him without warning, and all he can do is thrash and yell until it's passed. Somehow he's gone from the armchair to the floor; the room looks distorted, everything at the wrong angle. This could be it, he thinks vaguely, this could be how it happens, at long, long last. He wonders if Jack had a moment like this, in the flash of time he had to think before the bullet, the shrapnel, the explosion, whatever it was, hit home.

You're in luck. That had been the final verdict, the day he'd been summoned for his conscription exam, twenty years ago. *You're in luck,* as though the whole process had been nothing more than a coin toss, the rolling of a die. Lying on the floor in the youth hostel's tiny parlour, he can remember it so clearly it's as though he's back there. Sitting in a hospital corridor, ten or twelve young men alongside him, all of them twisting their fingers nervously, avoiding each other's eyes. Hearing his name, and feeling their eyes on him, weighing him up as he stood. *Good posture, young, still got all his teeth. Yes, he'll be among the first to face the guns.*

The doctor began by asking him to remove his clothes. It was a shock; at just eighteen, Keith had no conception of his own body. No one but him had seen it since he was a child, and he did his best to avoid seeing it himself. He was aware of it, of course, the various urges and compulsions that came with it, but he had only the vaguest conception of what it looked like. Skin that seemed too pale, too thin, beneath which veins seemed to sit uncomfortably close to the surface. Why were veins blue, he had wondered in moments when he caught himself looking, and why so vulnerable, why not bury them deep?

'Stand up straight, please.'

A tape measure was stretched from his forehead to his toes.

'Hold out your arms.'

From the tips of his fingers. The circumference of his chest.

'Please walk to the door and back again.'

The floor was cold. His feet slapped against it too loudly; he felt disgusted at the sound, at the thought of his naked body being viewed from every angle as he turned.

'Now hop there on your left foot, and back on your right.'

He could hear voices in the corridor, nurses coming and going. He imagined one of them choosing the wrong door and walking in to see him bouncing absurdly across the room, naked and exposed.

'Alright, now stand still, please, with your arms above your head.'

The doctor paced slowly around, taking him in from every angle. Keith thought of cadavers, hanging by a hook at the butcher's, swaying slowly from side to side. Without warning, the doctor's hands were on his testicles, turning them this way and that as though they were fruit in a market. He drew in a tight, sudden breath, feeling light-headed as he held it. Was there a way to cheat them? He wondered as he held on. To convince them he wasn't fighting material, that he'd be no use to them? It was an unthinkable idea; he erased it from his mind. He remembered the night on the rooftop before Jack had been sent out, felt again the thrill of fear which had run through him and tried to shake it away. Jack had wanted to go, and therefore so did he, because they did everything together.

The doctor let go and stood up again, and Keith felt the blood rushing to his face.

'Another deep breath, please.'

He took a stethoscope and wound it around his neck. The small metal circle was pressed against the centre of Keith's chest and he froze, staring down at his bare feet, the whiskers on his toes.

The rest of the examination was quick and, afterwards, difficult to remember. He moved his arms and legs as directed, opened his mouth to allow his teeth to be inspected fully. He answered questions about his medical history, called out various commands in a voice he hoped was loud enough, squinted at tiny symbols on a board hung up on the far side of the room. He stared down at his pale forearms, his torso, trying to imagine broken skin, bullet wounds, an explosion of unspeakable things.

'Alright, that will do.'

Dressed again, he was able at last to look the doctor in the face. He was middle-aged, with sad, wistful eyes. His hair was thinning and he had a tiny cut on his chin – shaving, Keith thought, and tried to imagine him that way, just an ordinary man like any other, wincing as he caught at his face with the razor, running his fingers across his jaw.

'You're in luck,' the man said.

'What?'

'Heart palpitations. I'll need to do more tests.'

Keith remembered his father, a sharp breath in, hands clutching at his chest. *Heart trouble,* his mother had whispered then, and made them promise never to bring it up again. It's in the blood, he thought, of course it's in the blood, of course I'm next.

'What do you mean, in luck?'

'What do you think I mean?'

His cheek feels numb against the cold flagstones of the youth hostel's parlour. There is a sound behind him. Somehow, he summons the strength to sit up and look round; a boy is peering at him through the half-open door.

'Clayton.' His voice sounds hoarse and hollow. 'Some water…'

After that, he must black out for a few moments; when he returns to the room, there is a glass beside him on the floor. He reaches for it, swallowing a mouthful quickly. It hasn't happened in so long.

'Thanks.'

Clayton is standing over him, wide-eyed with curiosity. He eases himself up, back into the chair, and indicates the armchair opposite, on the other side of the fire. Clayton slides into it, staring at him expectantly.

'Just…' What can he say? 'Just an old injury. Well, not injury, exactly…'

'From the war?'

'No, not from the war.' They meet each other's eyes. Keith fingers his medal in his pocket and searches for some sign of guilt on the boy's face. The day he'd shown it to them at school, Clayton had been so engrossed, so eager to hear the stories of his heroism. He hadn't meant to tell them so much, but once he'd started, it had been difficult to stop. 'Why aren't you in bed, anyway? Big day tomorrow.'

Clayton whispers something in a small voice.

'Eh?'

'Harry Prendergast put my bedding in the bath, sir.'

'I see.' Keith sighs. 'Happens a lot, does it? I mean – this sort of thing?'

Clayton nods.

'Alright. You shouldn't put up with it, you know. You should – ah – you should tell him what's what.'

'It's not just him, sir. I can't tell all of them that.'

'Course you can. How do you think wars are won? You have to stand up for yourself, even if you're smaller. Even if it seems like you won't win, you have to keep fighting.'

'Is that what it was like in the war, sir?'

'What? No. That is…'

It's very close now. Closer than it's ever been before. The whisky isn't advisable, he thinks as he pours himself another.

'Sir, did you kill anyone, in the war?'

Leaning forward on the roof with Jack, raising an imaginary sniper rifle, aiming at the men and women on the street below. The puff of cold air from his throat as he imagined pulling the trigger. He wants to tell Clayton to stop going on about the bloody war, but he can't do that. If he does that, the boy might ask him why he's told all his stories, why he's been so keen to talk about it, all these years.

'I didn't kill anyone.' Sometimes, when people ask him questions like this, he imagines he had. Jack had, countless times, it was all in his letters. He imagines their faces; young men with wide, intelligent eyes, unaware of the rifle that was tracking them across an empty street, a shattered hallway. He tells Jack's stories, when people ask him what it was like. He remembers them all, can conjure them up like an archive in his mind. It's easy enough to imagine himself as his brother. Easy enough to imagine how it might have been, to take on another life and allow it to bleed through from some other place to cover up his own. He can't – perhaps it's the whisky – he can't seem to do it now.

'Is that because you were never there, sir?'

He looks up. It's a relief, to hear it spoken. Strange, that the relief should come from this small boy, who likely wouldn't survive a week out there himself, if it ever came to it.

'That medal isn't yours,' Clayton says, a bitter, disappointed tone in his voice. 'That's not your name that's written on it.'

Keith lets out a breath. 'People don't usually read the words around the edge,' he says. 'I wondered if you had.'

'My mum says I should say sorry.' He drew himself up in his chair. 'But I think it's you that should.'

He flinches at the memory, his hand on Sylvia's hand, their faces close together. The boy standing silently in the doorway. The father neither of them ever spoke about, that he knows nothing of. Or perhaps it's the lie, perhaps that's what the boy wants an apology for?

'That's enough, Clayton,' he says, trying to imitate the way his father speaks. 'Don't speak to your betters that way.'

'Why didn't you go?' Clayton demands.

This isn't the question Keith has been expecting. Why did you lie, perhaps, or whose medal is it really? How did you come to have it? This question, by far, is the hardest one to answer. He puts a hand over his heart.

'They don't let you, if… if…' He can't say the words. For a horrible moment, he thinks Cyril is going to say them for him. *If you're broken. Defective. Not whole. My heart,* he wants to say, *my heart is broken.* 'It's called grade four. Medically unfit. Jolly bad luck, that's all.'

He feels shame, is overwhelmed with it. He might as well strip naked in front of all the boys, let them laugh at him as he cowers in a corner. He knows now why his father stopped his mouth, when he tried to ask about it. And he has his father's blood. It isn't their fault they never had the chance to fight, is it? No one knows what they might have done with it, if they had.

'The medal belonged to my brother.'

Pouring himself another glass, he seems to see Jack where Clayton is sitting by the fire. Jack, sitting opposite him in his rooms at Cambridge, his head in his hands. *I'm sorry, I'm sorry.*

'What happened to him?'

'It was a long time ago.'

You wouldn't stick a war, Keith. You wouldn't last five minutes. The things I've seen...

He leans forward, his head heavy with whisky and the heat of the fire. Afterwards, he can't explain to himself why he says it, why this small boy he barely knows should be the one to draw it out of him.

'I did kill someone once, though,' he says. 'Never fought a war, maybe, but I did do that.'

Cyril's eyes widen. 'Who? Who was it, Mr Hughes?'

He can see Jack's face now, staring up at him, the tears running down his cheeks. *Please, Keith. Please, don't.*

The next morning, the morning of the climb, he wakes with the knowledge of what he's said, what the boy knows, all the lies he's told, ringing in his ears. In the cold early morning light, there really isn't any choice at all.

Chapter Forty-Eight

In an instant, Hilde's childish vision of Else – a glamorous, elegant woman living in a stylish city apartment – was gone. In its place was a tired, thin-faced woman who eyed her niece suspiciously as she pushed open the door and beckoned her inside.

The tiny flat – Hilde could see every corner of it from where she stood in the doorway – smelled of cigarettes and a heavy, sweet perfume. A small galley kitchen led to a bedroom; Hilde could see the corner of a carefully made bed through the half-open door. In the sitting room, two wicker chairs sat on either side of an unlit fire, and a table, pushed up against the window, bore a sewing machine and a basket of scraps. Hilde took it all in, trying not to stare. Where were the elegant, tall windows, the polished floors, the plump velvet cushions? She had imagined space for dancing, for holding salons and dinners, ladies in furs and men in tuxedos. The woman she had seen at the back of the church, her face covered with black lace. Had she studied the dress, the veil, had she looked at it up close? Or had she simply filled in the blanks with what she'd wanted to see?

'You can sleep on the sofa,' Else said, going through into the kitchen. 'The bathroom's through my room. So you're not to use it after I've gone to bed.'

They sat in the wicker chairs drinking tea which Else had made with a few scraps of leaves; it was pale, almost transparent in the delicate china cup she handed to Hilde. There was a chip on its rim; Hilde ran her finger across it, feeling the worn, smoothed edge against her skin. She wondered if she would be offered anything to eat – she hadn't had anything since the slices of bread and cheese they'd given her in her cell; it must be more than six hours ago now. The window was half open; car fumes and the dank smell of the river drifted in, with the occasional sounds of children scrapping on the street outside.

'So,' Else said, eyeing her niece with narrowed eyes. 'What happened?'

Hilde told her, leaving out as much as she could: she'd learned her lesson, you had to be careful, it wasn't safe to trust anyone, even family.

'A rally, in Hofsgrund,' Else said. 'My God. Whatever for?'

'Those children, on the mountain.'

'The English children. I read about it in the papers.'

'There's a boy still missing. They thought he might be in the mines. But they're not searching any more.'

At the mention of the mines, she hesitated, thinking of her father, Else's brother. Could she see him in the angles of her aunt's face, the slant of her chin? She tried to, but all she saw was a stranger.

'Well,' Else said, leaning forward a little in her chair. 'You were lucky. That is, if they really have let you go.'

'What do you mean, if?'

'They'll still be watching you, that's certain. You'll need to keep your head down for a day or two.'

'How do you know these things?'

Else shrugged. 'You get used to it. I don't know many people who haven't been hauled over the coals a few times.'

'I thought things would be better here.'

'Better?' Else laughed dryly. 'You have no idea,' she said,

sounding suddenly angry. 'No idea at all. Out there in the…' She hesitated, searching for the right words. 'In the nowhere.'

Hilde felt indignant at that; hadn't she been interrogated herself? Living on the mountain hadn't protected her from that. 'It wasn't always easy there either, you know,' she said, feeling emboldened by the cold, her exhaustion. 'They didn't exactly leave us alone. They wanted to take Anna away from me,' she added, wondering, for the first time since leaving the mountain, what that would mean now. Would they let Anna come to Freiburg, or would she be kept like a prisoner in the Hubers' farmhouse, until she was ready to marry Paul, to start her own family?

'Wasn't always easy,' Else muttered. 'With your own food, your own supplies, all that land. None of you know what it's been like here. Since the war, how we've scraped.'

Hilde looked up at her, shocked again by the contrast between the woman opposite her and the one she'd imagined for so long.

'What happened?' she asked, and saw a faint smile flicker in the corners of Else's mouth. 'I mean,' she looked away, embarrassed. 'I just mean—'

'You mean, why am I like this? Why is my life like this? Your parents never told you? Well, I suppose it's not the sort of thing people talk about, is it?' She gave a tired sigh. 'It's the same old story.' She looked as though she was waiting for Hilde to say something; Hilde only stared back at her, waiting. 'It's always some man, *Liebling*,' Else said at last. She was speaking as though Hilde was a tired, grown-up woman herself, as though their lives had been the same. 'Haven't you noticed that? That's what's happening to the whole damned country, isn't it? Some man, and all his ideas.'

Hilde wasn't sure she understood, but she didn't want her aunt to know that. Else was eyeing her closely now, an appraising look on her face.

'So,' she said slowly, 'what are you going to do?'

'I thought…' Hilde felt foolish now, saying it out loud. 'I thought I might stay here.'

'Did you now?'

'Anna could go to school. We both could.'

'They'll only fill you up with their muck.'

'What muck?'

'My God. You really have fallen from a tree, haven't you?'

'I thought about training for nursing, like you.'

Else looked at her: a hard, cold look. 'You really don't know, do you?'

'Know what?'

But her aunt only shook her head. Easing herself out of her chair, she took a bottle and two glasses down from a shelf, pouring them out and handing one to Hilde, who sniffed at it suspiciously before taking a tiny sip. The liquid burned in her throat, warming her insides and making her cough.

'You missed all the fun, up there in the nowhere,' Else murmured after she'd swallowed hers. 'The boycotts, the rallies. We had the führer himself here, back before they called him that. Stirring us all up.'

'Why did he come?'

'Just to get votes, back when they needed them.' Else smiled. 'Seems a long time ago now, doesn't it?'

'Did you see him?' Despite herself, Hilde felt a thrill at the thought.

Else nodded. 'Threw stones at his car. One of them hit him in the face.' She laughed a hollow, throaty laugh.

'You hit him?'

'Well, someone did. Why shouldn't it have been me?' She laughed again. 'Your pa would have enjoyed that, wouldn't he? How much did he tell you, about me? About his life here, before he gave it all up to go live in the nowhere?'

'Hardly anything at all.'

Else nodded. 'He was never much for talking, was he? That's how you get by, after all. I don't normally tell people that, about the car, the stones. But it sounds like you might have done the same, if you'd been there.' She leaned forward. 'I'm right, aren't I?'

Hilde stared back at her. She wanted to nod, to say anything, but even though she felt sure it was safe, the old instinct was too strong to push down. *Dear God, make me dumb.*

Else nodded. 'I see.' She poured them both another drink and swallowed hers quickly with a flick of her wrist. 'God,' she said quietly. 'When I think of it, all those promises, all that hope. He was going to fix everything, wasn't he? Inflation. Poverty. Our *souls*. It boils my blood,' she said slowly, staring into her glass.

'It isn't all bad, is it? I mean...' Hilde didn't know how to finish. She didn't want Else to think she was on some other side, that she didn't feel the same way. But would she really have thrown stones, if she'd been there that day? She wasn't sure.

'It isn't all bad,' Else repeated slowly. She stood up and took a folder from a shelf. She handed it to Hilde, who didn't want to open it. She felt suddenly sure that, whatever was inside, she didn't want to see it. 'You want to be a nurse? You take a look at those and tell me that again. I can still help, if it's really what you want.'

Hilde leafed through the papers; they were medical records, names and details in smudged type, and a handwritten paragraph of text.

'Why do you have these?'

'I don't know,' Else said. 'I took them from the hospital, years back. I thought, if people only saw them – I didn't know, you see. It was only just starting back then. I thought people would be shocked. Now I know they wouldn't be.'

The paragraph of text began to resolve itself; at first, she hadn't been able to take it in. The words spun in front of her eyes, blurring and shifting. She took them in in pieces, 'fallopian tubes tied off'... 'two-centimetre long portion excised'... 'treated against periodontitis'...

'What does it mean?'

'What does it look like?'

Hilde cast her mind back to the posters she'd seen on the Huber's walls, in her own *Stube,* the slogans on flyers, her neighbour's chatter. 'Bad genes enter a village.' She knew, she realised, she'd always known. But somehow, it hadn't felt real.

'They decide who can have children, and who can't,' Else said. 'It's happening everywhere. The whole country. There are courts to decide for you. And if they decide you can't, they make sure. That's what I'm doing with my time, if you really want to know.'

Hilde felt herself instinctively reaching her arms around her stomach, holding herself tight. 'How do they decide?'

'How do you think? It's quick, with some of them. They're blind, or deaf, or some other thing you can see right away. With the rest, it's more difficult. *Feeble-mindedness.* That's what they call it. They talk to your neighbours, examine your home. I had a woman brought in once because she couldn't keep the house clean enough, though you can never be sure whether those are the real reasons. There's no one to check, you see. They decide, and that's that. You want to be careful they don't come for you, after what you did.'

'I don't even know if I want to have children.'

'But do you want them deciding for you?'

'No.' She wrapped her arms more tightly around herself. 'Of course not.'

'I don't do the procedure. Just the aftercare and the paperwork. And do you know what the worst thing is? It starts to feel normal, after a while. Just another normal day. The way some of them look at me – we're allowed to use force, you see. Some of them come in screaming. Some of them come in not able to say a word. And one day, I'll be asked to do something worse, and by then…' Else closed her eyes, gripping the edges of her chair. Hilde stared at her, so shocked she couldn't think of anything to say.

Later, as Else clattered about in the kitchen, Hilde sat at the small table by the window, listening to the noises from outside. How did anyone sleep here, how did they manage to think? The hum of cars and trams rattling past, the chatter of children in the street, and behind it all, the tolling of the cathedral bell, reverberating through her like a warning siren. It was all wrong, it wasn't what she had imagined at all. And now, even her vision of the future, of the life she could have away from the mountain, all of it was gone. How did Else stand it, day after day, how could she live with herself? *We're allowed to use force.*

'We have to do something,' she said as Else brought two plates of food, grey slabs of meat next to boiled potatoes, through from the kitchen.

'What's that?'

'Sterilisation. Everything they're doing – we have to tell people.'

'Hilde. Everybody knows. You knew, didn't you?'

The horror of it, finally, sank in. There was no one to tell. What had happened to Fritz, to all those women. All of it, being done in the open, in front of them all, it was part of the law, not separate to it. She looked down at the food, feeling sick.

They ate in silence, listening to the sounds of the city, their own breathing, occasional bursts of laughter or shouts from Else's neighbours. Afterwards Else lit a cigarette, contemplating Hilde as she breathed out wreathes of smoke.

'You have to do something else,' Hilde said.

Else laughed an angry, bitter laugh. 'And how would I do that?'

'You have to!'

'You think it's easy to leave, to change your life just like that?'

'I don't understand.'

'You will, though. We all have to, in the end.' She sighed.

'You don't throw away work when you've got nothing. Less than nothing.'

'But—'

'He was a silver merchant,' Else said, as though Hilde would know whom she meant. 'Silver tongued too, that's what we all used to say. Didn't I tell you? It's always some man. He was here to visit those mines, long before your father went to the mountain. Thought there might be something left in those old tunnels after all, something better than lead and stone.' She shook her head. 'He was a fool from the start.'

'What happened?'

Else sighed a weary sigh. 'What happened to all of them back then. He went to the war. Didn't come back.'

'Did he – was he killed?'

'No such luck! He went, and' – she waved the hand holding the cigarette, tossing the smoke around and about her head – 'he's still there, I suppose.'

'But the war ended.'

'Not for him. What I mean is…' Else leaned forward, looking irritated that Hilde hadn't yet understood. 'He liked it too much. Being away from me. He didn't *die*, or anything like that. He just didn't come back. I had a letter from him, all nonsense about debts and obligations. Well, we had enough of those here. I suppose he's got some other woman now.' She cast a glance around the tiny flat, and Hilde understood that it had once been a marital home. She tried to imagine Else being carried over the threshold, planning dinners and choosing curtains. Light pouring in through the dirt-smeared windows. 'Your pa was furious,' Else said, smiling. 'Wanted to track him down, make him pay. But we had enough trouble of our own. And of course, by then he was off on his own adventure. Playing at being a farmer.' She closed her eyes.

'Is it true Pa was a deserter?'

Else looked up. 'Who told you that?'

'Everyone but me seemed to know. I think that's why – they

came for his things, a few days back. They took everything, boxes and boxes.'

Else leaned forward and seized her hand. 'What did they find?'

'I don't know. They never said – I hadn't even looked at most of it. It was just books and papers.'

'Did she burn anything, after he – after he was gone? Your mother, did she burn anything?'

Hilde nodded slowly. 'Just some seed packets. He used to print them in the basement, try to sell them on. She put them all in a firepit.'

'Alright.' Else nodded. 'Good. That's good.'

'Why? What does it matter about some old seed packets?'

'Never you mind, Hilde Meyer.'

'I saved one,' she said nervously. 'Just one. Hid it in the floorboards.'

'It's still there?'

She nodded. 'I think so. Yes, I think so.'

Else looked at her hard, saying nothing.

'So, is it true? About his being a deserter?'

There was a long silence. Eventually, Else said, 'He didn't enjoy killing, if that's what you mean. He didn't have the stomach for it. That's not the same as desertion. Believe me.'

She smiled. 'I know.'

She spent the night on Else's worn-out sofa, waking up every time she heard footsteps outside, a fight breaking out or a car rolling past. By morning, her head was pounding and she ached with hunger. She'd hardly been able to eat anything the previous night, too sickened by what Else had told her, the thought of people being dragged to some clinic, what was being done to them, the cold, hard words she'd read on the pages Else had stolen.

'You can't stay.'

She looked up; Else was standing in the kitchen doorway, a dishcloth in her hand.

'For another night or two, while we make sure you're safe. But after that – I can barely keep myself going as it is. You do see that, don't you?'

She nodded, unable to speak.

'It's no good, Hilde. I'm no good. You've got to go back.'

Chapter Forty-Nine

The sun had visited London in the time Sylvia had been away. The grey, damp skies she had left behind were pale and bright, dust and fog cleared by the rain. The University College buildings gleamed as though they had been freshly painted.

A small crowd had gathered outside the Galton Laboratory building, handing out leaflets and holding up signs. Sylvia recognised some of the leaflets; they were the same she and Ruby had been given at the Women's Cooperative Guild meetings, entreaties to marry wisely, to consider your genetic heritage, your genetic legacy. 'Sterilisation – pledge your support now!' A woman pressed a paper into her hands and she pushed it hurriedly away.

Chi-square rubbed against her ankles as she pushed open the door to the laboratory; she knelt and ran her hand along her arched back. It was the middle of the day, and the building was busier than she'd seen it before; two women and three men were sitting at the long benches in the serology lab, and as she went upstairs, she could hear the chatter from the common room leaking into the corridor.

She slipped into the cleaning cupboard and collected the few things she'd left there: an umbrella, her overalls, a few bits of loose change. On her way out she saw Dieter coming along the corridor towards her.

'Sylvia!'

'I'm just here to collect some things,' she said, closing the door behind her. 'I sent in my letter – I've resigned.'

They walked back downstairs together as she took in the building for the last time, the polished wooden benches, the gleaming laboratory equipment, all the hopes she'd had for herself, for the future.

'How's it coming along?' she asked him as they reached the serology lab.

Dieter shrugged. 'No joy yet. They haven't found any linkages, just random patterns.'

She stared at the rows of slides, the palettes of blood, papers covered in scrawled tables of numbers and letters. 'Maybe you were right then,' she said. 'Maybe people aren't just blood and bones.'

'We have to keep looking, though,' he said, taking his seat at the bench. 'There has to be something we haven't seen yet.'

A newspaper was folded on the desk beside him. Sylvia recognised her own face, the photograph of her and Keith in Hofsgrund, a child offering them both a Nazi salute. She flinched, feeling ashamed. Below it was a headline: 'German Interior Minister declares 'Gypsy plague': round ups begin'.

'I read about your son,' Dieter said, following her gaze to the newspaper. 'I'm sorry.'

'I'm sorry for...' But she didn't know how to go on. Then, on an impulse, she said quickly, 'These linkages you're looking for.' It was her last chance to ask. 'All those diseases they want to cure. Is it possible they've got it all wrong?'

'Wrong?'

'Is it possible sometimes things just happen, and it doesn't matter who your parents are, what they did?'

He stared at her. 'You didn't think – Sylvia, of course. It's never one way or the other. Of course some things just happen.'

'And that means we can put them right?'

He hesitated then. She could tell he wanted to get back to

his work, that his mind was already racing forward to the next problem, the next question. She thought of the photograph of his father in Germany, the glare of the sun obscuring his eyes behind wire-rimmed glasses, his hands held formally at his sides.

'Do you think...' But she'd run out of words. Dieter pulled a microscope towards him and turned to look at her one last time.

'What I think,' he said, bending to peer through the lens, 'is that we have a long way to go.'

It was early evening by the time she reached the park surrounding Alexandra Palace. The transmission tower had been built now; Cyril would have been jumping up and down excitedly, trying to guess how many people tall it was, asking her if they could climb it. She took the toy figure from her pocket and held it up against the tower's peak.

Sitting on the steps which led towards the palace, she watched as people tidied away their picnics and hurried homewards, children pulling on their mothers' arms, the sun still warm enough that others lay in the grass, stealing a few more moments, coats and bicycles and magazines discarded in a heap beside them.

She didn't recognise Kit at first. She looked older, in a smart tweed suit with her hair pinned carefully back. Sylvia got up, and for a moment they stood opposite each other, awkward and unsure, until one or other of them laughed and the moment was over.

'Thanks for coming,' Kit said. 'You didn't have to.'

'You said you had something to show me?'

Kit led her towards the palace and they walked along its perimeter, in the shadow of the ornate red and orange brickwork, arches and columns and church-like windows reflecting the evening light. It was hard to imagine the prison it had once been, the cavernous hallways and exhibition spaces turned into dormitories and refectories, walls of fences and barbed wire breaking up the rolling parkland, cutting out the views of London skies.

'You're the only person who knows he was here,' she said as they paused by a doorway. 'Outside of family, anyway.'

'Your dad?'

'I can't have the paper finding out. Not now I'm – well. It's better to keep quiet about some things, isn't it?'

She knelt to the stonework, laying one hand on the bricks.

'He was going to be deported when they let him out,' she said. 'They would have sent him back to Germany.'

'What happened?'

'He died, just after he got out. He's buried not far from here.' She looked up. 'Some families never got put together again, afterwards. People got lost forever. So, at least we didn't have to put up with that. At least I know where he is.'

Leaning closer, she took a nail file from her pocket and began scratching at the stone. When she stood up, Sylvia could see 'Rudolph Harnisch, 1882–1919', etched into the base of the wall.

'He'd be proud of you,' Sylvia said as they walked back across the park. 'Getting that job at the paper. Everything you did.'

'It was wrong, what I did. I should have told you the search was off, I should have asked more questions about what they were planning. I'm sorry.'

They sat on a bench by the edge of the park; through a fence, motor cars and buses rattled past, and the fumes of the street mingled with the scent of chrysanthemums and primroses in their neat beds. Kit lit a cigarette and leaned back, stretching out her legs.

'I've quit the lab,' Sylvia said. 'Didn't feel right, somehow.'

'What will you do now?'

Sylvia hadn't given much thought to the future. She had been paid for her time at the laboratory, but that would hardly get her very far. She'd have to apply again, go back to the beginning – wanted ads, all that letter writing and waiting. Leaving the lab had seemed like the right thing to do, a fresh start, but she hadn't had any idea what to do next. As soon as Kit asked the question, though, she knew.

'I'm thinking of going back into nursing. Then, I don't know. A degree, perhaps.'

Kit nodded, as though she'd expected her to say exactly that. 'I never asked you why you stopped in the first place.'

'Something happened…' She stopped, realising she hadn't been visited by the boy in France for so long, she was almost beginning to forget his face. 'Something that was my fault.'

'I suppose a lot of people came back feeling like that. I'm sure you did your best, anyway.'

'I did,' she said, feeling suddenly sure. 'I think I really did.'

Kit stood up, stamping out her cigarette. 'Anyway,' she said, 'that wasn't what I wanted to show you.' She took something out of her pocket. 'I've been thinking about what you said in Germany. About your husband. About how you lost him.'

'I shouldn't have told you.'

'You said his name was Arthur? Arthur Clayton?'

'That's right.'

'Well.' Kit gave her a small, awkward smile. 'I couldn't stop thinking about it. And – well, I did some digging about. Thought I should make that new job mean something, you know? I thought this might help.'

She slid a piece of paper into Sylvia's hand.

Chapter Fifty

The train out of London was half empty, only a handful of couples on day trips, elderly women weighed down with baskets of gifts for grandchildren, to keep Sylvia company. The city slid quickly away and through the window she watched as they stopped at an endless stream of increasingly tiny village stations, at which more people alighted than embarked. By the time they reached the end of the line, Sylvia was the last passenger remaining.

It was a short walk from the station and she took it slowly, pausing to read the noticeboard on the tiny church, to pick flowers from the verge, where dandelions and daisies were pushing their way up through cracks in a crumbling stone wall. She did her best to take it all in, unsure if she would ever come back, unsure if she would be able to keep going. The red brick of a school building, stark against the pale grey slate and honeyed sandstone of the rest of the village. The low-roofed cottages in rows along the main street, and the larger, heavy thatched houses set a little back from the road, with their neat, carefully crafted gardens and brightly painted doors. It was impossible to imagine that a war had happened here too, or that one ever could again.

When she imagined the parents of that boy in France, it was always in a place like this. She saw them sitting down to breakfast in a quiet, bright room, a pile of letters on a tray. Then, one of them opening the letter she'd sent them a few days after he'd died, full of stories of his bravery, his goodness, his grace. Nothing about what had happened at the end, what she'd done. She saw them holding hands across the table and reading the letter aloud to each other. She imagined a room upstairs which, occasionally, one of them would step into for a few moments, before leaving and closing the door carefully behind them.

She had one of Arthur's letters in her pocket, along with another which had arrived that morning. Both of them, the old letter and the new, were folded up inside an old card case to keep them safe. Her hand curled around it as she walked, and the words in both were running through her head in time to her footsteps, the endings and the beginnings of stories which, until now, she had never expected to meet.

'15 March 1924

Dear Sylvia,

I hope this letter finds you and Cyril well. Is he walking yet? Thank you for the photograph you sent. I wish you'd sent a picture of yourself as well. I had one to take out to France with me, but I'm afraid it didn't survive the trenches. I should like to have another.

I think about you every day, and all the terrible things I did after I got back. I can't take them back, and you did the right thing sending me away.

I'm writing to let you know that they think I'm alright again, and they're going to send me home, wherever that is. I was hoping it might be with you and Cyril.

Will you write to let me know?

Yours always,

Arthur'

When she reached the right road she paused for a second, listening to the contented silence, the hum of crickets and, somewhere in the distance, a motor car purring by. She held on tight to the card case, hearing Arthur's letter in her head, all the time that had passed since, all the stories she'd told. All the stories she'd listened to; about blood, about strength, about how to be brave. A person can't be made over again, can't be cured if they're feeble-minded, if they're broken. Adversity only shows up the cracks that existed inside us all along. She'd thought her own story was written and sealed, that it was too late to change it now. And then Kit Harris, reporter, had slid a piece of paper into her hand.

A light-headed, floating sensation threatened to overwhelm her as she took her first steps along the path; she wished there was something, or someone, to hold on to. She held on instead to the thought of Cyril pushing his way through a storm, fighting to save himself, to keep going.

'Hello there!'

She looked up suddenly, shocked at the sound of a voice calling out to her, an ordinary voice coming from an ordinary-looking man. He was standing in the centre of a flower bed in one of the front gardens, surrounded by the shoots and leaves of newly emerging plants, a gardening fork in one hand, the other raised to greet her. He was perhaps fifty, dressed in overalls, with a gentle, welcoming smile which she couldn't help returning.

'Beautiful day, isn't it?'

'Yes, it is.'

'Perhaps you're visiting someone?'

'Arthur,' she said. The name felt strange in her mouth. 'I'm looking for Arthur Clayton.'

'Oh, rather.' He beamed at her. 'Number sixty-two, just a little further that way.'

She wondered, as she walked on, feeling stranger and more weightless with every step, what she would tell him. There were so many versions of what had happened, she felt she would have to choose. She'd brought the newspaper article with her, 'Tribute to Hitler Youth who Rescued British Boys'. Half the page was taken up with photographs of her and Keith shaking hands with children standing tall and proud in their uniforms, their chins held high, their hands held out in a salute. 'A special report by Katherine Harris in Hofsgrund'. There was another photograph too, much smaller, tucked in the corner of the page. A group of men and women gathered together holding the skis they'd worn on the night they'd brought the children in. Arthur had probably seen the newspaper articles already. He would have stared at both photographs, and wondered which of them was true.

And what would she tell him about his son? For so long, she'd been steeling herself for his loss. She felt ashamed at how she'd anticipated it, thought only of his weakness. And then Keith's letter had come, and it had felt like being handed another story, permission to believe in a different life.

She stopped outside number 62. A man was kneeling with his back to her, bent over a flower bed, working at the earth. She watched him, the familiar contours of his body, the thinning hair, the curve of his neck. She was about to change his story too, and when he turned around, he wouldn't ever be able to go back.

She took the card case from her pocket and opened it, taking out Keith Hughes' letter. There was no date, and when she tried to imagine him writing it, she found it difficult to picture his face, anything about him at all. She could only see a figure on a mountain, walking slowly away without looking back.

'Dear Sylvia,

I hope you don't mind my writing. I'm still in Germany. I don't think I'll be back for a while.

I didn't do my best for Cyril, but I'm going to now, and I won't be giving up. We've heard about some things being found in the tunnels under the mountain, they think someone's been living there, after all. If it's true, and he's still somewhere out there, I'm going to bring him back.

It might be too late for me, but it isn't too late for him, and I think everything will come out right.

Keep your head up, and I'm very sorry for everything that's happened.

Regards, Keith Hughes'

'Arthur.'

He stood up, and for a moment, just as he turned, she thought she saw her son's face smiling back at her.

Chapter Fifty-One

Cambridge, September 1918

There are only five men in Keith's morning lecture. Yesterday there had been seven; he has no idea where the other two are, but it happens like that sometimes, they vanish without warning. Despite their number, the students are sitting at a distance from one another, as though they expect the room to gradually fill up. Sometimes Keith wonders if they're doing it as a nod to all their missing comrades: *We've saved a space for you, lads, see you back any day now.*

The lecturers, too, are dwindling. Most are too old for active service, but they are slowly drifting into other roles: munitions, field surgeons, chaplains. Keith is left with the dregs. He looks around him; Langley is here, and Stephenson. Anand and Perry, both sent back from the front barely days after going out. Anand's crutches are leaning against the wall beside him; he was lucky, he keeps telling Keith, he ought not to be here at all. Lucky you have to sit through two hours of analytical chemistry, Keith replies, trying to make a joke of it, but it comes out wrong, as it usually does.

He's tried asking Anand and the others what it's like out there, but no one wants to say very much. He reads the papers, tries to see himself in the reports of skirmishes, bombings, raids and battles. Tries, too, to imagine himself bedding down in the trenches, waiting through long hours of darkness, swapping stories of home. It's not enough. Jack's letters are getting shorter, their details less vivid. The shame of his own safety, his inability to understand, is pressing more heavily every day.

He keeps Jack's letters in a drawer in his desk, in his impossibly large set of rooms at the college. There are so few of them now, they might as well take over multiple rooms, establish themselves over several floors. He reads the letters every night, picturing himself in Jack's place. Years from now, if the world is still around and people ask him what it was like to fight a war, he'll have all those memories stored up ready.

They never ask him why he hasn't gone. At first, some of the men thought he was an objector, but it soon became clear he's something else; all the conscientious objectors were slowly taken from their classes, one by one, and sent out anyway. He doesn't know of anyone who managed to avoid it. The looks they used to give him; he could feel them trying to diagnose him, or else work out who he was paying. He doesn't get the looks any more. Most students have long since stopped caring about the reasons behind anything; men come and go, some come back, some don't, and that's just the way of things. No point in asking why.

He walks to the quad with Anand, who chatters on at him about their upcoming examination. Keith wants to laugh, or scream at him. The world is ending, Vijay! We might not have long to go. Last night they received a notice about air raids; from now on, each man is to be responsible for the fire extinguishers on their staircase, and to be ready when the whistle sounds. It used to be the porter's job, but the porters' numbers are dwindling too.

They reach the courtyard, where men in military uniforms are massing. The war office has taken over the north quad; Keith's previous room was reassigned. No one knows what they get up to in there, but there's talk of everything imaginable; codebreaking, bombs, chemicals, Germans held prisoner in the wine cellars. Nonsense, probably, but all the rules seem to be shifting and disappearing.

'Come back for a drink?' Anand says, sounding bored. He's not supposed to drink, but he seems to have abandoned all of his rules too. Keith shakes his head. 'My brother's due,' he says, checking the time again. 'Any minute now.' It must be soon, he thinks, my heart, my heart is beating so fast.

'Your brother? Isn't he—'

'In France. He's on leave for a few weeks.' Showing off his medal, Keith thinks bitterly, but he won't tell Anand about that.

'Alright. Good luck then.'

At some point during the past few terms, they've all taken to using that phrase in place of goodbye. It comes, Keith supposes, of not quite knowing if you'll see each other from one day to the next.

Back in his rooms he begins rearranging things; replacing books on shelves, sweeping up the grate, plumping cushions. He realises he's nervous – he hadn't expected that. He's been looking forward to Jack's visit for so long, but now he isn't sure – will he be the same person? Will either of them be?

The newspaper is lying open on the side table; Jack's face beaming out of it. 'Heroism of sniper saves regiment' the headline reads, followed by half a column of text. Keith can't stop reading the reports. He collects them in piles about the room, and then has trouble looking at them. Hardly anything is said about Jack's family, at least, and Keith is glad of that. No one would connect it with him. It does mention the medal, though. Keith tries to imagine it, glittering on his brother's chest. He puts a hand to his own chest, imagining the space where a medal of his own might have been, resting just above his broken heart.

He heaps more coals on the fire and leans back in a chair beside it. He wonders if Jack will be game for a climb; his rope is coiled by the window where he dropped it last night when he came back in, hot and breathless with exertion. He has it in his mind that they can explore the roofs together, the way they used to. He'll show Jack the Wedding Cake, the gothic tower that sits atop his college like a jagged mountain summit, which men scale in darkness, clinging to the intricately carved stone, reaching up for the weathervane at the summit. Or perhaps, he thinks, Jack won't have the stamina for it. Perhaps he's come back broken down, exhausted, weakened, and he can stay on the roof and watch as Keith climbs on alone.

By the time the sun begins to go down, his anxiety has risen higher. He pours himself a whisky then sits and stares at the glass, twisting it in his hands, allowing the flickering light from the fire to shine into his eyes. Jack should have been here by now. He was going to take a taxi directly from the station to the college; what could have happened in the meantime?

Then he hears a sound on the stairs; a slow shuffling. For a moment he pictures his brother crooked and bent over; he was right, he thinks, he's picked up an injury, he won't be able to go back. It's all over. In a rush, Keith swallows the whisky in one and stands up, pulling himself taller and straighter.

The door opens, and Jack looks just the same; a little thinner, perhaps, a little older, his uniform a little rumpled. Keith scans him quickly for the medal, but Jack isn't wearing it on his chest.

They stare at each other for a moment, neither of them saying anything. 'I hardly recognised you,' Keith says eventually, and feels his face breaking into a wide smile, which Jack doesn't return.

'I look like you,' Jack says.

'I just mean... I mean you look better than I thought you would, anyway.'

He pours Jack a drink.

'What about this medal, then?' he says, trying to sound unconcerned. 'Let's have a look.'

'It doesn't mean anything, you know. Just the luck of the draw.'

'Still. I want to see.'

Jack reaches into a pocket and produces it, dropping it into Keith's hands. Keith feels a surge of pride; strange, when it isn't even his.

'You should wear it tonight,' he says, handing it back. 'Everyone should see.'

He can feel the whisky still stirring in his stomach.

They have dinner in a tiny, smoky restaurant. There's no fish, hasn't been for months, and the wine is prohibitively expensive. He can't say any of that, of course. Jack exclaims over everything: the soup, the meat, the fresh butter. Each time it feels like a reminder to Keith of how lucky he is to be here. Men shake Jack's hand as they pass, women glance at him over their menus. He wishes now he hadn't persuaded Jack to wear the medal; it glitters on Jack's chest just as he'd imagined it would, catching the light and drawing eyes towards him. That was what Keith had wanted, but now it's happening, he realises it puts him in the shade. They can't share it, this light, there's only enough for one. All of a sudden, sitting there opposite his brother, he wonders why on earth Jack came here at all – did he really want to see Keith, or was it because he knew it would be like this?

A young woman approaches them from another table, where she has been sitting with an older man. She's dressed in a neat burgundy suit, but as she comes closer Keith can see the places where she's stitched it up, the ragged hem, the faded patches. He waits for her to shake Jack's hand, to exclaim over him, praise him for his bravery, his sacrifice, but instead she reaches into her handbag, takes out a small white feather and lays it on Keith's plate.

There is a long silence while she stares at him. Keith wonders if he ought to say something. Eventually they watch her walk away, both of them silent, and Keith feels the rest of the restaurant's eyes turning towards him. *Coward*, he can feel them thinking. *Useless coward.* He picks up the feather and slides it into his pocket, as though he might need it for later.

'How's the studying?' Jack says at last.

'Fine. I came top last term, but that hardly signifies, does it?'

'Still on for medicine then?'

Keith hesitates, wondering if he ought to say. 'Actually, I'm thinking about teaching.'

Another uncomfortable silence. Keith knows what Jack's thinking. *Can't even stomach this, bloodless cadavers laid out neatly on slabs. You have no idea, Keith Hughes, no idea at all.*

Back in his rooms, he pours more whisky and eyes the rope lying beside the window. When he finally summons the courage to suggest a climb, Jack is against it; he cites his exhaustion, the cold, the unnecessary hour. *We're not children any more, Keith.* Keith gets his way, though, same as he always has, and they climb the staircase, haul themselves awkwardly through a window frame, out into the still dark.

On the roof, he feels immediately safer. It's some vestigial instinct of his childhood, this need to be up high above the world. He wonders if that's how Jack feels, if that's why he chose to become a sniper. Did it feel like this, every time he cowered in some bombed-out building, inched his way along some window ledge, peering down his scope?

They crawl along the ramparts and up onto the vaulted college roof, perching at the apex, an inversion of the valley they had cowered in as children. The air is still and as he feels the lingering warmth of a sunny day, Keith half wishes a harsh wind were cutting at their faces, so he can prove he doesn't mind.

'There.' He points to the Wedding Cake above them. Jack stares up at it uncertainly.

'I don't know…' he starts, and Keith makes to go without

him, but Jack puts a hand on his arm. 'Stay,' he says. 'It's alright here, isn't it? Can't we just stay here?'

They sit together on the sloping roof, and Keith wonders if Jack's thinking about it too. Their father, clattering about below them, the two of them safe from the world, high above it. The day he'd run, and left Jack behind to face the blows. Below them, the last lights of the city are twinkling like stars.

He turns to Jack. 'Tell me what it's like. What it's really like, I mean. Out there.'

'I don't want to talk about that.'

'Come on – I know there's more than the letters.'

'Really. I don't know what to tell you.'

'You think I couldn't do it, don't you?'

'What?'

He knows what his brother is thinking. *You couldn't stick a war, Keith. You wouldn't last five minutes. The things I've seen...*

'I don't care, Keith,' he says. 'I don't care about that. I'm glad you're safe here. At least one of us is.'

There is a long silence. Jack shifts his position uncomfortably. He wants to go inside, Keith thinks. He wants to, and I won't let him. Why won't he talk about it, why won't anyone?

'I'm not going back,' Jack says quietly. Keith thinks he's misheard him, perhaps the wind is rising after all, perhaps he's hearing voices.

'What?'

'France. Or anywhere. I can't go back.'

'Jack—'

'I know, I know. It's what I said I wanted. Always. But I can't do it any more.'

'But – your letters—'

'What about them?'

'You made it sound...' What was the right word? Exhilarating? Important? *Fun?* 'Worthwhile.'

'Keith, you know they're not real, don't you? What I put in my letters – I can't say what it's really like. Not properly. It's all stories. If I told you the truth—'

'So tell me now.'

Jack closes his eyes, as though he's trying to think himself back there. Keith waits, but he doesn't say anything more.

'What are you going to do then?'

'I don't know. Hide, I suppose. Go to London, maybe, leave the country. I don't know.'

'They kill deserters.'

'I know.'

'Please, Jack. You can't.'

Is he worried about desertion, about the penalty? Of course he is, but there's something else too. He's thinking about those letters, all the anecdotes he has of a war he's never seen, all the people he'll share them with one day. All the ways Jack is atoning for his own sins, his own weakness. He can't be Keith Hughes, brother of a deserter, not on top of everything he is already.

'Here,' Jack says, unpinning the medal from his uniform and handing it to his brother. 'You can keep it. It's all hopeless, it doesn't mean a thing.'

Keith stares down at the silver disc in his fingers. It feels right, the weight of it in his palm.

'They're expecting me back in two days,' Jack says, hunching himself against the cold. 'Keith, can I stay here? Can I stay with you? Just until I've decided what to do next.'

Keith looks over the edge, down into the dark. He imagines taking his brother by surprise. A sharp, quick shove, and it would be over so quickly, so silently. It would be an accident, and he'd have got his medal. An honourable death. He even feels his fingers flinch.

'Of course you can,' he says, wrapping an arm around Jack's shoulders. 'You can stay as long as you need.'

He's already decided what he'll do next.

Chapter Fifty-Two

Hilde left Freiburg just as the summer was beginning to burst into life; the soft, muted colours of spring were suddenly bold and vivid, the red roofs and painted doorways brash against the sun. The cart Else had hired was waiting for her at the edge of the city, by the side of the newly paved road which led towards the mountain; Hilde could already see the carpets of green-yellow wheat on the horizon, the sky a deep blue behind the grey shadows of the Schauinsland beyond them. Fritz should be painting sunscapes now, mixing yellows and oranges, splashes of bright reds and purples where primroses and violets sprung up from the verge. She thought of the last time she'd seen him, running from the square, and felt a wave of guilt and fear so strong she paused for a moment with one hand on her stomach, counting down.

'I packed up some food.' Else pressed it into her hands. They looked at each other. The driver, a boy of about fourteen with a long whip in his hand, huffed and coughed impatiently. 'I'm sorry it's not more. And this is for you.' She pushed an envelope into Hilde's hands.

'What is it?'

'Don't open it yet. I wasn't even sure whether to give it to you, but I can see it now.' She smiled, and the lines of her faces seemed to soften. She looked suddenly how Hilde remembered her father; gentle, kind eyes. 'You're his daughter, aren't you? So I think you should have it.'

'Come with me,' Hilde said, surprising herself. 'You can help me run the farm, get away from – all this.'

'Oh, Hilde, I'm getting old. Older than I should be. Don't open that until you're alone,' she said, indicating the envelope. 'And don't keep it, afterwards.'

'Alright.'

'I mean it. When you get home, when you've read it, you burn it right away.'

'Alright.'

'And you might open up that old seed packet too. When you have, you burn that as well. Understand?'

Hilde shook her head, but Else only smiled, her head on one side.

'And keep looking for that boy,' she said. 'There's life in those old tunnels yet, Hilde. Sometimes the dead don't die. You'll understand, I think, once you've seen it.'

She turned as the cart pulled away, but Else was already walking back towards the city, her satchel swinging at her side. The smoothed, paved roads began to give way to rougher, narrower paths, the cart bouncing and shaking as they climbed higher. The donkey let out a high-pitched whine as they hit a pile of stones and the boy with the whip swore under his breath. Hilde grasped the rail and stared resolutely ahead, not wanting to look back at the city, at the ruins of the life she had held out so much hope for. Instead, she focused on the road ahead: the ragged pine trees, the patches of yellow gorse, the road growing steeper and their passage slower as they approached the slopes of the Schauinsland. She hadn't told Else about the sale of the house, the animals. She hadn't wanted her to feel guilty, but now, unsure of where to go next, she wondered if she should have done. She unwrapped Else's parcel; the bread was stale and the cheese a sweaty, fatty lump. Beside her, the boy turned his head slightly; Hilde broke the bread in two and handed him a piece.

It was late afternoon by the time they reached the village. The main street was empty, and Hilde supposed everyone must be out in their fields or inside preparing meals. She was relieved; she didn't want to face them now. She kept her head down, pausing to hand the boy a coin before she climbed down from the cart and took the narrow path towards the house.

She hadn't expected to find Anna there, but it was still a shock to find it cold and empty. Gretel's place by the fire was empty too, and she was glad; Anna must have taken her to the Hubers' with her. She didn't like to think of her sister there, not Gretel either, but it was better than finding them here in the dark. There was no sound from the barn; if her buyers hadn't come for the animals already, she supposed the Hubers would have taken them in themselves, along with everything else.

There was still fuel in the stove, and she knelt in front of it in the kitchen, spending an anxious few minutes coaxing it into life, holding out her hands to the flames which, mercifully, began to flicker and flare. It felt strange to be so completely alone. She remembered Else's envelope and pulled it from her pocket, holding it up for a moment and imagining throwing it into the fire. Did she want to read it, really? It was clear from the past few days that Else wanted nothing to do with the remains of her family; she might have put anything in the envelope, something Hilde didn't want to know, something to punish her. She held it out to the fire, then changed her mind and opened it.

Inside was a ten-mark note and a small piece of paper. She unfolded the paper; an address was scrawled in smudged pencil.

'Walter. 110, Stare Mesto, Prague.'

She stared at it, wondering if Else had made some sort of

mistake. Her father had mentioned Prague once, years back, he had visited when he was a young man and still had friends there. Other than that, they had no connection at all. Was she supposed to write to the address, did he have friends still living there? She wished they hadn't taken his things from the basement; she could search through them, find some meaning there. What was it Else had asked her, when she'd told her they'd taken them? *Your mother, did she burn anything?* And Hilde had told her, yes, she burned the seed packets, and something in Else's face had relaxed, as though a weight had been lifted.

She stood up quickly and pushed open the door to the tiny room in the kitchen where she and Anna had slept as children. It was used for storage now; barrels filled with grain and meat drying in the rafters. Back then, they had slept on one mattress which took up nearly all of the space. Hilde remembered pushing up the loose floorboard and folding up the seed packet, sleeping with the knowledge that something of her father, the very last piece of him, was in the ground beneath them.

She moved some of the barrels to one side, feeling a sudden fear that the men who had searched the house might have found it already. But when she pushed up the loose board, there it was, covered in dust and soil.

The packet's colour hadn't dimmed in the two years it had spent in the earth. She brushed the last of the soil aside, 'finest tomato seeds', and three ripe, shining fruits. The tomatoes were nestled in a bed of green vines, and behind them a mountainscape rose in the distance. She held it closer to her face and looked hard at the brushstrokes, the speckles of light on the horizon, the sun, hazy among clouds. She thought of the painting in Fritz's *Stube*, the way the light filtered through the fog and snow.

I did some printing work with him once. It was a long time ago.

Carefully, she opened the flap and shook out a piece of

paper that was folded inside it. It was covered in tiny print, punctuated by two bold headings.

'A manifesto against fascism.

How you can fight back.'

She sat down on the cold floorboards. In the silence of the house, the fire cracked and spat.

She'd gone over that day in her memory so many times. The news of the cave-in, her parents, closeted for a few stolen moments in their bedroom, whispering. Her father, calling out to Anna, then shrugging on his coat, hardly looking back at them. *I have to go. There are people trapped, I have to help them.* And her mother saying nothing, her face set into a mask.

And suddenly, she knew.

She remembered Else's warning, and after making sure of the address, threw everything but the banknote into the flames. She thought of her mother doing the same, her expression hard and determined, the smoke rising and forcing tears that Hilde had tried for days to hold back. All those nights he and Fritz had disappeared into the basement, the comforting shunting and cranking of the press, all those journeys to Freiburg, the boxes piled up on the cart behind him. All the times, since, Fritz had told her to keep her head down.

How you can fight back.

What had Else said, as she'd handed over the envelope? *There's life in those old tunnels yet, Hilde. Sometimes, the dead don't die.*

He's collecting lives for his army, deep underground. Soon they will rise up, and defend the country against a great peril.

He takes the strongest. Leaves no one behind but weaklings like you.

110, Stare Mesto, Prague.

Sometimes, the dead don't die.

Chapter Fifty-Three

He is climbing. Behind him, the slopes of the Schauinsland rise gently towards a sky flecked with pale clouds, and the sun is high and bright. He can feel the skin on the back of his neck reddening in the heat; sweat dampening his shirt beneath the heavy pack. His body sings with energy; his feet pressing firmly down on grass and stones. He can feel the beginnings of pain in his soles, the nerves and tendons stretching and complaining, but he doesn't mind it now, it doesn't slow him down, and when it does he will simply wait for the pain to pass. His heart, at last, is strong.

Fritz has struck out in front of him, his broad body already disappearing on the path ahead. In a little while, he will slow down and Keith will catch up with him and overtake him, and then they will begin the pattern again. It's easier than walking alongside each other, needing to be alert to one another's pace. There's no need for talk either; they both seem to understand what the other needs without the necessity of asking.

They don't talk about that night, the night Keith was rescued. Sometimes he wonders if he should try to explain. How could he explain how it had felt, sending Cyril Clayton alone into the dark, not wanting him to be found? *We need to know if there's anyone else out there.* Keith had cast his eye around the room, taken in his boys, sitting dazed and shivering by the fireplace. He'd seen the bodies too, that had been carried down into the cellar. Clayton was out there, struggling in the storm, strength and youth and blood surging through him, while Keith had lain helpless in the snow. For a moment, he'd really allowed himself to believe it, there really were only twelve boys, there had never been any more. If Clayton could only disappear, if the knowledge he had of Keith's weakness, of all the lies he'd told, could disappear with him.

Fritz pauses by the side of the road; when Keith catches up with him he is breathing heavily, a hand on his chest.

'I'm alright,' he says slowly. 'We need to head east, through the forest. The next tunnel entrance is about a day's walk away.'

They're going under the earth. With each step forwards, each new rumour – the remains of a fire found by one of the midwives using the tunnels, a piece of clothing, footsteps ahead of her or behind – he feels the burden of his guilt easing just a little. He has imagined it so many times. Handing the boy back to his mother, some of the heaviness lifting from him. Not forgiven, but halfway closer to understanding himself. Are they imagining hope that isn't there? How many others are hiding underground, in this new world which only has a place for a carefully chosen few? He isn't sure, but he knows there's nothing to go back to now. For now, the climb is their only choice.

As the sun begins to fall they push their way deeper into the forest, pausing in a wide clearing. Fritz gathers up dry leaves and sticks and begins to construct a fire, chopping the larger logs with an axe he carries on his back like a rifle. Keith can feel his old life gradually fading; the trees rising up around him, keeping out the last of the light, hiding him from anyone who might still care to look. They eat roasted rabbit that Keith catches in a wire trap, triumphant that his scouting skills are finally of some use.

Fritz tells him again the story of a king who is sleeping under the Schauinsland, collecting an army, and Keith laughs and tells him, yes, we have that story too, a king under the mountain, a sleeping army, perhaps everybody does. But Fritz carries on gravely, talking of an army that will be roused, blood that must be spilt, and Keith stops laughing and listens to him. Fritz's face is lit up in the flames. It's coming soon, he says, it won't be long now. They're gathering underground.

Who? Who is gathering? Keith shuffles closer to the fire. But Fritz only stares into it, that almost smile on his face, and pushes another branch into the flames. Keith wonders if Fritz means that the two of them are the soldiers the stories speak of. This is the start of something, he thinks, the two of them on an empty road, the very first foot soldiers in a new war that hasn't yet begun. He has no idea where they will go or what will happen to them, but perhaps, one day, there will be three of them.

He had tried, that night after the climb, when his brother had lain stretched out on the sofa of his rooms in Cambridge. He really had. He'd stood watching Jack sleep, trying to imagine him a deserter, shamed and despised, the two of them no better than each other, unable to live off each other's stories, hiding from the world's disapproval. *My heart, my heart is broken.* He had tried to imagine living like that, what it would mean, and known he couldn't. When Jack had woken briefly, it was as though he had known it too. *Please*, he'd whispered to his brother. *Please, don't.* But by then, it was already done.

He'd crept down to the porter's office, where the only telephone still connected was kept. None of them were supposed to use it, except in an emergency, but hadn't it been an emergency of a kind? He'd wondered who he ought to telephone. The government? The police? When the operator's clipped voice had sounded over the line, he'd asked instead for Jack's regiment, expecting her to be confused. But she wasn't; the line had clicked neatly, and a man's brisk voice had rung out clear.

When he'd said the words, his voice had sounded like someone else's; he hadn't recognised himself.

I'm calling from St John's College. I want to let you know that my brother – yes, that's right, one of yours. Jack Hughes. To let you know he's here. No, there's nothing wrong. He'll be on the next train. I'll make sure of it.

'Did you never think of deserting?' he says, just as Fritz is nodding off. He looks out beyond the circle of light from the fire, listening to the crackling of the forest, the hiss of dying flames.

'Of course,' Fritz's voice comes sleepily. 'Doesn't everybody?'

'What stopped you?'

'I don't know. I suppose just being afraid.'

Keith stares at him through the dark. 'I thought desertion was the coward's choice.'

'Knowing what will happen if you're caught? What people will think of you? I'm not so sure.'

'I suppose…' He hesitates. 'I never thought of it like that.'

He waits for a reply, but nothing comes. He leans back in his bed of leaves and straw, watching the light flickering at the centre of the clearing, Fritz's face gradually growing peaceful and still.

'I killed my brother,' he says aloud. It's the first time he's said it since that night, the night he'd whispered it to the woman in Hofsgrund, and she'd stared back at him with wide, uncomprehending eyes. But no one is awake to hear him. The sky is black, Fritz Feldberg is dead to the world, his brother lies underground, his body shattered and broken, and the boy is out there somewhere, deep under the earth, following a trail that no one else can see.

Author's Note

This is a work of fiction. It was inspired by the true story of the 'Black Forest Tragedy' – a hiking trip in April 1936 led by the Strand School's Kenneth Keast, that left five children dead. Their names were Francis Bourdillon, Jack Alexander Eaton, Peter Harold Ellercamp, Stanley Michael Lyons and Roy Martin Witham.

The Eugenics Society's campaign for the legalisation of voluntary sterilisation in Britain reached its peak between the two World Wars. Following Parliament's rejection of a bill in 1931, a committee was established to look into the question, and in 1934, the Brock Report concluded that 'allowing and even encouraging mentally defective and mentally disordered patients' to be sterilised was justified. The report also suggested extending the policy to those with physical disabilities. Despite continued campaigning, particularly directed at women's groups such as the Women's Co-operative Guild, public and scientific opinion remained divided, and the report's recommendations were never enacted.

Following the introduction of the 'Law for the Prevention of Hereditarily Diseased Offspring' by the Nazi Party in 1933, approximately 400,000 men, women and children were forcibly sterilised. In 1939, the 'Aktion T4' programme of killings began.

For further reading

Jenny Bangham, 'Blood Relations: Transfusion and the Making of Human Genetics', 2020

Julia Boyd and Angelika Patel, 'A Village in the Third Reich: How Ordinary Lives Were Transformed by the Rise of Fascism', 2022

Kate Connolly, 'The fatal hike that became a Nazi propaganda coup', The Guardian, 6 July 2016

Bernd Hainmüller, 'Lost in the Black Forest', 2022 (Translated from the German by Peter Barker)

Richard Overy, 'The Morbid Age: Britain and the Crisis of Civilisation, 1919-1939', 2009

Acknowledgements

Thank you:

To my brilliant agent Juliet Mushens, whose wisdom made this book so much better, to Kiya Evans who saw it home, to Rachel Neely for her help and support, and to everyone at Mushens Entertainment.

To my editor Lauren Wolff-Jones for her insight and enthusiasm, and to all at Legend Press, especially Cari Rosen, Lucy Chamberlain, Olivia Le Maistre and Ditte Loekkegaard.

To Ross Dickinson for a fantastic copy edit, and to Rose Cooper for a beautiful cover design.

To Peter Francis and the whole team at Gladstone's Library and their wonderful Writer in Residence programme. Much of this book was written, unwritten, torn up and put back together again in your beautiful space. And especially to Louisa Yates, who more than once put me back together again.

To everyone who helped generously with my research, including Joe Cain, Subhadra Das, Jenny Bangham (in whose book, *Blood Relations*, I first read the Donna J. Haraway quote on page 11), and Robert Winckworth and the team at the University College London Special Collections. Thank you to Jude Heaney for the science, Kate McNaughton for the German, my dad David Day for first-hand accounts of night climbing in Cambridge, and Helen Wilson for the agronomy (get yourself an agronomy consultant). Any errors, misunderstandings and missteps are all mine.

To intrepid early readers Helen Wilson, Anna Mazzola, Claire McGowan and Matt Williams, and to all the friends who've provided support and encouragement along the way.

To Lucy for the Wednesdays.

To Kate Connolly for the article 'The fatal hike that became a Nazi propaganda coup' in the Guardian that got me started, and to Bernd Hainmüller for his painstaking research into the true story of the Black Forest Tragedy.

To my parents, to whom I owe everything, my sister Jess for keeping me sane/in supply of memes, and the gang, Freya, Grace and Stu.

To Matt, for being the best.